NIGHTMARE TIME

A profound horror seized Mira, paralyzing her. Even her mind had frozen. Yet she heard the frantic, wild beating of her heart and had a rudimentary awareness of some inner voice shrieking, *It's them, the cons, it's them*. But the sight of the man and the woman in her house, both of them armed, had rendered her incapable of linear thought.

"Hey," the man snapped. "I asked you a question."

Question. She blinked. Her mouth moved but nothing came out. She recognized these two as Billy Joe Franklin and Crystal DeVries, both of them drenched, their clothes filthy. Where was Tia Lopez? *I didn't just open the door to this nightmare; I blew it off the hinges.*

CATEGORY FIVE

T. J. MACGREGOR

KGL

PINNACLE BOOKS
Kensington Publishing Corp.

PINNACLE BOOKS are published by

Kensington Publishing Corp.
850 Third Avenue
New York, NY 10022

ISBN 0-7394-6069-2

Printed in the United States of America

For Kate Duffy and Al Zuckerman
Without them, the book wouldn't have a home

Acknowledgments

As always, love and thanks to Rob and Megan,
who put up with me while I wrote,
and thanks to Nancy McMoneagle,
astro coconspirator

On the Saffir-Simpson scale, hurricanes are classified according to windspeed:

Category 1: 74–95 mph
Category 2: 96–110 mph
Category 3: 111–130 mph
Category 4: 131–155 mph
Category 5: >155 mph

In the twentieth century, there were only three category 5 hurricanes: the Labor Day Hurricane of 1935, Hurricane Camille in 1969, and Hurricane Andrew in 1992.

PROLOGUE

JUNE 21, 1:38 AM

Billy Joe Franklin loved the darkness. Always had. He could pull it around himself like some sort of magical cloak that endowed him with special powers or he could lean into it and disappear, as he was doing now.

He stood alone on the upper deck of the Tango Key Ferry, a tall, muscular man in jeans, a black T-shirt, and a black cap pulled down low over his forehead. Black was his favorite color. Even his hair was black these days, and long, pulled back in a ponytail. You could project anything you wanted to on blackness, he thought, and often wished he'd been born black.

He stared out across the rough, dark waters at the island lights in the distance, a festival of lights, a wonderland, a sleeping paradise. He drank it in, the promise and exquisite beauty of it all. In a little while, he would descend on the island and, like some angry, vengeful god, would plunge it into chaos.

Behind him, a baby cried. Off to his left, a couple huddled close together, arms around each other. Directly behind him lay the stairs to the ferry's lower deck, where the strollers were stored, the bikes were carried, the cars were parked. The customized black Hummer waited for him down there, more than a hundred grand worth of car that weighed in excess of three tons and would do the job it was designed to do. And parked several blocks from the Hummer's final destination, in a parking lot where other residents kept their cars at night, was the innocuous black van with walls where the side windows should be. It would take him and Crystal to the cabin in the Tango wilderness preserve.

The cabin had enough food and supplies to last them a month if they were careful. He had planned well. He felt good about everything. He was water, that element that assumed the shape of the vessel into which it was poured. But without Crystal, he was just a vessel half-filled with diluted, impure water. He needed her. And for her, for them, his vessel tonight would be called *successful businessman* and that was how he would look when he was behind the wheel of the Hummer.

Stars appeared and vanished behind the rapidly moving clouds. Earlier, he'd been worried about hurricane Danielle four hundred and some odd miles out there in the Atlantic, who couldn't seem to make up her mind about where she was going. A front moving down from the north had been steering her southward, keeping her at coordinates that would bring her over the south end of Cuba so that she would miss the Keys and South Florida altogether. The front might be weakening, though, which meant that Danielle could turn to the north.

This possibility was why the National Hurricane Center probably would issue a hurricane watch sometime after sunrise for Monroe, Dade, Broward, and Palm Beach Counties—in short, everything from the Keys northward for three hundred miles. If that happened and the front continued to weaken, the center would upgrade the watch to a warning sometime later tomorrow. Either way, it didn't matter to him. He and Crystal would be safe in the cabin even if the hurricane struck. She, too, was water, and together they would become the Amazon, the Nile, or even the Pacific. They would do just fine in the cabin's forty-foot-deep cellar. It was well stocked, with enough money hidden on the property to cover just about any unforeseen eventuality.

Even if a warning was issued, it didn't mean Danielle would hit Tango Key. The center usually erred on the side of caution.

He knew all about the center's caution.

Until five years ago, he was one of its meteorologists, a behind-the-scenes weatherman with a TV-friendly face and a voice as smooth as old scotch. In those days, he'd had blond hair and a Pepsodent-white smile and should have been in front of the camera. But when he didn't get the promotion that he deserved, he lost it and made a scene. He was fired. The center mistrusted instability in employees as much as it distrusted instability in storms. End of story.

Twelve years of service, Christ knew how many hurricanes, and suddenly he was gone, out of work, a has-been. He'd grown bitter. His bitterness had rooted so deep inside him that he'd felt forced to change his outward appearance. He wore contacts now instead of glasses. He sported a neatly trimmed beard. His body was muscular, slender, strong, sculpted through endless hours at the gym. And of course, his hair was different. He had poured himself into the vessel called darkness and become the night.

The Billy Joe of today could afford to blow a hundred grand plus on a custom-made Hummer. This Billy Joe, he thought, had luxuries that five million from a federal bank heist allowed him. Stupidly, he and Crystal had pulled that job during the day and things had gone wrong. She had taken the fall and he had escaped.

But he wouldn't think about her right now. Instead, he would become water and pour himself into the nearest vessel and assume the shape of that vessel.

The ferry began to slow as it neared the island. From the air or on a map, Tango Key looked like a misshapen cat's head, with the right ear a wilderness preserve that spilled down into the cat's cheek and across a part of its forehead. The town of Pirate's Cove was located between the cat's eyes and everything else above the eyes and into the cat's left ear was occupied by homes and small businesses. The island's north half was hilly, filled with fields, old farms, citrus groves. The highest point—110 feet, to be exact—was also in the north. The entire island was a geological oddity, an anomaly amid a curving string of flat islands that jutted out into the vastness of the ocean with impunity. *Hit me*, these little islands seem to shout. *C'mon, I dare you.* Tango Key was the only place in the Keys and the lower half of the Florida peninsula with *hills.*

The ferry would bring him in just below the cat's mouth, where the land curved inward, forming a natural marina for the ferries and other boats that docked here. Well below the mouth, where the land was as flat as a postage stamp, lay the town of Tango, home to government offices, attorneys, doctors, the usual white-collar crowd, and the county jail. Dozens of small, family-owned businesses occupied the maze of narrow, shaded streets, some of them still paved with cobblestones that dated back to the 1700s.

Franklin shrugged his pack onto his back. He had plenty of cash in it. In addition to the cash on his wilderness property, he also had more cash in the Bahamas and in a Swiss bank. He'd been busy, efficient, thorough.

Down he went to the first deck, into his Hummer. How he loved the solidness of this vehicle, the smell of new, black leather, the way his hands fit over the steering wheel. A sexual feeling. That was what the Hummer did to him.

In addition to the brush grille guard at the front, both the front and the back were reinforced with steel plates. At the touch of a few keys on the computer under the dash, the Hummer could become nearly as impenetrable as a tank. The rear storage carried explosives that could be ignited by punching a three-digit code into the computer. The vehicle's design was impeccable. Too bad that he had to sacrifice the Hummer to spring Crystal.

As he drove off the ferry, he felt a bit edgy, nervous, the inside of his mouth dry and tight. Perhaps this was a good sign. He couldn't become complacent, careless. He brought a black cell phone out of the glove compartment and punched in a number. It rang at the other end, once, twice; then he disconnected, waited a few moments, and redialed. A single ring this time. Disconnect, call again, one ring, disconnect, two rings. There. Two, one; one, two: that was their signal. But would she remember it?

Yes, he believed she would.

Now it was past two AM. The graveyard shift at the jail would be in place and just one cop would be on duty, a bear of a woman who looked like a sumo wrestler.

He turned off Old Post Road and onto Lincoln Boulevard, which took him past the county government buildings, the library. The road twisted and a small fairground appeared, ringed by pines. Then, on his right, he saw the county jail that housed the female cons. An ugly building, low and squat, not well lit, with a ten-foot wire mesh fence crowned with nasty rolls of barbed wire. The front doors weren't behind any fence, though, and that was where he would enter. Two cruisers were parked along the front of the building, both empty.

Top of the morning to you, ladies, he thought, and smiled to himself.

Franklin continued to the end of the street, turned, and reached under the Hummer's seat for his weapon of choice, a newer version of the pump-action shotgun Arnold had used in the *Terminator* movies. He set it across his thighs, made a U-turn in the middle of the empty street, and started back toward Lincoln Boulevard. As he came into the turn, he picked up speed, the Hummer's powerful V-8 growling. Then he floored the accelerator and the Hummer leaped forward, raced over the sidewalk, tore up grass and flower beds, and barreled toward the jail's double glass doors.

Electronic doors. Two sets, glass. Not a problem. He pressed a button on the dashboard and the armored panels for the windows moved into place—rear window, side windows, and now the windshield itself, with just a strip of glass left clear along the width of it so he could see. Metal panels descended halfway over the tires, protecting them from bullets, flying glass. A thick metal mesh now covered the brushed grille guard and protected the headlights.

Seconds later, the Hummer crashed through the two sets of doors. Glass exploded, the alarms shrieked, and the sumo wrestler whipped around, her plump face vivid, eyes squinted against the brilliant glare of the headlights. She leaped out of the way with surprising swiftness, then spun and aimed a .30-06 at the Hummer.

Franklin swerved right. The Hummer struck her before she got off a shot. Her massive body seemed to burst like a balloon, spewing blood and bones, and he kept on going, the Hummer's engine roaring as it slammed into the wall.

It broke apart as though it were no more substantial than balsa wood. Bits of concrete rained down on the Hummer's roof and pinged against its armor. A cloud of dust drifted like smoke through the brilliant beams of the headlights. The ceiling sprinklers came on, the alarms kept shrieking. As the water from the sprinklers dampened the dust, he suddenly saw Crystal in the next cell, gripping the bars, her eyes startled, as huge as UFOs. Beside her stood a tall, black woman, her wild hair seeming to glisten in the brightness of the headlights, her long arms thrown up as if to fend off the Hummer. An Amazon warrior queen.

He flashed the headlights, the Amazon grabbed Crystal's arm and jerked her out of the way. He threw the Hummer into reverse, then forward, and jammed his foot against the gas pedal. The Hummer lunged with the hunger of a predatory beast and burst into the next cell. The impact jolted him to the roots of his teeth. But he was in and Crystal ran toward the Hummer, her slim legs carrying her as fast as they would move.

He hurled open the passenger door and Crystal bolted inside—and the Amazon shot in right behind her. "There's only room for two!" he shouted and swung the weapon up.

Crystal slammed her fist against the barrel, shoving it down. "She's my friend," she bellowed over the shriek of the alarms.

"Fuck it." He slammed the Hummer into reverse and tore back through the holes in the wall. "Guns under the seat. Grab them and get in the back. Can you shoot a gun, Amazon?"

"Not with armor on the windows," she shouted.

Very funny. A comedian. He swung the massive vehicle around and aimed it at the door, cops pouring through it. *Move, now, fast, mow the fuckers down.*

He gunned the engine and tore toward them, one hand clutching the steering wheel, the other pressing buttons on the dash that lowered the glass in the side and rear windows and opened gun holes in the armor. Some of the cops leaped out of the way, others weren't fast enough, and the body of one slammed into the armor over the windshield, his cheek smashed up against the slit of glass right in front of Franklin.

As the Hummer raced through the ruined doors and spun onto Lincoln Boulevard, he pressed another button and a sunroof opened up. Bits and chunks of concrete and wood and dust rained into the car. He shouted at the women to get the body off the windshield. The Amazon popped up through the sunroof like some giant jack-in-the-box, and peeled the cop off the armor.

As the Hummer roared up Lincoln, the Amazon and Crystal used the sunroof as a shooting perch. "Five in pursuit!" the Amazon shouted, and she and Crystal opened fire simultaneously.

One cruiser spun out of control. Another crashed into a tree. A third slammed into a parked car and both exploded. Franklin grinned and headed for Vine, a road so narrow that when he swung the Hummer around so it formed a ninety-degree angle to the road, it blocked it completely.

"Out," he shouted. *"Out!* Meet me in the woods."

He punched in the three-digit code, slung his pack over his shoulder, and clambered out of the Hummer with the economical swiftness of a hummingbird. The explosives had a thirty-second delay, long enough for them to take cover.

He sprinted for the woods, the squeal of sirens so close now that they echoed eerily through the darkness. Then he plunged into the trees where Crystal and the Amazon waited for him, and they raced deeper into the woods. A heartbeat later the Hummer blew.

It sounded like Armageddon. They instinctively threw themselves to the ground, rolled. A tremendous fireball shot into the sky, spewing volcanic light and debris. The air smelled scorched. A second explosion rocked the darkness and they leaped up and ran hard and fast through the trees, stumbling over protruding roots, the night springing alive now with other sirens, other shrieks, a third explosion.

At the edge of the wooded area, they paused, he and Crystal gasping like fish out of water, while the Amazon had barely broken a sweat. "What the hell was in that Hummer of yours, boy?" the Amazon asked. "All of Vietnam?"

That and then some. There wouldn't be enough left of the Hummer for a single fingerprint.

"Across the alley," he hissed. "To that four-story building. The van's on the second level."

The Amazon darted out ahead of them, her long legs eating up the distance between the woods and the parking garage. Franklin grabbed Crystal's hand and felt the suddenness of it, how he instantly felt whole again. They raced after the Amazon, across the alley, their shoes slapping the old cobblestones, and ducked into the shadows on the other side. This garage didn't have an attendant. You just bought a sticker for a week or a month or whatever time frame suited you, slapped it on the inside of your windshield, and it was read like a bar code on a grocery store product as you entered and left the garage. His sticker—like the van—was registered to Jerome Carver, a nowhere man who didn't exist.

Into the garage, penlight on, up the stairs, fast, faster. Below, more sirens. Something had caught fire out there on Vine Street—trees or bushes, someone's yard, loose garbage, he wasn't sure. But he could smell it, a stench that mixed with the odor of gasoline, burning rubber, ruin.

They reached the second level of the garage. He ran over to the black van, unlocked the back of it, and they scrambled inside. The backseats were gone, but there were two bunk bed platforms fitted out with sleeping bags, blankets, pillows. A built-in cooler occupied the other wall and, next to it, camping gear and a couple of duffel bags. He pushed the green one toward Crystal. "Become someone else, babe." He looked at the Amazon. A fine sheen of sweat covered her face. Her eyes, as black as bitter chocolate, revealed nothing. "You six feet or so?"

"Six, yes."

"I didn't plan for a third person, but there should be something in this bag that fits you." He shoved the navy blue duffel toward her. "When you're done, crawl into the bunks, cover yourselves."

He moved quickly to the front of the van, slid his weapon under the seat, and went through a routine he had rehearsed so many times he could do it in his sleep if he had to. Glove compartment: out came the electric razor, a pillowcase. He spread the pillowcase across his thighs, set the razor on the dashboard, reached under the passenger seat. Baseball cap, clean shirt. He folded his ponytail, hiding it under the cap, put on the shirt, brought out the glasses tucked in the pocket, slipped them on.

From between the seats, he brought out a bag of toys—Legos, stuffed animals, alphabet blocks, a couple of Dr. Seuss books—and dumped them in the passenger seat. He ran the razor over his face, shaving off his beard as he backed out of the space and started down the ramp. The hair fell onto the pillowcase and when he was finished, he would fold it up and stick it under the seat.

Franklin turned right out of the garage, away from the fire, the sirens, the stink, and headed west through downtown. *Keep to the speed limit. You are water. You have been poured into a vessel called camper and family man.*

He rubbed his hand over his face, feeling the unfamiliar smoothness. He folded the pillowcase and dropped it between the seats. The razor went back into the glove compartment. *We're going to make it.*

And then, up ahead, he saw two police cruisers, lights spinning. "Shit. They're cops up here. Get in the bunks. Fast."

"We're in," Crystal said.

CD player, a little music. *I am water. I am a camper.*

As he approached the cruisers, one of the cops stepped out into the road and motioned with a flashlight for him to pull over. A pulse hammered at his temple. *The sticker, Jesus, the sticker is still on the windshield.*

He started to peel it off, but was afraid to make any sudden movements. He pulled to the curb, stopped. "Don't move," he said under his breath.

The cop swaggered over to the van. "License and registration, sir," he said, and shone the flashlight into Franklin's face.

He squinted and handed the requested items to the cop, who examined them in the beam of his flashlight, shone the light on the toys and stuffed animals in the seat, then leaned a bit too far into the window and shone the light in the back. "And you're headed where, Mr. Carver?"

"I was trying to get back to the campground and apparently took a wrong turn. My son developed a fever and I had to find some children's Tylenol."

"Just a minute, please."

The cop walked back to the cruiser with Franklin's phony ID. He would run it and find that Jerome Carver was a safe driver who lived in Titusville, Florida, and worked at Cape Canaveral as an engineer. Married, one child, no arrests. An ordinary citizen.

Unless something goes wrong.

Franklin waited. Beads of perspiration erupted on his forehead, his palms. How fast could he pull the weapon out from under the seat? Not fast enough. "Ladies, keep the guns close. If I say shoot, start shooting."

Minutes ticked by. He heard more sirens, could see the glow of the flames in the side mirror. The inside of his mouth had gone bone dry.

Now the cop started toward the van. *I am water. I am a camper.*

"Here you go, Mr. Carver," the cop said, and handed him the ID. "You need to go east four blocks, turn onto the Old Post Road, and head north to the preserve. Stay clear of Vine."

"Will do. Thanks very much."

The cop stepped back, Franklin turned the key, and pulled out onto the road, his hands shaking.

PART ONE

THE WATCH

"A hurricane watch issued for your part of the coast indicates the possibility that you could experience hurricane conditions within 36 hours. This watch should trigger your family's disaster plan . . ."

National Hurricane Center

Tips from the FEMA Website for a Hurricane Watch:
— Listen to a battery-operated radio or television for hurricane progress reports.
— Check emergency supplies.
— Fuel car.
— Bring in outdoor objects such as lawn furniture, toys, and garden tools and anchor objects that cannot be brought inside.
— Secure buildings by closing and boarding up windows.
— Remove outside antennas.
— Turn refrigerator and freezer to coldest settings.
— Store drinking water in clean bathtubs, jugs, bottles, and cooking utensils.

— Store valuables and personal papers in a waterproof container on the highest level of your home.
— Review evacuation plan.
— Moor boat securely or move it to a designated safe place. Use rope or chain to secure boat to trailer.
— Have a family disaster plan.

1

"Ready or not, I guess."
                Governor Lawton Chiles, in the hours before
                Hurricane Andrew struck South Florida

Her eyes snapped open, air rushed from her lungs. Mira
Morales bolted upright in bed and looked wildly around the
bedroom, certain that her nightmare had sprung into waking
life with her. Intruders in the house, people with guns, Annie
in danger. . . . But even as she thought this, the images began
to fade, her frantic heartbeat slowed, her fear bled away.

She remained as she was for a few moments, drawing in
the familiarity of the house around her. The night noises
comforted her—the soft whispering of cool air through the
vents, the rhythmic click of the ceiling fan as it turned,
Sheppard's snores beside her. Farther up the hall, the old pipes
clattered in the walls as someone—either Annie or Nadine—
used the bathroom. Probably Annie, she decided. Now that
school was out for the summer, her teenage daughter kept
erratic hours. Besides, if it were Nadine, Mira would hear the
wheelchair's rubber tires squeaking against the tile floors.
She doubted that Nadine would get up at all tonight.

Her grandmother had been as exhausted as Mira when

they finally had returned from the ER around nine last night. They had spent ten hours in the emergency room yesterday, more than half of it waiting for a doctor to see Nadine. It had taken Sheppard's arrival to get things moving and then only because he'd flashed his FBI badge and made a stink about keeping an eighty-two-year-old woman with a broken foot waiting in pain for so long.

After X-rays and consultations among various physicians, it was decided that Nadine's foot didn't require surgery and they had put on a cast. But her personal doctor, worried that she might have sustained a concussion when she'd tumbled off a ladder at the bookstore, had ordered a CAT scan. Nadine, who had no tolerance for hospitals or doctors, had told him to forget it, she was fine and intended to go home. Her physician, accustomed to her stubbornness, had refused to allow her to leave until she gave him her word that she would stay in bed for two days, except to use the bathroom, and that she would use a wheelchair for two weeks. And, oh yes, he'd added, if she felt dizzy or nauseated, she would come in immediately for the CAT scan.

Mira suspected that Nadine, like a small child, had crossed her fingers when she'd agreed. Given her druthers, Nadine would be at the store tomorrow, working the register and teaching her yoga classes from her wheelchair.

Mira stretched out again and shut her eyes, her foot seeking the warm comfort of Sheppard's toes or the soles of his feet. Any physical connection would do. She felt his toes and pressed the sole of her foot against his. Occasionally when she did this, she tuned in on a dream he was having, a surreal experience and something that never had happened with anyone before, not even Tom, the man to whom she'd been married years ago. But now nothing came to her.

Mira pulled her leg back to her side of the mattress. It was a king-size bed she and Sheppard had bought two months ago, when he finally had moved into the house. Neither of them was accustomed yet to sharing a bed with another person. Although they had been lovers for more than five years, this living together stuff was a new chapter that required a whole new lexicon, the creation of new habits and grooves. She certainly hadn't gotten the hang of it yet and knew that Sheppard hadn't either. The habits one learned in marriage, she thought, were unique to that relationship. Tom had been dead for eleven years, Sheppard's marriage had been over longer than that, and now here they were, a couple in their forties who had grown accustomed to sleeping alone in smaller beds.

Sleep didn't come—and she knew it was because a part of her feared that if she fell asleep the nightmare would pick up where it had left off. The intruders. Mira tried to conjure their faces, more details of the nightmare, tried to determine if it was just a bad dream or a warning of some kind. But her efforts didn't yield anything more than Sheppard's foot had. Frustrated, she threw off the sheet and got out of bed. She was hungry.

As she entered the kitchen, all three cats joined her, winding between her legs, meowing to be fed, let out, petted. Whiskers, the alpha male, a black and white tuxedo cat, belonged to Nadine. Powder, a white cat with spooky blue eyes, belonged to Sheppard, and the tabby, Tigerlily, was hers. Now here came Annie's animal, Ricki, a gorgeous golden retriever with reddish gold fur who wagged her tail at the sight of the cats, her extended family. Mira fed everyone, fixed herself a plate of chilled papaya, slices of ice-cold mango, half of a toasted English muffin slathered in real butter, and cut up some sharp cheddar cheese to go on top.

Nadine, a vegetarian for sixty-some-odd years, disliked even the sight of cheese and eggs in the fridge, and nearly had a fit every time she saw the fish or chicken that Sheppard had bought. Both Annie and Mira had started eating fish again when Sheppard had moved in, one more grievance in the long list of things that Nadine held against him. But what the hell? Mira thought. Her vegan diet never had been a religion. She doubted she would ever go so far as to eat chicken, but after years of consuming vegetables, fruits, and soy, now cheese, eggs, and fish were a welcome change.

Mira carried her plate of goodies outside, sat down at the edge of the pool, and lowered her feet into the deliciously warm water. Stars were strewn across the glorious summer sky, but here and there, they vanished behind swiftly moving clouds. Down here on earth, that swiftness translated into a pleasantly warm and humid breeze that occasionally picked up, but not enough to blame it on Hurricane Danielle. In fact, until just this moment, she'd forgotten all about the hurricane.

The last she'd heard around five yesterday afternoon was that it had taken aim at southern Cuba and would miss the Keys and South Florida entirely. Good thing. She had enough to worry about without a hurricane too.

Her immediate concern was that one of the three authors scheduled to sign books tonight during the store's solstice celebration had canceled due to a family emergency. She hoped to find a local author who could fill in on short notice, but wasn't counting on it. She also had to cancel Nadine's yoga classes for the next six to eight weeks—or find a substitute. But a substitute would cost twenty-five bucks an hour, two hundred a week, eight hundred a month, and that would be on top of Nadine's regular salary. She just didn't have the money now. Yet, without a sub, she would have to teach the classes herself and that meant she would have to make one of her part-time employees full-time or get Annie to fill in while she was doing the teaching.

Mira moved her feet through the warm water, set her empty plate on the worn brick that surrounded the pool. The water beckoned. She pulled her T-shirt over her head, slipped off her gym shorts and panties, and eased her body into the water. She swam two laps underwater, her eyes open, luxuriating in the silken feel of the warm water against her bare skin. Only one of the pool's underwater lights was on and it cast intriguing shapes against the bottom of the pool. Now and then, the bubbles of her expelled breath floated upward, disturbing the symmetry of shadows and texture.

As she surfaced again at the shallow end, she was shocked to see Wayne Sheppard standing there, all six feet four of him buck naked. He was grinning. "Now this looks like a fine idea," he said, and came down the steps and vanished into the water.

Mira watched him, his stroke as smooth and effortless as that of an Olympic swimmer, then she sank beneath the water and swam after him. They met up at the deep end, where a ledge jutted out, and sat there under the stars.

"You think Nadine has a concussion?" he asked.

He was asking for her psychic opinion, not her medical one. Sheppard knew that she was empathic, but apparently didn't connect that with hospitals. He couldn't imagine what it was like for her to open herself psychically in a place where pain was the standard by which everything else was judged.

When Nadine had broken her hip more than five years ago, Mira had tried to read her in the ER while they had been waiting to see a doctor and she'd been assaulted by the symptoms of everyone around her. Aches, sniffles, coughs, fever, then pain and agony. The man in the cubicle next to Nadine that night had had pneumonia and it was those symptoms Mira ultimately had taken on, the fever, a horrid rattling in her chest, a terrible lethargy in her limbs. The symptoms had been real enough so that she too nearly had ended up in the ER as a patient.

"I don't know. I didn't try to read her."

He nodded, but she didn't know if that meant that he understood why she hadn't tried or if the nod was merely a polite response. Pearls of water dripped from his khaki-colored beard, from the tips of his eyelashes. "So read me," he said, and slipped his arms around her and nuzzled her ear.

He planted soft, cool kisses against her neck, the curve of her chin, her eyelids, her mouth. He was the only man she'd ever known who regularly kissed her eyelids, sometimes with his mouth, sometimes with his eyelashes—the butterfly kiss, he called it. Mira relaxed in his arms, her mouth opening against his, her blood quickening with desire despite her fatigue, despite the events of the day, despite everything.

And suddenly they were groping at each other in the water, on the jutting ledge. Her hunger for him often crashed over her at strange, inopportune times—in the car, the garage, the garden behind her house, in her bookstore, the grocery store, and in places like this, a private space where, any moment now, Annie might step out the porch door and see them.

His hand slipped between her thighs and Mira moved her hips against the delicious pressure. "Annie may walk out here," she murmured, her mouth against his neck, her hips moving, sliding.

"She's asleep. I checked."

His left hand came up under her chin, touching it, tilting her head back, exposing her neck to his mouth. Good thing they weren't standing. Shameless groping was so much easier in the pool, where his height and gravity weren't issues. Mira suddenly longed for their bed, that privacy, but she couldn't stop herself, couldn't stop the movement of her hips as his mouth devoured hers.

The heat. The exquisite pleasure. The sensation of the water surrounding them, licking at their bodies. Her fingers flexed against his back, nails digging into his skin. She groaned and arched her back, begging him for more, more.

She heard the noises that she made, the groans, the mur-

murings, the animal sounds, but all of this seemed distant and unconnected to her. Then her body convulsed and he was inside her, impaling her against the edge of the swimming pool, moving fast and hard, to his own completion.

And when it was over, they clung to each other, the water holding and sustaining them, their breathing like that of marathon runners. Mira felt a rush of gratitude. He understood that Nadine was Mira's last link to who she had become and an injury to Nadine was an injury to Mira, a reminder of just how deeply this woman had shaped her life, her abilities, the core of who she was. In the last ten or twelve hours, she had shut down emotionally and psychically, turned off, gone away, and Sheppard had understood that and brought her back.

Never mind that he was also one of the horniest men she'd ever known, that he could screw anywhere, any time, any place. Never mind that. This one, she knew, was about her, and her connection to Nadine. He had forced her to feel again.

Ricki popped out through the swinging animal door on the porch and stalked the edges of the pool, tail wagging. The dog figured it was all some sort of wonderful game, Mira and Sheppard in the swimming pool while the stars were out. The dog's emotions instantly drew Mira in, a psychic trail that shadowed her and wasn't so different from the trail that shadowed humans. And in this trail, Mira saw her daughter earlier in the evening, feeding Ricki dinner, then training her with too many dog treats. *Do this, do that, jump through hoops for me and you get a big fat treat.* No wonder Ricki had gained weight since she'd joined the family six months ago.

"You read Ricki," Sheppard exclaimed, watching her.

"Actually, I was reading Annie through her."

"So what'd Annie do tonight while we were at the hospital?"

"Fed Ricki treats and talked to her buddies online and on the phone."

"Mira, you're the ultimate voyeur."

"Is that what you call it?"

"That's what it is."

"You're so full of shit, Shep." She laughed when she said it and they looked at each other and laughed again, and swam together to the shallow end of the pool.

He got out first and offered Mira a towel. She wrapped it around herself, one of the huge beach towels that Sheppard had bought at a shop in downtown Tango, and then he wrapped a second towel around himself. "So what do you call it?" he asked as they settled into chairs at the side of the pool.

"Infringement."

"On?"

"My consciousness. I didn't go looking for information from a dog, Shep. It was just there."

"Entanglement."

"What?"

"Entanglement," he said. "That's what physicists would call it. In the moments that Ricki appeared and you read her, your life became entangled with hers."

"My life is entangled with hers because she lives here."

"But she doesn't know that."

"Oh, I think she knows."

"Pretend that Ricki is a human stranger. You become entangled when the human passes by you and you read him. Or her."

"But the man or woman doesn't know it because I don't say anything."

"That doesn't matter. The person you read doesn't have to know. Let's say you have two couples—Bob and Carol, Ted and Alice."

"Like the old movie."

"Uh-huh. This is from a book I'm reading, okay? Slightly

different names, though. Alice goes on a business trip. She meets Bob, who's also on a business trip. They fall in love. Their spouses, Carol and Ted, who are on the other side of the world and have never met, are now entangled with each other, even though they don't know yet that Alice and Bob are involved. So when you read this person—or this dog," he added with a chuckle, "the two of you became entangled even though he wasn't aware that you read him. Every time you read someone, entanglement happens."

She slid down in her chair and let her head rest against the back of it. "Spooky action at a distance. That was Einstein's name for it." Then she added, "Hey, you actually read the books I pass on to you."

"Thanks a lot."

"I figured they were just piling up under the bed or in your car."

"You obviously didn't read this one."

She held up her hands. "Guilty."

Sheppard laughed and reached for her hand. She suddenly felt herself zoning out, going elsewhere . . .

Rain whips across the road in sheets, he can't see more than a few inches in front of him. The wind howls, the Jetta shakes, and suddenly a tree crashes to the ground in front of him, blocking the road. He slams on the brakes and the Jetta skids left, right, left again, and plows into the mammoth tree. He snaps forward, his head hits the steering wheel, then the air bag inflates, trapping him against the seat . . .

Mira jerked her hand free of Sheppard's and knew that her shock showed on her face because he immediately said, "What? What is it?"

Entanglement. "I . . . I saw you in a car accident. In the Jetta. A tree had fallen across the road, it was storming . . ."

"We haven't had rain in three months, Mira."

So now he was going to argue with her. "In case you forgot, there's a hurricane out there."

"Yeah, and the last I heard, it wasn't coming anywhere near the Keys."

"You hit the tree, the car skidded, the air bag inflated, trapping you against the seat, Shep. The storm was so powerful the winds shook your car."

He started to say something, but a phone rang the theme song of E.T., Sheppard's cell phone.

"If that's work-related, I want you to take my van," she said.

"But it's not raining," he said. "So how can what you saw come true if it's not raining?"

"If it rains, then one of the conditions is present. Please take my car."

Third ring. "Let me get this call." He got up, the huge beach towel wrapped around his waist, and swept his cell phone off a nearby patio table. As he walked to the far end of the pool, Mira pulled on her nightclothes—and none too soon.

The door to the porch banged open and Annie rushed out into the pool area. "Mom." She sounded breathless. She wore her funny PJs from American Eagle, long blue cotton pants with a cloud motif and a sleeveless solid blue shirt. She didn't seem to notice Sheppard at the other end of the pool.

"I thought you were asleep."

"I was. But I set the alarm because I knew they were going to issue an interim tropical update. Danielle's now a cat three, with winds of 130. They're showing a twenty percent strike probability for the lower Keys. We're under a hurricane watch now, Mom, from the Keys to Palm Beach County. That means it could be here within thirty-six hours. Now's the time to evacuate. We can't stay on Tango. Not with winds this high. And the storm surge . . . my God, it's going to put the bookstore underwater. If the storm turns a little more north, which it could do, they'll issue a warning for the Keys. We need to get outta here."

"Honey, calm down. A watch is just a watch."

She sounded calm, but immediately wondered if this was what she'd seen, Sheppard driving through the storm that was Danielle. It didn't necessarily mean Danielle would make landfall on Tango, but she definitely would come close enough for high winds and a shit load of rain.

But whether it hit or was a very near miss, how could she evacuate? Nadine wasn't allowed to travel, it would take her hours to put up the aluminum shutters on her bookstore, and even then, they wouldn't prevent flooding. The store's stock right now was at a three-year high. She couldn't afford to lose it. No flood insurance. Since Andrew, many insurance companies had stopped issuing policies for South Florida and none would write flood policies for any home or business at the south end of Tango.

I'm fucked.

But only if Danielle made a direct hit.

Sheppard hurried over to her and Annie. "You heard." It wasn't a question. "We're under a watch. Sheriff Emison thinks the National Hurricane Center may issue a warning by midmorning."

"Shep, we need to evacuate," Annie said.

"Annie, I'm not in any position to evacuate," Mira told her.

"Right now," Sheppard said, "no one's evacuating. Some maniac drove a Hummer through the front doors of the women's jail. Cops are down, two inmates escaped, and Emison has closed the bridge and stopped the ferries until they're found. If a hurricane warning is issued later today and the inmates still haven't been found, he'll start the evacuation, but with cops checking every single car as it leaves the island. There're two conventions here right now, campers up in the wilderness preserve, and Emison figures all total we've got five to six thousand people who might leave. I need to get dressed and shove off."

"To look for cons?" Mira asked. "Or coordinate possible emergency plans?"

"Right now, it's just the cons."

"Make sure you take my van," she called after him. "The keys are on the kitchen table."

After Sheppard rushed inside the house, Mira sat there, staring out over the pool, Annie glaring at her. "Mom, we can't just sit here."

"Nothing's certain," she replied. "We should both just go back to bed."

Annie rolled her eyes in her typical teenage way. "Yeah, right." She marched off and slammed the door as she went back inside.

Mira couldn't decide what she should do first—or if she should do anything at all. A *watch* wasn't a *warning*. But even if she decided to do something—like top off the tanks on the cars and the store's delivery van or stock up on food and supplies—only Winn Dixie was open at this hour and you shopped there at your own peril. The fresh food was a week old, the fruits and vegetables looked parched and wilted, and the canned goods probably were riddled with botulism. But how bad could their bottled water be? She could at least get bottled water and pet food.

House? It had accordion shutters and it wouldn't take her more than twenty minutes to pull them shut, so that wasn't pressing.

ATM? She could get cash from the ATM on her way to the bookstore in the morning.

But if a warning had been issued by then, there might be long lines. During the frenzied hours before Andrew had slammed into Homestead, many ATMs from the Keys to

Palm Beach had run out of money. And in Andrew's aftermath, cash had been as valuable a commodity as water and food.

How much cash did she have on hand?

She recalled that in September 2003, Hurricane Isabel—a strong category four—kept the entire East Coast on alert when it was still over a thousand miles from the U.S. By the time it came ashore around North Carolina and Washington, D.C., cities were largely deserted, it was a weak category two, and broadcasters stood around in rain and wind reporting on virtually nothing. Even if a warning was issued, it didn't necessarily mean Danielle would arrive. And right now, Danielle was only a category three. Maximum winds of 125.

Mira went inside. Annie had the TV on, tuned to a Miami station. The broadcaster, one of those blondes who looked like a Stepford wife, was going on about what everyone should be doing *now*, under a watch. Annie had a printed sheet of paper in front of her and was checking off everything the woman said and jotting notes. Then a meteorologist came on to discuss Danielle—her birth in the Cape Verde Islands ten days ago, her erratic path across the Atlantic, her similarities to Andrew. Annie now unfolded a hurricane tracking map and spread it open on the table. Mira saw that she had drawn two lines on the map—one blue, the other red.

"Which one is Danielle?" Mira asked.

"The red. The blue is Andrew. Now here's the spooky part, Mom. Other than the fact that steering currents are carrying Danielle farther south than Andrew's path, these two hurricanes could be clones. Identical twins born twelve years apart. They've accelerated at the same pace, they're nearly the same size, but different categories, and—"

Mira's head began to ache. "I'm going to shower, then we'll decide what to do, okay?"

Annie nodded and went back to her calculations.

As Mira showered, she considered Plan B: close the house shutters, do what she could for the bookstore, take a chance by moving Nadine, and be ready to evacuate if a warning was issued. But evacuate to where? No hurricane shelter took animals and neither did most motels. She wasn't about to leave three cats and a dog alone here during a hurricane. Then there was the distance. How far would be safe? The watch extended to Palm Beach County, more than two hundred miles up the coast. That meant the forecasters still weren't sure of Danielle's exact track. Suppose they evacuated only to find that the storm came right to where they were?

If you flee from what terrifies you, it follows you. One of Nadine's axioms. And when it came to hurricanes, Mira felt it was true. When the watch had gone up for Andrew, it was close to a cat five, with winds in excess of 140. Thousands of people from the Keys to the Palm Beaches had fled and quickly turned I-95 and the Florida Turnpike into a river of chrome, bumper-to-bumper vehicles for hundreds of miles. People had been on the highways for as long as fourteen hours and if Andrew had been a larger storm, it would have taken out the lot of them.

Plan C?

She didn't have a Plan C.

Banging on the bathroom door. "Mom," Annie shouted.

"Shit," Mira muttered. She shut off the shower, stepped out onto the mat. "What is it?"

"The central pressure of this storm is 931. Andrew's was 922."

Great, just great. "Get dressed. We're going to the ATM and to Winn Dixie for bottled water and pet food."

Should she wake Nadine?

No, let her sleep.

*   *   *

Five minutes later, she, Annie, and Ricki were in Sheppard's car, the Jetta, with the key in the ignition, but Mira didn't turn it. She felt a deep reluctance to put her hands on the steering wheel. After all, Sheppard spent a lot of time in this car, with his hands against this steering wheel. Even though it was wrapped in leather, which usually wasn't a great conductor of psychic energy, virtually any material could hold emotional residue, particularly when it had built up over time. But since she wasn't going anywhere without touching the steering wheel, she finally brought her right hand against it. Closed her fingers around it. Nothing. Left hand now.

Safe.

She started the car and backed out of the driveway. As she turned north on Old Post Road, images surfaced, but nothing startling or horrifying, nothing that distracted her. They were scenes from Sheppard's daily life, music that he played on the way to and from work, he and his partner, John "Goot" Gutierrez laughing, Sheppard with her and Annie, Sheppard with Ricki. The stuff of ordinary life. No accident. No crashing tree. No blinding storm.

It seemed that by changing cars, they had changed the future.

From her experience, though, she knew that by changing a detail in something she'd seen, another alternate path was created. Not always, but frequently enough so that she should have read her van with him inside it before he'd driven off.

"How much money can we withdraw?" Annie asked.

"Five hundred at a time."

"That's not enough, Mom. In the days after Andrew—"

Annie, the Andrew expert. "Hon, I have more cash at home and cash in the safe at the store. Five hundred is plenty."

The bank was deserted. Not too surprising. At this hour, most sane people were asleep. She slipped her card into the slot, started punching in her PIN, and something happened. The bank, the ATM, Annie, and the dog, vanished . . .

Fire, sirens, smoke filling the air. Homes are on fire, trees burn like money, yards the drought has turned to tinder go up in flames. She turns away from the ruin and finds herself inside a parking garage. A vehicle backs out of a parking space and as it passes her, she glimpses the driver, a man wearing a baseball cap and glasses . . .

The vein dried up as abruptly as it had opened and Annie was saying, "Mom? Hey, the money's there. Mom."

Mira squeezed her eyes shut, opened them again, took the money, her card, a receipt, and drove forward, a part of her consciousness still stuck back in that garage, the stink of smoke and fire lodged in her nostrils. She sneezed.

"You okay?" Annie asked worriedly.

"Uh, yeah, sure."

But what the hell had just happened?

2

"The average hurricane can travel up to four hundred miles a day."

National Hurricane Center

The jail's emergency lights cast a surreal glare across a scene that looked like a bomb blast site, something beamed through satellite TV from Israel or Baghdad. Streams of water, which Sheppard guessed were from the ceiling sprinklers, ran through the mess, turning the dust to mud, the mud to sludge.

Off to Sheppard's right, paramedics lifted the ruined body of Granny Moses, the cop in charge of the jail's midnight shift, onto a stretcher. Bile rose in his throat. He hadn't known Granny well, he doubted if anyone had. But she always had been helpful to him and was known to treat her female charges well.

He turned away from the carnage and focused on the gaping hole in the wall. It made him think of the open jaws of a giant shark, the protrusions of wires and metal and broken concrete as jagged as teeth. Lights darted around inside the hole, voices echoed eerily. Sheppard stuck his head inside, into the cell block, turned on his flashlight, and stepped inside.

Without electricity, the gloom, dust, and heat were extreme. Sheppard tied a handkerchief over his nose and mouth so that he could breathe with a minimum of dust clogging his throat and lungs—and suddenly found it almost impossible to breathe. His heart slammed into overtime, sweat oozed down the sides of his face, his stomach lurched, he thought he might puke.

Open fields, vast skies, deserted beaches: he conjured all the images of openness that he could think of, repeated his mantra against anxiety—*I am safe, I am safe*—and these techniques at least allowed him to move. He stumbled forward farther into the cell until he reached a spot where he could breathe. It wasn't apparent what was so different about this space that his mind would release him from panic, but it was enough that air flowed freely into his lungs again, that his heartbeat settled down, that his stomach calmed.

He glanced quickly around. Had anyone seen it happen? Unlikely. Only three other cops were in the cell block and they were at the other end.

Sheppard wiped his face with the hanky and groped in his pocket for the pack of mints. He popped one into his mouth, sucked hard. For some unknown reason, the mints helped mitigate his attacks of claustrophobia. When he had forewarning about an attack, sucking on peppermint could stop it dead in its tracks. There was no medical evidence that mints could mitigate or stop claustrophobia. But as his doctor had observed, *If it works, use it.*

He'd never been claustrophobic until a year ago. Mira felt certain it was a side effect of having gone through the black water mass. His doctor, who knew nothing about the black water, attributed it to the vagaries of aging. *Hey, Shep, some guys have sex problems, others get high cholesterol, you get claustrophobia. The luck of the draw.* That explanation seemed to be the standard one doctors issued when they didn't know the answer. In his heart, Sheppard suspected that Mira was right. You couldn't go back thirty-five years in time, as he had done a year ago, without some sort of side effect.

Now that he felt better, he moved forward, flashlight illuminating his way. The Hummer had broken through the wall of the next cell, too, slamming into the concrete strip that held the bars in place and knocking loose enough of it so that whoever had been inside could get out. The cell block doors stood open and he went through the closest one and moved slowly down the aisle, shining his flashlight into each of the cells.

The jail had a dozen cells, in each of which two or three women could be housed. But from the looks of it, only two had been occupied—those closest to the hole. Sheppard saw the pay phone on the wall, where inmates were allowed to make weekly calls to attorneys or family members. He made a note of the number, then called his contact at Tango Bell and left a message, asking her to check for incoming and outgoing calls from this number over the last twenty-four hours. He doubted anything would come of it, but since this certainly had all the markings of a planned jailbreak, he might just get lucky.

"Shep? Hey, amigo, you in here?"

"Yeah, Goot." He turned his flashlight toward the hole, flashed it twice, and saw Goot making his way through the debris.

John Gutierrez was the first person Sheppard had hired for the bureau's Tango office four years ago, when he was lured back to the FBI by the man who headed up the Southeast division. Cuban-American, he was blessed with hardy genes and a handsome face that women, both gringas and Latinas alike, seemed to find irresistible. In the time that Sheppard had known him, he had been involved with dozens of women, but the latest relationship had been going on for six months now, a record for Goot. The man's love life was so tempestuous that Sheppard didn't understand how he had any energy left over to do anything else.

Goot hailed from a family of santeros, practitioners of a Cuban mystery religion that had originated in Nigeria, an amalgam of Catholicism and paganism. Even though he wasn't a practitioner himself, his exposure to Santeria had made him far more open to Mira's abilities than anyone else Sheppard had worked with in the bureau. And, of course, it helped that he and Sheppard were also close friends and had spent countless hours discussing the more mysterious parts of life.

"I find it difficult to believe a Hummer did all this." Goot threw out his arms. "It looks more like a tank."

"My sentiments exactly. Have you seen the sheriff?"

Goot shook his head. "One of the locals said he's in the employee kitchen. Probably stuffing his fat face. How many cops are down?"

"Other than Granny Moses, I don't have any idea."

Goot went into one of the cells that had been occupied and shone his flashlight around at the woman's meager belongings. "We got names on these cons?"

"We don't have anything." Except a call from Sheriff Doug Emison, asking for help. Sheppard followed him into the cell and while Goot rooted through the woman's belongings, Sheppard poked around and finally lifted the mattress and turned it on its side.

Several photos were taped to the bottom of it. A color Polaroid showed a man and a woman, who was pretty in a trashy way, with blond hair that was short, curly, and wild. Her thin body was pressed into very short shorts and a tight-fitting blouse that revealed substantial cleavage. She looked to be thirty or thirty-five. The man looked older, early forties, Sheppard guessed, with short, black hair and a movie star smile. In one picture, he and the woman stood on a beach at sunset, arms around each other's waists. In another photo, they were on a balcony, the woman standing with one hip thrust out provocatively, her laughter almost audible, and the man standing with his arms wide open, as if begging her to come into them.

He flipped the photos over. *Billy & me, Bahamas, 1999,* read one. *Billy & me, St. Augustine, 12/02,* read another. The other photos didn't have anything on the back of them. "Find anything?" he asked Goot.

"Maybe something Mira can read." He handed Sheppard a Baggie with a pair of earrings in it. "If she's so inclined."

"She probably won't be," Sheppard replied. "Not with a hurricane possibly on the way."

"She thinks it's going to hit?" Goot suddenly sounded worried. "That they'll upgrade to a warning?"

"She thinks I'm going to be in an accident and insisted I take her van."

"And because you're in her van and she's now driving your car, the event won't happen?"

"Something like that."

"You live in a strange world, amigo."

"You've got that right."

"But what about the hurricane?"

Sheppard didn't know. He'd left the house before they could discuss it. But he knew there were certain phrases that immediately triggered a Mira Mental List of Things to Do and he was betting that she was going through her list now, especially with Annie pressuring her about evacuating. "I don't know what Mira feels about the storm." He told Goot about Nadine, who traveled in the same Cuban circles that he did. "She's at home, but we don't know if she can even travel."

"My *abuelita* tossed the bones on Danielle last night. She says we'll get wind and rain, but won't take a direct hit."

"Let's hope she's right." Sheppard handed Goot the photos. "I found these under the mattress."

Goot went through them as Sheppard held his flashlight over them. "So we're looking for Billy?"

"Who drives a Hummer. Yeah. Maybe. C'mon, let's go find Emison."

The sheriff was on the other side of the damaged wall, pacing back and forth across the debris, his cell phone pressed to his ear. He looked to be on the verge of a stroke. He was a short man of perhaps fifty, going soft in the gut, his hairline receding, with the hair he had going gray. A southern cracker through and through, he hailed from the good ole boy school. He and Sheppard rarely saw eye to eye about the often thin line between local and federal investigations, but over the years they had learned that cooperation benefited them both. Even so, Sheppard and Goot didn't entirely trust the man.

"Shep, John, where've you two been?"

His rolling good ole boy twang grated on Sheppard's nerves. It always did. "In the cell block."

"C'mon," Emison said gruffly, stabbing his thumb toward the employee kitchen. "We threaded the security images through a laptop. Mira didn't come with you, Shep?"

"Why would she? You know what time it is?"

Emison glanced at his watch. "Oh. Yeah. Well. I guess I just assumed she would come. We could use some additional input."

Sure. For free. Everyone wanted psychic input for free, Sheppard thought, even the idiots who professed to be skeptics. Emison had benefited in the past from Mira's input, but he stuck to the party line. *Psychics? There's no such thing.* That was the thing about skeptics. When they needed help, they weren't skeptics anymore.

"You didn't ask for her help, Doug."

Emison spun around, cheeks burning with color, eyes bulging as though he'd been struck in the stomach. "Some maniac roars in here in an armored car, springs two cons, kills some of my people, blows up the Hummer on Vine, and the fire catches onto trees, yards, two homes. . . . Bet your ass I need help." He kicked open the kitchen door, marched in there, went over to the laptop that was up and running on the table. He hit a key. "Here's what we have of what happened."

Sheppard and Goot watched several minutes of streaming video. The Hummer was impressive, all right, outfitted with metal plates that covered the rear and side windows and all but a slit of glass on the windshield. Even the tires were partially protected by metal plates. There wasn't a single image of the driver. The only view of the two cons was within the cell block, right after the Hummer had slammed through the walls. But thanks to the swirling dust, the images weren't clear.

When the video stream was finished, Emison unhooked a memory stick from his belt and inserted it into the USB port on the laptop. The stick—the newest gizmo in digital storage units—was about the size of a man's thumb and could store anything that was on a computer. Its capacity ranged from sixty-four megabytes all the way to one gig. Sheppard never had figured Emison for a tech geek and found it fascinating that the sheriff even knew about memory sticks, much less owned one. And why was he backing up the video stream?

"So what's with the memory stick, Doug?" Sheppard asked.

"My kid got me into this." He looked embarrassed. "Whenever I got pissed at Windows XP, trying to back up data on CDs, my son would be laughing. He bought me this for my birthday. Cool, huh?"

Cool. Yeah. Cool, awesome. Weird. Emison just didn't say words like *cool*. "Okay, here're the photos," Emison said, and brought up photos of the two women—the blonde from the mattress pictures and a mulatto woman. "The blonde is Crystal DeVries. She was arrested six months ago for a federal bank robbery that she committed with this guy . . ." He hit another key and up came an image of the man in the mattress photos. "Billy Joe Franklin. He got away with five million bucks—the real figure, not what the press reported—and she took the fall. Whole thing happened in broad daylight. DeVries has been in the Tango jail since late February, while Dade's jail is being renovated."

Sheppard thought he'd seen this guy's face before, but couldn't place the when and the where.

"Who was he before the heist?" Goot asked.

"That's where it gets mighty interesting." Emison pressed another key, bringing up a photo of a blond-haired man, surfer type. "Meet William Franklin, weatherman at the National Hurricane Center."

Bingo. Sheppard often forgot specifics—names, where, when—but never forgot a face. The hair color was different, certain small details had changed, but the face was the same.

"He was mostly out of sight," Emison continued. "But occasionally they put him in front of the cameras. Five years ago, he apparently didn't get the promotion he figured he deserved, so he beat up his competition in front of several dozen witnesses. He got fired. He would've done time except the guy he beat up dropped the charges."

"Weatherman to bank robber," Sheppard murmured. "That's a significant leap backward."

"What bank?" Goot asked.

Emison named a federal bank in Miami, but it didn't ring any bells for Sheppard. No reason it should. He didn't do banks. "Did DeVries have any priors?"

"Key question, Shep. A juvenile record for B and E. About half a dozen of them. Never did time, though. From around 1995 to 1999, the year that Franklin got canned, she worked for a local Miami TV station as a researcher for the weather department. That's when she met Franklin. After he got fired in 1999, she lived in Pensacola—and so did he, same address, according to Motor Vehicle—and in Tallahassee, so did he. Same address."

"What'd they live on?" Goot asked.

"I'm waiting for IRS and Social Security records," Emison said.

"And the mulatto woman? What's her story?" Sheppard asked.

Emison slipped a pouch of chewing tobacco from his pocket, opened it, pinched a wad between his thumb and index finger, and stuck it in his cheek. Now he looked like an overfed squirrel. "Tia Lopez. Her trial venue was changed from Jacksonville to Miami. She got moved down here in January, because of the Dade jail renovations. Frankly, I think they transferred her here because she spooked the other cons. Arrested for quadruple homicides. The ex-boyfriends, spouses, lovers, pimps, whatever, of her abused women's support group in Miami. Nine years ago, she was also the primary suspect in the disappearance of her husband, a city councilman. The cops never came up with squat for evidence. After seven years, he was officially declared dead and she left Jax and moved to Miami. He was white, by the way."

As though that exonerated him of any crime, Sheppard thought.

"Disappearance," Goot repeated. "What does that mean?"

"What the hell do you think it means?" Emison snapped. "One day he was at work, the next day he wasn't. In seven years, they never found a body, a weapon, nada. The only thing they had was hearsay that he was abusive."

"I smell a money trail," Sheppard remarked.

"You got it. He was worth a couple of mil, courtesy of his family. After he was declared dead two years ago, she moved to Miami with her mil. And not too long afterward, the exes started dying. The court ordered a psych evaluation."

"And?"

"Well, Lopez is an Andrew survivor. That's what they call themselves these days. She was one of thousands who wandered through the devastation around the Metro Zoo during the aftermath. She was pregnant at the time, went into premature labor. The baby died, Lopez buried it in the ruins. The court shrink thinks it damaged her."

Emison uttered this as though he didn't have a clue why burying your premature newborn in the ruin of Andrew would damage anyone.

"What else?" Sheppard asked.

"She's very bright, IQ way up there, but self-educated."

"Does she know Franklin?" Goot asked.

"Nope. She and DeVries were cell mates for a while, then had cells right next to each other." Emison looked at Sheppard with supplicating eyes, liquid eyes filled with regret, pain, sadness, anger. "Call Mira, will you, Shep?"

"And ask her what, Doug?"

"To help us out."

Now it was suddenly clear to Sheppard why Emison had called him; he wanted Sheppard to run interference with Mira. "You call her."

"She doesn't like me."

"She doesn't like me, either. But she knows that I, at least, pay for her services," said a voice behind them.

A familiar voice. Sheppard turned just as Leo Dillard hurried into the room, all puffed up with his own importance. His face was just as plump as Sheppard remembered, his nose just as crooked, and the mole on the curve of his jaw looked darker. Melanoma? Oops, too bad. His thick white hair looked as though it had been coiffed lately, probably at taxpayers' expense, and his skinny body was jammed into tight-fitting jeans more appropriate for John Travolta than an FBI bureaucrat.

Dillard was second in command of the bureau's Southeast division and twelve years ago, during Sheppard's first stint in the bureau, Dillard had been his boss. He was Sheppard's immediate boss now, too, but only on paper. It was understood that Sheppard answered to the man who had hired him, Baker Jernan, Dillard's superior. Dillard lived and worked in Birmingham, Alabama, and Sheppard's contact with him was mostly through e-mail and an occasional phone call. This arrangement suited Sheppard just fine. He and Dillard didn't get along. Never had. Never would.

"Well, Leo, what brings you here?"

"One of our Key West agents had gotten a lead on Billy Joe Franklin, so I came down here to help out."

Uh-huh. And to claim the credit if and when the perp was brought in, Sheppard thought. The one thing Dillard did very well.

"You know about the bank heist, boys?" Dillard asked.

"We don't do banks," Sheppard reminded him. "But Doug filled us in."

Mira usually referred to Dillard as Sheppard's "karmic cross," but he felt it was simpler than that. The bad blood had begun twelve years ago in Miami and had gotten worse when Sheppard had been hired to head up the Tango Key office, a job Dillard had wanted. A demotion for Dillard, but Tango was a better place to live than Birmingham. Sheppard suspected that Dillard had envisioned himself whiling away his days on the beach, sipping margaritas and surrounded by babes in string bikinis, all at the taxpayers' expense.

The bad blood had grown more intense during the black water events of last summer. After Mira and Annie had disappeared, Dillard had tried to remove Sheppard from the investigation. Sheppard was sure Dillard still had questions about what, exactly, had happened during that episode and Shep wasn't about to enlighten him. Besides, what would he say? *It's like this, Leo. That black water mass was nature's time tunnel and Mira and Annie went through it, back to 1968. And then I went back to find them.*

Right. That would land him in a padded room. And if Dillard ever discovered the extent of Sheppard's claustrophobia, he would use that against him.

"So, Shep, any chance you can get Mira down here? These cons vanished into thin air. I'd like to take her over to the spot where the Hummer blew up and go from there."

"And you're paying for her time." It wasn't a question.

"Of course."

"I'd like that in writing, Leo."

Dillard snapped his fingers and Emison, dutiful foot soldier, brought up a consultant template on the laptop, printed it out, handed it to Sheppard. He glanced through it and laughed.

"She won't do it for this price, Leo."

He looked indignant, as though Sheppard had said something he found personally offensive. "That's our usual consulting rate."

"Good. Then call a psychic nine hundred line. I think the going rate there is three or four bucks a minute. I'm sure you'll get incredibly valuable information."

Dillard pursed his mouth. "Look, we don't have time to shit around here."

"Then you should have contacted her directly to begin with rather than calling John and me down here under the pretense that you needed our help."

"But we *do* need your help." He gritted his teeth, lips pulling away from them in Dillard's version of a smile. "In the event that a warning goes up and the cons haven't been found, we'll need you boys to check ID for anyone evacuating the island."

Goot, who had been uncharacteristically quiet, jammed his hands in the pockets of his khaki slacks and said, "Yeah? And where're you going to be, Leo?"

"Checking ID, helping to set up shelters, going wherever I'm needed."

Leo Dillard, good Samaritan? Maybe he'd had a religious epiphany since Sheppard had seen him last. Or perhaps the bank was offering a juicy reward if Franklin was brought in and Dillard had figured out a way to cash in on it. Never mind that it would be illegal. Rumor had it that Dillard had big gambling debts and in desperate times, desperate men took desperate measures. As much as Sheppard wanted to believe that Dillard would stoop to something illegal, it seemed more likely that he believed nabbing Franklin would win him a significant raise and/or a promotion.

"But a warning hasn't gone up and may never go up," Dillard was saying, his eyes darting toward Sheppard, eyes that resembled beads of water sliding across some grossly dark surface. "So in the meantime, Doug and I need you to convince Mira this is a worthy cause. What fee would she accept?"

"Beats me, Leo." Sheppard pulled out his cell phone and punched out Mira's cell number. "Just press the SEND button and ask her yourself."

Those slippery dark eyes now turned to stone. Dillard regarded the cell phone as though it were a creature that might take a hefty chunk out of his hand, then he snatched it away. Sheppard tried hard not to snicker.

3

"Between 1900 and 2000, sixty hurricanes made landfall in the 'Sunshine State,' the most direct hits from
hurricanes."

National Hurricane Center

It took them a dozen trips from the van to the house and
back to unload the supplies Mira had bought at Winn Dixie.
Even the dog helped, carrying the lighter packages inside in
the hopes that she would get a treat—maybe even a treat for
each package.

Mira had gone for water and pet food and had returned
with all sorts of canned goods, cheeses, coffee, jars of peanuts, sunflower seeds, trail mix, batteries, flashlights, pack-
aged juices, eight bags of ice, three dozen eggs, and fresh
fruits and vegetables. She'd intended to wait until Publix
opened to buy the fresh stuff, but once she and Annie were
in the store, it seemed more prudent to buy everything now.

Prudent or stupid? she wondered as she and Annie began
rearranging items in the floor freezer in the garage. At this
rate, she was going to need another fridge to hold everything
she'd bought. And why had she bought flashlights? There
were eight flashlights in the garage. She knew because

Sheppard had informed her of the number several days ago. Informed her in that irritated tone of voice that made it clear he believed that two flashlights for every person who lived in the house were at least one too many per person. But the three she'd bought were hurricane lanterns, powerful and supposedly long-lasting.

And if the flashlights annoyed him, just wait until he saw the water. Ten gallon jugs of distilled water and three twelve-packs of distilled bottled water. Shep considered bottled water to be an environmental hazard. Plastic killed fish, dolphins, whales, and fouled ocean ecology. It took centuries to disintegrate. That famous line in *The Graduate*—the future is in plastic—had come true in spades, Sheppard said, and to what end?

They'd had this discussion several times since he'd moved here and she knew they would have it again and again because he just didn't get it. She detested the taste of faucet water. She detested that bureaucrats had decided that she and everyone else on Tango Key had to be protected against cavities and had added fluoride to the water supply. She'd told him as much, too, laid it out clearly. She, Annie, and Nadine would continue to drink their bottled water and he could drink out of the toilet if he wanted to. Flashlights, water, and what else?

Five years together, she thought, and the real issues hadn't come up until they'd moved in together.

Her cell rang for the second time in ten minutes. Neither she nor Annie had recognized the number the first time, but not that many people had her cell number, so what the hell? she thought, and took the call.

"Hello?"

"Mira?"

She didn't recognize the man's voice. "And you are . . . ?"

"Leo Dillard."

Fuck.

"I apologize for calling at this hour."

Then why did you call? "I'm awake, Leo. What's going on in Alabama?"

"I'm on Tango. In fact, I'm here at the women's jail with Shep."

Hey, that's wonderful news, Leo, oh pal, oh buddy. "Okay." She paused. She could hear noise in the background and felt like wringing Sheppard's neck for giving her cell number to Leo Dillard. "And?"

"We need your help."

Her help. Uh-huh. She had helped Dillard on investigations several times in the past, sometimes by phone, once in person. Either way was the same thing for her, a challenge because Dillard's energy was a wall of cynical skepticism that was difficult to get around. But it wasn't just his skepticism; she'd read for plenty of skeptics over the years. It was her fear that she might inadvertently read Dillard himself, a complete gross-out event, on a par with reading some neocon who believed that a woman's role in life was to give birth, obey her husband—or her father, brother, uncle, or some other man—and to basically shut up and not be seen. Yeah. Just what she needed. Leo Dillard.

As he explained the situation, her reluctance to get involved deepened. Yet, even though the feds didn't pay quickly, they paid well. She would need extra money to cover the expenses of Nadine's absence. All of this flew through her mind as Dillard explained what he needed and Annie stood there, glaring at her, aware of what was going on.

But of course she was aware. Her antenna probably had gone up the instant Mira had said Dillard's name. Annie knew the score.

Mira's eyes met her daughter's and Annie mouthed, *No, tell him no.*

"And your fee, Leo?" Mira asked, looking away from her daughter.

She had learned that with Dillard, the business part of this had to be up front and spoken before she consented to anything. He named an absurdly high fee and she suddenly knew that Sheppard had negotiated it. She smiled. Sheppard might be a prick about flashlights and bottled water, she thought, but he knew what her psychic input was worth.

She started to say that the fee was fine, but Annie now waved her arms, telling Mira to hang up, they needed to talk. "I'll call you back in five minutes, Leo."

"Five minutes? I need an answer now, Mira."

"Five minutes, Leo." Her frigid tone ended *that* conversation. She disconnected and looked at Annie. "What?"

"Why help him out, Mom? He nearly prevented us from . . . you know . . ."

The unfinished sentence hung there between them. Annie didn't need to finish it. Mira knew she was about to say that when Dillard had meddled in Sheppard's investigation into the black water events, he nearly prevented her and Annie from returning to their own time. But that was then, this was now.

"What he's willing to pay will cover the extra help I have to hire with Nadine out of commission for six to eight weeks. I can't afford *not* to do it."

"Shep can help make up the difference," Annie argued.

"The store belongs to Nadine and me, not to Shep."

Annie started to say more but Mira touched her index finger to her lips; she heard Nadine's wheelchair clicking up the hallway. When Nadine rolled into the kitchen a few moments later, she looked pointedly at each of them, as if in admonishment.

"You two are carrying on so loudly out here I couldn't help overhearing." She stabbed her fingers through her short salt-and-pepper hair and eased a pencil down inside her cast to scratch an itch. "And just for the record, Mira, I can still teach yoga classes and help out at the store from a wheelchair, you know."

"I know you can. But I don't want you to feel obligated, that's all."

"Why should she do a job for that despicable Dillard guy?" Annie burst out. "Tell her, Nana Nadine. The man's a real idiot."

"This isn't for us to decide, Annie."

"But we should be making preparations for getting off the island, for evacuating."

"We can't evacuate," Mira said. "Sheriff Emison has closed the bridge because of the jailbreak."

"What?" Annie looked horrified. "How can he do that? There's a hurricane out there and Emison shuts the bridge? What's *wrong* with him? It's got to be illegal, right?"

Mira shrugged. "I don't know."

Nadine patted the air with her hands. "Calm down, *mi amor*," she told Annie. "Right now, we're only under a hurricane watch. That doesn't mean the hurricane's going to hit us."

Annie threw out her hands. "I live with two psychics and neither of you has any feeling one way or another about whether this storm's going to hit? Is that what you're telling me?"

Mira and Nadine exchanged a glance and Mira knew they were thinking the same thing—that when it came to hurricanes, it was difficult to separate fear from a genuine psychic impression. *Fear*—not psychic certainty—had prompted her to spend over a hundred bucks on food and supplies.

"It's too difficult to read something like a hurricane," Nadine said finally. "And besides, the hurricane isn't the point now. Dillard is." She turned her dark eyes on Mira again. "If you want to help out Shep by doing this job for Dillard, then by all means do so. But just remember that every time you read a crime scene, Mira, you open a psychic door between you and the perpetrators."

Entanglement, Mira thought.

Annie rolled her eyes, her exasperation obvious. "Wait a minute here, Nana Nadine. How come you're not raving about Shep pulling Mom into something like this? You always have in the past."

Nadine rolled her wheelchair over to the fridge, opened it, and helped herself to an apple. Then she moved over to the counter and proceeded to slice the apple into quarters.

"Nana?"

"I heard you," Nadine said. "I'm thinking about it."

"What's there to think about?"

She turned the chair, facing Annie. "I've never pretended to like Shep's line of work, Annie. But the fact is that he's a member of this family now and this Dillard man is his boss. If your mother reading the crime scene will help Shep, then that's one thing. But if she's doing it for money, that's something else."

"But Shep didn't ask," Annie said. "Dillard did. *He* called her cell, not Shep."

"Shep probably told Dillard that if he wanted my help, *he* should call me," Mira said. "That means Shep's okay with whatever I decide."

"It means, of course, that Sheppard is also opening that door," Nadine cautioned. "Is he willing to live with the consequences? Are you?"

"Are we?" Annie chimed in, looking at Nadine. "We're part of her decision, too."

"Oh, forget it. I'll call him back and tell him I can't do it," Mira replied, exasperated.

"Wait a minute," Annie said, holding up her hands. "If they catch these people, will they open the bridge?"

"That's what Dillard led me to believe."

"Then you have to do it, Mom. The sooner the bridge is open, the sooner we and everyone else can evacuate."

An exuberant about-face, Mira thought. Welcome to the world of teenage hormones and angst. "*If* it's necessary,"

Mira said, and didn't bother pointing out all the details that would have to be tended to before they left the island.

"Just remember," Nadine said, "if you run from what you fear, it follows you."

Annie frowned. "Meaning that if we evacuate, the hurricane will follow us up the coast?"

"Meaning that one way or another, you'll have to confront your fear."

"Whatever. Call him back, Mom. I'll go with you. As a team. Okay? I'll help."

"Is it okay with you, Nadine, if we leave you here alone for a while?"

Nadine looked indignant. "Just because I broke my foot doesn't mean I'm incapacitated, you know."

"I just meant—"

"I know what you meant." She reached into a small canvas bag that hung from the arm of the wheelchair and brought out a necklace that Mira recognized. It was a malachite sphere that hung from a silver chain. It had been given to Nadine by a Chilean healer long before Mira's birth, as payment for Nadine's help to the man's family. Mira remembered seeing this necklace first when she was maybe four or five and being entranced by it.

What kind of stone is that, Nana?

Malachite, mi amor. It keeps records about the planet. It heals. It protects. It allows us to hear the music that's in our hearts, our bodies. It helps us to become more.

Nadine's poetic description had been fine when she was a kid, but now, as an adult, she didn't understand why her grandmother believed the stone was so magical. Nadine wore it on special occasions and the fact that she insisted Mira put it on meant she was worried about her reading a crime scene for Dillard.

"What am I supposed to do with it?" she asked, running her finger over the cool, green stone.

"Nothing. It knows what to do."

"It's your amulet, Mom," Annie remarked.

"Exactly," Nadine agreed. "Now get on the phone and tell Dillard you'll do it. But be clear about your parameters. He'll try to push you around."

Fat chance of that. Frankly, she was more worried about Nadine's remark that by reading a crime scene, she was opening a psychic portal between herself and the perpetrators. *Entanglement*, just as Sheppard had said. But once the reading was over, the entanglement ended and the psychic portal slammed shut, didn't it?

After all, she had tuned in on a lot of perps over her years with Sheppard and only three had affected her directly. Hal Bennet, the man who had killed her husband and inadvertently been responsible for her meeting Sheppard; Patrick Wheaton, who had nabbed Annie, taken her into the black water mass, and thus been responsible for her and Sheppard's journeys back thirty-five years in time; and Allie Hart, who had abducted Mira as revenge against Sheppard—and been responsible for Mira's experiences with her dead husband.

All these events had been extremely personal. But reading a crime scene did not have to be personal, she reminded herself. Besides, if she helped Emison and Dillard find the perps, then Emison would open the bridge, and people who wanted to evacuate would be able to do so. Therefore, her efforts would be serving a greater purpose.

"Mom? Are you going to call him or not?"

Still not entirely certain she was doing the right thing, Mira punched out Dillard's number.

4

Hurricane/Typhoon John, which developed in the Pacific Ocean in 1994, was the longest-lasting hurricane. During its thirty-one-day duration, it was both a typhoon and a hurricane.

I am water, Franklin told himself as the bedroom door shut behind them. And he was about to be poured into the vessel called *Lover.* That meant romance, whispering sweet nothings, taking his time, moving the way a slow river moved, savoring the shape and texture of the banks that contained him. It meant savoring the completion he'd sought ever since Crystal had been arrested.

But it didn't happen like that. The instant the door shut, he and Crystal tore at each other's clothes like hungry wolves and fell back on the waterbed. The inside of his head exploded. His skin burned to a crisp. He became fire. And it was all over in five minutes.

Then they lay there, fingers laced together, both of them sweaty and breathing hard. The air-conditioning unit in the window, which ran off the solar panels now, gasped out cool air that eventually brought goose bumps to his skin. He reached down and pulled the black sheet up over them.

"That was heaven," Crystal said softly. "Just like this bed."

She flung her arms over her head and the bed bounced and jiggled. She laughed and did it again. And again. Franklin started doing it, too, and pretty soon they were rocking and rolling on the king-size waterbed, laughing and snorting and trying to be quiet about it because the Amazon was asleep in the front room.

In the early days of their relationship, when they had both been in the weather business, they used to spend most of their free time in a waterbed at his town house in Coconut Grove. Sometimes, they never left the place. They had food delivered that they ate in bed, they watched movies in bed, and once, when the waterbed had broken because they were jumping on it, they had made love in the sea of water that had covered his bedroom floor. In those days, they both had been water.

But in the first several months after he'd been fired from the Hurricane Center, he lost the center of himself and ceased being water. Some days he had been earth, other days air. And sometimes fire, the element he liked least of all. On a few occasions, he had become what he thought of as a fifth element, metal. And it was as metal that he and Crystal had planned the heist that had gone wrong.

Metal was dangerous. When he lived from a place of metal, he was consumed by aggression, hostility, bitterness, a hunger for revenge. When he was metal, he couldn't see the larger picture.

He suddenly wondered what element Crystal had been after they had left the weather business and moved to northern Florida. Air? Earth? In retrospect, it seemed obvious that during that dark time, Crystal had been whatever he had been, as though she were an extension of his flesh, his soul. But perhaps that meant she had been the very paragon of water, able to assume the shape of whatever vessel contained her.

So what was she now? She was still fire in bed, but what about the rest of the time?

The waterbed finally settled into stillness. In his head, he saw the water inside the bed as a lake at dusk, the very center of it shimmering with silver, the edges lost in shadows. He could float in that lake forever.

"I've always been kinda curious about something, Billy. When we pulled the job, how'd you know all the details about the money transfer that day?"

Interesting question, he thought, *and too long a story to go into now.* So he lied. "I spent weeks observing the routine at the bank, that's how I knew."

"Yeah? So anyone could, like, observe a bank and learn the routine?"

"Well, no, the routines vary. But there're patterns to watch for, just like with weather systems."

"Patterns." She repeated the word carefully, as if it were new to her.

He didn't like the direction of this conversation, so he changed the topic. "Tell me about jail, babe." He raised her hand to his mouth, kissed each of the knuckles. "What was it like?"

"Like? It wasn't *like* anything."

"Describe it."

She jerked her hand away from him, rolled onto her side, lifted up and rested the side of her head in her hand. The light seemed to tunnel through the curls of her wild blond hair just so that it could kiss the curve of her cheek. She brought her index finger up the center of his chest, his throat, up over the curve of his chin to the tip of his nose. "Why?"

"Because for days and weeks I tried to imagine you in jail and I couldn't see it. I couldn't see you there. I just couldn't conjure your face and body in a shit hole."

She flopped back against the bed, making it jiggle and

rock, and folded her hands under her head. Eyes glued to the black ceiling, she said, "Dade was the shit hole. There, your life belongs to the state. You're an indentured servant. You're a slave to fucked-up guards. You learn to sleep with your eyes open." She paused. "We used to get out for exercise in the yard for a while every day. And one day, these black chicks started hassling me. They started with the stupid blond jokes, then things went south from there."

Franklin shut his eyes as she spoke and her voice flowed like water across the inner screen of his eyes. He could see her, see the yard, the hot light, see it all.

"Suddenly, I . . . I was surrounded by six or eight of these dykes, all clutching shanks. They hissed like snakes, they said if I agreed to fuck them, they would protect me. Then . . . then this tall mulatto chick—Tia—strolls out into the yard and suddenly everything stops. She shouts at a dyke who'd been talking shit to me. The dyke spins around, threatening Tia. The other women drop their shanks and split. But Tia and this woman keep moving closer to each other, and then . . . then they're, like, going at it, okay? Except that Tia doesn't have a shank. She doesn't have anything. She spins, she dances, she laughs, and then she's moving so fast she's a blur.

"I blink. I . . . yeah, it was that fast. I blinked, Billy, and suddenly the dyke's on the ground, shrieking, and Tia coming toward me, grinning like it's all been a big fat joke, and she says, 'You are one stupid white girl, getting yourself into a mess like this. C'mon, girl, I need to talk to you about what's what around here.' And that night, I hear the dyke is in the clinic, with burns on her hand."

"From what?"

"From the shank. It was metal. I heard it got so hot that it burned the dyke."

Franklin felt certain that he'd missed something here. Or that Crystal had. "How'd it get hot?"

"I don't know."

"That doesn't make sense. Did she have matches? A lighter? Something flammable?"

"I don't know. But anyway, after that, no one bothered me. Word got around that I was under Tia Lopez's protection. She was in for a bunch of homicides and everyone knew it and even the dykes didn't fuck with her. Then, in late January, Tia's trial got switched to Tango and they transferred her out. A month later, I went, too."

"Because?"

"I thought it was because they were renovating the jail. But Tia said she'd heard there'd been a payoff somewhere up the line."

Franklin smiled to himself. Yes, indeed. A hefty payoff. But he wasn't ready to tell her about any of that yet. *When you were water,* he thought, *other people had to step into you to find out what you knew.*

"When I got to Tango, there were a bunch of women in the jail, they were short on cells, so Tia and I became cell mates. After the other women left, we had cells right next to each other. We had it pretty good there. Granny Moses treated us well, brought us home-cooked food, makeup, free-world shampoo. Once a week, she'd bring in movies and we'd have a Hollywood fest in the main room. I . . . I couldn't kick her out of the Hummer, Billy. I owe her a lot."

Spoken like a true water person, he thought. "And who'd she kill?"

"Some guys who were beating up on their women."

"Where'd she learn to shoot?"

"I don't know. But she's good, isn't she?"

She said this with a kind of enthusiastic admiration that worried Franklin. The last thing he needed was a third party tagging along. "She can't stay here indefinitely, babe. I planned enough food and supplies for the two of us for a month. A third person will cut that time too drastically. We'd have to leave Tango before it's safe."

"I think she knows that.*"*

Assume nothing: it was one of his rules. "I'll give her some money, clothes, a disguise, whatever she needs. There's also a Harley in the storage unit out back that she can have."

"A Harley? Since when do you drive Harleys?"

"It was here when I bought this place. This property is old, really old. It dates back to the Civil War. I bought it from the last descendant of the slave who inherited it from the master who freed him. There's even a tunnel that runs from the cellar into the storage unit. They used it to hide slaves and then ship them off the island."

"Cool."

Cool? What the hell kind of response was that? The history of the place wasn't just *cool*, it awed Franklin.

"How long have you owned it?"

"Nearly six months."

"And how much did it set us back?"

"All total, the price for the cabin, springing you, supplies, all the rest of it came to about two million." *And that included payoffs,* he thought, but didn't say it.

"*Two* mil?" She bolted upright, her expression horrified. "But . . . but that leaves us just three million out of our take, Billy, and where the hell are we going to live? We're going to have to buy another place? And how're we going to sell this place? We killed . . . I don't know how many people today and everyone's going to be looking for us. Jesus, Jesus, I had no idea, no—"

"Hey, calm down." He touched his hand to her bare back. "I've planned it out. I've got us a little place in the mountains in North Carolina. We can live a very long time on three million, babe. We're doing fine. Really. But not if we have to pull a third person around with us. Come light, our pictures are going to be everywhere and no matter how you dress up your Amazon pal, she's tough to miss because she's so tall. If she stays, we'd have to split up and all of us go solo just to get off the island."

She stabbed her fingers into her hair, shook her head, flopped back down. "I . . . I'll say something to her. But we need to know about the hurricane first. What it's doing, where it's—"

"We'll check the updates when we get up. Just make sure that she's clear on the ground rules. A couple of days, then we give her cash and whatever else she needs. Okay? We agreed?"

"Yeah. Sure. Of course. But suppose the storm hits? What then?"

"She rides out the storm with us, then splits."

"Does this place have hurricane shutters?"

"We'll be fine."

"Fine how? Are there shutters?"

This was something new, he thought. In the past, Crystal never had questioned him when he'd said something was fine, that he'd take care of it. She had trusted him. Did this mean she was no longer water?

"There's a cellar, fully stocked."

"They have *cellars* on this island? Wow."

"The hills make it possible."

"But a cellar might flood during a hurricane."

"Doubtful. It's in the garage."

"My God, you've thought of everything." And with that, Crystal rolled on top of him, covering his face with quick, soft kisses. Even though his body responded, a niggling doubt had crept into the back of his mind. *Is she still water?* Of course she was. Crystal would be water forever.

But what's it mean if she isn't?

* * *

Tia Lopez lay on a very long couch, on sweet-smelling free-world sheets, with a deliciously soft, free-world pillow under her head, and she was so deliriously happy she didn't know if she could sleep. It had been nearly a year since she'd slept on anything except hard jail cots, in cells where the air was either too hot or too cold and it was either too noisy or too silent. In jail, the air always stank of something—sweat, bleach, puke, violent emotions.

But here, God, the living room windows were open and the summer breeze carried the scents of pine, jasmine, gardenias, melaleuca, the richness of wilderness. The complex sounds of darkness created the most perfect music. She wasn't sure where, exactly, they were, but her senses told her it was deep in the wilderness preserve. On the Tango map in her head, the preserve was marked with a large red X. It was one of several spots she had selected as a possible sanctuary. She hadn't figured that her escape would come about because of someone else, but now that it had, she needed a plan for what would happen next.

She couldn't stay here. She liked Crystal well enough and it was because of her she was here at all. But in the end, she was a stupid white girl who'd gotten taken in by a good-looking prick with a slick line. Tia knew all about women like Crystal. Hell, she used to be one of them. She also knew a lot about men like Franklin, a guy with a reckless bravado borne of some deep insecurity that he didn't measure up. Dipshits like him usually had major childhood issues that they never got rid of. They weren't introspective. They couldn't look far enough inside themselves to ask the questions that would free them. So they repeated the same dumb patterns over and over until the pattern crippled or killed them.

Her husband had been that kind of dipshit. And his pattern was abuse—mostly toward her. And for months, she had taken it, tolerated it, lived with it because she believed that she had incited it, had done or said something that had triggered it. But in the end, she had broken her pattern by smothering the bastard while he slept off a drunken stupor.

Franklin's pattern, she thought, wasn't abuse. It was power. When she'd seen that monster Hummer come crashing through the cell wall decked out in all its armor, she'd thought the island had been invaded by terrorists or by the U.S. military. That kind of power. Franklin was toxic. He was like sarin or anthrax, a shock-and-awe sort of guy.

Tia pressed the heels of her hands against her eyes and told herself to sleep. She needed to sleep. Her body begged for it, her brain demanded it. But she had to find answers about tomorrow, the next day, the day after, about whether Danielle would hit or miss, about how she would get off this island. On the mainland, she had money, her books, people who would help her. On the mainland, she had made preparations for when she would no longer be Tia Lopez and would become someone else.

Now she struggled to remember what those preparations were, but a sweet, seductive darkness swam through her—and took her away.

The hums and songs of the wind chimes filled the air with a haunting, almost ethereal music that was, Mira thought, like listening to a spiritual rendition of something by Chopin or Mozart. Accompanying these glorious sounds was the song of the wind clicking branches and strumming leaves, an orchestra's equivalent of oboes, small drums, castanets, tambourines.

Annie heard it, too, and they both paused on the sidewalk at the bookstore's front door, and listened. Even Ricki, pursuing some stray scent along the ground, stopped as if understanding that something extraordinary was happening out in the yard. The music was as layered and complex as a language, yet held a simplicity that startled Mira.

"I've never heard the wind chimes quite like this," Mira remarked.

"Me neither." Annie took Mira's hand. "Can you read the bookstore, Mom? To find out how it will do during the hurricane if we have to stay?"

She could try, yes, but if she saw the bookstore collapsing or flooding . . . well, what could she do to prevent it? The store had good hurricane shutters—but lay in a flood zone. Concrete block fared better than any wooden structure in a hurricane, but what good would concrete be if her stock got ruined by water? The store lay several blocks from the Tango pier on the flattest part of the island, which surely would suffer a storm surge if Danielle hit. Even though her deep beliefs prompted her to trust that her world would be safe during the hurricane if it struck, her left brain threw up countless wild, dire scenarios that marched through her with impunity as she unlocked the front door.

One World occupied a corner lot three blocks north of the Tango pier, an unassuming concrete block building with decorative blue wooden shutters on the front windows, a wonderful wooden porch that wrapped around three sides of the structure, and a front yard filled with gracious old trees. The gumbo-limbos had endured fifty years or more of weather; the banyans were at least as old. The mango and grapefruit trees were younger, had shallow root systems, and probably wouldn't make it through the storm. She didn't expect the white picket fence or the porch to make it, either. But porches and fences could be rebuilt, trees could be replanted, yards could be replenished. The building would endure, she felt certain of that, but could it survive a storm surge of fifteen or eighteen feet if Danielle made a direct hit?

And what about the restaurant next door? Mangrove Mama's was strictly an island place—laid-back, colorful inside and out, and looked as if it might blow away on even a marginally windy day. Yet, it had stood here for years—as had its twin on Sugarloaf. She noticed that the owners weren't up and about right now, *they* weren't worrying about flooding, wind damage, or losing everything. They were genuine Tango Fritters, never worried about hurricane *watches* and took a wait-and-see attitude about hurricane warnings.

Nonetheless, here she was, Mira Morales, Consummate Worrier. She had insisted on meeting Leo Dillard at the bookstore rather than at the jail because she had to come here first. Before she could take preventive and protective measures, she needed a clear sense of what she could do to mitigate a worst-case scenario. She needed to walk through the aisles and touch the shelves, the books, allowing her intuition to speak to her. And she needed to do this before Dillard and his crime scene came into the picture, before his energy tainted hers, before, before.

Mira turned on the lights and she and Annie stood just inside, taking it all in. Right now, her stock was close to forty thousand volumes, the highest since she and Nadine had opened the place five years ago. And she couldn't move everything. That would take days and require more space than she had. At the very most, she could move the stock on the lowest shelves to higher spots and box up the stock that sold the best—romance, suspense, some young adult fiction, nonfiction political best sellers, some self-help and health/ diet titles.

For her own peace of mind, she also would move certain metaphysical titles that meant a lot to her—and immediately felt panicked by what that would entail. Where to start? The tarot, yoga, the *I Ching,* runes, astrology, and palmistry to mythology, quantum physics, reincarnation, and anything by Terrence McKenna Louise Hay, Caroline Myss, and Mona Lisa Schultz, to . . . oh, Christ, too many books and not enough time.

"Mom, we need boxes," Annie said.

"In my office closet. There're plenty of boxes." They had

received a large shipment earlier this week and she hadn't had time yet to flatten the boxes and put them in the Dumpster. "Masking tape is in there, too. We're going to need a lot of that."

Annie looked dismayed. "Where should I start?"

"With the books on the lowest shelves and with your personal favorites. Pretend you're living in *Fahrenheit 451*. Where would you start?"

"Harry Potter. *The Gossip Girls. The Golden Compass.* And John Edwards's books."

"Really? John Edwards? The TV medium? Why him?"

"I like his stuff. Also . . ." And now she grinned. "He's hot."

"We've got room for genuine. We do *not* have room for hot."

Annie laughed. "Where should I put the boxes?"

"Start stacking them on one of the dollies."

Annie hurried off and Mira moved farther into the store. In addition to books, she carried music and made an immediate decision to pack away as many of the CDs as she could. No telling how many boxes that would require.

Over three thousand square feet and at least a third of that belonged to the aerobics area and to the coffee shop. The only items she would move from those areas were the espresso machine, which had cost her a small fortune, and the computers.

"Mira?" called a man at the front of the store.

It took her a moment to recognize the voice, and when she did, she hurried through the aisles. Ace stood near the counter, a tall, sinewy black man with hair as tight and wiry as a Brillo pad that was turning white at the sides. He wore psychedelic board shorts and a blazing red T-shirt with the words *Sunset Performer* screaming across the front of it in brilliant yellow.

"Ace. I thought you never got up before noon."

"Only for you, sweet thing." And he threw his arms around her, hugging her hello as though he hadn't seen her in years when, in fact, he'd been in last week for a reading. "I saw the lights on. I hope it's okay that I came in."

"For you, Ace, always. What's going on?" She touched his elbow. "C'mon, walk with me. I'm taking inventory."

He didn't walk; he bopped along next to her, his gangly body loose, rubbery. His sandals slapped against his heels. "Is she going to hit?"

"I don't know."

"Then what're you doing here?"

Good question. "Fear, paranoia, maybe it'll hit." She shrugged. "What're *you* doing here?"

"Luke thinks the storm's going to hit big time and wants to evacuate. I told him I'm not getting stuck on the road outta here. We compromised and decided to ask you."

Luke was Ace's long-time partner. Every evening, about an hour before the sun sank, Ace and Luke joined dozens of other performance artists on the Tango pier and entertained tourists, locals, and whoever else was around—Ace as an escape artist and Luke as a tightrope walker. They'd started their acts twenty years ago on the Key West pier and had moved to the Tango pier seven years ago, when they'd bought a bungalow in the Tango hills, at the edge of the wilderness preserve.

"I can't tell you what to do, Ace. But right now, no one's evacuating. The bridge is closed." She explained about the jailbreak. "And frankly, I think it's going to be a nightmare out there on the roads with thousands of people headed north, and running into more thousands in Dade and Broward."

"Uh-huh, just like I told him. We've got shutters, food and supplies, a shortwave, a generator, and our place sure isn't going to go the way of Noah's ark. We're fifty feet above sea level."

"Then you should stay." Mira reached the metaphysics

section and began pulling books off the lower shelves and stacking them on the floor to be boxed later.

"That's your psychic opinion? I can tell Luke that?"

"It's just my, uh, regular opinion."

Ace thrust his long arms forward, palms turned upward, as if he were about to take something into them. "Read me, Mira. I gotta tell Luke your psychic opinion. I don't need a full reading, just your take on this."

Mira's gaze went reluctantly to Ace's slender, beautiful hands. She didn't want to read anyone right now. Bad enough that she would have to read a crime scene when Dillard and Sheppard arrived.

"I—"

"Please?"

The supplicating look in his eyes elicited a reluctant nod from Mira. She brought her smaller, whiter hands to his callused palms, and felt a tingling that seemed almost electrical. As soon as she shut her eyes, two paths opened up in her head. One was lined by gnarled trees that created dark, spooky tunnels of wet leaves and branches that appeared to angle deeply into a thick, black wooded area. She didn't know whether the image was a metaphor or an actual scene. The other path crossed a bridge and she understood this to be the path to evacuation.

Mira focused her inner attention on the bridge, crossed it, and saw a wall of water crashing across mile marker 40, at the beginning of the seven-mile bridge. It swept away everything in its path—beaches, rocks, brush and trees, cars and people. In the instant before she jerked her hands away from Ace's, she heard shrieks and screams, the death throes of hundreds that would be washed away.

"Unless you can leave right now, don't evacuate."

When she opened her eyes, Ace's face had seized up with terror. "We die," he breathed. "That's what you saw, right?"

She was sweating profusely and suddenly felt so nauseated that she leaned against the shelf and wiped her arm across her face. "A storm surge, Ace. Around mile marker forty. And you and Luke are stuck in the traffic when it happens."

"But if we were going to evacuate, we'd do it as soon as the bridge opens. The storm isn't due for another seventeen hours. So we'd be way farther north."

He was right. It didn't make sense. But as soon as she had touched his palms, linear time had vanished. "I'm just telling you what I saw."

"And if we stay?" He held his hands out again, like a young child eager for the present hidden behind the adult's back. "Can you tell me what happens if we stay?"

"I can only tell you what I see, Ace."

"That's what I mean." He shifted his weight from one foot to the other, as though the floor were hot and his feet were burning.

She hesitated, wiped her hands on her shorts, then pressed them against Ace's palms again and he went still. She asked for information on the path that led into the dark, spooky woods . . .

. . . and barrels through the woods in a huge six-wheeler truck, the kind that hauls refrigerated foods. It crashes over fallen trees, through pools of standing water so large that the wind whips across them, creating waves. The headlights bounce up and down, twin balls in the wet darkness. Rain pummels the windshield. Ace's beautiful dark hands grip the steering wheel.

"Over there," Luke shouts, pointing at the heap of debris and rubble.

"Jesus God," Ace hisses. "They're in a cellar under all that. We . . ."

The vein dried up. Mira gripped Ace's hands. The pit that opened in the center of her stomach meant that what she had seen was connected somehow to herself, Sheppard, perhaps even Annie or Nadine. But how could that be? They wouldn't go through the storm inside a cellar in the woods.

Give me more.

"What?" Ace asked. "What is it?"

Scenes appear and vanish faster than her heart-beats. There, the truck nearing the turnoff for the by-pass that cuts from east to west across the island. Here, Ace and Sheppard, commiserating in the back of the truck, surrounded by the strange contraptions Ace and Luke use in their acts. Now the truck trundles up-hill through the remains of a neighborhood. Trees lie in the road like fallen giants, fences are gone, roofs are gone, garages have collapsed. And with growing horror, Mira understands what she's seeing.

Mira stumbled back, her arms swung to her sides, she ached all over. "Ace, do you own a refrigerated truck?"

"Yeah, for when we haul Luke's tightrope gear and the crane that pulls me upside when I'm in a straitjacket and wrapped up in chains. Why?"

"Make sure you keep that truck near your house during the hurricane. You're going to be using it to rescue people in different areas."

And one of those areas, she thought, was her own neighborhood.

"So we stay."

"On the path that I just saw, yes."

"Do we make it through?"

Do they? She felt a quick, hard tightening in the center of her chest, then heard a soft, resonant *yes* in her head. "Yes."

Ace threw his arms around her, hugging her again, then stepped back, grabbed her hand, and kissed the back of it. "I could be straight again for a lady like you, Mira. Thank you, thank you . . ."

And he danced backward up the aisle, spun, and moved swiftly toward the door, snapping his fingers and swinging his hips in rhythm to music that only he could hear.

Mira continued to lean against the bookshelf, arms clutched to her waist, and wondered why she could see choices for other people but not for herself.

5

"Forget the weather computer models.
Forget the strike probabilities.
Forget predictions.
A hurricane has a mind of its own
And it's not telling us where it's going or why."

Tia Lopez

When Annie, her mom, Shep and the others reached the area where the Hummer had exploded, the morning light was the color of tartar sauce, the air was still, thickly humid, and stank of scorched earth. Smoke clung to the frail light. Annie saw pieces of smoking debris, blackened yards, denuded trees, tree trunks wrapped in black soot or the scorched remnants of fire, she couldn't tell which.

Just outside the fire zone area, Dillard pulled the police van over to the curb and they all got out. The smell of the air nauseated Annie. Her reaction apparently showed because Shep touched her arm and asked if she was okay.

"The smell," she said softly, and suddenly wished she had stayed home.

He pulled a handkerchief out of his pocket. "Put this over your nose and mouth. It'll help."

But it wasn't just the smell of the fire that got to her. Beneath that odor lurked other scents—of fear, desperation, despair, each one holding the promise of a story or information. This had happened to her a few times before and she never knew what to make of it. Once in the school cafeteria, she'd caught a whiff of a cheerleader's perfume and, like some puff of smoke in a cartoon, it had turned into a beckoning finger and she had followed it into the girl's home. There, Annie had seen the tension in the girl's family, the parental misery with which she lived. Annie had thought the girl was just a snobby eleventh grader, but realized it was all a show, a cover-up.

"Hey, Leo, why'd you stop here?" Sheppard asked. "Mira said she saw a parking garage. There's one a few blocks down. Let's drive over there and save some time."

"But we aren't sure it's *that* garage." Dillard glanced at Annie's mother. "Right, Mira?"

Right, Mira? Annie repeated silently to herself, mimicking Dillard's slightly nasal tone, her mouth puckering just as his did. "You frickin' jerk," she murmured.

"It seemed like it was a parking garage, but I don't have any idea where it's located," her mom replied. "We can just start here."

"This isn't a place for kids or dogs," Dillard remarked to no one in particular, even though Annie knew it was directed at her.

"I'm not a kid." Annie stuffed the handkerchief in her shorts pocket. "I'm fifteen."

"Ah. Hormones." He and the sheriff traded secret glances, good ole boys sharing their joke. "Keep the mutt on a leash."

"She's a retriever, not a mutt," Annie snapped.

"Hey, we've had dozens of police dogs out here that couldn't pick up a trail. Your dog won't do any better."

"Police dogs don't compare to retrievers in the smell department. That's been proven."

Dillard finally looked at *her*. "You're awfully opinionated for a kid."

As he said this, he emanated an odor that was just as strong as the smoke, but in a different way. His scent brought her an image of Dillard as a nerdy kid, whose parents subscribed to the belief that children shouldn't be seen or heard.

"I'm entitled to opinions," she shot back. "Here, Ricki." She held out a shirt taken from one of the cells. "Find the scent."

Ricki sniffed and Dillard rolled his eyes as if to say he would tolerate Annie's presence only because he needed information that her mother could provide. Annie felt like kicking him in his skinny ass. Her mother sensed it. She touched Annie's shoulder, shook her head, and muttered a few words in their secret language. "*Nit noke.*" *Not now.* Why not now? Annie wondered. What was wrong with now?

But she kept her mouth zipped and she and her mother fell into step behind the men like second-class citizens. It burned her ass. *Guess what, Mr. Dillard, m'man. I've marched in D.C. with my mom, I'm pro-choice, pro–civil rights, pro–universal health care, pro–everything you're against. You're a bureaucratic asshole.* She itched to say it—but didn't.

Annie noticed that her mom's fingers went to the malachite necklace Nadine had given her. She doubted any stone, regardless of how magical an amulet it was supposed to be, could protect her mother against Dillard's negativity.

Annie knew all about the history between Dillard and her family—the bad feelings between him and Shep, the black water events that had changed certain things in Dillard's life that he might or might not be aware of. It wasn't that her mother and Shep talked specifically about Dillard, but that they rarely censored stuff in her presence. She was a good listener and smart enough to fill in the blanks.

Since last summer, her mother and Sheppard had been worried that there might be residual effects of their having gone back in time. They speculated these effects might manifest themselves in the future and involve everyone who was a part of those events. At first, Annie wasn't at all sure what those effects might be—permanent changes in their DNA? Something more serious? But in recent months, she'd discovered something tangible, evidential, solid. Her enhanced sense of smell, for instance, had started about three or four months ago, around the same time she'd noticed Sheppard's claustrophobia.

One evening he'd been in the attic, shuffling stuff around, doing his usual Shep organizing, and suddenly Annie heard him shouting. She had run out into the garage, scrambled up the ladder, and found him hunched over in a corner where the attic roof was very low, paralyzed with terror. Her mom had to talk him into moving forward. She knew he'd been to a doctor about it, but not any doctor associated with the bureau, and that her mother had given him visualization techniques to use whenever he began to feel claustrophobic. She also knew he kept a supply of mints on hand that supposedly helped. But he didn't talk about it, not with her.

She hadn't seen anything obviously weird in her mother yet, but her mom was tough to figure because she was always so weird. Now Annie felt she should be alert for oddities in Dillard. But she didn't know him personally, not really, not like she knew her mom, and didn't have the vaguest idea what to look for in a jerk like Dillard.

Ricki trotted alongside Annie, her nose to the ground as they skirted the explosion site, and headed for a thickly wooded area behind some houses. The dog whined, glanced up at Annie, and she snapped on Ricki's leash. The fires were out, but the air smelled scorched, ruined, and a two-block area was still cordoned off. Here and there people stood around, watching, waiting, some of them in pajamas, some in work clothes, some busy putting up hurricane shutters.

That was what they should have been doing, too, Annie

thought, getting prepared instead of catering to Dillard. But she reminded herself that if her mom could get a handle on where the perps were, then Emison would open the bridge and they could all get out. Not that anyone listened to her. She was just a teen, couldn't vote yet, so what the hell difference did her opinion make? They all talked about the family as though it were a democracy, but her vote didn't count, her voice wasn't heard.

Her mother held a Baggie that contained an earring Goot had found in a cell and as they walked, she pressed the earring between her palms and focused on her breathing. No one spoke as they made their way through the trees, the light spilling down through the branches. Ricki strained at her leash, so Annie removed it and the dog darted out ahead of them all, leading them through the woods. Her mother didn't comment, didn't even give Annie a reprimanding look. That meant she was in the groove, pursuing what no one else could feel or see—sort of like what Ricki did.

They emerged from the trees and everyone stopped—except for Ricki, who darted on ahead, crossing a deserted road and headed for a building on the other side. A parking garage.

"Hey, there goes your dog," Dillard snapped.

"She's onto something."

"She's running without a leash. That's against county ordinance."

Oh, gimme a break, you moron. "In Birmingham, maybe, but not here."

Just the same, Annie ran after Ricki—across the street, into the parking garage, then into the stairwell.

Here, the dog paused, tail wagging, and Annie snapped the leash on her collar and held the shirt up to her nose again. "You're doing great, girl." She gave Ricki a small treat. "Keep looking, girl."

Ricki headed up the stairs and Annie hurried after her,

clutching the leash. The dog darted over to an empty parking space and, nose to the ground, circled the area, tail wagging. Then she sat down, looked over at Annie, and barked. Annie ran over to her. "What?"

The retriever stood, revealing a thin gold chain. A bracelet or an anklet, she thought. "Good girl." But where had this come from? Had one of the perps lost it?

Annie crouched, turned on her flashlight, and searched the area around the chain. She didn't see anything else. Annie picked up the chain, closed her fingers around it and, following what she had learned from her mother and Nana Nadine, silently asked the chain to yield its secrets. Nothing happened. She brought it up to her nose, sniffing it, and caught the vaguest fragrance of something—body odor, sweat, and the smell of the metal itself. She had a sudden, vivid impression of a woman with wild blond hair. But that was all.

Sheppard, her mother, and the others reached the spot and Sheppard came over to her. "Did Ricki find anything?" he asked.

"This." She opened her palm, revealing the gold chain. "I think their getaway car was parked here."

Annie appreciated that Sheppard didn't pick up the chain. He knew his touch might contaminate the residue of psychic energy that the gold held. But shit, *she* had touched it. *Bad move, very bad move.*

"Maybe your mom can pick up something from the chain."

"That's what I was trying to do."

"Remember how you and Nadine did your mind meld thing at that cabin in Asheville?"

"Yeah, so?"

"Can you do that with your mom? Maybe with you holding the chain and your mom holding the earrings, you'll be able to come up with more."

Annie often felt intimidated by her mother's abilities, but

it was worth a try. She and Sheppard joined her mother, Goot, and the others. Her mom was just standing there, frowning, her hands pressed against the Baggie that contained the earrings. Annie knew by the expression on her face that she was having trouble picking up the thread of whatever had brought her to the garage.

"Ricki found this," she said, showing her mother the chain. "Do you want to—"

"Jesus," Dillard burst out. "You aren't supposed to *touch* anything you find." He snapped his fingers at Emison. "Give me an evidence bag, Doug."

Her mother gave Dillard a sharp look. "Back off, Leo. She's trying to help. And forget the Baggie, Doug. She already touched it." Her mother reached for Annie's hand. "Let's see what we can find, hon."

Annie noticed the irritation etched into Dillard's features and caught a sharp, unpleasant scent of anger. But Dillard didn't voice his displeasure and Annie and her mother moved away from them. "He shouldn't be here," Annie whispered.

Her mom nodded. "I have trouble picking up anything when he's too close to me. But let's push him away and focus." They paused inside the parking space where Ricki had found the chain.

Annie shut her eyes and after a few moments, was aware that Sheppard and Goot stood behind them. She didn't sense Dillard nearby and suspected Sheppard had told him and Emison to stay back.

"I'm seeing a black van," her mother began. "It doesn't have side windows. The man and two women are scrambling into the back of it. No rear seats."

And an image popped into Annie's mind, shocking her. "It's a converted camper. With bunks, a cooler—"

"Can either of you see the license plate number?" Sheppard asked.

"No," they answered simultaneously, and began moving,

as though circling a parked car. "There's a sticker on the front windshield," Annie said. "I can't read what it says."

"It's a blue sticker," her mother went on. "There don't appear to be any markings on the van, no other colors, no designs. I don't know what year it is. He's talking, the guy is talking. *Become someone else, babe,* he says." She paused and Annie heard the rest of it.

"He says he didn't plan for a third person. . . ."

Her mom, still holding Annie's hand, dropped into a crouch and Annie dropped with her. They set the items they'd been holding on the ground and, simultaneously, placed their free hands on the pavement. Dozens of different scents swirled into Annie's nostrils and she understood immediately what it meant. "They became other people. Put on new clothes, disguised themselves. The guy . . . he's shaving off his beard."

"His beard?" Dillard interrupted.

And just that fast, everything dried up. It was as if the sound of Dillard's voice had slammed a door. Annie glanced back at the others.

"Jesus, Leo," Sheppard exploded. "You're supposed to keep your mouth shut."

"Hey, I just want to know about the beard—"

"Keep your distance, Leo," her mother snapped, releasing Annie's hand as she grabbed the Baggie and got to her feet. She started moving again, down the ramp, past the men.

Annie remained where she was for a few moments, staring after her mom, astonished at what she'd been able to pick up, and pissed that Dillard had broken the flow. Ricki came over and licked her face, telling her to c'mon, hurry, or she would be left behind.

She and Ricki trotted after the others and fell into step alongside Sheppard. "You did great," he whispered, and gave her a quick hug.

"He spoiled it," she replied.

She spoke a bit too loudly and Dillard heard it and gave

her a dirty look. He jabbed his finger at her and mouthed, *Shep, keep the kid in line.*

Annie's eyes locked with Dillard's and her third finger slid up her cheek. *Fuck you and the horse you rode in on.*

She knew he saw it, but he looked quickly away.

6

"Whether your roof comes off in a hurricane, exposing your home, might come down to a three-cent nail."

Palm Beach Post

Mira's awareness split like an atom. A part of her was conscious of Annie at her side, of the others behind her, and another part of her could still see the cons' van in her mind's eye.

The driver turned right, so did she. The driver picked up speed, so did she. The energy of the woman whose earring Mira held pulled her into the van's psychic slipstream, along the early morning street, into an alley several blocks later.

Then Dillard moved closer to her—and his energy distracted her, teased her, drew her in. She didn't have any desire to read the man, so she shut down completely. *Be clear about your parameters*, Nadine had told her. *Spell out the boundaries.* She hadn't done that.

She stopped, spun, snapped, "You can't do that, Leo."

He drew back, startled by the savagery in her voice. "Do what?"

"You can't come up behind me like that when I'm reading a scene."

"Oh. Okay. Sorry. I, uh, thought maybe I should go get the car so that we can drive the route you're seeing."

"I have to walk. I can't do it from inside a car." Walking helped to ground her, to connect her with the solidity of the real world. She didn't bother explaining any of that. But because she would be able to read more deeply if he wasn't anywhere near her, she quickly added, "You can follow in the car if you want."

"I'll go get it," Emison offered, and extended his plump hand for the keys.

Dillard dropped the keys into his palm and he waddled off. Mira, disappointed that Dillard hadn't left, now established rules, parameters, boundaries. "If you have a question about what I'm doing, ask Annie or Sheppard. You can't ask me. It interrupts the flow. If I say something, please don't ask me to repeat it because I probably won't remember what I say. I'll read until the vein dries up, and after it runs dry, don't press me for more answers."

"Reading the scene. Interrupting the flow. The vein." He nodded as he repeated what she'd said, then tried to make light of it by laughing. "You speak another language, Mira."

"The last time I checked, it was English. If you have problems with English, Leo, then I'll do it in pig Latin."

Color rushed up into his neck. She had embarrassed him, but Christ, he deserved it. He raised his hands and patted the air as though he were dealing with a wild, unpredictable Doberman. For some reason, she noticed that he bit his nails, a rather odd habit for a grown man. "Okay, continue. I'll shut up."

Sheppard and Goot stood silently behind Dillard, suppressing their amusement that Dillard had been put in his place.

"You should be back there with them." Mira gestured toward Sheppard and Goot. "Stay back at least ten feet so I don't pick up anything on you."

She turned again, walked quickly forward, Annie and the dog keeping pace with her. Her focus had been compromised and she had to will herself back into the flow using the techniques that Nadine had taught her years ago: alternate nostril breathing, rolling her eyes upward toward the middle of her forehead, deep diaphragmatic breaths, bringing her focus into the center of her solar plexus. Gradually, she felt an inner shift and was able to enter the slipstream again.

A block later, she stopped, pointed off to her left. "He got stopped by a cop."

"Here?" Dillard came up close to her, but not too close. "Right here?"

"Yes."

"The black van."

"Isn't that what I've been talking about?"

Her irritability sailed right past Dillard. "Jesus, this is great, Mira. This is perfect."

He immediately got on his cell phone and barked orders to Emison and Mira stood there, wide open, the Baggie with the earring inside still pressed between her palms. Why was it in a Baggie? It wasn't evidence. They knew who it belonged to and she needed to feel the metal earring against her bare skin. Metal was an excellent conductor of emotional energy, but with a layer of plastic between her and the metal it was like trying to feel the warmth of a vine tomato while wearing winter gloves. She tore open the baggie and plucked out the earring.

It heated up almost instantly and just as she began to pick up images, Dillard rushed over and touched her arm . . .

. . . And she sees him in a bank, a casino, arguing with a woman, speaking in hushed tones on his cell phone, meeting someone on a dark street . . . money passes hands . . .

. . . Now Dillard and a man in a military uniform survey a ruin strewn with bodies and speak in urgent, terrified tones . . .

. . . he's arguing with his wife . . .

. . . with his kids . . .

The images shoot toward her so fast and furiously she can't draw air into her lungs . . .

Mira wrenched back, startling herself as much as she did Dillard, who stammered, "What? What is it?"

"You can't touch me while I'm doing this!" she screamed at him, her reaction so completely out of proportion to what he'd done that she instantly felt ashamed of herself. She rubbed her eyes and when she spoke again, her voice was lower, but as tight and tense as a newly strung guitar. "When I'm wide open like that, Leo, and someone touches me . . . that energy is what I see." Her hands moved instinctively to the center of her chest again, rubbing at a lingering ache there. "You had pneumonia recently." She hadn't meant to say it, hadn't tagged it consciously yet, but the words spilled out. "You got sick after you and your wife had a major blowout and . . ." She stopped. *Shit, shit, shut up.*

"How . . ." He paused. "When I touched you?"

She nodded and looked quickly away from him, certain that he was about to ask her what else he'd seen. *That your life is a fucking mess, Leo, and you're in debt up to your eyeballs. And what's with the strewn bodies? Where was that?*

Mira dropped the earring back into the Baggie, shoved it at Dillard. Her fingers stroked the stone around her neck that Nadine had insisted she wear. She felt a tingling in her fingertips, like a mild electrical current, and suddenly a block of information fell into place.

"He's not using his real name. Not for the van, not for the sticker. . . . His last name rhymes with something . . ." She cocked her head, listening to an inner whispering, but couldn't hear it all. "It's like Carter, Jimmy Carter, but that's not it. It's close, though."

Dillard's eyes glistened like stars. "Anything else?"

"No. I'm done here. I can't do anything more, Leo."

She walked swiftly away from him, wanting only to put distance between them as fast as her legs would carry her. The sun was fully up now and everywhere she looked, she saw signs that people were taking the hurricane watch seriously. Trucks loaded with plywood made their way up the street, into driveways. People were out putting up shutters, trimming back trees and shrubs. While she had been zoned out, the world had moved into a new day fraught with uncertainty.

She felt a sudden urgency to get back to the bookstore and begin loading her stock into the delivery van, putting up shutters, bringing in the patio furniture. Her unease was too acute to ignore.

Annie broke the silence first. "If we're walking back to the bookstore, it's kinda far, Mom."

"You get a ride with them if you want. I can't bear to be near him."

"What'd you see about him?"

Mira didn't want Dillard to overhear her. She thought a moment and in their secret language, said: "He's got gambling debts. It's wrecking his marriage. His house is mortgaged to the hilt. And I think that if he brings in this bank robber guy . . ."

"Franklin," Annie said, then told her that Dillard had moved out of hearing range.

She switched to English. "Yeah, him. If Leo brings in Franklin, he's getting a payoff from someone. Or he'll benefit somehow financially." There was more, a deeper layer here about Dillard and this whole business that she couldn't reach. "I'm not sure of the specifics."

"Where're the cons?"

"They're still on the island. Other than that, I don't know. Hey, can you get us a weather update on that PDA of yours?"

"Sure." She whipped out the Palm Pilot that Sheppard had given her for her birthday. "If the wireless stuff is working. Sometimes it's tricky." Annie leaned against a tree and, with the little black stylus, played the device with the ease of a pianist.

Sheppard caught up with them, his expression unreadable. Mira couldn't tell if he was feeling happy, remorseful, or somewhere in between, and she wasn't about to try to read him. Right now, she didn't think she could read her big toe if she had to. "Don't you want a ride?" he asked.

"With Dillard in the car? No, thanks."

Sheppard jammed his hands into the back pockets of his jeans and kicked at a pebble or a twig on the sidewalk. She sensed that he was choosing his words—and his timing— carefully, deliberately. "Half a dozen dark vans were stopped in this vicinity since the jailbreak. The names are being run now. You gave us a key piece of the puzzle, Mira."

"But the name's phony," she said.

"It will give us a place to start. We're pretty sure it's Billy Joe Franklin, but once we have the name he's using, we'll be able to check for bank and property records under that name. We . . ." His hands came out of his back pockets and he crossed his arms on his chest. "Hey, don't be pissed at me, Mira. Dillard wanted me to run interference with you, to get you down to the station. I think that's the only reason he called me. So I told him to call you himself."

"If he ever asks again, just tell him flat-out no, Shep. Don't put me in this situation again."

Sheppard's jaw went rigid, his expression shut down, and a terrible silence flooded his eyes. "No one put you in any goddamn position. You could've just told him no when he called."

Never mind that he had given Dillard her number or had dialed the number for him. Never mind that. She knew he had a good point. She'd been seduced by Dillard's fee and the silly notion that she might be serving a higher purpose. Yeah, right. "We're out in the middle of the street, Shep. I don't want to have this conversation here."

"I don't want to have this conversation at all." Terse, blunt.

She hated it when they reached an impasse like this. It would take them hours to get back to a normal level, she thought, so it was a good thing that they would be going their separate ways now. She gestured toward the police van coming up the street. "Here comes your ride."

"I'll call you later."

"I need help putting up the shutters."

"I know. I'll call."

"Uh, hey, wait." Annie hurried over, her face flushed with fear, excitement, both. "Look at this."

She thrust the PDA at Mira and Sheppard, forcing them to move closer to each other so they could see the little screen on the device. And what Mira saw was a sentient but alien being with a perfectly formed and single, ubiquitous eye, churning less than four hundred miles off the South Florida coast. According to the stats at the bottom of the screen, it was moving swiftly, had top winds of 135, and was southwest of the Keys. A red line streaked up the coast, indicating the probable strike areas, from Tango Key to northern Palm Beach County. A hurricane warning for this stretch of the coast was expected to be implemented at eight AM, ten minutes from now.

A near panic hurled open Mira's inner floodgates. Adrenaline poured through her, her muscles twitched and shrieked to flee or fight. Confronted with the real possibility of winds strong enough to shear bark from trees, everything else paled in comparison.

She instantly imagined the chaos on the single highway out of the Keys, as some thirty or forty thousand residents all took to the two-lane road at once only to join three or four times that many drivers in Dade County and more tens of thousands fleeing from Broward County. She began imagining millions evacuating all at once.

There were three main arteries north out of South Florida—I-95, the Florida Turnpike, and I-75. Those roads would take you into Georgia, assuming you could even get out of Monroe or Dade Counties, she thought. The other roads like U.S. 1, Dixie Highway, and A-1-A would be jammed with local traffic as residents ordered to evacuate low-lying beach areas tried to move inland to shelters.

Madness. And right then and there, she decided she would stay. She would stay in her house, with her family and animals and as much of her bookstore stock as she could cram into the delivery truck and the garage. She would make her home and her business as secure as possible and ride out the bitch in a house that, in forty years, had withstood other hurricanes. She would do it because the alternative—being stuck on a highway as winds of 135 miles an hour or more whipped your car to dust—was unthinkable.

Mira struggled to do the math in her head, but she was so drained that her brain refused to work. "How long?" she murmured. "How long do we have?"

Annie already had done the math. "At her present speed, the eye will make landfall in about fifteen hours. But we'll be feeling it a long time before then. The outer bands are filled with violent weather."

"Hey, you all need a ride?" Dillard called.

Mira thought about it for about five seconds, then hurried toward the van.

Fifteen hours.

She would have to make every minute count.

7

The word "hurricane" comes from "Huracan," the god of violent storms and thunderbolts among the Yucatan Carib Indians.

The wind woke her, two strong gusts that rattled the windows like ghosts in chains. Tia Lopez bolted upright from the couch, body braced for imminent disaster, eyes pinned to the windows. Daylight. She couldn't see anything except trees—green piled upon green.

She threw off the black cotton sheet and swung her long legs over the edge of the couch. Her bare toes curled and uncurled against the smooth wood floors. Real wood, not the laminate shit. She liked that and hadn't noticed it earlier this morning when it had been dark. Her eyes moved slowly around the room, drinking in the details.

It wasn't a huge room, but when you'd spent months in a seven-foot cell, this space seemed as vast as Russia. The pine furnishings wouldn't win any *Good Housekeeping* awards, but she liked what she saw. Pine, lots of color in the throw rugs, colorful pillows here on the black couch, a couple of afghans tossed over the backs of chairs. One beautiful wooden rocker looked to be old.

Photographs of weather systems covered the walls. Tia remembered that Crystal had told her Franklin had been a meteorologist, but these photos indicated an obsession with storms—dust storms, whirlwinds, tornados, summer rainstorms, snowstorms, hail storms, solar storms, space storms, ice storms, desert storms—and satellite photos of hurricanes. The pictures pulled at her in a visceral way, with a compulsion that could make her panic.

Tia dropped to the floor and did seventy-five push-ups, forcing her attention away from the photos. Whenever panic threatened her, she channeled it into something physical. It occurred to her that near panic must be her daily condition since every day for nearly a year she had been doing push-ups, sit-ups, yoga, and lifting weights when weight had been available. She was probably in better physical shape than she had ever been in her life—thanks to all the screaming banshees locked behind a door in her head.

Tia went over to the window. The woods looked dense, thick, deliciously primitive. No utilities strung up out here, she thought, and wondered how the place was powered. Solar panels? Wind? Generators? After months of studying the layout of Tango, its topography and geological anomalies, Tia knew that the preserve covered several thousand acres and was as wild and untouched as it got anywhere in the Florida Keys. So if they were in the preserve, how far into it had they gone?

Even more to the point, how long had she been sleeping? What time was it? *And where's the hurricane?*

Her chest tightened at the thought. *Not yet. Don't think about that yet.*

She quickly patted her back pocket—and felt an immediate relief. Her fat little spiral journal was still there. Granny Moses had given them out to all the cons who had passed through her jail and told them they should write in it daily, even if it were just a sentence or a paragraph. She seemed to consider it a form of therapy or rehab. Most cons didn't bother—Crystal never had—but Tia had discovered a friend in the journal. Through writing, it was easy to swim back through the chaos of her life and order it. Now the journal represented the center of herself, her true heart.

She turned, looking for her weapon, the one Franklin had tossed her when they'd escaped. Gone. Okay. Franklin had taken back his gun. He was the boss, the Man. Yeah, fine. She got the message.

Tia went into the kitchen, a long room with a window behind the sink that looked out into more trees. It had both a fridge and a floor freezer and they were jammed to capacity. It looked as though he'd intended to stay here for a long while. You break your *chiquita* out of jail and instead of fleeing the island, you lie low in a predetermined hiding place. Smart. He now had points in her book.

She started a pot of coffee and whipped up a feast for herself—omelet, buttered toast, slices of crisp bacon. God, oh God, *free-world* food, in a *free-world* kitchen, on her first day as a *free-world* woman. After nine months, one week, and three days in jail, the experience of selecting and cooking her own food, of drinking real coffee, and of standing here at a kitchen window in such blissful silence filled her with awe and wonder and profoundly humbled her. Never again would she sit in a jail. Never. She would die first.

She washed off her plates, marveling at how cool and fresh and sweet smelling the water was. She cupped it in her hands and sipped, savoring it. In the aftermath of Andrew twelve years ago, she would have killed for water like this. She wanted to feel this water washing over her body, through her hair, but she hadn't seen a bathroom and figured it was connected to the bedroom where Crystal and Franklin were.

In fact, as soon as she could figure out how to escape the island, she would get out of their lives. But that would take money, clothes, transportation. She would make it clear to

Franklin that she intended to repay him for everything, but first she had to get to the mainland so she could retrieve her money. Before she could plan anything, though, she needed to know what the cops were up to.

News, she thought, and turned on the small TV that sat on the kitchen counter. Surely the jailbreak had made the news. She flipped through the channels, loving the freedom of it, that no one was standing over her, directing her to go to this channel or that one, as Granny Moses and some of the cons used to do in the common room. She could watch anything that she wanted to watch. The cooking channel. Oprah. Cartoons. Who would give a shit?

Given the sheer number of stations, she figured Franklin had satellite TV. What hadn't this guy thought of? He probably had a shortwave radio, another set of wheels, bicycles, a stash of weapons, maps, additional generators, maybe even fuel cells. The source of the cabin's energy intrigued her. Fuel cells, solar panels, a generator: was there anything she was forgetting?

Too bad he didn't have a plane.

She settled on a Miami channel. Commercials. Tia dried off the plates and silverware she'd used and returned everything to the cabinets and drawers. The commercials ended and she turned up the volume.

"In case you're just tuning in with us this morning," a pretty broadcaster said, "the top story is Hurricane Danielle. Around eight this morning, the National Hurricane Center in Miami upgraded the hurricane watch for South Florida and the Keys to a hurricane warning.

"Danielle is now packing winds of 140 miles an hour and may strengthen to a category-five storm over the next several hours. At eleven this morning, Danielle's central pressure was 929 millibars, just seven millibars higher than Andrew's when he slammed into Homestead twelve years ago. Only two hurricanes have been more powerful than Andrew—

Hurricane Camille in 1969, which had a central pressure of 909, and the Labor Day Hurricane of 1935, which devastated the Florida Keys and had a central pressure of 892.

"Mandatory evacuations have been ordered for all residents living between Key West and Tavernier. All visitors and nonresidents throughout the Keys are ordered to evacuate. In Dade and Broward Counties, evacuations are ordered for anyone who lives east of U.S. One. In Palm Beach County, the warning has been downgraded to a watch, but emergency officials there are requesting voluntary evacuations of the area east of U.S. One.

"The governor is expected to drop tolls on the Florida Turnpike and to open all lanes for northbound traffic only. As of thirty minutes ago, only emergency vehicles are permitted to enter the Florida Keys and all boats and marine vessels in the area are urged to move farther north immediately. We'll now take you live to the National Hurricane Center for the latest update on Danielle. . . ."

Blood roared in Tia's ears, she couldn't swallow. Her mind pedaled backward twelve years. She began to shake and stood there with her arms clutched against her, paralyzed with shock. *Not again, sweet Christ, tell me it's all a mistake.*

But now the male forecaster appeared, sitting at his desk, with a huge map on the wall behind him and a satellite photo of the storm imposed over it. "Jesus God," she whispered, her voice so tight she nearly choked on the words.

It was Andrew all over again—small, compact, immensely powerful. The eye, like Andrew's, was so perfectly formed that she could see the swirling bands of violence in the eye walls. It was slightly farther to the south than Andrew had been and the bands of rain reached out a bit farther. The eye was also larger, but otherwise, Danielle could be Andrew's clone, his spawn twelve years later.

Statistics appeared at the bottom of the screen, but she

couldn't make sense of them. It was as if some vital connection between her eyes and her brain had broken down, blown out, gone haywire.

She brought her fisted hands to her eyes, pressing hard. "Pay attention, pay attention," she murmured.

But his words darted around in the air like fireflies and were difficult to seize. Her ears rang, her stomach clenched. ". . . strengthening . . . slowed . . . fifteen miles an hour . . . present course . . ." The forecaster's stick moved to the map and traced the red line that snaked up the eastern coast, from Tango Key to northern Broward County. ". . . by late this evening . . ."

Tia stumbled back, groped behind her for something to grab, pulled out a chair, sank into it. When she looked up again, the forecaster was gone and some local newswoman was doing what they always did when a hurricane threatened: talked about what you should be doing. Food, supplies, provisions for your pets if you were evacuating, how to secure your property, where to put your important papers.

Tia burst out laughing and instantly slapped her hands over her mouth. Right, sure, important papers. Food. Supplies. A first-aid kit. Like a Band-Aid and iodine would get you through it all. *Morons, morons, all of them.*

Now another aerial shot, of Tango, where cars snaked back for miles, waiting to get on the bridge. "Earlier this morning, the Tango bridge was closed while police sought two inmates who escaped the Tango women's jail." Now: photos of Crystal, of Tia herself. Her mug shot made her look edgy, unstable, maybe insane. "Tia Lopez, forty, was being held at the Tango jail while awaiting her trial. She's accused of killing four Miami men. Crystal DeVries, thirty-two, was awaiting trial for a federal bank robbery months ago in Miami. Both women are armed and considered to be extremely dangerous."

Now the cameras cut to a tall, bearded man, who was

identified as FBI Agent Wayne Sheppard. "We believe DeVries and Lopez are still on the island, perhaps in hiding with the individual who aided in their escape. This necessitates our checking the ID of every driver and passenger seeking to evacuate the island. We apologize for any inconvenience this may cause."

Tia stared at this man, Sheppard, and suddenly knew she had seen him somewhere before. But where? When?

And then it came to her, December, while she'd been sitting in the can in Miami, Sheppard had been on CNN because of a quadruple homicide outside of Asheville, North Carolina. Four people dead, his fiancée missing, believed to be kidnapped. It had stuck in Tia's mind because the CNN guy had smirked when he'd reported that Sheppard's fiancée was a psychic. Tia couldn't quite wrap her mind around that, a fed and a psychic, engaged. Now here he was again.

And suddenly she wondered if his psychic fiancée had been found and if he'd enlisted her help on the breakout. Tia had only one experience with a psychic, a woman who had come to speak to their support group in Miami. She'd been dressed like a Gypsy and talked New Age shit. *As I come into your vibration . . .*

She had the uneasy feeling that the fed's fiancée wasn't that kind of psychic. He just didn't look to be the gullible type.

She pressed her hands over her face and struggled to focus, to think, to plan. But she knew too much. In fact, if she had known as much about hurricanes twelve years ago as she did now, she would have fled Miami the Friday before Andrew had hit. On that day, the director of the National Hurricane Center had assured viewers that it was doubtful Andrew would hit South Florida and that beautiful weather was predicted.

Only last year, the U.S. Army Corps of Engineers and the Federal Emergency Management Agency—FEMA—had released the results of a test that had cost eighty grand about the evacuation of South Florida in the event of a catastrophic hurricane. They'd determined it would take sixty hours— two and a half days—for all the people who fled to get out. *Sixty hours,* she thought, just to get to some place safe like Orlando. This time could be cut to about a day and a half if the Florida turnpike made all its lanes northbound from Fort Pierce to Kissimmee. But another study had determined it would take ninety-nine hours.

Her head snapped up. The time. What time was it? She had to know the time.

She bolted upright and rushed back into the living room, searching frantically for a clock. She finally found one in a study—it was one PM. Dear God, one PM. Nowhere near a day and a half to get out.

She ran back into the kitchen and flipped through the channels until she found CNN. And there it was, living proof. The aerial photos of the Keys showed a slow-moving river of glass and chrome, inching along the two-lane road north. She started shaking and suddenly she was *there,* inside her apartment near the Metro Zoo twelve years ago, her windows sealed up with plywood, the wind picking up, her TV on, her dog pacing frantically. She still had power and was on the phone with her sister, who lived a mile south with her three kids, and was trying to convince Tia to get her ass over to her place, where it would be safer.

It had sounded so reasonable, so sane, what her sister suggested. But Tia kept saying no, no, she was fine, really, and she and the dog had food and supplies and were surrounded by more than four hundred neighbors. The baby, her unborn baby, wasn't tossing or turning. And then the phone had died, the TV had gone blank, and the words *emergency broadcast* had pulsed across the screen, and a trembling voice had said, "This is an emergency broadcast. Andrew is coming ashore at Homestead. Winds exceeding 155. Do *not* evacuate. Stay where you are and take shelter in a window-less room and stay tuned to the emergency broadcast. . . ."

The power went off, the dog started howling and leaped onto the couch next to Tia, and the walls of her apartment began to shake. Tia had leaped up, shouting at the dog to come, fast, and they'd fled into the windowless bathroom, where her supplies were. Minutes later, the world had exploded with sounds—jet engines, colliding high-speed trains, like Hiroshima at ground zero.

Then there was nothing.

She came to in the dark, buried under a pile of rubble, her body curled around her dog's or his curled around hers, both of them whimpering. He was licking her face, digging, licking, and she moved her hands, digging her fingers deeper into stones, dirt, shit, she didn't know. She passed out, came to, passed out, and came to so many times she thought she had died. Air finally poured into the space where she and the dog lay and rain and more wind swept over them, through them. They finally managed to crawl out of the rubble together and collapsed in the unforgiving dark.

The next time she came to, the agonizing pain in her abdomen told her she had gone into premature labor—four months premature—and she shrieked and screamed and no one came to help her. The dog tried to comfort her, to keep her warm and dry, and then she'd felt the rush of blood and tissue between her thighs. She passed out again.

Light and dark melted together. She didn't know how long she and the dog lay there. Eventually, the dog went off to find food and her thirst drove her forward onto her hands and knees. She found a damp stone and licked it for moisture, but it wasn't enough, she needed more, more. She finally found a freezer half-buried at an angle on its side, trapped by the muck and debris, and she pried open the lid. Most of the frozen food had melted and left pools of cool water. The dog stuck his head inside and drank and drank and Tia scooped her hands into the water, drank, vomited, drank again and again. She filled a dirty cup with water and brought it over to her baby and pressed the edge of it to her baby's dried and bloody lips—and realized the baby was dead, half-formed.

After that, she didn't know what happened. Her mind took flight.

And that had been only the beginning.

Struggling to pull air into her lungs, Tia stumbled out of the kitchen and into the living room and threw open the front door. She lurched outside, into the breeze, the extreme humidity, all the quivering green. She tripped over something and fell to her knees and oh, sweet Jesus, the smells right then were the smells of Andrew, the richness of wet earth mixed up with the storm's violence and the complete indifference to human life. That bitch Danielle was coming, she was. Tia knew it, felt it. She pressed her hands against the ground and pushed up, rocking back onto her heels, and looked frantically around.

Trees, more trees, everything moving, flapping. The wind wasn't strong yet, but the branches swayed back and forth like dancers. It began to rain—not hard, but just enough so that it released more smells, and she shot to her feet and spun around. The house. Could it withstand a cat four?

She took one look at it and a peal of hysterical laughter escaped her. Fuck, fuck, it wasn't even concrete block. It was wood, just a wooden cabin that looked as if it had been slapped together from driftwood, spare plywood, and fallen trees.

Shutters. Were there shutters? Was there plywood to nail over the windows?

She hurried from window to window, praying that she would spot runners where aluminum panels would go or, at the very least, evidence that plywood had been nailed over these windows at some time in the past. But she found nothing like that. Some distance behind the house, up against the dense woods, stood a concrete block, windowless building. At first, she thought it was a one-car garage, but then she saw the ordinary door, a padlock on it. Tia broke open the padlock with a large rock and peered inside.

The only source of light in the building streamed in through the door, but it was enough to determine the building was used for storage—boxes stacked in a corner, things hidden under tarps, a workbench, a fridge. She peeked under the tarps and discovered a Harley Davison. The Harley was a Screamin Eagle, a beautiful monster with the key in the ignition—her way off the island?

Not now, not with police checks on every vehicle leaving Tango. But maybe in a day or two, after Danielle had blown through.

Tia left the building, shut the door, then walked quickly along the back of the cabin, hoping to see concrete or evidence of shutters somewhere, but didn't. She came out again by the front door, discouraged and scared. No shutters, no plywood, nothing at all to keep the wind out. But with winds at cat four or higher, what difference would the best shutters in the world make if you had a roof made of shit? It was the old fairy tale about the three little pigs and how the wolves would be huffing and puffing and when the roof went, the entire place would be history.

She would have to head out on foot, steal a boat, and get off this island while there was still time to get somewhere farther north. Uh-huh, on foot. That part stumped her. Getting out of the preserve on foot might take more hours than she had. Worst-case scenario, she might get caught in the open as Danielle made landfall. If she took the Harley, she would never make it through the line of evacuees going through the police check. In short, she needed a miracle.

Tia ran back inside. Crystal was in the living room, folding the sheets, Ms. Domestic. She wore a T-shirt that covered her skinny ass and not much more. One look at her and Tia knew she'd been fucked silly during the last several hours, and had loved every second of it. She glowed.

"Tia, where you been?"

"Tasting the wind," she said. "You seen the news? The bitch is coming."

"I'm watching it now," Franklin called from the kitchen.

Tia hurried into the kitchen, the skinny white girl padding along behind her. Billy Joe Franklin stood at the stove in jeans and an unbuttoned shirt, his feet bare. He kept watch over strips of bacon and mushrooms simmering in butter, and four eggs crackling in oil. He munched noisily on a crisp, red and yellow apple.

"You have shutters for this place, Billy?" she asked. "Sheets of plywood?"

"Nope."

"Do you have an extra car? A bicycle?"

"Nope."

"What about that Harley in the storage unit?"

"Unless it turns into a boat, it's no use to us now."

"Is it coming here, Billy?" Crystal asked, biting worriedly at her lower lip. "Is that what the news is saying?"

"Uh-huh." Another bite of apple, then he scooped the mushrooms out of the frying pan, dropped them on a bed of paper towels, and flipped the bacon.

"And we're going to stay here?" Crystal burst out.

He pointed the clicker at the TV and changed channels. "You want to get stuck in *that?*" Aerial shots streamed across the screen, two hundred miles of cars that had come to a complete stop.

Crystal's blue eyes widened. She looked stupefied.

"And when Danielle makes landfall," Franklin went on, "she's going to be pushing a storm surge of at least fifteen to eighteen feet, probably more. And all that water is going to crash over that skinny piece of highway and wash every god-damn car into oblivion."

"Maybe we can steal a boat and get the hell out of here on the Gulf side."

Franklin's burst of laughter made it clear he thought Crystal came up way short in the intellect department. *Nothing worse than a patronizing man,* Tia thought, and felt the old rage turning over in its long slumber and stirring awake. She shoved it back into the crevice where it had lain hidden.

"Not with them seas," Tia pointed out.

The poor grammar was for Dipshit's benefit. She wanted him to think she was just a dumb nigger killer. She gestured toward the TV, where the water on the Atlantic side of the road churned fiercely, waves crashing against the narrow, rocky beaches. Within a few hours, those waves would be washing across the road.

"Damn straight," Franklin agreed.

"I'd rather be here than there," Tia said, and looked point-edly at Franklin. "But if we stay here, it can't be in this cabin."

"Hey, we'll be fine here. The trees are so thick and dense they'll form a wall against the wind."

Huh? This guy had been a meteorologist? He was talking like a nutcase. She struggled to speak calmly. "Excuse me, but nothing forms a wall against winds this high. Them trees out there are going to be stripped nude, trunks torn up and branches like flying missiles. Every piece of glass in this place is going to go, your roof peeled back like the top of an aluminum can. Even if this place was rebuilt after Andrew, when they had stricter building codes, it won't matter if we take a direct hit because at the end of it, Tango will look like Hiroshima. We'd be better off in that concrete storage unit. It felt pretty solid to me. No windows. A tile roof."

Franklin was looking at her strangely, as if actually seeing her for the first time. "Sounds like you've been through a couple of hurricanes, Lopez."

"Just one." The one that mattered. "Andrew."

"Where were you living?"

"Two blocks behind the Metro Zoo, in an apartment building that had more than four hundred people living in it. After Andrew roared through, the building had been leveled and sixteen survived."

"That's impossible. The official tally of dead from Andrew was twenty or twenty-five, something like that."

"You buy *official* if you want. But I counted the fucking bodies myself. We spent ten days without water, food, or first aid. We rummaged in shit. We fought monkeys for food. They'd escaped from the zoo, along with an assortment of panthers and tigers. We had to hide from them. But none of this ever made it into the news, either. And there was never a goddamn word about the nuclear power plant ten miles south, about the cracks in the smokestacks."

She had his attention now. And Crystal's, too. They were seated at the kitchen table, eating the scrambled eggs and mushrooms, their eyes riveted on Tia.

"You never told me any of this stuff," Crystal remarked. "We were cell mates for months and I never heard shit about this. But, Tia, Billy used to be a meteorologist, so I think he knows a little more about hurricanes and all this stuff than you do. No offense," she added quickly.

Outside, the wind gusted again, hurling rain against the windows, and then the rain began to fall in earnest. Franklin cocked his head, listening to it in a way that suggested he understood the rhythm of the rain and the wind the way a musician understands the rhythms of the instrument he plays.

"The outer bands are starting to move in," he said.

"Yeah, great." Tia leaned forward, hands on the table. "So do you have anything around here we can use to board up the windows? That would be a start."

"I have something better." He winked at Crystal. "Remember, babe?"

"Oh. Right." Crystal grinned. "You'll love this, Tia."

They both pushed away from the table and Franklin gestured for them to follow him.

They went out into the double-car garage, a *wooden* garage, she saw with dismay, where the van fit snugly between walls of boxes, a workbench, a stack of spare tires. Something else was in the corner, covered with a large yellow tarp. He moved boxes to the side and opened a door in the floor. New. Metal. "We've got a cellar. Probably one of the few cellars in South Florida. But hey, we're over a hundred feet above sea level here."

He reached in and turned on the light and Tia and Crystal huddled in next to him for a look down the long stairwell. "There's running water, a freezer stocked with food, sleeping bags, a generator, we'll be fine down there. C'mon, I'll show you."

They followed him down the stairs into a small room crowded with *stuff*. Sink, washer and dryer, small floor freezer, dozens of gallons of water, boxes of canned goods, all of it lit by a forty-watt bulb that hung, nakedly, from the ceiling. *And no other exit.* A coffin, it was just a coffin supplied with stuff to take into the afterlife.

A ball of panic hammered in Tia's chest, she couldn't pull air into her lungs, she broke out in a cold sweat, and backed toward the stairs, shaking her head, unable to speak around the intense and crippling terror that she felt. She'd been buried alive during Andrew and no way was it going to happen again.

Tia stumbled and grabbed on to the railing, whipped around, and tore up the stairs, her bare feet pounding against the old wood, the stink of mold, dirt, and death clogging her nose, nearly choking her. She burst into the kitchen, her chest heaving, air whistling through her gritted teeth, and kept right on going, through the living room to the front door.

She hurled it open and stumbled out, into the wet wind, sucking air deeply into her lungs, struggling not to sob, to scream, to run like hell. Everywhere around her the woods trembled, shook, danced. Birds took to the skies in huge flocks and winged their way northward. Frogs jumped around, croaking in the rain. Way back deep in those woods, she knew, wildlife made their own kind of preparations, some digging in, others scurrying for safety, wherever that might be. She sank to the stoop, her mind roaring.

"What the hell's your problem, Lopez?" Franklin demanded, coming up behind her.

Tia shot to her feet and turned on him with such ferocity that he looked momentarily stunned and drew back. "What's wrong with *me?* Wake up, dipshit. You may have been a meteorologist, but I'm telling you that cellar's a death trap. What happens when the house and the entire garage collapse, trapping you inside? There's no other way out. And who's going to hear you shouting way down there? And how long's your air going to last? And if we get a foot or two of rain, that cellar is going to fill up with water mighty quick. So you think about *that.*"

The rain picked up, as if to underscore what she'd said, and Franklin stepped back under the porch roof, staring at her, then out at the rain. A variety of emotions flickered across his face, here one instant, gone the next, but Tia saw them all and some of what she saw scared her. This man, whoever the hell he really was, had dark, shadowed places in him, she thought, where no one was allowed—and where no sane person would want to go, anyway.

When he spoke, she sensed he had gone through the many possibilities, had played them out in his own head, and realized that she might be onto something.

"You have some good points, Lopez. But what other choices do we have? Let's hear your ideas."

She moved up under the porch roof with him, to get out of the rain. "The storage unit. We can take all the cellar supplies over there."

"That building has drawbacks. The roof isn't as solid as it looks. I did it myself, so I know."

"Then maybe a house at the northern end of the island that has good shutters and no one home. We stay there until the storm passes. We take some of your supplies with us. But we can't take the van and since I don't see any other vehicle around here, that could be tough to do."

"There's a VW Bug in the garage. Under a tarp. I have to put in a new battery and do a few other things to it, but I can have it running in thirty minutes. One of us can scope out a neighborhood first, find the right house, then come back for the others. While one of us scopes, the other two start hauling supplies out to the front room, emptying the freezer and putting what we can into some coolers."

"You said you didn't have another car."

He smiled, a quick, charming smile. "I lied."

"Uh-huh. Well. Okay. So we should have some way of keeping in touch."

"I've got two cell phones."

No one could accuse him of not being prepared. "I'll toss you for who goes out to scope."

He grinned. "So you're a gambling woman, Lopez?"

"Hon, my whole life has been a gamble. And I've got more to lose than you if I get caught."

"How's that?"

"If convicted, I go to death row." Either Crystal hadn't enlightened him or he was playing dumb.

"What the hell did you do, anyway?"

"Crystal didn't tell you?"

Another grin, a flash of beautiful white teeth. "We weren't exactly talking a lot."

"I killed four men." Five, with her husband, but she didn't say that.

"How'd you kill them?"

What a revealing question, she thought. Most people were interested in motive, not method, and asked why. "I don't know. I don't remember the specifics." She'd been in the Red, that place beyond reason, beyond thought, beyond memory. In the Red, she became a primal being. "The police shrink told me they all died the same way—they bled out and the third vertebra in each guy's neck was broken."

"Bled out?" Franklin looked extremely uneasy now. "From what?"

She shrugged. "Beats me. I guess the moral of the story is don't piss me off, huh?" And she tapped his chest with her index finger and laughed. After a moment or so, Franklin laughed, too, an edgy, nervous laugh, as though he were anxious to put some distance between them—and fast.

The wind swept across the clearing in front of the house, whistled through the eaves above their heads, and bent the trees like straws. And it wasn't just a gust. This wind was now steady at fifty or sixty miles an hour, she guessed, and could imagine it three times stronger, roaring over this little cabin in the woods as though it were no more substantial than a pile of hay. She shivered and stepped back closer to the open front door.

"Let's toss that quarter, Franklin, and get the show on the road."

He slipped a quarter out of the pocket of his jeans. "Heads goes on the scouting mission. You call it."

"Heads," she said.

He tossed the quarter, she caught it, flipped it into the palm of her hand, and opened her fingers. Tails. *Shit.*

"I'll go get the VW ready," he said, and went into the house.

Tia stood there a few minutes longer, her nose turned into

the wind like that of a dog, hoping to catch some telling scent that would indicate what the bitch had in store for them. But at the moment, Danielle wasn't surrendering any hints about her plans for Tango Key—or for Tia Lopez.

8

"When the National Hurricane Center makes five-day forecasts for storms, 'the best they can say is that a storm that appears to be headed straight for Palm Beach could hit anywhere from North Carolina to Jamaica.'"

The Palm Beach Post

The line of cars stacked up at the bridge, waiting to evacuate, extended back for more than a mile, blocking several intersections, then turned a corner and extended another mile or so beyond that. It had been like this for more than six hours, Sheppard thought, and didn't show any sign of diminishing.

He had lost count of how many car windows he had rapped on, how many times he had said, *FBI. I need a driver's license or picture ID for everyone in the car.* He had thoroughly searched perhaps two or three dozen vehicles, most of them vans and campers large enough to hide several people, had run another several dozen IDs on individuals who, for one reason or another, struck him as suspicious. And so far, no sign of the women or of Billy Joe Franklin, confirming his suspicion—and Mira's contention—that they were in hiding on the island.

He, Goot, and a handful of local cops had been working

the line on rotating shifts. Whenever a car cleared inspection, a bright orange sticker was slapped on the windshield so the vehicle could pass onto the bridge without being stopped again. During the periods when he was off the line, he biked to his car three blocks south, then drove over to the bookstore to help Mira, Annie, and Nadine load endless boxes of books onto her truck.

It was now half past three and as the bands from Danielle moved closer, the rain alternated between dribbles no worse than that of a usual summer day and driving, horizontal sheets that stung his face and cheeks. The wind had picked up to a steady fifty-five, with gusts ten miles higher. The bridge supposedly could tolerate sustained winds of a category three around 125 miles an hour. But Emison and the mayor, working with emergency officials, had decided it would be shut down when the winds reached eighty-five or ninety. And passengers in the cars left behind would be directed to the hospital, an official hurricane shelter.

No one wanted to think about what would occur on the other side, as the evacuating vehicles joined the endless procession of evacuees headed northward out of the Keys. As Dillard so succinctly put it, *Let them become someone else's responsibility.* Unfortunately, the cars still stuck in the massive two-hundred-mile-long traffic jam might still be sitting there when Danielle made landfall. And then they'd become statistics.

A cop in a bright yellow rain slicker hurried toward Sheppard. He knew it was Goot by the manic swagger to his walk that broadcasted his annoyance. He would rather be at home with his new love, battening down the hatches and settling in for the siege. Sheppard sympathized. He understood exactly how he felt.

"Dillard said you're relieved for thirty minutes," Goot announced. "And keep your cell phone on. They're close now to some leads and he may need you to handle it."

"Not that many dark vans were stopped. Why's it taken them so long?"

"The computers keep going out, the phones go bananas, the employees are spread too thinly . . ." He shrugged. "What the hell do I know? Just be back in thirty minutes so I can take my break, okay? And just between you and me, Shep, I'm going home on my break and I'm not coming out again until it's over."

"AWOL?"

"You got it."

Sheppard felt tempted to do the same. What purpose did any of this serve? His gut told him the two women and Franklin had dug themselves a very deep hole and weren't about to come out until the storm had passed and the island had gone into the aftermath mode. And in that aftermath, he thought, there might not be a bridge to cross or a boat to flee in.

"I may be joining you. Listen, Mira made a remark that's been bugging me."

"Just one?" Goot asked with a grin.

"Yeah. Well. What were two high-risk inmates doing in a minimum-security jail like Tango?"

Under the hood of his raincoat, Goot frowned. "Renovations to the Dade jail, right? Isn't that what Emison said?"

"All we have is Emison's word. I'd like to see the actual files."

Goot jammed his hands into the pockets of his raincoat. "Okay, so it's a valid question. How can we get the files?"

"I'll go by the jail. The files may not tell us anything, but we need to look."

"We always need to look when Dillard is involved," Goot reminded him.

"I'll keep you posted."

"Hey, did you hear? Danielle is officially a cat five, with sustained winds between 155 and 160."

"One sixty?"

Danielle had sneaked up on them, just as Andrew had, he thought as he made his way through the traffic to where he'd left his bike. He vividly recalled that on Friday, August 21, 1992, Bob Sheets, the director of the National Hurricane Center at the time, had sent South Floridians out to enjoy what he predicted would be a beautiful weekend. Andrew had weakened to a tropical storm, with maximum gusts of fifty miles an hour, comparable to what South Florida some-times got on a windy day. Even though Andrew staggered to-ward the Southeast coast and could hit anywhere between Florida and the Carolinas, Sheets had told his audience that Andrew could miss the coast entirely. So Sheppard, like thousands of other South Floridians, had partied hard on Friday night, slept in that Saturday morning, then headed north to Lauderdale later that day to go fishing with friends.

He was divorced by then from his first wife, living with his cat in a town house in north Dade County, on what would become the last leg of his first stint with the FBI. It had been his first weekend free in months and he had intended to make the most of it.

When he'd gotten to his friend's house in Lauderdale, Andrew was nine hundred miles from the coast and strength-ening. By two PM, it had become a hurricane again, but its path was still uncertain. Just the same, the National Hurricane Center issued a hurricane watch that covered a 350-mile area from Cape Canaveral to the Dry Tortugas off the coast of Key West.

Twelve hours later, at two AM on August 23, Andrew had reached category-three status, with winds of 120, and was 475 miles from Miami. Computer models predicted that Miami and Marathon, in the Middle Keys, had a 23 percent probability of being hit by midday on Monday, the twenty-fourth, and Palm Beach County had a 20 percent probability. Hurricane winds extended thirty miles from the eye and tropical-storm-force winds reached out eighty-five miles from the center. The entire hurricane was only two hundred miles across, compared to Hugo, a category four that had measured four hundred miles across.

By seven AM Sunday, a hurricane warning had gone up for Florida's southeast coast and the Keys, mandatory evacuations had begun, and Dillard, who was Sheppard's boss at the time, had called him in to work. Sheppard spent the next eight hours helping with evacuations and coordinating disaster relief with the Red Cross and local shelters. For the most part, shelters were overcrowded and understaffed, some didn't open on time, and some didn't open at all because volunteers didn't show up. In Dade County, there weren't enough shelters for all the evacuees.

By five Sunday afternoon, when he'd finally left work, shelves at grocery stores and hardware stores had been stripped bare, the roads were choked with cars, gas pumps had been sucked dry, and many ATMs were empty. Andrew was packing winds of 150 by then and pushing a wall of water fourteen feet high. It would be the first major hurricane to hit Florida in forty-two years and the third most powerful hurricane ever to hit the U.S.

He vividly recalled that by two that morning, the rains and winds had started. An hour and a half later, Andrew's fury had seized downtown Miami. The ferocious wind snapped trees as though they were no more than matchsticks, whipped away street signs, stoplights, anything and everything that wasn't nailed down. It flattened trailer parks, neighborhoods. But Sheppard didn't know any of that at the time because he had lost electric power. His battery-operated radio reported that they were no longer receiving information from the National Hurricane Center because their equipment had been destroyed.

Around three, he'd gone to bed. Four hours later, he'd been awakened by a call from Dillard, demanding that he report to the county's emergency operation center seven miles from his town house. Sporadic ham radio broadcasts from Homestead and near the Metro Zoo were reporting unimaginable devastation and the emergency services personnel needed all the help they could get. Considering the state of things in his own neighborhood, the reports of devastation seemed vastly exaggerated to Sheppard. Trees had come down, some power lines had fallen, places had flooded. But generally, his neck of northern Miami seemed to have come through a category five in extremely good shape.

He joined a caravan of federal trucks that made their way into southwestern Miami, and it was then that Sheppard realized what kind of storm Andrew had been. Small, compact, and so powerful that it had wiped twenty communities off the face of the planet. Country Walk, which had once been a neighborhood of upscale homes, was gone, wiped away, obliterated. The Metro Zoo, which covered nearly three hundred acres, had been devastated. Monkeys had gotten loose, panthers had escaped, the aviary had collapsed, and thousands of birds had escaped or been killed. Domestic pets—dogs, cats, ferrets, rabbits, exotic birds—he had seen all sorts of animals—wandered around in shock.

People stood outside the rubble of their homes armed with shotguns and signs. NEED MEDICAL HELP. NEED WATER AND FOOD. NEED ALL STATE INSURANCE COMPANY. The paramedics in his truck tried to save the wounded, the traumatized, the dying. But they were pitifully short on medical supplies. Sheppard witnessed surgeries without anesthesia performed in the midst of filth. He saw bleeding patients turned away, children roaming the wasteland, crying for their mommies.

The twin smokestacks of the nuclear plant ten miles south of Homestead had been so badly damaged that radiation surely had escaped. No one knew how much or what it would mean to the surrounding neighborhoods. An entire community of migrant workers had been killed and their bodies eventually buried in mass graves in the Everglades. Hundreds of bodies were strewn across the ruins in southwest Miami and refrigerated trucks from Burger King arrived to haul the bodies away.

He saw the unspeakable. And hardly a word of it ever made it into the press.

By his fifth day there he'd felt as if he were living inside a Salvadore Dalí nightmare so grotesque that he exited the area in a kind of shock. He went home and slept for eighteen hours straight—not a piss, not a dream, not a rumble of hunger. He had sunk so far down into a black slough that when he surfaced, he considered it a miracle that he had emerged at all.

The next day, he had submitted his resignation to the bureau with a letter detailing what he had seen and experienced. Several weeks afterward, Dillard visited him, accompanied by some DOD officials. They informed him that he hadn't seen or witnessed what he detailed in his letter, that he'd been suffering from post-traumatic stress and could seek treatment at the government's expense, if he so desired. Sheppard got the message.

Two weeks later, he leased out his town house, asked a friend to take care of his cat, and left the country.

He spent three months in South America, maxing out his credit cards, clearing his head, and ridding himself of everything he had seen and experienced in the aftermath of Andrew. When he returned, he was broke and deeply in debt. Going back to the bureau wasn't an option. Since he had a law degree, he went to work with a friend who was a litigation attorney. He hated it, but it paid his bills and bought him time to explore other options. He eventually landed a job as a homicide detective in Broward County. He sold his town house, moved, and never looked back. It was in Broward where he had met Mira.

He'd never told her what he'd seen during those five days. He'd told no one. And it was this secret, held for so many years, pushed into the back of his consciousness, that surfaced during his bike ride to the jail.

No, it didn't just surface. It came roaring back in full Technicolor. It was why he had spent the bulk of his day helping with hurricane preparations rather than helping Mira. With Andrew, he'd seen the end result. With Danielle, he had been trying to do what he could to offset that. And how ironic, he thought, that Dillard was present both times.

Two empty police cruisers were parked outside the jail, which looked to be wrapped up in yellow crime tape. A cleaning and maintenance crew of half a dozen men were boarding up the shattered doors and cleaning up the main room. Not a cop was around, though, which wasn't surprising. They'd been recruited for emergency and evacuation duty.

Just the same, he showed his badge to the head guy on the crew, then hurried through the main room and made a beeline for Emison's office. Emergency power was still on, so he turned on the lights in Emison's office and shut the door. He knew that despite computers, the Tango jail kept hard-copy on every inmate that passed through its system.

Sheppard went over to the row of filing cabinets against the wall, glanced at the labels on each drawer, and determined that the files were organized in two-year periods. In the 2004 drawer, he found the folders on Crystal DeVries and Tia Lopez.

He was looking for transfer dates and any other information that would answer Mira's question about how two high-risk inmates ended up at a minimum-security jail. In Lopez's case, it was perhaps understandable since her trial venue had been transferred here. Even so, the Key West jail would have been more appropriate. DeVries's transfer bothered him more because she was Franklin's girlfriend and the reason he'd pulled the jailbreak.

A break, he thought, that Franklin wouldn't have been able to pull off at the Dade jail.

According to DeVries's file, she had been transferred to Tango on February 21 of this year. So where was the transfer paperwork? Where was an explanation about why the transfer was made? The only thing Sheppard found was the sign-off on the transfer, which included the name and a phone number for the employee who had turned DeVries over to the transfer driver. He jotted down the information, then scanned the rest of the DeVries file, not sure what he was looking for.

Her history before the bank heist and the specifics of how she'd gotten caught were pretty much the way Emison had laid them out. After her arrest, she'd been questioned by federal investigators about where Franklin might be and that report was part of her file. The investigator noted that DeVries claimed she didn't know where Franklin was, didn't care, and never wanted to see his face again. She felt betrayed that Franklin had run out on her.

Sheppard flipped to the end, looking for DeVries's official visitors' list. There were two individuals—her mother and a female cousin. No men.

He paged through the rest of it, scanning it for anything useful. He came across an intriguing bit concerning two incidents at the jail that had been investigated by correctional officers. One occurred in the exercise yard, where a group of inmates apparently had threatened DeVries with metal shanks. Someone had intervened—possibly Tia Lopez, but that was never confirmed, the report noted—and one inmate had ended up in the jail clinic with burns on her hands and a gash on her chin that had required stitches.

Burns on her hands? From what?

The second incident concerned unauthorized use of the computer in the jail library. DeVries was suspected of having gone online and contacting someone through e-mail, but nothing was ever proven.

Contacting whom? he wondered.

He went on to Lopez's file and learned that she'd been transferred out of Dade on January 6, 2004. Her transfer papers were attached and appeared to be in order. These papers provided a reason: trial venue changed, just as Emison had said. The transfer order was signed by a different employee than the one who had signed off on DeVries. Sheppard scribbled down this employee's name, then went back to his notes on DeVries and called the number that had been in her file.

He waited through a recording, a list of options, then punched in the woman's extension. "Classification. This is Betty Pandrino. How may I help you?"

Different name. Sheppard identified himself, gave his badge number, and Pandrino ran it through her computer. "How may I help you, Agent Sheppard?"

"I'm checking on the transfer sign-off of one of your inmates to the Tango Key jail. Crystal DeVries, February twenty-first of this year. I was just wondering why she was transferred to Tango. I can't seem to find any reason listed in the transfer papers."

"I just stepped into this job on March first, Agent Sheppard. My predecessor is on maternity leave. But hang on, let me bring this up on the computer." Keys tapping. "Okay, here she is. We scan their photos onto the computer now. I remember her. Pretty girl. Bank robbery. Hmm. Odd. There's no reason listed here, either."

"When did the request come though? Is that in your file?"

More tapping. "The request came through in early January, but there's nothing here that indicates why."

"Wasn't the jail undergoing renovations?"

"Well, yes. In January we transferred about thirty female

inmates to other facilities. But by the time DeVries was transferred, the renovations were done. So that can't be the reason."

"Overcrowding?"

"Not likely. That's why we were renovating."

"How was the transfer made? Does Dade do it or does the receiving jail pick up the inmates? What's the usual procedure?"

"We usually do it if it's within the state. But DeVries was being tried on federal charges, so it's possible that a federal employee made the transfer. I guess that would be your department, Agent Sheppard."

Sheppard sensed he was onto something, but that he wasn't asking the right questions. "Does the driver sign off when he accepts the prisoner?"

"Yes. In fact, our people are supposed to give the entire file, with transfer papers, to the driver, who delivers them to the new jail."

"I don't seem to have that in the file. Could you see if you have anything on it?"

While she was tapping away on her computer, Sheppard heard voices coming his way. He quickly removed the transfer orders on both inmates, folded them, stuck them inside his pack, and pocketed his notepad. He shot to his feet, returned the files to the drawer, turned off the light in the office, and hurried out into the hall and into the men's room, where he promptly lost the cell phone connection.

No matter where he moved in the room, he couldn't pick up a signal.

He waited a few moments, hoping that whomever he'd heard had left, and stepped out of the restroom.

There stood Emison in his wet raincoat, barking orders at one of the maintenance men, his back to Sheppard. He slipped his cell phone in his pocket. "Hey, Doug."

Emison spun around, his face bright red. "Shep. What the hell are you doing here?"

"Bathroom." Sheppard stabbed a thumb over his shoulder. "This was the closest one. What's up?"

"I need to move files and some other things out of the office. We're shipping everything up to the Tango hospital. Can you give me a hand?"

"Uh, yeah, sure. I can't run them over there for you, though. I need to help Mira secure the bookstore."

"Just help me get them into the truck."

As they loaded the files into cardboard boxes, Sheppard's cell phone rang. He saw the Dade County jail number in the window and knew it was Betty Pandrino calling him back. "Agent Sheppard," he said, stepping into the hall to put some distance between himself and Emison. "Hi, Betty. I've got a stronger cell connection now."

"I found the driver signature, Agent Sheppard. It was Doug Emison, with the Tango PD."

Well. How intriguing. "Thanks, I really appreciate this."

"I tried calling my predecessor, Jan Phillips. She apparently headed north because of the hurricane. But I've got her cell number."

Sheppard jotted the number in his notepad. He could think of several legitimate possible reasons why Emison would be the transfer driver and foremost among them was that there had been no one else to do the job. But why hadn't Emison mentioned it? Why had he said that DeVries had been transferred because of jail renovations when, in fact, the renovations had been finished before her transfer?

"Trouble?" Emison asked as Sheppard returned to the office.

"No. Just Mira, asking where I am."

"Trouble of a different sort," Emison said with a chuckle.

They loaded boxes onto two dollies and pushed them out

into the hall. "So, Doug, how come you were the driver the day DeVries was transferred here?"

Emison's glance was sharp, filled with suspicion. "Dade's drivers were all hauling cons to other jails. She was coming here, so I said I'd do it."

"Key West would have been more appropriate for both DeVries and Lopez."

"They were full. Since when do you check up on what local law enforcement is doing, Shep?"

"Since you called me at three this morning. Besides, I had some unanswered questions."

"Then ask me." Emison's voice turned tight, angry. "Don't go sneaking around behind my back."

"Okay, here's another question. How come there's no paperwork on the transfer in DeVries's file?"

Color seeped up Emison's neck. "I don't like your tone, boy."

"And I don't like getting jerked around, Doug. It's a simple question."

"How the fuck should I know why there aren't any transfer papers? The Dade people must've left them out."

"They're supposed to be given to the driver, who delivers them to the new jail."

"Look, the only thing I was given was her file, okay? And I don't do the paperwork and I don't usually do the transfers. The paperwork slipped through bureaucratic holes, Shep. That's nothing new."

Emison grabbed a tarp from a nearby chair, threw it over the boxes on his dolly, and pushed it out into the rain.

Sheppard stared after him, certain now that Emison wasn't telling the whole truth, but unable to connect any dots that would explain why. It bothered him enough so that he called Goot to let him know what he'd discovered. It wasn't that he felt threatened by Emison or that he believed he'd stumbled upon some vast and intricate conspiracy. But throughout his years in law enforcement, he'd come to realize it was only prudent to cover your ass and that was what he and Goot did for each other.

He reached Goot's voice mail and left him the *Reader's Digest* condensed version. Then he borrowed a tarp from one of the workmen, covered his boxes, and hurried out into the rain to Emison's truck.

9

"The government never told the full story about Andrew. Twenty-one communities disappeared that night. Hundreds of people died. The confiscated bodies were hauled out on Burger King trucks."

K.T. Frankovich (www.kt.cjb.net)
Hurricane Andrew Survivor

Annie stood in front of the small TV in the bookstore office, gripping the handle of a dolly loaded with boxes of books, and stared at the satellite images of Hurricane Danielle.

THe storm did look like some living mutant, her eye small, perfectly defined, and round as a poker chip. The bands of wind and rain that swirled violently around the eye looked impenetrable to Annie, as though the speed of the winds somehow had turned the storm into a solid object. Her path had grown unstable in the last eight hours, dipping slightly southward, then northward, then veering back on track, now heading straight for the Keys. It was as if Danielle were magnetized to move toward the area of greatest fear.

The statistics appeared on the screen. Forward speed had dropped a little, winds were a steady 160, and central pressure had dropped to 924, just two millibars above Andrew's when it had slammed into Homestead. That alone terrified Annie. The gale-force winds extended outward from the eye for about seventy miles, but the forecaster said there was a lot of weather preceding Danielle. A storm surge of fifteen to twenty feet was expected.

She leaned toward the TV screen and sniffed, but of course the storm on the screen had no smell. She pressed her hand to the screen, as she'd seen her mother do, but nothing came to her. She shut her eyes, trying to find a scent in the office air that might belong to Danielle. But all she smelled was a hint of dust and rain.

"Hey, kiddo."

"Shep, you startled me." He'd come through the delivery door at the side, where the store's van was parked.

He, too, stared at the TV screen.

"It's bad," Annie whispered. "We should've left."

"That'd be worse. Look."

Sheppard switched to a Miami station and an aerial view of the two-lane road out of the Keys. Both lanes were now northbound and jammed bumper to bumper with cars, trucks, SUVs, campers, RVs, many of them towing boats. On either side of the narrow road, palm trees flapped like flags. The water on both the Atlantic and the Gulf was turbulent, swollen with whitecaps.

"And that's not even at high tide yet," Sheppard said. "That doesn't come until later tonight."

"My God," she whispered, and trailed her finger up the screen, following the road. "Somebody's got to *do* something, Shep."

"FEMA is going to open a shelter on Sugarloaf, at the new school, just to ease the burden, and they may open a shelter farther north, like around Marathon. The Sugarloaf shelter is probably a big mistake, given Danielle's track, but being on that highway would be disastrous."

Sheppard's voice faded like an echo. Her ears rang, blood

pounded inside her skull, and her finger, pressed against the TV screen, had assumed a life of its own. It circled an area around Bahia Honda . . .

. . . and she sees the Bahia Honda bridge collapsing, cars plunging through the wet darkness, some turning end over end, the people inside shrieking, screaming . . . bodies spilling from them. . . . And the smells, my God, the smells, of ozone, excessive electricity, violence, sea-weed . . .

Horrified, Annie struggled to jerk her hand away from the screen, but it was as if her nerve endings had rooted in there. Her muscles refused to cooperate and her finger pressed down with such pressure that her fingernail turned white. She knew what was happening, that by touching the screen she was touching the future. It zipped into her finger with the power of an electrical current, and forced her hand back, back, so that her finger moved down the road to a point be-tween Sugarloaf Key and Bahia Honda . . .

. . . and huge swells of water, tipped with moiling white, seem to rise into the darkness like sea monsters and crash over the road, washing away trees, cars, people . . .

She gasped, a ball of grief and terror surged in her throat, but her finger remained pressed to the screen, moving now across the bay to Tango Key, forcing her to see . . .

. . . the right corner of the Tango pier collapses and within seconds, another piece of it goes and then an-other and another, like a line of dominoes. A tremen-dous surge of water sweeps upward and Annie follows it with her eyes, as if she is standing right in front of it.

*Ten, twelve, maybe fifteen feet high, it looms above her
and then it begins to fall and she jerks back . . .*

And, with her fists pressed to her eyes, she stifled a sob
and tripped over Nadine's wheelchair.

"What'd you see, Annie?" Sheppard asked, sliding an arm
around her shoulder.

"Stop!" Nadine snapped. "You're making it worse, Shep."

"It's okay, Nana." Annie's arms swung to her sides. "I just
wasn't ready for such . . ."

"Intensity?" Nadine offered. "Rawness? Immediacy?"

All of the above. "Yeah. And my hand wouldn't do what I
was telling it to do."

Nadine nodded sagely, watching Annie with her dark,
hawkish eyes. "Then it would seem you were seeing very
real possibilities."

"These weren't *possibilities,* Nana. These events were
happening, okay? A wall of water washing away cars somewhere between Sugarloaf and Bahia Honda, the bridge at
Bahia Honda collapsing with cars on it, the Tango pier collapsing . . ."

"Only possibilities," Nadine said.

"But since there's no way to change what's going on out
there," Sheppard said, "then that makes what Annie saw even
more probable, right?"

Nadine looked infuriated now. "You're talking about
things that are beyond your ability to know, Shep."

"Why're you so angry at him, Nana?" Annie asked.

"Because he should have been here helping us secure the
store. Because his job is more important than his family.
Because—"

"Hey, Ace and Luke were here to help and I'm sorry I
asked." Annie threw up her hands. "And what you said isn't
fair. Shep has been here every opportunity he's had. He put
up the back shutters on the store, he—"

"Thanks, Annie, but I can defend myself."

His mouth, she thought, looked tight and grim, and Annie suddenly felt sorry for him, always fending off Nadine's attacks and criticisms, and trying to deal with her mother's psychic impressions. Who could blame the guy if he moved out?

"I think a truce is the best idea," Annie said, and started pushing the dolly toward the side door.

Sheppard took over. "I'll get this. Go load up some more boxes and tell your mom I'm here, will you?"

"Uh, sure."

Annie gave Sheppard's hand a quick squeeze, making it clear that she was on his side, that she thought Nadine was being unfair—and had a sudden image of him inside some dark, tight place. Claustrophobia had seized him, paralyzed him, and he could hardly breathe. Sweat poured off him, she could smell it, a strong, sour odor of unwashed skin and dirty clothes and total, outright terror. The image of Sheppard so crippled, so powerless, so stripped naked of all the qualities she loved in him, horrified her every bit as much as the images she'd seen moments ago.

She left the office fast and for the first time ever, had an appreciation for the way her mother somehow had learned to balance her psychic life with the demands of her ordinary life.

As soon as Annie was out of sight, Sheppard and Nadine glowered at each other. He had plenty to say to this old woman, beginning with how sick to death he was of her regarding him as the gringo bastard son. It didn't matter that he had been born and raised in Venezuela or that he spoke Spanish nearly as well as she did. To Nadine, he was still a gringo who worked in one of the most despicable professions on the face of the planet and she still didn't understand why Mira was engaged to him. He supposed that in the privacy of her own thoughts, Nadine wrote the relationship off to karma and thought of Sheppard as her personal karmic cross to bear.

"I'm going to take this out to the van," he said.

"Where do you plan on riding out the storm, Shep?"

"At the house." The question irked him. "Where the hell else would I be, Nadine?" He unplugged the TV, disconnected it from the cable, and put it on top of the boxes.

"Oh, out chasing escaped convicts."

He suddenly didn't give a shit if she was eighty-two years old and confined to a wheelchair with a broken foot. "Look, Nadine, if you've got a bone to pick with me, then let's get it out in the open. I'm not in the mood for innuendos."

"*A* bone to pick?" She laughed. "I have several. You should be here, helping Mira, instead of working, that's at the top of my list. She helped you out by reading the crime scenes, the least you can do is help out here."

"And Mira has said that, Nadine?"

"Well, no, not in so many words."

His blood pressure shot for the moon. "Then stop judging me." The words came out as sharp as glass and she looked taken aback. Sheppard turned and pushed the dolly outside and up the ramp that led into the van.

He quickly unloaded the boxes, stacked them, and went down the ramp to load some more. Nadine was gone, but Mira came pulling a dolly across the room and smiled when she saw him. "I heard Nadine got all over you," she said quietly.

"Just the usual shit."

Mira made a face and leaned across the dolly to kiss him hello. He loved the softness of her mouth, the faint coffee taste that lingered on his own mouth as she rocked back on her heels and turned the dolly over to him. "She's about as cranky as I've ever seen her. She hates the cast, being in a wheelchair, and so on and so on. You're her convenient whipping boy."

Sheppard didn't want to talk about Nadine. He pulled the dolly up into the van and she followed him carrying a couple of boxes of stuff from her office. "Where're you unloading all these boxes?" he asked.

"Against the walls in the garage, in our closet, and in the family room. I hope we'll still have enough room in the garage to get our cars inside. I thought it'd be good to park this vehicle outside, parallel to the garage door as additional reinforcement."

"Good idea. You have gas for the generator?"

She nodded, her beautiful hair moving in such a way that it seemed to cup either side of her jaw, like dark hands. "And we're set with food and supplies."

As they unloaded and stocked the boxes, they talked about the evacuation, about which room in the house would be their safe room, and how they would deal with Nadine in an emergency. Their conversation seemed strangely calm to Sheppard, as though they were discussing what they would have for dinner. But that's how it often was with Mira when she was uneasy. Her voice remained soft and fluid, hypnotic.

"Look, if there's a crisis, I'll carry her out of the house. But there isn't going to be a crisis. We're in good shape, Mira."

As soon as he said the words, he felt as if he'd hexed them. And he saw the sudden tightening in Mira's jaw, the shadows that darted through her eyes, as quick and sly as foxes, and knew the same thought had crossed her mind. She moved closer to him and put her arms around him. A simple embrace, meant to provide and to draw comfort. Except that things with Mira were rarely simple.

She made a soft, strangled sound, and yanked away from him, her eyes wild and strange, moving as though they had torn loose from the muscles that held them in their sockets. She gasped and doubled over, arms clutching her waist, and sank to her knees. There, she rocked, groaning, unable to extricate herself from whatever she was seeing or experiencing or feeling or whatever the hell was happening. Sheppard knew better than to touch her, knew that he had to allow whatever it was to work its way through her. He didn't understand what that meant. It was one of Mira's rules and he respected it—but only through sheer force of will.

The first time he'd seen this, she was reading a crime scene for him and had taken on rope burns at her wrists, the same burns that she claimed the victim had on hers. He'd witnessed the phenomenon dozens of times over the years, but it never ceased to shock him. Mira explained that it happened because she was primarily an empath, as though that said it all.

However, from everything Sheppard had read throughout the five years he'd known her, he had come to understand that "empath" rarely referred to taking on someone else's injuries—experiencing them, yes, but not physically taking them on. And when it did happen, it was commonly among cultures that accepted it. He'd witnessed it among some of the santeros in Goot's family, among Haitian voodoo practitioners, and among medicine men in the Amazon. But he knew he never would get used to seeing it in the woman he loved. In his more desperate moments, he wondered what it would be like to love an ordinary woman, someone for whom an embrace was merely an embrace and not an invitation into the inexplicable.

After a few moments, she rocked back onto her heels, raised her head. Her eyes were still unfocused, glazed, the pupils huge, as though she'd ingested a tremendous amount of some illegal drug. She held up her right arm, the soft underside exposed. It was covered with dark, nasty bruises. The left arm was the same. She lifted her T-shirt and looked down. Bruises spread across her ribs on the left side, as if she'd endured a vicious beating.

"I don't know how this happens," she whispered.

He stood there, speechless, paralyzed, his head screaming. Was this what lay in his future? Physical injuries?

Now the bruises began to fade and she looked up at him, her eyes liquid with residual pain. "But . . . it's soon. Around the next corner."

"What can I do to prevent it?"

She shook her head, pressed her palms to her thighs, stood. "I don't know, Shep. Only the pain registered. I can try again, see if there's anything else."

"Can you block the pain and physical manifestations?" He couldn't stand to see her in pain again.

"Maybe." Her smile then struck him as almost sad, resigned. "We'll see." She shut her eyes, alternated her breathing, and after a moment or two, extended her hand.

Sheppard hesitated, then grasped her hand, lightly as first, the muscles tensing, preparing to jerk his hand away. But the touch, however light, was all that she needed.

"You're in a wooded area. It's raining hard, the wind's really blowing, and you're assaulted by surprise, complete surprise . . ." She winced, grasped his fingers. Seconds ticked by. She shook her head. "That's all I'm picking up, Shep."

"Assaulted by whom?"

"I don't know."

He didn't find that the least bit comforting and gently withdrew his hand. "Let's go load some more books."

Comfort in routine.

They were loading the last of the books when a Ford truck pulled to a stop in front of the van. Dillard got out, his raincoat flapping wildly. He loped over to the ramp and ducked under the awning and out of the rain. He slid off the raincoat's hood and shook himself like a dog, spraying Sheppard and Mira.

"You're not answering your cell, Shep," Dillard said.

Yeah, the cell was off. "The battery's low," Sheppard lied.

"Hello to you, too, Leo," Mira said dryly.

Dillard grinned in that irksome way he had, teeth gritted as though he were constipated. "Jerome Carver. There are three of them on the island and we know where one of them is. Aka Billy Joe Franklin, we're sure of it. I need to borrow Shep for a while."

He sounded manic, Sheppard thought, and suddenly wondered if Dillard, in addition to his other charming and endearing qualities, was bipolar. "We're pushing the eleventh hour, Leo. I need to finish up here first."

"And how long will that take?"

"Until the weather forces us to take shelter," Mira snapped. "Give it up for now, Leo. Even if you bring these people in, you can't stick them in the jail because it, like everything else here at the south end, may be underwater by the time Danielle passes through."

He drew himself up straighter and regarded Mira as though she were an annoying insect that he might swat any second now. "Let me worry about where we'll put them. Shep, it's you, me, Goot, and Doug. We go in, we get out."

How interesting, Sheppard thought. The last he'd heard, Goot was going AWOL. He wondered what Dillard had promised him—triple overtime? Hazard pay? A raise? Would any of that seduce Goot? He sincerely doubted it. He suspected that Dillard had threatened to can Goot if he didn't accompany him and Emison. "And Goot knows that?"

"He's on his way over here."

"Excuse me," Mira said, stepping between them to shut

the van's rear doors. Then she deliberately moved between them again and asked Dillard to move his truck so she could get out. "I need to shove off."

"So do we," Dillard replied, and darted off into the rain to move his car.

"Go fuck yourself, Dillard," Sheppard breathed. "I think he threatened to fire Goot and figures he'll threaten me, too, if he has to."

"Probably."

"So let him. I'm getting fed up with the job anyway. I still have plenty of money left from my aunt's estate."

In the wet light, Mira looked tired, worn, thin, and when she spoke, her voice sounded the same way. "Goot's not in the same position, though. If you don't go, then he's out-numbered."

"If I go, it may play into what you saw."

She considered this, nodding slowly. "You were definitely in a wooded area and attacked by surprise. But if you and Goot watch each other's backs, you should be okay. Just in-sist on it." She paused. "Look, I know what Nadine said to you, Shep, and she had no right. I'm okay with this. I mean, I wish I hadn't read the damn crime scene, but I did. We opened this door and now we have to walk through it and see where it goes. Just be careful. And try to get to the house be-fore the real heavy winds start."

"It'll give Nadine one more reason to keep thinking of me as the gringo bastard son, you know."

Mira laughed and made a dismissive gesture with her hand.

Then, very quickly, he told her what he'd found in Emison's office. He also gave her the papers he'd taken from the files and asked her to put them some place safe. More backup. What the hell.

Moments later, a caravan of cars pulled away from the bookstore—Sheppard with Dillard in his truck, Goot with

Emison in a Jeep Cherokee, and Mira driving off in the bookstore van alone, headed to the house.

Sheppard watched her van in the side mirror, the rain rendering the image to a vague blur of chrome, paint, and taillights. He had a bad feeling about the choice he had made.

10

"A Mike Tyson storm."

Gil Clark, hurricane expert,
referring to Hurricane Andrew

I am water and I am being poured into a vessel called perfect refuge. Is this the refuge?

It looked perfect, Franklin thought, eyeing the house. Set back in a plush neighborhood, the trees on either side of it providing ample privacy from the neighbors. The hurricane shutters were in place, a combination of aluminum panels and accordions, and no cars were in the driveway. Now he had to find out if the house was as empty and as perfect as it looked.

He glanced up and down the street, didn't see any cars coming his way, and pulled into the half-moon driveway. He parked close to the front door, the VW Bug, his beautiful re-furbished 1968 *black* Bug, shielded from view by shrubs and stunted palms. He pulled the raincoat's hood over his head—and hesitated. Suppose someone was home? What then? Even more to the point, suppose this person recognized him?

I am water. He would pour himself into a vessel called *lost driver* and ask directions to some fictional place. As for being recognized . . . well, that seemed very unlikely. The cops who had stopped him on his flight from the parking garage hadn't recognized him and there was no reason for him to suspect some ordinary citizen would do so. Besides, he was dressed entirely in black—black jeans, black T-shirt, a black raincoat, and black shoes. Looking at him, someone would see whatever they wanted to see.

As he opened the Bug's door, the wind flung it out of his hand and hurled rain into his eyes. A new sense of urgency claimed him. He shut the door and hastened up to the front porch. He rang the bell twice, waited, rang twice again. No one answered the door. Franklin hurried along the side of the house, looking for the best way in, and quickly realized that it wouldn't be a problem. The accordion shutters still had the keys in their locks.

He pushed open the gate to the backyard and moved quickly across the lawn to the nearest shutter. He turned the key, pulled the shutter open, and peered through a sliding glass door into a living room. The door wasn't locked and he slid it open and stepped inside.

Whoever lived here hadn't left that long ago, he thought. A faint residue of perfume lingered in the cool air. And behind that scent trailed others—of soap or shampoo, food, animals, all the smells of ordinary life. He checked out the windows, doors, whether there were skylights. The house was concrete block, had no skylights—a vulnerable spot during a hurricane—and the windows and outside doors appeared to be well sealed by the shutters. The phone worked, the place had running water, and the fridge was large enough to hold the supplies they would bring with them. He jacked down the temp in the fridge and the freezer to the absolute coldest, so that by the time they got back here, both would be cooled to the max. Even when the power went down—as it most surely would—the fridge and freezer would remain cold for as long as eight or ten hours.

He wandered into the master bedroom. The windows were standard, but the shutters sealed them well, and the room itself felt solid, secure. He didn't see any signs of water leakage on the ceiling or on the walls or even around the baseboards. The adjoining bathroom was large and window-less, but the metal door felt flimsy to him. Forget the bath-room as a safe room, he thought, and went into the walk-in closet.

No windows, quite snug. He loved the female scents in the closet, of that tantalizing perfume he'd smelled when he'd come into the house, of silks, softness, mystery. The cubbyholes of the closet organizer were filled with panties, bras, slips, nightgowns, everything neatly folded. Franklin picked up a pair of lavender silk bikini panties, saw the Victoria's Secret logo on them, and held them up. He whis-tled softly. The woman who wore these must be an itty-bitty thing, he thought, and wondered why she wore anything at all. He rubbed them against his cheek, loving the cool smooth-ness of the silk, and breathed in the scent of them.

It made him hard.

It made him want to curl up on the floor with them.

The temptation to take the panties with him tantalized him. But he was water, completed now that he had his Crystal back, and he stuffed them into the cubbyhole where he'd found them.

The closet would be their safe room, he decided, and hur-ried out and up the hall and through the sliding glass doors. He left everything as he'd found it and even remembered to turn the key in the shutter lock.

The wind whistled through the yard, shaking bushes, trees, driving rain into his face as he made his way back to-ward the gate. He kept lifting his fingers to his nostril, sniff-ing them. The scent of the panties lingered on his skin. Years ago, he had stolen a pair of panties from his sister's friend, skimpy bikinis like these—but not from Victoria's Secret—and he'd kept them tucked under his pillow for weeks. Every night, he had stroked them and fantasized about her, and one spring afternoon his sister's friend had come on to him and they had done it in a field near his house. She was seventeen, he was fourteen, and their relationship continued until she had gone away to college in the fall.

Even now, he believed those panties had been somehow magical, providing a connection between himself and his sister's friend that had drawn her to him, to that field of grass, beneath that spring sky so many years ago. He wondered what it was about Crystal that had connected them all their months apart. Lust and love were part of it, he thought, but their truest connection was that they were both water.

Franklin loped along the side of the house, staying close to the wall where a tall hedge offered some protection against the wind. He paused at the front corner of the house—and saw a police cruiser moving slowly up the street, headlights burning through the heavy rain.

He stepped back, flattening against the wall, his breath balled in the center of his chest. Even if the cop ran the plate on the Bug—and there was no reason he should—it wouldn't tell him anything useful. It was a New Hampshire plate, legal, up to date. He should just walk out to the Bug with his head down, get in, and drive away as though he had every right to do so. *I am water,* he reminded himself. *I am water.* But he still didn't move.

He squeezed his eyes shut, struggling to will himself into that frame of mind where he could slide into any role and make it believable. He'd learned this skill as a kid, in a household of raging maniacs. But his brain wasn't listening. His brain was stuck in that familiar childhood groove that had grown out of confrontations with his father, the ultimate authority. *Just what the hell do you think you're doing, Billy?*

his old man would demand whenever he caught Franklin playing pretend or doing something else that his father didn't want him to do.

Nothing, sir.

And the arguments and the shouting would start and his mother would come running in and his younger sister would start wailing and pretty soon the entire household throbbed with screaming.

I am water.

He forced himself to take one step forward, then another and another. He moved with his head down, the raincoat's hood covering it completely. And when he finally moved out from the protection of the house, the cruiser was no longer in sight—and the wind rushed up inside the hood and flung it off.

As soon as he was inside the Bug, the fear that had seized him when he'd seen the cruiser now crashed over him. He started to shake. He grabbed a towel off the floor in front of the passenger seat and rubbed it over his head and face. He swiped it across the windshield, trying to clear the fog, and got the hell out of there.

The rain came down so furiously now that Franklin couldn't see a foot in front of him. The wipers on the refurbished Bug were the originals, tired and rusted, and even on full speed they didn't move fast enough to keep the windshield clear enough to see anything. And the wind, Christ almighty. Every time he entered a stretch of road that wasn't bordered by trees, the wind howled out of the east and the Bug coughed and shuddered. Even though it was late afternoon, and summer, when it didn't get dark until nearly nine, a gloomy twilight clung to everything.

Franklin drove in third gear, hunched over the steering wheel, his hands clutching it so hard that his knuckles looked like pale knobs. His foot never strayed far from the brake pedal. He passed an occasional car, but all indications were that the evacuation was over, the bridge was closed, and most people who had stayed were holed up wherever they were going to ride out the storm.

Cell phone out. He called the number of the phone he'd left with Crystal. He wanted to tell her the good news, that he'd found the perfect house, and that she and the Amazon should load the food and supplies into the van. Given the scarcity of traffic, it would be safe to drive the van to the house and it would give them more room for food and supplies than the Bug. But the phone rang once, then he got a message that the service was busy. He tried again and a *No Service* message popped up.

"Shit."

Cell towers couldn't be out of commission already, could they? Maybe it was just his location, here in the hills. *And maybe it's a sign, Billy Joe.* That was what his mother used to say all the time. Whenever something went wrong, it was a *sign*. But a sign of what? And who sent this mysterious sign? God? Satan? Saints? She never said, never revealed the mysterious workings or the source of these signs, but she had lived her life by them.

The day his father had split for parts unknown, his mother had confided that there had been many signs it was going to happen. Well, yeah, he thought. Signs like the endless shouting matches, the arguments in the middle of the night, the constant bickering. Those kinds of signs he understood and the early years of his life had been riddled with them.

It wasn't that his parents had alcohol or drug problems or that either of them ever physically abused him or his sister. It was just that they were as mismatched as wolves from enemy packs and the only thing that held them together for the first eight years of Franklin's life was religion. Good Catholics didn't separate or get divorced. Good Catholics went to Mass every Sunday, to confession at least once a month, took communion, were baptized, confirmed, and adhered to the sacraments. But by the time Franklin reached third grade, even the glue of Catholicism hadn't been enough to keep his old man around.

After that, his mother worked two jobs and was rarely home. The rooms had been filled with exquisite silences. He could indulge his fantasy play as long as he wanted, whenever he wanted, without fear that his old man would barge into his bedroom, demanding to know what he was doing.

His sister had grown up to become their mother and he hadn't seen her in fifteen years. The people he had worked with at the National Hurricane Center hadn't understood him at all. They shouted at each other—and at him—all the time. Do this, do that, where's that forecast, that computer model, that file? For most of his twelve years there, it seemed he had walked around with his jaw clenched, the muscles in his neck strained, his nerves always on edge. But he'd done the job better than nearly anyone else and his knowledge of hurricanes far surpassed that of his colleagues. So when a promotion he deserved had been awarded to a man who didn't have a clue about hurricanes, all those years of shouting and arguments, to do this and that, had collapsed into one huge tsunami of fury.

And by the time the fury had passed, he had decked his boss, two security officers, and had beaten the shit out of the guy who'd gotten the job. He would've done time for it, too, but his competition hadn't pressed charges. How Christian of him.

He turned onto the rutted dirt road that led into the preserve. The wind whipped the trees back and forth, shook leaves loose, snapped the branches in two. But the trees provided a buffer from the worst of the wind and rain and he could finally see through the windshield again. Leaves flew about in the air like exotic birds. Branches had fallen across the road. He tried the cell number again, but still got the No Service message.

He hated to admit it, but the Amazon was probably right about the cellar in the cabin's garage. One way in and out was never a good policy. He, of all people, should have remembered that. If there had been only one way in or out of that bank he and Crystal had robbed, neither of them would be here now. Even though he didn't particularly want to ride out a hurricane in the same place as the Amazon, Crystal felt she owed the woman. And because he felt guilty that Crystal had taken the fall for him, he would do this for her. He would allow the Amazon to tag along.

He turned on the radio, but got only static. He pulled a NOAAH radio out of the glove compartment. It worked better than the car radio and the dryness of the language comforted him. Danielle's coordinates, wind speed, forward motion, gust speeds. Straightforward, factual. It was the kind of information that had comforted him as a kid. He supposed his interest in hurricanes had started then. Surrounded by rage, he had found solace in the most violent of nature's storms.

But what he heard from NOAAH didn't offer either solace or comfort. Danielle was now about two hundred miles off the coast of Key West, although that was an estimate because the next official report wasn't due for another hour. The hurricane hadn't deviated from the path that would bring her ashore in the Keys. She was two hundred miles across, large enough to brush southern Palm Beach County, but only half as large as monster Hugo, which had stretched some four hundred miles from one end to the other.

Danielle's central pressure had dropped steadily over the last six hours, and she was packing sustained winds of a hundred and sixty miles an hour. That meant the gusts were higher. It meant wind powerful enough to strip paint from cars, bark from trees. It meant the hurricane would be pushing more than an eighteen-foot storm surge in front of it.

All that water would wash across the two-lane road out of

the Keys, a strip of pavement that divided the Atlantic from the Gulf of Mexico, and take thousands of people with it. Good-bye, bridges, good-bye, Bahia Honda, good-bye, Hemingway house, restaurants, businesses, homes, trailers.

The surge certainly would flood the southern end of Tango, but it wouldn't run uphill, he thought, and everything from just below the ferry dock northward would be safe from a surge. But the winds were obviously something else. Andrew's winds—and not the nearly seventeen-foot storm surge it had pushed into Biscayne Bay—had caused the most damage. And, like Andrew, Danielle had caught the experts unaware. South Florida should have been evacuated three days ago to get everyone out that should leave, he thought. But that would have meant a watch issued when Danielle was a tropical depression out somewhere near Puerto Rico and barely a postscript on the evening news.

Bottom line? Weather, like the behavior of his parents, was rarely predictable. You could read all the patterns you wanted, do all your computer models, but in the end, nature did what she pleased, even if it flew in the face of logic. Danielle, like Andrew, was a prime example. And if he had been paying closer attention to what the storm was doing, instead of following his dick, he wouldn't be in this situation now. He would have made plans to get the hell off the island last night and make it to some faraway spot in a preserve elsewhere, like maybe the Ocala National Forest.

He slowed and shifted into second gear and followed the sharp turn in the road. A quarter of a mile later, the road forked and he went right. Another mile and he spotted the path no wider than a foot trail that led to the cabin. The trail had deteriorated considerably since he'd seen this place for the first time six months ago. The old codger from whom Franklin had bought the cabin had kept the path cleared of undergrowth and the branches around it trimmed. Franklin had allowed everything to revert to its natural state in the hopes it would provide greater camouflage—and thus, greater safety. At the moment, though, it was just a big fat hassle.

Halfway up the path, the Bug got stuck in a slough of mud and muck. He gunned the accelerator, the engine flooded, he turned the car off and counted. One thousand, two thousand . . . the wind whistled, the trees sang, the rain poured down. At ten thousand, he tried to crank the car again, but nothing happened. He called Crystal's cell number and although the number now rang, he got his own recorded message.

Franklin pressed his fists to his forehead, fighting a terrible sense of futility, defeat. How long would it take him to walk the distance to the cabin in the mud and rain and wind? Too long. Pretty soon, the wind would ratchet into the high-risk zone, somewhere just above 125 mph.

"Start, please start," he pleaded with the Bug, and turned the key.

The engine sputtered to life, he gunned the accelerator, slammed the Bug into reverse, first gear, reverse again, first, trying to rock it out of the mud. The tires spun, spewing mud.

He jerked the Bug into neutral and swung his legs out and his feet sank into the mud. With the door open, he pushed the car forward, pulled back, grunting like a pig, trying to work up a momentum that would rock the car out of the mud. But the car was stuck good, deep.

Franklin kicked the door shut.

He stumbled back, hating the stupid car, the mud, the storm, the whole stinking package. He should have kept a Hummer in reserve, not a van. Even the van would have trouble getting out of here, especially if they didn't start out before the winds slammed into a high category three.

And how would he drive the van out of here with the Bug blocking the way? Through the brush.

He kicked the door, the tires, the front fender. He threw

himself against the Bug's hood and pummeled it with his fists. "You piece of shit!" he screamed, and stumbled back, fumbling for his weapon, and blew out the windshield, the tires, and riddled the body with holes.

And when his little tantrum was over, he felt marginally better. Okay, yes, he had lost it for a few minutes. He had become fire. But he was fine now. He was becoming water. How could he ignore water? Rain pouring down, puddling everywhere he stepped. Rain, water, rain, water.

I am water.

So why was he breathing air?

I am water.

So why wasn't he swimming?

I am water. Two-thirds of the planet is water. The human body is ninety-eight percent water. Blood, semen, spit, tears, embryonic fluid, spinal fluid. Have I forgotten anything?

Twilight, wet and hungry, like some orphan stray dog. Mud, seeping into his shoes. His socks, pasted to his ankles. His clothes, sticking to him like a second skin. How much farther?

I am water, I will swim.

But he couldn't swim. He could barely walk upright, the wind pushing against him, fighting him, declaring that it was stronger, that air was more powerful than water.

Franklin sank to his knees in the mud. The trees around him bent inward. Branches clawed at his spine, at the back of his neck, his skull. The wind became a concrete barrier against which he struggled, fought, railed. He lost his weapon. One moment he had it, the next moment the air pried it from his hands and the earth sucked it away.

He was now on his belly, arms moving as though he were swimming, mouth puckering like that of a fish just so that he could breathe. In, out, went the air. Up and back, went his arms. Bend, push, went his legs. And then he could see the clearing where the cabin stood, and his heart turned to ice.

Two vehicles. A truck, a Jeep. Cops. They had found him. Found his refuge, his sanctuary. Found him how?

The truck was closest.

He would get to the truck. He would dive deep into the mud like one of those freshwater catfish that lived in South Florida lakes, a mud sucker, his old man used to call them, and he would swim to the goddamn truck.

11

"Not a one of them has been the same."
Greg Bast (flight engineer who has flown 251
missions into the eyes of hurricanes)

Tia didn't need eyes and ears to know that the momentum of the storm was building. She felt the drop in barometric pressure in her ears, in the hard, persistent throbbing behind her eyes, in her joints, her teeth. And it made her edgy, nervous. Franklin should have been back by now.

She and Crystal were in the garage, loading food and supplies into the van. They had decided it would be safe enough to drive the van a short distance, and besides, they might not have a choice about it. If Franklin didn't return, the van was their only way out of here.

"You think they caught him?" Crystal asked, voicing what Tia had been thinking.

"I don't know."

"What's your gut say?"

"My gut's in knots."

"No, I mean, what's your gut say about Billy?"

"My gut is screaming that we get outta here while we still

can. If your man isn't back when we're done here, I say we leave. But we're going to need a weapon. What'd he do with that gun I was using?"

"I don't know. Where would we go?"

"Find a house."

"But that's what he's doing."

"Then where is he? Why isn't he back yet?"

Crystal rolled her lower lip between her teeth, shook her head, and looked as if she might cry. "I . . . I don't know. I've called his cell number half a dozen times and he doesn't answer or it's busy or it says there's no service. Maybe something happened. Maybe he . . . got caught."

"Exactly. That's why we need to split."

"But we won't have any way of getting a message to him. No, I can't do that. He risked his ass for me. I . . . I can't just leave, Tia."

"Excuse me, but he wasn't as worried about you the day he took off outta that bank, Crystal."

"He didn't have a choice. He saw a way out and took it. If he hadn't, we'd still be sitting in jail."

Good point. But it didn't change Tia's mind about anything. "You want to stay, then stay. But I'm leaving. You take half the food and supplies. And we'll both need weapons. You have any idea where he keeps them?"

"He took one with him. I don't know what he did with the others. Hid them somewhere, probably. Tia, I can't stay alone here. I won't have a car. I . . . won't have anyone to talk to."

Yeah, that's what alone means, hon. "Then come with me."

"But I don't want to leave without Billy."

"Look, leave or stay. Just decide. I'm going. You want me to take some of this stuff out or not?"

She stood there, arms crossed, rolling her lower lip, her blue eyes watery. "I . . . let's give him ten more minutes, okay? Then we'll leave. I'll go look for the guns and then I'll take a look outside. Maybe the car got stuck in the mud or something."

"I'll finish up here. While you're inside, look for the keys to the van, too."

"The keys," she repeated, looking confused. "I . . . shit, suppose he took the keys with him?"

"Look for them first."

Crystal hurried through the door that led into the house. In the moments the door was open, the racket from the generator—which she and Crystal had moved into the kitchen—made the throbbing ache in Tia's head worse. She decided to look for weapons in the cellar and got out of the van. It made sense that Franklin wouldn't overlook weapons in his cache of supplies, she thought.

She flicked the switch upward and a dim pool of light came on way below. She hesitated at the top of the steps, staring down. *Under the earth.* She licked her lips. *A tomb.* But she wasn't staying down there, she told herself. She was going to look for weapons.

Tia started down the steps, her heartbeat accelerating, the inside of her mouth flashing dry. Thirty-one steps. She had counted the first time she'd gone down here. Not so far. *Keep moving.*

The noise of the rain grew more muted, distant, like sounds in a dream. It would be okay. The door to the cellar stayed open. Yes, she could do this. Would do it. Was doing it.

She reached the bottom step and hit the switch to her left. The bright florescent lights came on. Better, so much better. Despite everything they had loaded into the van, the cellar still held plenty of food, water, and other supplies. But where would Franklin have stashed weapons?

Tia searched through a couple of cartons on a shelf, rifled through the contents of a scruffy duffel bag, and pawed through the clothing in another duffel. At the bottom, she found a beautiful hunting knife tucked neatly away in a leather holder, outfitted with leather straps that buckled at a belt or an ankle or even an upper arm. The blade was as sharp as a razor.

She preferred a gun, something less up close and personal, but this would do in a pinch. Tia buckled the knife around her calf, let her loose pants slide over it. It didn't show.

Lights off. She took the stairs two at a time, the darkness below licking at her spine, the stink of earth and wetness already thick in her nostrils. She shot up through the door—and stopped cold.

A tall man stood at the front of the van, a shotgun aimed at her. "Lock your hands behind your head, and move away from the door, Ms. Lopez."

A pulse beat in her throat. She recognized the weapon, a Remington twelve-gauge with a tubular magazine and a modified choke barrel, a weapon favored for riot control. She wasn't about to argue with it. She also recognized the man. Sheppard, the fed with the psychic girlfriend, the guy she'd seen on CNN. She slowly raised her arms, locked her fingers behind her head.

"Where's Franklin?" Sheppard demanded.

"Ask his girlfriend."

"We're asking you, Lopez." That familiar rolling southern voice came from behind her.

"Sheriff Emison," Tia said without looking back. "How nice to hear your voice again."

"Cuff her," Sheppard said. "And check her."

She grinned. "Oh, by all means. I guess your psychic girlfriend must be pretty good to have found us, Sheppard."

"Shut up, Lopez," the sheriff spat. "Bring your hands down from your head and behind your back."

"I saw you on CNN," she said to Sheppard. "Last year.

Around Christmas. Quadruple homicide, your lady friend missing—"

"Arms down," Emison barked.

She lowered her arms, Emison cuffed her hands, then frisked her expertly and thoroughly and found the knife she'd strapped to her calf. "You're slick, Lopez, I'll give you that much. Nice knife. Oh, and what's this?" He pulled her journal out of her back pocket.

Tia struggled not to say anything; otherwise Emison would use it against her.

"You write, Lopez?" He laughed. "I didn't realize you were bright enough."

Fuck you.

He came out from behind her, holding a nine millimeter, *her* journal sticking out of *his* jacket pocket. He was a despicable Southern cracker with a pot belly and an abusive mentality. He was four or five inches shorter than she was and had to look up at her. She liked that.

"Move, Lopez." He gave her a shove.

"No need to get physical, sheriff."

"You killed Granny Moses. That entitles us to get as physical as we damn well please."

"Dipshit hit her with that Hummer. I didn't have anything to do with it. I liked Granny."

"You didn't hesitate to run, though, Lopez. That'll bring you another fifteen for attempted escape."

She laughed. "What the fuck difference does that make? I'm headed for the chamber, we both know that. A black woman, charged with killing some men, a couple of them white boys just like yourself."

He moved back, his gun still pointed right at her chest, his finger just itching to pull the trigger, and stepped up into the house. Behind her, the fed said, "Keep moving, Lopez. Inside."

She went into the kitchen, the living room, and everyone stopped. Crystal was sitting at a table stacked with books, CDs, clothes—Franklin's stuff. Her hands were cuffed in front of her, resting on the surface of the table, and her eyes were wide, terrified. A Latino stood close by, his weapon trained on her. Another man stood nearby, as skinny as a shoot of bamboo, with thick white hair. A bureaucrat, Tia thought. The head honcho.

"Sit down, Lopez," Emison demanded, and pulled a chair out for her at the far end of the table.

"I'll stand," she said.

"You'll sit your black ass down," Emison demanded, and shoved her into the chair.

"So, Lopez," said the man with the white hair. "Where's Franklin?"

"And you are . . . ?"

The man's eyes darted to Emison and the sheriff suddenly whacked his police baton against the table in front of her. The CDs slid across the table. A crack sped through the wood. Crystal jerked back and began to cry.

"Let's try this again," said the man with the white hair, grinning so that his teeth lined up in his mouth like a newly painted white picket fence. "Where's Franklin?"

"How the fuck should I know? I was asleep when he left."

"That's not what Ms. DeVries said," the white-haired prick continued with a sly smile.

"He . . . he hit me," Crystal sobbed, turning her face so that Tia could see the dark bruise that spread across her jawbone. "I . . . I . . ."

"Where's he looking for a house?" the honcho asked.

"If I knew that, Mr. Man, I wouldn't be *here,* now, would I?"

Emison got right up into her face. "Answer the question, Lopez."

She looked at Emison, at Crystal, at the Latino, at Sheppard, then back at Emison again, and spat in his face. "You got a small prick, Sheriff, that's your problem."

Emison slowly rubbed the back of his hand across his cheek. Color seeped into his neck, his face. Fury blazed in his eyes. He swung the baton and slammed it down against her left shoulder.

Agony exploded through her, stars burst inside her head. She shrieked, Crystal screamed, the men shouted at her and at each other, and Sheppard lunged toward Emison and wrenched the baton out of his hand. She saw it all through a blur of pain, lightning quick, as though it were unfolding in fast forward.

"You stupid fuck!" Sheppard shouted. "What the hell're you doing?"

"Now just a goddamn minute, boy," Emison yelled. "No nigger is going to spit at me, you hear? No—"

An explosion of gunfire silenced Emison, silenced everyone. "Get the women out back, into the Jeep," demanded the honcho.

Tia's vision remained a blurry fog. But the taste of hot peppers flooded her mouth, a sign that the old rage had come fully awake inside her. She felt the rage through the agony that burned through her shoulder, felt it against her skin as the handcuffs heated up, felt it in the adrenaline that suddenly surged through her. The Red seized her, filling her mind, consciousness, her entire being. And suddenly the cuffs were gone, her arms flew free, she no longer felt pain, no longer felt anything at all. The Red had claimed her completely.

As she shot to her feet, she grabbed on to the underside of the table and heaved it over. She spun, her body tight where it was supposed to be tight, loose where it was supposed to be loose, and kicked out, spun, kicked again and again, one, two, three—Emison, Sheppard, and the Latino all went down. She had her journal—and the Remington. She pumped it and fired at the white-haired bastard, missed him, but blew out the picture window. The wind caught the explosion of glass and hurled it everywhere.

Tia whirled and ran toward the back of the house, stuffing the journal down inside her front pocket. The agony in her shoulder lit up the inside of her skull like fireworks on the Fourth of July. More shouts and gunshots echoed through the tempest. Crystal sprinted along slightly ahead of Tia.

Another gunshot. Splinters of wood flew away from the wall inches from Tia's face, then she rounded a corner and crashed through a porch door.

The driving rain stung her eyes, the wind fought her. Crystal cleared the corner of the house first, vanishing from sight in a windblown vision of denim and pale yellow. Tia ran hard, pain biting into her ribs, her lungs, her injured shoulder. She skidded around the corner—and Sheppard appeared in her line of vision, an obstacle between her and freedom. Tia leaped before he even saw her. Her feet left the ground, her body became an airborne missile.

Seconds later, she struck him, but he grabbed on to her foot and they both crashed to the ground. She lost her grip on the Remington, they rolled through the mud, and she immediately knew he had the advantage. He was taller, heavier, strong, and her shoulder sang with agony.

Tia struggled to summon her rage, to leap into the Red, but she couldn't do it. It took everything she had to keep him from pinning her to the ground. She finally managed to jack-knife her body, throwing him off, and scrambled through the mud on her hands and knees to reach the Remington. He seized her ankle and jerked her backward, something her husband had done to her the night of their last argument, when he, in a drunken rage, had accused her of having an affair. That horrifying taste of hot peppers flooded her mouth and she catapulted into the Red.

She twisted, turned, kicked, and the next thing she knew,

Sheppard was curled up on his side, gasping for air, groaning, and she had the barrel of the Remington pressed to the side of his neck. "I got no karma with you, Sheppard, and I don't aim to create any. Just leave me the fuck alone."

His eyes rolled toward her face and for a single, terrible moment there in the wet, gray light, she recognized that this man was different from the others. She pulled the Sig Sauer from his shoulder holster, backed away from him, the Remington still aimed at him. She scooped up the stuff that had fallen from his pockets—wallet, a cell phone, keys— and spun when she heard a car behind her.

A truck raced toward her, Franklin at the wheel, Crystal hanging on the open passenger door, shouting, motioning wildly with her cuffed hands. Tia pumped the Remington and blew out the tires on the Cherokee. Then she blew out the windshield and riddled the rear end with holes until she hit the gas tank and the Jeep exploded.

She scrambled into the front seat of the truck, screaming, *"Drive, drive!"*

The truck swerved into a wild, erratic circle, then raced forward. Gunfire erupted from the shattered living room window and she pumped the shotgun and fired back. Moments later, the wet woods swallowed them.

The truck crashed through the trees. Branches clawed at the windshield and slapped at the windows. The wipers whipped back and forth in a maddening rhythm. No one spoke. Crystal fumbled with the keys Tia had dropped in her lap and finally succeeded in unlocking the cuffs.

Tia's clothes, soaked straight through, felt like a second, heavier skin. Mud covered her, her shoulder throbbed, she knew it was swelling. Her right hand slapped at her pocket, feeling for the journal. Yes, okay, she had it. As long as she had the journal, her talisman, she would be okay.

Crystal was breathing hard, gripping her thighs, and she broke the silence first, her voice low, almost a hiss. "Where the fuck *were* you, Billy?"

"The VW . . . it got stuck in the mud on my way in here. I couldn't get it free and had to come in on foot. I saw the Jeep, the truck, and I knew the cops had found us. I—"

"You were outside that *whole fucking time* and you never tried to *help* us?" Crystal shrieked, and then turned on him, beating him with her fists, clawing at his face.

He tried to drive with one hand and fend her off with the other and failed at both. He slammed on the brakes, nearly catapulting Tia through the windshield, and grabbed Crystal's wrists and pinned her down against the seat, her head pressed into Tia's thigh. "Listen to me," he yelled. "Just listen to me."

Tia slammed the shotgun against his upper arm. "Back off, Dipshit."

"Jesus, what the hell're you doing?" he shouted, rubbing his upper arm.

"Get out, get the fuck out." Tia pointed the shotgun at him. "Go on, get in the backseat. *Now.*"

"Okay, okay." He looked at Crystal, who was slowly sitting up. "Babe, I—"

"Get out!" she screamed. "I don't want you near me!"

"I'm driving," Tia announced, and climbed over Crystal, her vision blurring again with pain.

Franklin slammed the door, got into the back, and slammed that door, too. He immediately leaned forward. "I found a house. It's perfect."

"Where is it?" Tia demanded, and started the truck.

As he told her, she tried to clear her vision, to keep her eyes on the space directly in front of the truck. The map of Tango Key went up in her head. Too far, she thought. She wasn't sure she would be able to stay conscious that long. They needed something very close.

She brought Sheppard's wallet out of her pocket, fished out his driver's license, glanced at the address. She wasn't sure of the exact street, the map in her head wasn't *that* precise. But she was pretty sure she could find the neighborhood and that it was closer than the place Franklin had found. Since Sheppard was a fed and probably an orderly man, she was betting his place was sealed up and well supplied. And she doubted if he would be returning to his place any time soon, not unless he was walking out of here. If he had half a brain, he would crawl into the cellar with his copper buddies and shut the door. His own home was the last place he or anyone else would think to look for them.

"I have a better choice," she said, and slammed the truck into gear.

Struggling against pain, the Remington resting across her thighs, she drove fast, the truck careening out of the woods and onto Old Post Road.

PART TWO

THE WARNING

"A Hurricane Warning issued for your part of the coastline indicates that sustained winds of at least 74 mph are expected within 24 hours or less. Once this warning has been issued, your family should be in the process of completing protective actions and deciding the safest location to be during the storm."

National Hurricane Center

12

Hurricane Gilbert, which struck the Yucatan Peninsula on September 13, 1988, remains the strongest hurricane ever recorded in the Western Hemisphere, with a central pressure of 888 millibars.

Mira's house sat at a weird angle on an acre of land high above the Gulf. It had been built at this angle, she supposed, to maximize the spectacular view of the Gulf and for the most efficient use of the land. But because it was an older home that had been added to over the years, the shape of the house smacked of chaos rather than design.

Shaped like a bracket, the north end of the house featured three bedrooms and two bathrooms, one of which Annie and Nadine shared. At this end, the master bedroom and bathroom occupied the jutting edge of the bracket. The front entrance, recessed so that it formed a screened porch, opened into the living and dining room in the middle of the house. The utility room and garage occupied the southern edge of the bracket. Then came the large kitchen, with French doors separating it from the family, Sheppard's office, and the cabana bathroom, all added in the seventies. This section of the house was wood frame instead of concrete block, and there-fore less secure in a hurricane. That worried her.

Connected to the family room was a screened porch ac-cessible by a pair of pane-glass doors. Beyond the porch lay the backyard, with Nadine's beautiful Japanese garden, and an unscreened swimming pool. The trees that bordered the rear of the property probably wouldn't survive category five winds, she thought, and that meant the back of the house would take the full brunt of the storm. Those windows and sliding glass doors all had hurricane shutters, but even so, how effective would shutters be in winds stronger that 155?

She thought about all this as she pushed the dolly into the house and down the hall toward her bedroom. It was loaded with cartons of books from the store, which she was stack-ing in the bedroom closets, on shelves and low platforms that usually held shoes. She felt the closets were the safest areas in the house.

When these areas were filled, she put some cartons in Sheppard's office closet, stacked others on top of the book-shelves in the family room, on top of the washer and dryer in the utility room, and then had to retreat to the garage. Here, she stacked boxes on every elevated surface—the work-bench, the shelves that held Sheppard's windsurfing gear, the tops of old metal cabinets. Even if she had wanted to stack boxes on the floor of the garage, there wasn't room. She had parked the delivery van in the garage with the Jetta, the first glitch in her plan to secure the house. But she hadn't fore-seen that the weather would be this bad by the time she fin-ished at the bookstore. Rather than haul the books in through the rain, it had seemed simpler to just pull the van into the garage, which had created a space problem.

She quickly ran out of room in the garage, so she left the remaining books in the van. It seemed clear that she had overreacted. It was possible that the bookstore would make it through the storm just fine. It had good shutters, a solid roof, the building itself had withstood forty years of hurricanes, and since it was located several blocks inland from the Tango Pier, it might escape flooding.

Maybe, if, might . . . the voice of hope, she thought.

Twice today she had tried to read the bookstore—the structure itself—and hadn't picked up anything at all. She didn't know if that was because the bookstore would survive the storm, be flattened, or if meant something else altogether. For whatever reason, that information was blocked, forcing her to make choices in the same way that other people did and then live with the uncertainty of whether she had made the right choice.

A bit late for wondering now, she thought, eyeing the cartons with dismay.

As she finished stacking the boxes against the wall, her head continued to pound. She knew it was due to the dropping barometric pressure and noticed that the animals seemed sensitive to the drop as well. Ricki paced restlessly around the house, panting and whimpering, and the cats kept threading themselves between her legs, leaping onto the boxes, and trying to dig their way down inside them.

So how fast was the pressure dropping? She turned on the TV, hoping for the latest info on Danielle. The update was supposed to have come in at five, but it was late. Regardless of what local channel she went to, the news was the same: Danielle. She saw another replay of its birth two weeks ago as a tropical wave that emerged from the west coast of Africa. The wave spawned a tropical depression two days later and on the third day it became a hurricane. Danielle, like Andrew, dissipated four days ago as it encountered bands of upper-level wind shear, then regrouped and strengthened with alarming speed.

The TV weather map, like Annie's, showed Andrew's track and Danielle's, the two so similar it spooked her. The two tracks diverged, however, well below Cuba. Where Andrew had continued steadily northwest, eventually crossing the island of Eleuthra before slamming into Homestead, Danielle remained farther south due to a system to its north, and threatened Cuba. Fourteen hours ago, it had taken a sharp northward turn.

And now it looked as though it was aimed directly toward the Keys. She turned up the volume just as the local channel switched over to the National Hurricane Center.

"We now have an interim report on Hurricane Danielle," said the hurricane center director, a pale man with white hair and thick bags under his eyes. "Danielle is an extremely dangerous category-five storm," he began, stating the obvious. "She's now less than two hundred miles south of the Florida Keys and her forward movement has slowed somewhat, to about fifteen miles an hour. We expect her motion to slow even more the closer she gets to land. Her winds are holding steady at 160, with gusts of 175 miles an hour." The director pointed at Danielle's eye. "The eye of the storm is about fifty miles across, with the northern edge of the wall holding the most intense winds. The storm surge from Danielle is expected to be in excess of twenty feet. . . ."

Images danced through Mira's head: a wall of water several stories high crushing the Tango pier and crashing across the southern tip of the island for blocks, washing away everything—including her store. The image didn't feel psychic; it seemed to be born of fear.

"Since early this afternoon, Danielle's central pressure has plunged five degrees, to 919, three millibars below Andrew's central pressure when he made landfall. It's expected that Danielle's central pressure will continue to drop until the eye makes landfall in about . . ."

"My God," Annie breathed.

Mira hadn't heard her come into the room and glanced at her now, her beautiful daughter clutching the clipboard with her hurricane to-do list on it. Blood had drained from her face. She looked terrified.

"Mom, she's already stronger than Andrew. And if her central pressure has dropped five millibars in just a matter of hours, then by the time the eye makes landfall, her pressure could be as much twenty points lower—898. That's only six millibars higher than the worst hurricane to ever hit the U.S., the one that hit the Keys on Labor Day 1935. And it's only ten millibars above Gilbert's central pressure, and that storm was the worst to ever hit anywhere in the Atlantic basin."

"You've become a walking encyclopedia of horrifying knowledge about hurricanes."

"Only since I went through the black water."

Mira didn't know what to say to that. She, Sheppard, and Annie hadn't talked in any depth about going back thirty-five years in time and the possible repercussions somewhere down the line. And now wasn't the time to open that discussion.

"It's not going to drop twenty millibars, Annie."

"Yeah? That's your psychic impression?"

No, it wasn't. It was a mother's response to a daughter's fear. Fortunately, Mira didn't have to answer the question because the click of Nadine's wheelchair interrupted them.

"Instead of debating how strong this hurricane may get, we should make a decision about a safe room," Nadine said.

"I think the master bedroom closet should be the designated safe room," Mira replied. "No windows, it lies within three concrete walls, and it's in the part of the house that's concrete block."

"I know of a better place," Annie said, and gestured for them to follow her.

Annie led them into Sheppard's tidy office and opened the closet door. She pulled the string that hung down from the ceiling light, got down on her hands and knees, and pushed cartons out of the way. "I don't know if you can see it, but there's a hobbit-like door in the corner there. It's the same dark color as the wall."

Mira had crawled in beside Annie and she saw it, all right, hidden back in the shadows, and wondered if Sheppard even knew it was here.

"I think it's in the concrete block part of the house, Mom," said Annie. "C'mon, I'll show you."

Annie opened the hobbit door, turned on the light, and ducked inside, Mira behind her. The room was perhaps seven feet long, five feet wide, and just as high as its highest point. A metal staircase spiraled upward at the highest point, then just stopped in midair, as though the builder had considered adding a second floor, then changed his mind and had built the kitchen wall in front of it, to hide the mistake. Markings on the walls where shelves had once been attached indicated that previous owners of the house had known about the room and probably used it for storage.

"It feels solid," she said.

"It should. We're in between four thick concrete walls, Mom."

"Yeah, but there's only one way in and out. It could become a concrete tomb."

"The whole house could become a tomb."

Mira pressed her hands to the walls, hoping she could pick up something about the room, about whether it would be safe, but nothing came to her. It was a repeat of what had happened when she'd tried to read the store. So was this some sort of new pattern? Was her psyche storing up energy for when she might really need it?

"Okay, let's move quilts and some water and food and stuff in here," she said finally. "Great work, hon."

Annie beamed. "I'm going to move the cats in here, too, with food and a litter box."

"Good idea. We'll keep them in the office for now, with

the door shut. Then we won't have to chase them down if and when we think it's necessary to head into the safe room. How'd you find this, anyway?"

"Ricki found it. I was tossing her ball around one day and it rolled into the closet and I found her sniffing around at the back, behind some boxes, and when I moved them, I found the door."

As they moved out of the room and into the office again, Nadine raised her brows. "Well?" she asked anxiously.

"We're going to move some supplies in there. Your wheelchair won't fit, so you'll have to crawl in."

"I can hobble, you know." She lifted the broken foot. "I'm allowed to walk on this cast."

"But not for forty-eight hours," Mira reminded her.

Nadine rolled her eyes. "In an emergency, I can do what it takes to get wherever I have to get. Now, how much water do we have?"

"Ten gallon jugs and thirty-six bottles of bottled water."

"What?" Annie looked horrified. "You mean, you didn't buy any more water except what we picked up at Winn Dixie? It's not enough. The recommended amount is three gallons per person a day. That's twelve gallons a day for four people. But we've got pets, so let's say we need thirteen or fourteen gallons a day. That's ninety-one to ninety-eight gallons a week."

Not enough seemed to be Mira's MO for the day. She hadn't had *enough* time to clear out the bulk of her stock, didn't have *enough* space in the garage or bedroom for books, didn't have *enough* water, *enough* propane . . . "Even if we could get water now, where would we put it?"

"I'll fill the tub and the sink in the laundry room and the one in the garage. That'll give us a little more. And then I'll bring the cats and stuff into our new safe area."

With specific goals to accomplish, Annie hurried up the hall, her doom and gloom temporarily forgotten. Mira and

Nadine looked at each other. "If something happens, Mira, I may become a liability." Nadine spoke softly. "I want you to—"

"Nothing's going to happen. The house has stood here since the sixties, Nadine. The roof is new and conforms to the tighter standards that went into effect after Andrew. We have—"

"I'm just saying if. If something happens, I don't want any heroic measures, Mira."

"Look, we've got plenty of supplies and we'll all keep our cell phones with us. We'll be fine."

"And where's your cell phone?" Nadine asked.

"Right . . ." Mira patted her hip, but her cell phone wasn't there. She remembered she had left it in her closet, when she was moving supplies into it because she'd thought it would be their safe room. "I'll get it, don't worry."

"Where's Shep? Why isn't he here?"

"I don't know."

Outside, the wind now gusted into the high category one status, serious enough so that if Sheppard had been detained, he would have called. But he hadn't called. And when she had called his cell number, she had gotten either his voice mail or a message that he had traveled out of the calling area, clearly impossible. When she tried to tune in on him, it was like running into a brick wall. More of the same pattern? It wasn't uncommon for her to be unable to tune in on a loved one when she was stressed—and she was definitely stressed now—but it worried her nonetheless.

"His place is here," Nadine went on. "He could have done more to help us get the house ready."

Under normal circumstances, Mira could ignore Nadine's constant picking at Sheppard. But conditions had ceased to be normal when the hurricane warning had gone up. "Stop blaming him for everything, Nadine. He's got a job to do and he's doing it."

"I understand about his job. I admire his sense of responsibility. But once the evacuation ended, Mira, he should have come here."

Just then, the shutters made a strange, twanging noise, like that of a guitar string that wasn't properly tightened. Mira went over to the French doors that opened onto the porch. She had closed only one shutter here because she wanted a viewing point for the storm. This now seemed foolish. Mira flicked on the porch lights, opened the unshuttered door, and stepped outside.

Rain strummed the screens and slashed across the yard in sheets that were nearly horizontal. The trees thrashed, leaves floated on the surface of the swimming pool, a flotilla of miniature ships. The water level looked to be dangerously high. She figured the porch was elevated from the pool and yard level by perhaps an inch. Once that level was breached, the porch would flood and if the water rose another half inch and could find a way under the shutters, the family room would flood as well. Even worse, the porch now creaked and groaned as though the next gust of wind would collapse the whole thing like a house of cards. If that happened, the furniture they had brought in from the pool area could become airborne.

She started moving the furniture into the house and called to Nadine to get Annie to help her. Her daughter appeared moments later, eager to be of help, to have another goal. They stacked the table and chairs in the already crowded living room and Nadine followed them like a fretful mother hen, instructing them to move a chair over there, another chair here, to push the table more snugly against the wall. Mira struggled not to snap at her. She understood how frustrating it was for Nadine to be confined to the wheelchair. But she wished her grandmother would leave them alone.

Mira grabbed her poncho from the utility room and hurried back onto the porch to close the shutters. Once they were shut, she couldn't get back into the house through the French doors and had to leave the relative protection of the porch to run to the door of the cabana bath by the pool. The wind swept up under the poncho, inflating like a balloon, and then it slammed into her from behind, propelling her forward.

She sloshed through several inches of water. The cabana bathroom door was locked. She pounded her fists against it and when Annie opened it, the wind caught the door and flung it all the way open. It banged against the wall, torrents of rain blew into the bathroom. Mira grabbed the knob to pull the door shut, but the force of the wind was so great it was as if she were battling an invisible giant for control of the door, the bathroom.

When she finally slammed it shut, water covered the floor of the bathroom and bits of leaves, twigs, and chunks of gravel floated in it. Annie plucked towels from the linen closet and they spread them out to soak up the water. It quickly became apparent that water was seeping through the crack under the door, perhaps an overflow from the roof gutters. Mira rolled up two towels and pressed them against the crack while Annie cut long strips from the roll of electrical tape. When the floor and wood were dry enough, they sealed the crack with double layers of tape.

"Will the tape keep water out if the pool overflows?" Annie asked.

"That water should flow into the yard."

"We're not in such good shape here, Mom."

Mira rocked back onto her heels, threw off the wet poncho, and hung it up in the shower. "We're okay for now."

"I'm not talking about this. I'm talking about the skylights. I forgot all about the skylights."

The skylights. Christ. How had she overlooked the skylights? There were three—in the family room, living room, and a bathroom. They were domed, made of heavy-duty plastic. Several months ago Sheppard had built wooden frames for them that would act as buffers against the wind in the event of a hurricane. But he hadn't put them up yet. In the chaos of the day, the wooden frames had been forgotten and, as far as she knew, were still in the garage. Even if she knew how to install them, she wasn't about to get up on the roof in ninety-mile-an-hour winds. So now the skylights were liabilities. Lose one, she thought, and the wind would sweep into the house and the entire roof might go.

"Mom?"

"I'm thinking, hon, I'm thinking."

They hurried into the family room, the racket of the rain hammering the skylight now was so loud, so invasive, she wondered how she could have missed it earlier. She peered up into the well of the skylight, then hurried into the living room and stared up at its skylight. Yes, she thought, her plan might work. "Do we have any plywood in the garage?" she asked Annie.

"A couple of sheets."

"Let's bring some in here."

Nadine, who had followed them into the living room, looked dubious. "You should cut the sheets to size."

"We don't have that kind of saw," Mira replied. *Or the luxury of time.*

"We'll work with what we have," Annie said.

"You see?" Nadine's gaze slipped from Mira to the skylight. "This was Shep's responsibility."

"What's your point, Nadine?" she asked crossly. "You want Shep to move out? Is that it? You want me to break off the engagement?"

Annie, who was still standing there, just shook her head, as if to say the entire argument was pathetic. Then she whistled for the dog and they headed for the garage.

Nadine made a dismissive gesture with her hand. "What I want should be obvious. He puts his job above you and Annie."

"You *encouraged* me to help him out."

"Because he's a member of the family. But his place now is here."

"He did the best he could. He was at the bookstore during every break he got."

"But Ace and Luke had to help put up the shutters."

"Look, he probably just got held up somewhere. Besides, we can use that money to hire a substitute yoga teacher for—"

"And I told you before," Nadine went on, her voice rising, "I'm not going to be out of commission. I can teach yoga from a wheelchair. I can still come into work. I can . . ."

And then Nadine's lower lip started to quiver and her eyes brimmed with tears and Mira thought, *No, please don't cry, please* . . . She went over to Nadine, put her arms around her, and suddenly her grandmother was simply an eighty-two-year-old woman with a broken foot who felt helpless, frustrated, and scared.

13

In 1928, the San Felipe-Okeechobee Hurricane caused a six-to-nine-foot surge in the waters of Lake Okeechobee, an inland lake that is the second largest freshwater lake in the U.S. It flooded the surrounding area and more than 1,800 people died.

Sheppard came to, coughing and sputtering, and realized he was being dragged by the arms through mud and rain, against a barricade of high wind. At this angle, he might drown before his rescuer reached some place dry and still.

He tried to shout, but the wind swallowed his voice. He dug his feet into the mud, creating a drag that caught his rescuer's attention and caused his ribs to light up with pain. He suddenly remembered the bruises on Mira's sides when she had read him, and wondered if the Lopez bitch had broken one or more of his ribs.

His arms were dropped, he was now flat on his back. He rolled onto his side, the pain rolling with him, the darkness around him blurring, melting into a mass of painful sensations.

"Shep, hey, wake up, c'mon, man, I need to get you inside."

The shouts pierced his awareness. Sheppard fought to focus and Goot's face took shape inches from his own. One of his eyes was swollen shut, a bruise spread like ink across his cheek.

"Help me, amigo, I can't do this alone."

Sheppard rolled onto his hands and knees and shook his head, trying to clear it. He rocked back onto his heels and Goot helped him to his feet. They stumbled forward, alternately leaning on and supporting each other. Sheppard couldn't see worth a shit, every breath he took felt as if hot metal rods were being jabbed between his ribs. Goot limped, stumbled. A couple of times he stopped and doubled over at the waist, arms clutched against his own body. And then it was Sheppard who coaxed, urged, supported, dragged, pulled.

He felt a kind of terror that one of his lungs had been punctured and that he was now slowly suffocating. He sucked air through his mouth. It hurt, but he could feel the air moving deeply into his chest and guessed his lungs were okay. *What the hell happened?*

How had a handcuffed woman, injured from a whack from Emison's baton—a whack so brutal that Sheppard was sure he heard bones crack—managed to overturn a table, grab a rifle, take down three men, and then assault him outside? He could still see Lopez in his head, spinning, her legs kicking out at the speed of light, her face inscribed with such powerful emotions that it was as if she had entered some other sphere.

They made it into the house. Even though the living room window was blown out, the noise of the wind wasn't as great and the rain lessened. They weaved through standing water, shards of glass, piles of soggy leaves, and made it into the kitchen. The generator was still on, but sputtering. Lights flickered off and on, alternately illuminating the fridge, hiding the sink, dipping the floor into darkness. Everything seemed strange and disproportionate to Sheppard, as though he were a Gulliver, then a midget, then the White Rabbit, then Alice.

Sheppard turned on the faucet, splashed water on his face. It was cold and shocked him into the here and now. He drank from his cupped hands, sating a deep thirst, then pulled paper towels from a roll on the counter, wiped his face, and handed the roll of towels to Goot. His body seemed to creak and complain like that of a ninety-year-old man. Sheppard took a bottle of water from the fridge and rolled it over his face and the back of his neck, then drank down the entire bottle and refilled it with water from the tap.

He grabbed a dish towel off a rack and ran it over the top of his head and across the back of his neck. Then he and Goot went through the door that opened into the garage. He began to feel almost whole except for the excruciating pain in his sides, especially his right side. He pushed the kitchen door shut and the cacophony of the wind ebbed enough so that Sheppard could hear the ragged edges of their breathing. Even though it wasn't cold, he shivered. He stripped off his poncho. His muddied clothes were drenched and his skin felt wrinkled, as if he'd been in the shower an hour too long. He shut his eyes and gradually the darkness behind them began to stabilize.

When he opened them again, the world took on shape, texture, form, immediacy. Jerome Carver's place in the middle of Bum Fuck, Nowhere. Carver aka Billy Joe Franklin. Dillard, Emison, the blonde, the Lopez woman who moved with such quickness that she seemed to defy gravity. The images rushed through him with impunity.

How'd she do what she did? How'd she get loose from those cuffs?

He turned his head. It felt as though it had been removed from his torso and stitched back on the wrong way. He peeled his wet shirt up and saw that his sides were already discolored. Then he looked up at Goot and nearly went into shock. His friend's face glistened with bits of embedded glass. The skin had begun to swell and fester and drops of fresh blood appeared. His swollen eye, the bruise on his cheek, looked like the marks of Cain.

"Sit down, Goot." Sheppard crouched in front of him. "What the hell happened?"

"Wrong place, wrong time," Goot breathed. "When the window blew, I caught splinters." He pulled open his shirt, popping buttons. Glass glistened like diamond chips against his chest. "I . . . came to on the floor, face down in glass, glass in my mouth and wind and rain like the end of the world. I don't know . . . how I got outside."

"Where're Dillard and Emison?"

"Emison's hurt bad. Dillard dragged him down into the cellar."

"You have a phone?"

Goot shook his head. "Lost it somewhere."

Sheppard patted his own wet, muddy clothes. No phone, no weapon. He vaguely remembered Lopez scooping up his wallet, keys, phone, and everything else that had fallen from his pockets. "Dillard and Emison have phones."

"Emison and Dillard still have phones, but they're dead. Jesus, Shep. We need to get outta here. But they took Dillard's truck, blew up my Jeep, and the only way we're getting out is in that van, if we can get it started." He nodded at the van parked behind them.

"I'll check it. Goot, who knows we're up here? Do you know if Emison told anyone from the station?"

"He just told one of the lieutenants that we'd be back in an hour. As far as I know, he wasn't specific. What about Dillard?"

"I don't know." But if Dillard played his usual game, he had kept mum so he could make his dramatic entrance with the cons. For Dillard, it was all performance, the *show*. "Stay put while I check out the van."

Its windows were down, the doors unlocked. Sheppard didn't find a cell phone or a key, but the back of the vehicle yielded a treasure: it was loaded with food and supplies and the makeshift bunk beds in the back held sleeping bags and pillows. If the garage didn't collapse, the van would be a good spot to ride out the storm. But with the cabin's living room window gone, threatening the integrity of the structure, Sheppard worried the cabin and the garage might collapse once Danielle made landfall.

He found Ace bandages in one of the unopened cartons and wrapped two of them tightly around his torso. They enabled him to breathe more easily, with less pain. He scooted out of the van and popped open the hood.

Sheppard was no mechanic, but it sure looked as if Franklin had pulled out a lot of wires. Forget driving out of here, he thought, and dropped the hood. He climbed into the back again, opened some of the boxes, and felt a reluctant admiration for Franklin's thoroughness. He obviously had planned to spend a long time hiding out at the cabin and Sheppard was betting that somewhere in these boxes he would find medical supplies.

"Is there a shower in that cellar?" he asked, returning to where Goot sat.

"No. But there's a shit load of food and supplies."

"You should use the shower in the cabin while you still can and try to get out that glass. Maybe you can find us some dry clothes, too. I'm going to search the cartons in the van for medical supplies and anything else we can use. We're going to be spending this storm in the cellar with our two favorite people."

Goot made a face, pushed back against the wall for leverage, and slowly stood. The garage lights flickered off, winked on.

"That generator's going. Let me get you a hurricane lantern."

Sheppard hurried back over to the van, plucked two of the battery-operated lanterns off the floor in the back, turned them on. The lights were wonderfully bright. He handed Goot one, set his on top of a filing cabinet.

"What kind of power source is there in the cellar?" he asked.

"A generator."

Which meant it would need gas. "Is there extra gas anywhere?"

"Not that I've seen. Maybe we can siphon it out of the van."

If he could find something with which to siphon and a container to put it in. "Can you make it into the cabin?" Sheppard asked.

Goot let loose a stream of Spanish, basically telling Sheppard to fuck off. "Before I forget." Goot reached into his raincoat pocket and withdrew a pair of handcuffs. "These were on Lopez." He held them up.

The handcuffs were nickel-plated hardened steel with double safety locks, ditched and grooved jaws, and two keys. Yet, the chain links between the two cuffs had snapped and the jaws of the cuffs looked as though they had melted away. "What the hell?" Sheppard murmured.

"Yeah. How do you figure she did *that?*"

Burns on her hands: that was what he'd read in Crystal's file about an inmate whom Tia Lopez probably attacked. Burns on the hands, melted cuffs: more impossible things. He shook his head, took the cuffs, pocketed them. "Get moving, amigo."

As Goot opened the door to the kitchen, Sheppard heard the wind again, and knew that clean clothes were the least of their worries. He watched Goot cross the ruined living room and headed toward the back of the cabin where the bathroom was, then shut the door. He picked up the lantern and re-

CATEGORY FIVE   183

turned to the van, aware of the weight of the cuffs in his pocket.

Snapped. Melted. *Impossible.*

He worked fast, trying to ignore the discomfort that movement caused at his sides. He emptied cartons, reloaded them with food and other useful supplies, and finally found a box that contained medical supplies. It wasn't just a first-aid kit, either. From the looks of it, Franklin had been prepared for anything short of radiation poisoning. Of the six different kinds of antibiotics, Sheppard recognized only two—penicillin derivatives. Either would help ward off whatever infection might be brewing in Goot or Emison. *Right? Penicillin, miracle drug? Is that still true?*

Sheppard wished for some sort of mild painkiller for himself, just something to dull the ache in his ribs. No such luck. Instead, he uncovered two vials of cocaine and a fat Baggie filled with weed. He shoved them down inside one of the boxes, then carried the boxes over to the entrance of the cellar, moved the lantern closer to the metal door, and opened it.

"Leo?" he called.

Dillard appeared at the bottom of the stairs, his face haggard, his clothes dirty and torn. "Jesus, Shep. Doug's in a bad way down here."

"I found some medical supplies in the van. I'm bringing them down."

"Where's John?"

"Showering off the glass, looking for dry clothes. Are there sleeping bags down there?"

"A couple, yeah. And blankets. And a lot of food, water, batteries."

Sheppard heard the rattle and clatter of the generator. "How's the generator fixed for fuel?"

"It's not full, but I think we're okay for a while. The room's running off some other power source, too, maybe solar, but since the lights were so dim, I turned on the generator."

"Any cell phones? Radios? Weapons?"

"No weapons, just a shortwave and a weather radio. Also a small battery-operated TV with fairly good reception. There must be some sort of satellite connection topside."

Which wouldn't last long, Sheppard thought.

Dillard came halfway up the stairs and Sheppard saw the bandage on his arm, blood staining it. "Glass?" he asked.

"Yeah. But I got lucky. Emison took a much larger piece in the leg. At least, I think it was glass. Maybe it was something else. All I know is that it's bad."

He took the carton that Sheppard held. "Leo, did you tell anyone else we'd be here?"

"No."

"Not anyone?"

"I figured we'd be in and out in thirty minutes."

"With the cons."

"Of course."

"For maximum dramatic impact. That's good, Leo. Very good. And you were hoping this would get you—what? A raise? A promotion? The Tango office?"

Dillard's eyes narrowed and turned darker, menacing. "Fuck off, Sheppard."

For several minutes, neither of them spoke. Sheppard passed the boxes and additional sleeping bags down to Dillard. The medical supplies were last and he took them down himself. The cellar was perhaps forty feet down, ten feet by fifteen feet, but sectioned off by a bamboo screen that he guessed hid a bathroom of some kind, with some additional space under the stairs for storage, and a makeshift kitchen. It worked for two people, but not for four men and especially not for four men who included Leo Dillard.

Stacked against the far wall were boxes of supplies, most

of them open, some of the contents sitting on top of the cartons. The kitchen consisted of a sink with running water, a small camping grill with a propane tank, a card table with two foldable aluminum chairs, a garbage can with a large pack of garbage bags next to it. The generator stood against this wall, clattering away. It kept the cellar well lit and the portable fans circulating the air. He dreaded the thought that the generator would run out of fuel and the power would die.

To the south, the floor was covered with sleeping bags and here lay Doug Emison, sweating and shaking under several blankets. His face looked to be the color of stale white bread, his breathing sounded ragged. Sheppard's only medical experience was a course he'd taken a year ago that had included CPR and the most rudimentary EMT procedures. Even to his untrained eye, it seemed to him that Emison was going into shock.

"I told you it was bad," Dillard said.

Their harsh words of several minutes ago had receded in importance, Sheppard thought, and crouched on one side of Emison as Dillard knelt on the other side. He rolled the blankets upward from Emison's feet to his thighs, exposing the bloody towels wrapped around the lower part of his right leg. "The gash is maybe six inches long and deep, Shep. When I was wrapping it, I thought I saw bone. It's gotta be stitched up to stop the bleeding."

"Was the blood spurting at any time?"

"No." Dillard was firm about this. "It didn't puncture any arteries. But it's gaping."

The area wasn't sterile, Sheppard himself was a muddy mess, and none of them had the medical experience needed to care for a man who was going into shock and looked to be in danger of bleeding to death. He tried to remember what he'd learned in the course about how to treat someone for shock.

"First, we need to elevate his legs and loosen his clothing. Cut off his clothes if you have to. Keep him warm and dry. Then we need to clean the wound."

"Clean it with what?"

"How the hell should I know? Soap, iodine, Betadine . . . whatever's in there. Open that box of medical supplies, get his legs elevated."

Sheppard went over to the kitchen sink, stripped down to his boxers and Ace bandages, washed his hands and face. Goot reappeared, his arms laden with clean clothes, towels, sheets, and dumped everything in the sleeping area. He came over to Sheppard with clothes. His eye was still swollen shut, but didn't look as angry as before and it seemed he'd gotten most of the glass out of his face and arms. "You're taller than Franklin, but the cotton pants have a drawstring waist and should fit and the shirts are extra large." He lowered his voice. "What're we going to do about Emison?"

"Try to stitch his leg."

"You know how to do that?"

"No. But if we don't try, he's going to die down here."

"Christ." He combed his fingers through his wet hair. "What can I do to help?"

"Tear one of those sheets into strips. Find bandages in those med supplies." Sheppard pulled on the clean clothes, washed his hands again. "I need latex gloves and more light next to Emison."

"I'm on it."

Several years ago, Sheppard and Goot had gone wind-surfing off a beach here on Tango. Sheppard was new to the sport and at one point approached the shore too quickly. He was forced to leap off the board and landed on a broken beer bottle. The jagged edge had sliced across the sole of his foot, along the side, and onto the top of it. If the cut had been a quarter of an inch deeper, it would have struck the bone and required surgery.

Sheppard recalled that the ER doc had used copious amounts of Betadine to wash the wound before she had begun stitching and had injected the wound repeatedly with lidocaine to kill the pain. Even if Franklin's supplies had lidocaine, Sheppard didn't have any idea how to give an injection. And where should he start stitching? If memory served him, the podiatrist who had worked on his foot had started from the inside of the wound. *These inner stitches will dissolve.*

Christ, he didn't have a clue what the hell he should do.

He crouched next to Emison. Goot and Dillard had set up two hurricane lanterns nearby, the light spilling over Emison's elevated legs. A sheet was now spread out on the floor beside him with the med supplies lined up on it, and another sheet was spread out under his elevated legs. Goot handed Sheppard a pair of surgical gloves and knelt beside him, prepared to assist, his own hands gloved.

"Doug?"

Emison's eyes opened to slits in his pale, sweaty face. "Shep," he breathed. "Take me . . . hospital."

"We don't have a way out of here and no one's got a phone. We're going to stitch up your leg."

The sheriff sucked air in through his teeth. "You . . . know how?"

"Sure," Sheppard lied. "Just shut your eyes. We'll take care of everything."

He nodded at Goot, who began unwrapping the bloody towels. It occurred to Sheppard that bits of glass might be stuck in the wound and that before he cleansed the wound, he should wash it with water. He hesitated using the running water from the sink. He picked up a large bottle of distilled water and twisted off the cap. He opened the bottle of Betadine, got out sterile gauze pads. He asked Goot to look for a needle and thread and to sterilize both with alcohol. He was sure Franklin had all three items.

As the last bloody towel fell away, Dillard groaned and

stumbled away, gagging. Seconds later, they heard him throwing up behind the bamboo partition. Great, Sheppard thought. Dillard was going to be a whole lot of help.

Sheppard turned his attention to Emison's leg. It continued to bleed profusely except for the few seconds when Sheppard poured water over it. Then he could see what certainly looked like bone and realized he would have to do what the podiatrist had done for *his* foot: start stitching from the inside. The wound was too deep to do otherwise.

He kept pouring water over the wound until he no longer saw glistening bits of glass inside it, and picked up the Betadine. The first squirt through the wound elicited a horrendous shriek from Emison, who bolted nearly upright, eyes bulging in their sockets. Sheppard didn't think that Betadine stung, not like the Merthiolate his mother had used on his skinned knees when he was a kid, and wondered if the stuff had touched a nerve in the wound. Goot wrestled Emison back against the blankets and, mercifully, the sheriff passed out.

"More gauze," Sheppard said, holding out his bloody, gloved hand.

Goot gave it to him. Dillard, out of the bathroom now, remained on the other side of the room, one hand covering his mouth and nose.

Sheppard worked feverishly, squirting, cleaning, squirting, and when he finally began to stitch, he couldn't say with any certainty that he was doing it correctly. He wasn't even sure what the hell he was stitching. Tissues? Muscles?

Mira once had told him that in a prior life he had been a physician in France at the turn of the century, that the abilities he had honed during that life could be drawn upon whenever he needed them. Sheppard didn't have any conscious memory of such a life as a doctor, but if it was true, then he sure could use whatever he'd known right now.

After a while, he lost awareness of Dillard, of Goot, of

where they were. His world shrank to the size of a pea. He moved his hands, the gaping wound grew less gaping, the stream of blood became less profuse. Now and then he heard the wind, but the sound seemed distant and unconnected to him. Emison regained consciousness before Sheppard had finished stitching, but he was so out of it that he merely lay there and moaned, turning his head from one side to another. Sheppard thought that his color looked better and when Goot took his pulse, he nodded and mouthed, *Steadier.*

When Sheppard finally rocked onto his heels, his back ached, his eyes burned, and his fatigue was so great he wasn't sure if he could make it to the kitchen sink to wash up. He peeled off his bloody gloves, dropped them on top of the even bloodier towels and sheet. He shook two five-hundred-milligram tablets of Augmentin into his hand, and roused Emison, coaxing him to swallow the pills with sips of fruit juice.

Goot started gathering everything up, but he didn't look to be in such great shape either. "Leave it, Goot. It's Leo's turn."

Dillard, now hunched over at the kitchen table, listening to the NOAAH radio, turned and glared at Sheppard. "I can't stomach the sight of blood."

Sheppard's blood pressure soared, his anger swept into rage. He crossed the cellar in seconds, jerked Dillard to his feet, and shoved him toward the sleeping area. "*Go do your part, you sorry sack of shit!*"

Dillard wrenched free, color poured into his face, and he hissed, "You don't tell me what to do, Sheppard."

Sheppard thrust the pack of garbage bags at Dillard. "Your turn, pal. I did the stitching, Goot assisted, and you sat on your bony ass listening to the radio. Do it or you're gone."

Dillard looked at Sheppard as if he'd lost his mind, his dark eyes widening, and laughed. "Yeah, right." He dropped the box of garbage bags. "In case you don't recall the hierarchy in the bureau, Shep, let me remind you that I'm your boss and Goot's boss and I don't do towels and sheets."

Sheppard lost it. His arm swung up and connected with Dillard's jaw and even as Dillard was falling back, shock and surprise etched into his features, Goot rushed over, threw his arm around Dillard's neck, and pulled back until Dillard's eyes bulged. "Do *not* give me an excuse to snap your skinny little neck, Leo." A deadly calm gripped his voice.

Dillard, leaning back on his forearms, his head at a cock-eyed angle because of the way Goot held him, went utterly still. He barely breathed. His eyes slid right, left, as loose as marbles. Blood oozed from his nostrils.

"We each do our part," Goot said quietly, "and we'll get through this storm intact. Got it, Leo?"

"Yeah. Yeah, okay, man. I got it. Right."

Goot slowly withdrew his arm from Dillard's neck and Dillard sat up slowly, warily. He touched his throat, rubbing at the skin.

The three of them got to their feet. "Here's the deal, Leo," said Sheppard. "There're two of us, one of you. Don't fuck with us and you'll make it out of here alive. We all do our part. Put the soiled sheets and towels in a garbage bag and stick them under the kitchen sink."

Dillard didn't say anything. He went over to the sleeping area and Sheppard and Goot stood together, whispering. "We should sleep in shifts, maybe an hour at a time," Goot said. "You did the stitching, so I'll take the first shift."

"You sure?"

"Yeah, I need to ice my eye worse than I need to sleep."

"Wake me in an hour."

"I don't have a watch."

Sheppard didn't, either. He'd taken it off when he and Mira had gone swimming and hadn't put it back on. "Wake me when you get tired."

"What should I do if Emison takes a dive?" Goot asked.

"Wake me."

Sheppard went over to the sink to wash up again. He was so out of it that he didn't know Dillard had approached the sink with the garbage bags until he said, "Can you move aside?"

Sheppard straightened, water dripping off his face, and stepped aside. Dillard put two bags under the sink. "Just so you know, Sheppard, when this is over, I'll fire your asses."

"Hey, Goot," Sheppard called. "Leo here is promising that when we get outta here, his mission is to fire our asses."

Goot guffawed. "You could take him and I'd snap his neck and who the hell would know?"

"That sounds like an excellent idea."

Dillard stepped back and looked from Goot to Sheppard, his face rapidly draining of color. "You two fucks stay away from me," he said hoarsely, hands jerking into the air, balled into fists. "Just stay the fuck back."

"After I break his neck, we could scalp him with one of the kitchen knives," Goot went on. "On this forensics show, I saw how the Cheyenne used to do it. Or was it the Sioux?"

Dillard suddenly realized what they were doing and gave a clipped, nervous laugh. His arms dropped to his sides. "Yeah, very funny. Now that you two comedians have had your little laugh—"

His sentence died at the tip of his tongue as a kitchen knife suddenly slammed into the wall just inches from his temple. "It's the only sharp knife in the kitchen, Leo. And I've got the fucker." Goot jerked the knife out of the wall before Dillard moved or breathed a word.

"That . . . that was attempted assault," Dillard sputtered.

"What was?" Sheppard asked innocently.

"Who attempted to assault whom, Leo?" Goot asked. "I didn't see anything. Did you, Shep?"

"Nope."

When Dillard spoke again, his quiet voice shook with a barely controlled rage. "You won't get away with this."

"Yeah?" Sheppard laughed, a sharp, ugly sound. "So go take it up with the Christian Coalition, Leo. You and the rest of the neocons can join the fight to have the Ten Commandments posted at the courthouse in Alabama or you can file lawsuits about gay marriages or you can head to the Mideast and join the hunt for terrorists."

A pulse beat hard and fast at Dillard's temple. Veins and tendons stood out in his throat, his neck. "You're a disgrace to the bureau," he spat. "You didn't deserve to head up the Tango office and if it hadn't been for Baker Jernan, you'd still be a homicide cop in Broward County. And if we go farther back, Sheppard, back to Andrew, remember Andrew? The post-traumatic stress syndrome you suffered then is still alive and well."

"Yeah, yeah," Sheppard muttered. "Get some sleep, Leo. We're doing one-hour shifts and Goot's got the first one."

With that, he turned his back on Dillard, shuffled back across the room, and collapsed on top of a sleeping bag. The last thing he heard was the distant howl of the wind.

14

What to expect in a category-five hurricane: A storm surge greater than 18 feet; complete roof failure on many residences and industrial buildings; all shrubs, trees, and signs blown down; complete destruction of mobile homes; severe and extensive window and door damage; low-lying escape routes cut off by rising water three to five hours before arrival of the hurricane eye; major damage to lower floors of all structures located less than 15 feet above sea level and within 500 yards of the shoreline.

In the midst of her mother's argument with Nana Nadine, Annie had hurried into the garage to get the plywood and to seek refuge. Now that she was here, the sound of the wind and rain sounded raw, immediate, frightening. But as long as the power stayed on, as long as there was light and she kept focused on the goal—gathering up the sheets of plywood—she would be okay.

Light was good, darkness was bad. Darkness was the reason she needed a night-light in her bedroom, music to fall asleep to, friendly voices or lyrics that accompanied her into sleep. Some nights when none of those things worked, she asked her mom to tickle her back, to read to her, to tell her a story just so she could find her way into sleep.

It wasn't something she could admit to her friends. They wouldn't get it. How could they? When you'd been whisked back thirty-five years in time, you lost the ability to communicate certain stuff to your peers, and you learned the value of ordinary life. You learned that your mother, despite her oddness, was an anchor. You learned that your great-grandmother, another weirdo, was wise. And you learned, she thought, that your mother's boyfriend or fiancé, or whatever Shep was, was as close to a father as you were going to get. You learned that the impossible happened and that regardless, you simply moved forward one step at a time.

But tonight she seemed to be taking baby steps and no matter what she did, she couldn't move beyond her fear.

"Over here," she said to Ricki. The dog sniffed around at Annie's feet, following a scent that was every bit as mysterious to her as anything else that had happened in this long and puzzling day. "The plywood's over here."

Several sheets of plywood rested against the wooden shelves loaded with Shep's windsurfing gear and cartons of books. Sails, boards, booms, and several wet suits hung on a hook. Annie took comfort in the sight of his gear. It made her feel that he was somewhere nearby—in the house, in the delivery van—and that any second now he would appear and call her name. *Hey, Annie*, as if he'd known her for a hundred years.

She selected a flashlight from the neat row of flashlights that hung near the sheets of plywood, and when she tried it, the flashlight worked. Of course it did. Shep had seen to it that all the flashlights here had fresh batteries, new bulbs. When her mom had been in charge nothing had been ordered. Flashlights lay next to bottles of vitamins, the gardening tools had been stuck in with the cans of paint.

She turned the flashlight on, pleased with how bright the light was, brighter than the garage's overhead light, and turned it toward Ricki, who whined and moved between the delivery truck and Shep's Jetta. She pawed at the garage door, whining.

"What?" Annie said. "You have to go out? Forget it." She went over to squares of sod that Shep had stacked up near the side door and laid out eight pieces, creating an oasis of green. "Ricki, go here. This is your litter box, girl."

The dog ignored her and moved swiftly along the length of the door, nose to the ground. All the cats were inside, in Sheppard's office with their food and litter box, so it couldn't be one of them. Ricki probably had picked up some other scent, maybe of some wild creature seeking a haven from the storm.

She turned off the flashlight, tucked it under her arm, and returned to the plywood. She slid the front one out and pulled it over to the door that led into the house. She set it against the old shelves that held shoes—and immediately smelled something sharp, like old cheddar cheese, and felt . . . *weird*. Goose bumps broke out along her arms, the hairs on the back of her neck bristled, the inside of her mouth flashed dry. An image popped into her head of a black woman wrapped up in duct tape, in what appeared to be the family room off the kitchen. *What's that mean?*

Ricki continued to paw and whine at the garage door. Annie shrugged off the sensations, grabbed the plywood sheet, tugged it toward the utility room, opened the door. "Mom? Can you c'mere? Mom?"

Her mother appeared, her face drawn with worry, anxiety, and other emotions that Annie couldn't identify. "There's just this one sheet?"

"There're four or five," she whispered urgently. "Listen, you know how I tuned in on stuff in that parking garage? Well, something like that just happened again."

"Good, hon, that's good. C'mon, let's get the plywood into the house. Can you get the ladder?"

With that, her mother pulled the sheet of plywood into the house. Tears stung the backs of Annie's eyes and she hurried into the hall, shouting, "Would you listen to me? I'm telling you something important."

Her mother dropped the sheet of plywood and spun around. "You don't have to yell," she yelled.

"Then you need to listen to me. I . . . I experienced something really weird a few seconds ago. It scared me. I need to understand what it means, Mom."

"Fine, we'll talk about it. But get the ladder and more plywood, will you? We have to cover up these skylights."

Her frustration boiled over. "I need answers *now,* not when it's convenient for you."

"This isn't about you or me," her mom snapped. "It's about securing the house while we still have time."

Annie started to say something hateful, but the peal of the telephone prevented it. She was closest to the kitchen phone and hurried over to it. "Hello?"

"Uh, yes, this is Sergeant Humphrey at the Tango Police Department. I'm looking for Sheriff Emison or Detective Sheppard."

"They aren't here. Would you like to talk to my mother?"

"Yes, thanks. I appreciate it."

"Mom, it's someone from the Tango PD." Annie set the receiver on the counter, turned away, and stepped back into the garage.

Ladder. Nails. Hammer. *She's blowing me off.* Her mother blew her off because what *she* picked up was the only thing that counted. She seemed to regard Annie as her apprentice, the psychic in training. What bullshit.

Annie marched over to the tool bench for a hammer and nails. What kind of nails would work for this job? She didn't have a clue. She jerked out one drawer after another in Shep's neat chest of nails and screws and finally selected long, skinny nails that looked as though they would do the trick. She had read somewhere that the 8d ring shank nail could substantially improve the odds of a roof staying in place during a hurricane and wondered what kind of nails *their* roof had. Her mother had said the roof had been replaced after Andrew, when new building codes had gone into effect, but the findings on the 8d nails were recent, no more than a few months ago. The 8d nails were supposed to be so effective that the Florida Building Code would require the ringed nails in all new home construction in Dade and Broward Counties in 2005.

Not in time for Danielle.

She put the nails in the pocket of her shorts, clamped the hammer between her teeth, picked up the ladder, and stepped back into the utility room just as her mother was getting off the phone.

They looked at each other, she and her mom, and Annie thought her mother's face seemed ravaged, despairing. Annie removed the hammer from her mouth. "What?"

"No one has heard from Shep, Emison, or Dillard," her mother said, her voice tight. "The sergeant thought they might . . . be here. I told him that Dillard claimed to have narrowed the Jerome Carver choices down to one guy and knew where he was."

"Shep's okay, Mom. He just isn't here yet." Annie didn't want to hear about Sheppard. He was an adult who could take care of himself. Right now, *she* needed help understanding what had happened to her. Maybe it was nothing. But suppose it was important? "I need your help, Mom," Annie said softly. "I saw a black woman wrapped up in duct tape in our family room. What's that *mean?*"

Her mother resumed pushing the plywood sheet along the floor. Her back was to Annie. "I don't know what it means. How did you feel when it was happening?"

"Weird. Disturbed. I didn't like it."

Her mother picked up the ladder, turned away from her. "Can we talk about it in a few minutes? After we secure these skylights?"

"Can't it wait for sixty goddamn seconds?" Annie exploded. "You're always doing that to me. Blowing me off or telling me later, later, because you have a client coming or Shep needs you or you have to do something at the store. . . . Just give me your full attention for once, Mom."

Her mom pulled the ladder over to the skylight, opened it, then gave Annie her full attention. Hand on her hip, expression resigned. Nadine, positioned halfway between them in her wheelchair, just shook her head.

"Dios mio," Nadine muttered. *"*This is no way to understand anything. Listen to yourselves."

"I didn't know she felt that way," her mother snapped at Nadine.

"Hello, I'm right here, Mom." Annie stabbed at her own chest. "Talk to *me.* I asked the question."

"I . . . I didn't know you felt that way, Annie."

"I've told you she feels this way," Nadine butted in.

"You have not."

Nadine rolled her eyes. "Oh, *please.* You're impossible sometimes, Mira."

"Yeah," Annie agreed. "You are. Sometimes you treat me like . . . like, I don't know, like I'm a postscript in this family. I need to understand what I saw. I . . . who else can I ask? Who else is going to know this stuff? Just you and Nana Nadine."

Her mom rubbed her hands over her face; then her arms dropped to her sides. "Tell her what it means, Nadine."

Nadine raised her arms and shook her head. "She's asking *you,* not me."

"Someone tell me *something,"* Annie shouted.

"It's not like using a dream dictionary, okay?" Her mother

threw out her arms. "You can't just turn to a page and find an entry for black woman or duct tape or family room. It's not that simple. What you experience is unique to you. Maybe it's a symbol for how you feel right now, incapacitated, silenced . . ."

"But suppose it *wasn't* a symbol? Suppose it's literal? Huh? And suppose the black woman is the one who escaped the jail? How can you tell the difference?"

"I doubt that it was literal, honey. You're too young to—"

"What?" Annie couldn't believe what her mother had just said. "Too young? You were in pre-school when you started picking up psychic impressions. Besides, you're not in my body or inside my head—"

"Stop shouting."

"I'm not shouting." But she was. She dropped the nails and the hammer and spun around. "Just forget it. I'll get the other ladder." She hastened out into the garage and slammed the door.

She struggled with feelings of betrayal, failure, and began to doubt what she had experienced. *Incapacitated, silenced . . .* well, yeah. That about summed up how she felt. She picked up the second ladder, then glanced around for Ricki and saw her now squatting on the square of grass. "C'mon, girl, we need to go inside and get these skylights done."

Ricki refused to budge. As Annie glanced around for her leash, she heard a woman shout, *"Get back, just get the fuck back, and no one will get hurt here."*

Everything inside Annie went cold, still. *Did I really hear that?*

She moved swiftly to the utility room door, turned off the overhead light and her flashlight, pressed her ear to the wood.

"Is it just the two of you here?" a man demanded.

Oh my God, it's real. Annie jerked away from the door, grabbed Ricki's collar, and pulled her back into the shadows next to the side door that opened into the yard. She hunkered down, head in an uproar.

How had they gotten inside the house? She hadn't heard the doorbell—but Ricki sensed them, that's why she was sniffing along the edge of the garage door. They had come in through one of the windows, sure, it made sense. Even though the shutters were all closed, covering the windows and the French doors, they weren't locked. Just pull them open, remove the screen, raise the window.

There were at least two of them, a man and a woman. *And a black woman, who eventually will be wrapped up in duct tape.* The escapees. She suddenly was certain of this. Maybe her mother hadn't opened the front door for them, but she had opened a psychic door when she'd read the site where the Hummer had exploded. *And I helped. I helped open that door. I'm as much to blame as she is.*

She felt the warm, wet air of the storm seeping through the crack under the door. *Need to hide. And fast.* She considered hiding in the back of the delivery van, but it was too obvious. She could think of only one spot where she wouldn't be seen when the intruders came into the garage. And they *would* come, of course they would.

Annie crawled over to the tool bench, urging Ricki to follow. She pulled the bench away from the wall just enough to expose part of the hollow space beneath it, and ducked under. Ricki, thinking it was some sort of game, eagerly climbed into the space with her. Annie grasped the handle of a large green plastic bin that was nearby and pulled it over to the tool bench so that it hid the opening. She pushed back as far as possible into the space and made Ricki stretch out on the floor next to her.

"You have to be quiet," she whispered, and touched her fingers lightly to Ricki's muzzle. "No growling, no scratching."

Instead of hiding, maybe she should grab a shovel and rush into the house swinging it.

Right. One kid against three armed cons. She would get them all killed.

She slipped her cell phone out of her back pocket and punched out Shep's cell number. It rang and rang until she reached his voice mail. "Shep, it's me," she whispered. "I don't know where you are, but we need help. There're intruders in the house. I'm in the garage and . . ." And what? Just what the hell did she expect Sheppard to do? The Tango PD had called *here* looking for him.

Something had happened to him. Otherwise he would be here.

Annie ended the call, panic scrambling her thoughts, squeezing her choices to absolute zero. *Calm down, calm down . . . The Tango PD, of course, duh, hello.*

Her fingers trembled as she punched out 911. She got a busy signal.

She disconnected, pressed Redial, got a busy signal again.

This was what happened when the World Trader Center got hit, she thought, and suddenly knew this was *her* nine/eleven, *her* Iraq, *her* war with terrorists.

Stay hidden.

She threw her arm over Ricki's back and pressed her face against her thighs.

15

"In 1992, Hurricane Andrew went from a category one to a category four in thirty-six hours."

from *The Weather Book*

A profound horror seized Mira, paralyzing her. Even her mind had frozen. Yet she heard the frantic, wild beating of her heart and had a rudimentary awareness of some inner voice shrieking, *It's them, the cons, it's them*. But the sight of the man and the woman in her house, both of them armed, had rendered her incapable of linear thought.

"Hey," the man snapped. "I asked you a question."

Question. She blinked. Her mouth moved but nothing came out. She recognized these two as Billy Joe Franklin and Crystal DeVries, both of them drenched, their clothes filthy. Where was Tia Lopez? *I didn't just open the door to this nightmare; I blew it off the hinges.*

"Hey, lady." He rolled onto the balls of his feet and got right up in her face. "Answer the question. Are you two the only ones here?"

His breath smelled like rotten cucumbers. She turned her head away. "Yes."

He grabbed her chin. "Look at me when I'm speaking to you."

Don't touch me, don't touch me . . . Brief images flickered through her of Franklin in a black room, on a bouncy bed covered with black sheets, making wild, violent love to the blonde. "Yes. I said yes. We're the only two here."

"That's better." Grinning, he released her chin and rocked away from her. "Babe, get the Amazon in here."

The blonde, edgy and hyped up, danced around like she was high on speed. Even though her facial structure, the color of her eyes, her wild blond hair, and the pout of her mouth held the promise of beauty, her face lacked humanity. The result was a sort of white trailer trash kind of face that would be sagging, drawn, and old before she hit forty.

She held a gun, a Sig just like Sheppard's, and aimed it at Nadine. "I don't like how you're looking at me, old lady." And she danced right over to Nadine's wheelchair and jammed the muzzle of the Sig against Nadine's temple. "I think I'll shoot her, Billy. Okay? Is that okay?"

"Back off, babe. Just back off. You're—"

"C'mon, Billy. We've never wasted anyone together. Well, no, that's not quite true, is it?" She giggled like a silly teenage girl. "We wasted those cops who were chasing us. But that's not the same thing because you were driving, not shooting. C'mon, let's have some goddamn fun while we're here. I really want to shoot her, I hate old people."

Sweat glistened against Nadine's forehead, her eyes widened and darted to Mira, the message clear: *No heroics.*

"Leave her alone!" Mira cried out.

The blonde whipped around, her eyes like chips of steaming dry ice. "Who the fuck are *you,* telling *me* what to do, bitch?" And she danced backward and swung around, the Sig now aimed at Mira. "Let's just waste them, Billy. Who's gonna know?"

"What the fuck's wrong with you, girl?" A tall black woman weaved from the family room, right hand gripping her left shoulder. She was just as dirty and wet as the other two. "You're talkin' like a barbarian."

Franklin rolled his eyes and laughed. "Right. Barbarians. You've killed more people than Crystal and me together."

"Leave her alone, Billy. She's hurtin bad," Crystal said, and pulled out a chair at the kitchen table. "Sit down here, Tia."

She helped Tia Lopez into a chair at the kitchen table, exhibiting such solicitous concern she hardly seemed like the same woman who, only moments ago, had held a gun to Nadine's head. Mira pressed back against the edge of the counter, frightened that the dog might start barking, that this shit would find Annie.

"We just want a . . . refuge from the storm." Tia grimaced with pain and gripped her shoulder more tightly.

"Then go to a shelter," Mira said.

Franklin laughed. "Sure. Where's the dog?"

"What?"

"The dog." He gestured at Ricki's bowl against the far wall in the corner. "D-O-G. Dog. Where's the dog? I hate dogs."

"The bowls belong to the cats," Nadine said.

"Cats." Franklin wrinkled his nose. "Jesus, I hate cats as much as I do dogs. Babe, go find the cats and shoot them."

Mira's horror bit in more deeply. "That's not necessary. They won't bother you."

Crystal nodded. "There, see? And I'm not shooting any animals, Billy. Forget it."

"Damn straight," Tia muttered, raising her head from her arms, which rested on the table. "Animals sense things in storms. The animals stay."

"You're not in charge, Amazon. I am."

"I don't give a damn who's in charge, Dipshit. The plan

was that we find a house where we could ride out the storm. We're not here to shoot animals or people. That was the deal, right, Crystal?"

"Right." Her head bobbed. "You've got that exactly right."

Mira and Nadine exchanged a glance. Mira knew they were thinking the same thing, that the inner dynamics of this trio kept shifting because Crystal was the swing vote. She might be Franklin's lover and the reason for all the havoc he'd created, but Crystal seemed to feel a certain loyalty to Tia as well. Mira wondered how she might use this knowledge to her advantage and keep them out of the garage and away from Annie.

Franklin, who obviously disliked having two women lay down the rules, said, "Here's the deal, ladies. You do what we tell you and we'll all get through this storm in one piece. Just keep the cats away from me."

"I need ice and some aspirin," Tia murmured, resting her head against her arms again.

No one moved. Crystal whipped around and pointed her gun at Mira. "Get her some ice, didn't you hear her?" she shouted. "And aspirin."

"I can't be in two places at once." Mira spoke quietly, calmly, and remained where she was. "Which do you want first, the ice or the aspirin?"

"Oh, for Christ's sake." Franklin's exasperation rolled away from him in thick waves, like a foul odor. He grabbed Mira's arm and jerked her forward, toward the refrigerator. "Get the ice. Make a pack out of it."

Don't touch me. She jerked her arm free of his grasp. "I speak English. You don't need to push me. I understand."

He threw his head back, laughing, and rocked forward, into her face again, and the foul stink of rotten cucumbers nearly choked her. Then he grabbed her by the hair, jerking her right up against him, and jammed the barrel of the shotgun against the underside of her jaw. Mira gasped and struggled to throw up inner walls against him, against picking up anything about him, but his energy crashed over her, sweeping away her walls . . .

I am water, I am water . . .

"And I will touch you any time, anywhere, any place that I like," he hissed. "Are we clear on that?"

"Yes." She nearly gagged on the word.

I am a rushing, swollen tide of water and I will fill you . . .

"Billy, stop!" Crystal shouted. "Please." She hurried over to him and insinuated herself between Franklin and Mira, pushing Mira away.

Mira stumbled, her hands went to her throat, to the indentation the barrel of the rifle had left in her skin. She coughed, her eyes watered, she kept moving back, back, putting as much distance as she could between herself and Franklin. Crystal talked to him, trying to calm him down as though she were a preschool teacher and he, an intractable toddler with a bad temper.

Mira turned and opened the cabinet door where she kept the aspirin. Tylenol. A glass of water. A Baggie that she filled with ice. She went over to the table, Franklin and Crystal watching her with predatory fascination, and set the ice pack in front of Tia.

Tia raised her head and looked up at Mira with bleary, pain-filled eyes. "Thanks."

"What happened to your shoulder?"

"A cop slammed his baton against it."

"If it's fractured, Tylenol won't do much for pain."

"You're a doctor?" Franklin sneered. "A nurse?"

"No."

"And what is it you do?"

"I own a bookstore."

He pointed at the One World Books slogan on her T-shirt. "That store?"

She nodded and noticed that his eyes moved, briefly, to the malachite stone around her neck, then to her breasts and back to her face.

"And those boxes in there . . ." He pointed at the family room. "Are they all filled with books?"

"Right."

"Then shut up unless someone asks your opinion about books." He pointed through the utility room to the garage door. "Where's that go? The garage?"

Shit, no, don't go out there. "Yes, and it's got two cars and more books inside it."

"Would you check the garage, babe?"

Crystal hurried through the doorway, turned on the utility room light, stepped into the garage. "It's crowded with shit, Billy," Crystal called.

"Check inside the cars. And while she's doing that, ladies, we're going to need food, dry clothes, and towels, plenty of dry towels." He pointed the Remington at Nadine. "You. What's your name?"

"Nadine."

"Nay-dean. Okay, Nay-dean. Where's the closest linen closet?"

"In the cabana bathroom off the family room."

"Get us some towels from there."

"I'll get them," Mira said. "In case you haven't noticed, she's in a wheelchair and the chair won't fit through the doorway." *What's going on in the garage? Did the blond trailer trash find Annie? The dog? Dear God, no, please . . .*

"You stay where you are. She'll figure out a way to get them, won't you, Nay-dean?" He grinned as he said it. "You didn't get to be old without figuring out a thing or two."

Nadine's eyes held spit, fire, contempt, but Mira knew she wouldn't do anything foolish. She turned the wheelchair and slowly moved toward the cabana bathroom.

"Babe, what's going on out there?" Franklin shouted.

"Nothing." Crystal came back into the house, shut the door. "There's nothing out there. The van's half-filled with books, there're boxes of books everywhere. Look, I'm starved and I need dry clothes, Billy."

"Nay-dean is getting us towels. We'll get dry clothes in a minute. And your name is . . . ?" he asked, looking at Mira.

"Mira."

"Isn't that, like, Spanish for 'he watches'?"

"It's a proper noun. But if it were a Spanish verb, it would mean 'he looks.'"

"Wow, so precise." He reached out and stroked her cheek with his thumb. Mira jerked her head away and he laughed. "So how're you fixed for the hurricane, Meer-ah?"

"Just fine, Billllll-ee."

He realized she was mocking him; anger coiled in his small, dark eyes, shadowed as they were by his endless calculations, his strange shrewdness. *And what's the water mean?*

"I don't like the way you touched her cheek." Crystal spoke sharply, her eyes burning holes in the side of Franklin's head.

"Chill, babe." He glanced at Crystal, then reached out and stroked her cheek in the same way that he had touched Mira's. "Your skin is softer."

Crystal giggled and bussed Franklin on the cheek.

To Mira, he said: "You have a generator?"

"In the garage."

"How long will it last?"

"Until the gas runs out. I don't know how long that is. We've never used it before."

"And it looks like you have plenty of food and water."

"But we have three skylights," she said. "The family room, the living room, and a bathroom. I was about to nail plywood over the skylight openings. That's why the ladder is out there."

"Skylights. Shit."

Distract him, keep him out of the garage and away from Annie.

"Is that bad, Billy?" Crystal looked worried and rolled her lower lip between her teeth.

"It's not good. Keep your gun on her, babe."

Franklin strode quickly into the family room, turned on all the lights, and stood under the skylight for several minutes, staring up at it, just as Mira herself had done. It bothered her that she would have anything at all in common with this man.

Now he walked in small, tight circles, running his fingers through his hair, shaking his head, muttering. Then he stood under the skylight again, staring, ponderous, hands on his hips. Nadine came out of the bathroom with her towels piled in her lap.

"You've never seen a skylight before?" she asked Franklin.

He made a dismissive gesture with his hand and Crystal shouted, "Hey, old lady, get your ass in here. Don't bother him while he's thinking." She pointed the gun at Mira. "You, help her."

Mira went over to the wheelchair and pushed Nadine into the kitchen. She gave her shoulder a quick squeeze and Nadine patted her hand, as if to comfort her. Mira picked up the pile of towels and set them on the table. Tia raised her head, took a towel, and rubbed it over her face and wet clothes.

"I need dry clothes," Tia said. "And a shower. And food."

"Hold on, just hold on." Franklin's voice was all business now, sharp, authoritative. He strode back into the kitchen, looking worried. "We may have a problem with these skylights. When was your house built?"

"I don't know." Mira didn't feel like telling him anything about her house, her life, her family.

"Is the roof new?"

"It was supposedly replaced five years ago, before we moved here."

"Were the skylights replaced?"

"I don't know."

"Do you know the exact date the house was built?" he asked.

"No, why?"

"Because he's trying to figure out whether this place will still be standing in eight hours," Tia murmured. "That's what these guys do, see? They look at past patterns and make predictions based on computer models that have all these patterns on their hard drives. But computer models don't tell you shit, do they, Billy Joe? Not really. Not for monster storms like Andrew or Danielle or Hugo."

It was the most this woman had said since these people had broken in. It was immediately apparent to Mira that Franklin wished Tia would just shut up and disappear.

"So let's say the house was built in the 1930s," Tia continued, looking at Franklin. "What's that tell you?"

"That it survived the Great Labor Day Hurricane of 1935," Franklin replied.

"Exactly," Tia breathed, pointing her index finger at him, her eyes preternaturally bright. "And that storm had a central pressure of 895 millibars and winds estimated to be in excess of two hundred miles an hour. It was the most intense storm to ever hit the U.S."

She sounded like Annie, Mira thought, and gone was the awkward grammar, the tough broad act. "How do you know that?" Mira asked.

"What difference does it make?" Tia shot back.

"She's an Andrew survivor," Franklin said. "That's how she knows it. I'm betting she's got a whole lot of facts about hurricanes stored up in that pea brain of hers. Right, Amazon?"

"You got it, Dipshit. Over four hundred people died in the

Great Labor Day storm, most of them World War One vets who were building a new highway. Forty miles of railroad were destroyed. Most structures between Long Key and Plantation Key vanished. But that was long before this house was built because guess what? How many houses in the thirties had skylights? You're not so smart for a TV weatherman," she finished with a smirk.

"A weatherman?" Nadine exploded with laughter. "Fascinating. And how did you get from weatherman to murderer? And why do you wear so much black? Is it, like, you know, a Darth Vader thing?"

Mira understood that Nadine sought to distract Franklin, too. The longer he was in the house, the longer it would be before he went into the garage and made a thorough search. But he wasn't about to be baited. He walked over to Nadine and slapped her so hard across the face that her head snapped back, her nose began to bleed, and tears sprang into her eyes.

"You shut the fuck up. I don't like old people. I especially don't like you, Nay-dean."

Mira rushed over to her grandmother with a dish towel, pressed it against Nadine's nose, and glowered at Franklin. "You're a low-life bully."

"Yeah, I am." He flashed that despicable toothy grin again.

"Of course he's a low-life fuck," Tia said. "It's the one thing the three of us have in common."

Crystal looked indignant. "I am *not* a low-life fuck."

"Let's start over again," Franklin said. "When was the house built?"

"Summer." Nadine wiped the towel across her nose. "Nineteen sixty."

"Okay, that's a place to start. In September 1960, Hurricane Donna hit the Keys."

"But most of her damage was to the Middle to Upper

Keys," Tia said. "Where sustained winds were cat four, with gusts up to 180. Key West and Tango escaped with much lower winds, maybe low cat-three winds, if that."

"But she didn't do shit to Key West," Franklin added.

"Exactly. Then, look at Betsy, 1965. Defied all your fancy predictions. She was well north of the Upper Keys. But she was a seductive bugger and decided she could change her mind, right, Dipshit? Headed back to the Bahamas and then changed her mind again and damaged the Middle and Lower Keys, max winds in gusts as high as 160. But hey, the house is still here, so that must mean it did okay in Betsy. Next."

"Shut up, Lopez."

She dismissed him with a wave of her hand. "We should've ditched you back in the preserve. You're nothing but trouble. And just for your information, I know as much about hurricanes as you, probably more. And I'm telling you Danielle's going to do a tune on this house unless you fix the skylights."

He ignored her. "Inez, 1966, that was the next big one. Key West and Tango barely got cat-one winds. Minimal damage, mostly at the south end of Tango."

Tia rolled her eyes. "Well, shit now, that's a no-brainer. The southern end of Tango is going to vanish in Danielle. So we're up to 1987 and twenty-one years with no hurricanes to South Florida and along comes Floyd. Maximum sustained winds barely a category two. Minimal damage in Key West, but some flooding and roof damage at the southern end of Tango. And then 1992."

"Andrew," he said quietly, almost respectfully, Mira thought.

"Let's not go there," Tia said.

"Oh, let's. C'mon, Lopez, it couldn't have been all that bad. I was working for the National Hurricane Center then. And in terms of the Keys, damage was to the north—Key Largo—but that was spit in the wind compared to damage in

Homestead and Miami. But the storm destroyed power lines to the Lower Keys."

"Honey," Tia said, softly, shaking her head, "it destroyed a lot more than that."

"Nineteen ninety-eight. Hurricane Georges. High cat-two winds, destroyed Houseboat Row in Key West, did major damage to the marina on Tango, destroyed part of the Tango pier. Nearly nine inches of rain. Nineteen ninety-nine. Hurricane Irene. Rain, rain, rain. Not much damage from wind. Two thousand four. Danielle. Cat five."

"Uh-huh," Tia said. "We are *fucked.*"

Silence. The rain hammered against the roof, wind rattled the shutters. Mira knuckled her eyes and sent her daughter mental messages to stay hidden, to stay quiet, to keep the dog quiet.

"If the roof was replaced after Andrew," Franklin said, "when the building codes became more stringent, then the skylights might hold. And besides, plywood isn't going to do shit. It's not going to make us safer."

Us. Once again, Mira was struck by just what sort of Pandora's box she had opened when she'd agreed to read the Hummer site.

"But will post-Andrew codes hold in winds of 160?" Mira asked. *Will anything hold?*

"Forget the plywood. If the skylights blow, so will the plywood." He stopped pacing. "Fix us some sandwiches, Meer-ah. Grilled cheeses, a frying pan, butter on both sides of the bread."

"You're making a mistake," Tia said quietly. "This bitch is going to be worse than Andrew and we should be doing whatever gives us an edge."

"An *edge*?" He laughed. "The only edge you've got for this kind of storm is to be elsewhere. And unfortunately, we lost that option." He turned his small, dark eyes on Mira. "Food. We all need food. Then dry clothes."

Mira got out the frying pan, butter, cheese, bread. As she opened the utensil drawer, her eyes fixed on all the knives, many of them sharp. *Which one? Which is sharpest, longest?* Franklin suddenly slammed the drawer shut and clicked his tongue against his teeth.

"Bad idea, Meer-ah." He jerked the drawer out of the cabinet and slammed it down on the counter. "Babe, collect everything sharp and get rid of it." His eyes bored into Mira's and she felt so dirty, so sullied, that she glanced away. "Use this to cut cheese." He slapped a plastic picnic knife down on the counter.

And then the phone rang.

The sound rang out with a kind of terrible clarity, seizing them all. Franklin moved first and grabbed the portable phone and looked at the caller ID window. *Unknown caller.* Their eyes met, locked. "Who would that be?"

"Probably one of the neighbors, checking up on us," she lied.

He raised the shotgun and aimed it at Nadine. "You say the wrong thing, she eats dust."

Mira's body turned cold. She nodded.

The instant Mira touched the phone, she knew that it was Annie, calling from the garage on her cell phone. Mira was suddenly grateful she accidentally had left her cell in the bedroom closet. Otherwise, he would know she had a cell phone and would take it away.

"Morales residence." She never answered the phone in this way.

"*Eu coosi dao, Mikono,*" Annie said in a soft, quavering voice, in their private language. It was incomplete, this language, but they had created enough of it to converse in a limited way.

"*Santelo ni opeku tuman. Eu juraz non bokuto. Eu coosi dao, Suki. Timbo.*" It roughly translated as, *Stay hidden, I can't speak freely. I love you, Annie. We're okay.*

Annie began to cry and tried to speak through her muffled sobs. She suggested they communicate through text messages. She could use her cell phone or PDA as long as possible, and said she would wait for a signal from Mira before she came out of hiding. In the meantime, she would keep trying to get through to Shep or to 911.

Franklin suddenly grabbed the phone out of Mira's hand. "Hello, who is this?" he demanded. He listened, then slammed down the receiver. "Who was that? What language were you speaking?"

"A neighbor. She's Greek. She's worried because her husband hasn't come home yet."

"That didn't sound like Greek to me," he said.

"It's a dialect used on Crete." How smoothly the lie came out, she thought. And how convincing it sounded.

He jerked the wire out of the wall. "No more calls. When those sandwiches are done, bring them into the family room. We're going to get storm updates. Keep an eye on her, babe."

Then he herded Tia and Nadine into the family room, turned on the TV, and pulled up a chair where he positioned himself like a feudal lord in his castle. Mira struggled to keep her emotions under control. She finished the grilled cheese sandwiches, put them on paper plates. Her mind raced, but her thoughts kept circling one indisputable fact: she had opened this door when she'd agreed to help Dillard. This was her fault, not Sheppard's. Never in a million years could she blame this one on him.

Outside, Danielle's outer bands kept pounding the island.

16

Hurricane Gilbert, a category-five storm that struck the Yucatan Peninsula on September 13, 1988, had a central pressure of 888 millibars. It remains the most intense Atlantic hurricane on record.

A disembodied voice stabbed at Sheppard like a new, shiny needle, rousing him from a sleep so deep that even the heat in the cramped cellar room had failed to touch him. Now the heat wrapped around him, insidiously gripping him, as wet and heavy and intimate as an unwanted kiss. His eyes, sticky with sleep, opened reluctantly and he instantly shut them again, wanting nothing more than to scramble back into the soft haven where only the voice had reached him.

Whose voice?

"Shep, wake up."

Goot's voice.

Sheppard bolted upright, wondering why the battery-operated fan had stopped, why the lights were dimmer. Was the generator running out of gas already? He looked slowly around the cellar, and suddenly felt as if he were being squeezed into a coffin or a glass jar in which his body would float like a fetus. His throat went tight, his chest felt as if it had been carved open, stuffed with cotton, and set on fire.

Open fields, vast blue skies, space, space, space . . . He pulled his usual tricks out of the hat and within moments, the tightness eased, the heat in his chest went away, and he could speak. "What is it?" he whispered.

"I nodded off on my watch and when I came to, Dillard was gone."

"Good. We got lucky and he walked back to town."

"I thought I heard him talking to someone. That's what woke me."

Sheppard turned on his flashlight and shone it at Dillard's sleeping bag, tucked back into the shadows. The area around it resembled a picnic area trashed by juvenile delinquents— wrappers, crumbs, a can of Coke resting on its side, empty bottles, a dirty sheet bunched at the foot of the sleeping bag. Maybe claustrophobia finally had gotten to Dillard and he'd gone topside for a breather. How tempting it would be to lock the bastard out and if the garage blew away . . . well, too bad.

"Is he using the can?" Sheppard asked.

"Nope. He went topside. Left the trapdoor open, too, I think. That's probably why the storm sounds closer."

"Whatever he's doing, we know he's up to no good. Let's go take a look."

Sheppard reached for his running shoes, but they were still muddy and wet. Forget the shoes, he thought, and crawled over to where Emison lay. He was either sleeping or unconscious, Sheppard couldn't tell which. He felt for his pulse. A little fast, but better than before. He touched his hand to Emison's forehead; the skin felt hot. How hot? Was there a thermometer in Franklin's medical supplies? Any Advil or Tylenol that would bring the fever down? *And what about the wound?*

Before he dealt with Emison, they needed to find Dillard. He and Goot crossed the cellar in their bare feet. They helped themselves to water from the fridge and Sheppard grabbed a bag of trail mix. Hand into the bag, hand to the mouth, chew. He felt like an infant or an invalid, badly in need of help, direction, purpose. No, not purpose. His purpose was simple: to survive this storm in the company of a man whom he despised. Call a spade a spade.

Sheppard started up the stairs, his bare feet tingling against the rough texture of the wood. The cellar door was open, all right, and the fury of the storm grew louder with each step. He and Goot glanced at each other and Goot gestured that he would hold back just in case Dillard gave Sheppard trouble. Sheppard nodded and, at the top of the stairs, stuck his head out.

In the glow of the hurricane lamp, Dillard looked like a dark, hunched figure out of myth or legend, Kokopelli or the hunchback of Notre Dame. He skulked along the length of the garage door, turning his body this way and that, trying to pick up a signal on the cell phone he held. Hadn't Goot told him that the batteries on the other phones were dead? And hadn't Dillard himself said as much? *And since when do you believe anything Dillard tells you?*

Sheppard climbed out of the cellar and moved quickly toward Dillard, the cacophony of the storm masking any noise that he made. If Dillard had been honest about having the phone, they would have gotten Emison to the hospital and could have gone their separate ways. But now the winds were too high for any rescue vehicle to attempt a trip into the preserve. What the hell had Dillard been thinking, anyway? What plot had he been hatching? Had he believed that Franklin would return here? Was that it?

"Shit, shit," Dillard muttered, staring at the cell phone as though it had betrayed him. "Just pick up a fucking signal. C'mon."

"And all this time we thought the battery was dead," Sheppard said, and Dillard whipped around.

He immediately swung his arm behind his back, hiding the phone like a kid who knew he'd done something wrong. "I, uh, thought it was dead but the battery had a bit of juice left. I got a call in the cellar from the Tango PD, but now I can't get through to them. There's not enough juice to pick up a signal. It keeps cutting off."

"Uh-huh." Sheppard extended his hand. "Let me take a look at the phone, Leo."

He held it up, as if seeing it at a distance was the same thing as *Let me see it.* The last thread of Sheppard's patience snapped. He snatched the phone from Dillard's hand so fast that he actually looked down at his empty hand like some fool whose tired brain couldn't quite connect the dots. Sheppard turned away, fiddling with the buttons, navigating to the battery meter. Only one of the six little squares was darkened. Definitely low on power. But there was enough juice left for him to make one or two brief calls *if* he could get a signal.

"Give that to me," Dillard demanded, and ran up behind Sheppard and tried to grab the phone.

Sheppard slammed his elbow back into Dillard's ribs and whirled around. "You *lied*, Leo, and if Doug Emison dies here, it's on *your* head. Either way, there's going to be an internal investigation when we get out of here."

Dillard, hands pressed to his side, stammered, "You . . . you . . ." And he hurled himself at Sheppard, knocking him back, and to the floor of the garage.

Then Dillard was on top of him, struggling to grab the phone with one hand, his other hand gripping Sheppard's jaw with shocking strength, his knee jammed up against Sheppard's balls. Just as Sheppard wrenched his right arm free, Goot grabbed Dillard by the back of the shirt and jerked him to his feet as though he weighed no more than a sparrow. He threw Dillard up against the front bumper of the van and Sheppard rolled onto his side and scrambled to his feet, his balls aching. He took immense pleasure in the sight of Dillard rocking back and forth, his hands pressed against the back of his neck, as if to hold his head in place.

"Stupid fuck," Goot muttered, and wiped the back of his hand across his mouth.

Sheppard moved to the far right wall, seeking a stronger signal. He found it and punched out his home number. The phone rang and rang, ten, twelve, thirteen times. Instead of wasting power on more rings, he called Annie's cell number.

"Hello," she whispered.

"Annie, it's Shep. Are you okay?"

"Shep." Her urgent whisper tore at him. "My God, my God . . ."

"Annie, listen. Tell your mom we're in a cabin in the preserve." As he spat out directions, static erupted on the line, then Annie came back clearly.

"Shep? Shep?" She sounded as though she were underwater and sinking fast. "They're here. The cons. They're in the house. I'm hiding in the garage. I—" The call broke up, the connection went dead.

A numbness claimed Sheppard's limbs, his body, but his brain roared with savage scenes and worst-case scenarios. *They're here.* How? As soon as he thought this, he saw Lopez scooping up the things that had fallen out of his pockets—his cell phone, keys, wallet. Lopez had gotten the address off his license. It made perfect sense. It was the last place he and the others would have looked.

Goot hastened over to Sheppard. "Is there enough power for another call?"

"I don't know." Sheppard handed him the phone, the numbness clenched around his heart now. *They're here. The cons.* Nothing ambiguous about it.

"It's me," Goot shouted into the cell phone. "Graciella, can you hear me? . . . What?"

Sheppard's head shrieked with the static of his own confused and terrified thoughts. *They're here.* The killers were in the house and Annie was hiding in the garage. *And there's nothing you can do about it right now.* Did Franklin have a cell phone charger somewhere in the house? The tantalizing possibility drew Sheppard toward the door to the kitchen. With a functional cell phone, he wouldn't feel so helpless, so disconnected, so useless to help Mira, Annie, Nadine. He would be able to call the Tango PD. . . .

I'm hiding in the garage . . .;

How had she come to be hiding in the garage?

"Goot, call 911 if there's enough juice left on that phone."

"Right," Good called back.

Sheppard touched the doorknob—and felt the entire door shudder. He drew his hand back, hesitating. Inside the house, with the picture window in the living room blown out, the wind must be swirling like some Shakespearean tempest. As if to confirm this thought, objects slammed against the door.

Sheppard instinctively backed away, then whirled and shouted at Goot, at Dillard. *"We need to get into that cellar. Fast!"*

Goot, cell phone pressed to his ear, held up his hand, indicating that 911 was ringing. Dillard was oblivious. His head was under the hood of the van as he apparently tried to do what Sheppard had tried earlier—to get the vehicle started. "He cut the wires, Leo," Sheppard shouted at him.

Dillard kept fiddling. Sheppard went over to the front of the van, pointed at the cut wires. "Here and here. We're not leaving in the van and this door's going to blow."

"Yeah? You're a hurricane expert? A wind wizard?"

"Suit yourself."

Sheppard took one last quick look in the van for supplies

they might be able to use and hauled out another two cartons of canned goods and medical paraphernalia. He carried them down into the cellar, glanced at Emison—who seemed to have fallen into a restful sleep—and hurried back up into the garage. Goot and Dillard were arguing, shouting at each other, and Sheppard didn't bother trying to figure it out. "Let's go, c'mon, c'mon, hear that wind? That door is about to bl—"

The door to the kitchen suddenly blew inward, straight off its hinges, and shot across the garage like a missile. And right behind it screamed the wind, a raging beast so powerful that it whipped Sheppard off his feet, slammed Goot up against the filing cabinet, and shoved Dillard against the front of the van. The entire garage became a wind tunnel. Sheppard couldn't hear anything but the wind, could barely pull air into his lungs, and his muscles screamed as he struggled to crawl across the floor, against the force that had filled the garage.

Things flew around in the air, crashed against the walls—the lanterns, tools, boxes, anything that wasn't nailed down. Bits of glass and dust stung his face, his arms, and sliced into his skin like knives through melon. Sheppard reached the trapdoor to the cellar. It had slammed shut and he had to rock back on his heels and hunch over it, the wind a crushing weight against his spine, to even grab hold of the handle. The pressure of the wind was too great to get the trapdoor open.

Sheppard collapsed against it, shielding his face in the crook of his left arm, his right hand gripping the handle and his feet braced against something behind him. He didn't know how much time passed—probably only seconds—but at some point Goot crawled up next to him and grabbed on to the handle, too. Together, they managed to lift the trapdoor just enough for Sheppard to wedge his body between the door and the frame. His eyes blurred from the dust and grit that swirled in the ferocious wind.

Goot crawled through the door and, moments later, so did Dillard. Sheppard dropped his legs down through the hole, his feet found purchase on one of the upper steps. He pulled his head inside and wind slammed the door shut.

The echo rang out through the cellar and threatened to split Sheppard's head wide open. He sank to his knees and grabbed blindly for the rails so that he wouldn't tumble headfirst down the thirty or forty feet into the depths.

We're going to die in here. Suffocate. Drown. Worse. What could be worse?

17

"A category-five hurricane fills your head with noise. You feel edgy, weird, even sexual."

Billy Joe Franklin

Franklin heard it in the howl of the wind, in the intensity of the rain battering the shutters, and he could feel it in his teeth, an edginess, as though he were biting into aluminum foil. Danielle continued to strengthen and her barometric pressure kept dropping.

He went through the statistics in his head—wind speed, forward motion, velocity of the gusts, approximate location, amount of rainfall, height of the storm surge—and then checked his estimates against the official stats on the Weather Channel. Pretty damn close. That pleased him. He hadn't lost his touch. Back in the days at the NHC, he used to be able to hit most of the stats right on the head before the hurricane planes returned with the data. At one point he was so good at it that guys placed bets on how close he would be.

Good at prediction, he thought, but not so good at contingency plans. Why had he gone off in search of another house? Why had he listened to anyone else? In the beginning, he hadn't thought of the cellar as a hurricane shelter. It had been intended as a hiding place in the event that the cops located the cabin. But once the hurricane had been factored in, the cellar had seemed ideal. Then the Amazon had convinced him the cellar could flood.

How had she done that? How had she convinced him so readily? Why had he allowed himself to become something other than water?

He pressed the heels of his hands into his eyes, struggling to find the vessel into which he should pour himself now. Boss? He was already the boss. Weatherman? *Been there, done that.* Decision Maker. Close, but not quite right. CEO. He liked that, liked it very much. A CEO was the ultimate authority in a corporation, the place where the buck definitely stopped. And right now, this house and everyone in it was *his* corporation.

Franklin pressed the Mute button. "We need a safe room."

Crystal, pacing like a caged animal, now paused, lit a cigarette, and said, "What's wrong with this room?"

"It has windows. The skylight is nearby." He had nailed plywood over the skylights, but doubted plywood would do much if the roof was breached.

"And this section of the house is wood frame," the old lady said.

As CEO, he already knew that. But now he would brainstorm with the underlings. "You got any ideas, Lopez?"

She drew her glazed eyes away from the TV screen. "Yeah. But you won't like them."

"I'd really appreciate it if you wouldn't smoke in here," Mira said.

"Really." Crystal went over to the couch where Mira was sitting, pressed the barrel of the Sig up against the tip of her nose, took a deep drag of her cigarette, and leaned into Mira's face as she blew it out of her mouth. "So sue me." She straightened up again, the Sig now aimed at Mira's chest. "You're not my boss, got it, bitch?"

The Amazon, seated on the other side of the couch, just shook her head and looked at Mira. "Rule one, never put restrictions on an ex-con."

Crystal looked pleased with herself and nodded. "You got it. That's exactly right." She leaned toward Mira again, grabbed her jaw, squeezed. "And rule two, never *piss off* an ex-con. The . . ."

Something strange and terrible happened to Mira's face. Her mouth moved frantically against the pressure of Crystal's hand, but no words came out, just hissing, rasping sounds, as though she were suffocating. Then her eyes rolled up into her head, so that only the whites of her eyes were showing, and she wrenched her head to one side and gasped, *"Whack, whack, bad girl . . . whack those knuckles, squeeze that mouth, wash it out with soap, Crissie said fuck, fuck, fuck . . ."*

Crystal jerked back so fast she nearly stumbled over her own feet. "How . . . what the hell . . ."

Mira's eyes rolled back into place, she doubled over, and began to gag.

Franklin shot to his feet. "What's wrong with her? What just happened?"

Crystal kept dancing around, waving the Sig, screaming at Mira, tears coursing down her cheeks. "The nuns. They used to do that to me. Whack my knuckles with a ruler, wash my mouth out with soap, and then I'd be gagging . . ."

It was Lopez who told Crystal to shut up, Lopez with a smirk on her face when she said, "The bookstore lady's a psychic. When you touch her, she picks up shit about you."

Psychic? Franklin laughed and threw up his arms. "Sure, Lopez. That must be it. That's the logical conclusion."

"Then how'd she know that about Crystal?" the Amazon countered.

He didn't know, but was sure there was a reasonable explanation. "She's a fed's girlfriend. She read the file."

"That's not in my goddamn file," Crystal said.

"You saw your file?" he shot back at her.

"Well, no, but—"

"But nothing." The Amazon grinned. "A psychic, Dipshit, just like I said."

"You're really a psychic?" Crystal wiped at her rheumy eyes. "Like that John Edwards guy? Like him?"

"Similar," the old lady said. "But she doesn't just talk to the dead."

"Oh yeah, hey." Franklin waved his arms. "That's sure a great explanation, old lady. You keep your mouth zipped unless someone asks you a direct question."

Crystal's head snapped toward him. "I told you that about the nuns, Billy. Don't you remember?"

No, he didn't remember. He didn't give a shit about nuns in Crystal's life twenty years ago. Nuns were whacked, priests were whacked, rabbis and preachers and ministers were whacked.

"What else can you tell me?" Crystal moved closer to Mira, but didn't touch her. Didn't even threaten her with the gun. "What else did you see?"

"Nothing." Mira's voice dropped to a soft whisper and she shook her head. "Nothing at all."

"Don't you get it, Dipshit?" The Amazon leaned forward, eyes on fire. "That's how the feds found us. She read the jail. Or the place where the Hummer exploded." She looked over at Mira. "That's it, isn't it? I heard about you on CNN." She slapped her thigh and laughed and sat back and laughed some more.

Mira raised her eyes slowly, huge, blue eyes, gorgeous eyes, Franklin thought, and immediately felt himself getting hard. He wanted those eyes on him, not on Lopez, not on Crystal, not on the old lady, but on *him*. He lost track of the storm, of Crystal, of everything except Mira's eyes. He didn't realize he was moving toward her until Crystal insinuated herself between them.

"I want to know what you see for me," she demanded, leaning close to Mira.

And those eyes went to Crystal, pinning her like a butterfly under glass.

Franklin grabbed the back of Crystal's shirt, pulling her away from the woman's mesmerizing eyes. "She's playing with you."

But Crystal wrenched free of his grasp. "*I want to know.*" A voice like ice. "I want to know what she sees."

"Nothing." He leaned into her face, spittle flying onto her cheeks. "She doesn't see shit, babe, because she's a phony, a carnival sideshow."

Mira rubbed her hands over her face and sat back against the couch cushions as if she hoped she might disappear into them. Her hands dropped to her thighs. "Yeah. A carnival sideshow. That's what I am."

"Well, good, now that we've settled that . . ." Franklin aimed the Remington at Mira's chest. "Get up. You're going to take me on a tour of the house and we're going to find the safest room." He reached into his pack and pulled out a roll of electrical tape. "Babe, wrap up the old lady's hands and feet. Lopez, check out the food in the pantry, in the fridge, in the cooler. Take inventory."

"You're wasting time," the old lady said. "The cooler has plenty of food, there's water in the pantry, in the tub and utility room sink."

"Tape the old lady's mouth," he said.

"Please don't do that." Mira turned those gorgeous blues on him. "It isn't necessary. She's no threat to you."

"I'll decide who and what's a threat. Get up."

She pushed to her feet and he prodded her in the back with the Remington. "Show me the safest room in the house."

"I'll go with you," Lopez said.

I am water. I am the CEO of this operation and you are not *part of this picture, Amazon.*

Franklin spun around, pumped the Remington, and fired at a large ceramic flowerpot behind and just to the left of the Amazon. It blew apart with satisfying precision, pieces of ceramic, leaves, and dirt flying everywhere. The deafening explosion got Lopez's attention, all right. She just stood there with her mouth open, her eyes shocked, as wide as poker chips.

"You're helping Crystal. Remember?"

"You're a fucking maniac, Dipshit."

He pumped again and blew apart a pillow on the couch. Stuffing floated like white blossoms through the air. "The next one's got your name on it, Amazon."

"Stop it!" Crystal shrieked. "We're supposed to be working together, not against each other."

"Then make sure your buddy there understands it, babe." He stuck the shotgun in Mira's back again. *"Move."*

She didn't say another word. No one did. That was how it should be. Fuck the CEO shit. He had poured himself into a vessel called *dictator.* They moved through the kitchen and she started to turn down the hallway, toward the other part of the house. "No," Franklin said. "Into the utility room."

Mira hesitated, then stepped into the utility room. She turned on the light and Franklin came up behind her, enthralled by the perfect sheen of her black hair, a cascade of thick blackness that fell nearly to her shoulders. He leaned closer to her, sniffing at her hair, inhaling the delicious scent of it, of her skin. A woman like this had class, something Crystal wouldn't have no matter how she fixed her hair or what kinds of clothes she wore. This woman, he thought, had been born to class.

But she's a carnie act.

"You filled it with books, so you must think this room is safe."

"I ran out of space for the books, that's why they're in here."

"What about the garage?"

"I've heard that garages are the worst places to be." She turned, looking at him, those blue eyes like oceans into which he could sink and swim forever. "But you're the weather expert."

She was right about garages. "Uh-huh. Okay, let's move on."

Down the hall they went, Franklin slightly behind her. The lights blinked off, on again. "Is the generator rigged to go on automatically if the power goes down?"

"Yes. But the power has to be down for at least five minutes before the generator kicks in."

Maybe he imagined it, but it seemed that she replied too quickly. Yet, why would she do that? "Is there anything you didn't plan for?"

"Yeah. Intruders."

"Then you can't be much of a psychic, I guess."

"Right."

"The world's filled with suckers who fall for the psychic shit. You must be a good actress."

"Uh-huh."

They reached the first doorway in the hall. "Go in here."

She stepped into the room, turned on the light.

The walls were painted deep blue and pale green and were hung with framed posters of young celebrities—the stars from the *Harry Potter* movies, teenage singers, teen stars. Metal signs hung on the wall over the bed: ADULTS STAY OUT, said one. IF YOU'RE OVER 19 YOU'RE TRESPASSING, said another. ANNIE'S LAIR, read a third.

"Annie? Who's she?"

"My daughter. I sent her to Miami with friends when the watch went up."

"And she's how old?"

"Fifteen."

He touched her hair, just his fingertips, the lightest of touches, but she felt it and jerked around. "Don't *touch* me."

Franklin got a big kick out of that. *He* had the weapon and she was telling *him* what to do. He laughed, a low, husky laugh, and pushed her down onto the bed, jammed the barrel of the shotgun up under her jaw, and straddled her.

"Just like Crystal said. You don't tell us what to do. If I want to touch you, I will. And I'll touch you when, how, and where I want. If I want to touch you here . . ." He brought his hand to her breast. ". . . then I'll do it. If I want to touch you here . . ." He clutched her crotch and she squeezed her eyes shut and jerked her head to the side, refusing to look at him. ". . . then I'll do that, too."

Her breath came out in short, startled gasps, tears leaked from under her eyelids. He pulled her T-shirt up, excited that she wasn't wearing a bra, and feasted on the sight of her breasts, plump and perfect, her tummy as flat as a ruler, her skin like satin or silk or some other deliciously soft texture. But the stone she wore around her neck disturbed him, a vividly green stone with jagged edges. He pushed it aside and breathed, "My God, you're beautiful."

He felt an overwhelming urge to lick her skin, to nibble at her breasts, to make her scream with desire. Franklin unzipped her shorts, thrust his hand inside her panties, felt himself growing hard, and wanted nothing more than to be inside her, sliding into the hot intimacy of her body, lost in its seas, its oceans.

Now she pleaded with him—*don't, please don't do this*—but blood roared in his ears, he wanted her, had to have her, and didn't care what he had to do to get her. He dropped the shotgun to the floor, grabbed her arms, and pinned them above her head with one hand, while his other hand worked her shorts down over her hips.

"I know you like this." He whispered the words and

leaned close to her face, breathing in the scent of her skin. "I know you do." And then he drew his tongue up between her breasts, against all that deliciously soft skin, and his tongue circled one breast, then the other, and he nibbled at the nipple and his left hand struggled to get her panties off, so that he could push himself inside her.

Her eyes snapped open, but they weren't seeing him, they weren't seeing anything. The pupils had grown huge and black, like the vast darkness of outer space, and swallowed most of her irises. Shudders ripped through her. She gasped, "Your mother. Your mother used to make you touch her like this. It's how you learned . . . to become water . . ."

Franklin leaped away from her, his shock so profound that he couldn't shout at her to shut up, couldn't sweep the shotgun off the floor, couldn't do anything except stand there with his shorts puddled around his feet.

". . . immersed yourself in water so that you could forget. After your old man left and your mother used to come into your room at night and . . ."

He no longer heard her. He lunged toward her, a pillow in his hands that he didn't remember picking up.

I am water, I am water . . .

She rolled to the right, off the bed. Franklin hit the mattress facedown, twisted, bolted upward. She was on her feet, swung the shotgun, and as he ducked, it whistled past his head and struck him on the upper arm. Enraged, he leaped off the bed, but she pumped the gun and fired.

In the small confines of a shuttered room, it sounded as if a bomb had detonated. The shot flew wild and took out a chunk of Harry Potter's face. Franklin tackled her before she could shoot again and she crashed to the floor, kicking and clawing and biting. Despite the rage that fueled her, he had become a tsunami and cut off her air. When she finally stopped struggling, he lifted himself up, shocked to see that he had pressed a pillow to her face.

Franklin quickly threw the pillow away from her, pulled her shorts and panties up, tugged down her T-shirt, jerked up his own clothes—and none too soon. The Amazon and Crystal ran into the room.

"We heard . . . Jesus," Crystal said, her eyes darting around the room. "What the hell happened?"

"She tried to get the goddamn gun," he explained. "I knocked her out."

"You sure she's still alive?" Lopez asked.

"Yeah, she's breathing." He snapped his fingers. "Let me have that electrical tape."

Crystal passed him the roll. He tore off a large strip and wrapped it around Mira's wrists. A second large strip went around her ankles. "We'll put her in the master bedroom until we're ready to move into the safe room."

"Which is where?" Lopez asked.

She was testing him, he could hear it in her voice. *You been back here a spell, white boy, and you don't have a safe room yet? How come? How come this white girl's on the floor, her clothes rumpled?* He could almost see the thoughts swirling through the dark pools of her suspicious eyes.

Think fast. "The utility room. No windows and we'd be between solid walls. But she's got books stacked in there. We need to move those first. I'll get started in there. Babe, you and Lopez move her into the master bedroom."

"Grab her feet, Tia," Crystal said.

He noticed that Lopez hesitated and that in her dark, shrewd eyes lay suspicion of and disdain for humanity in general and for him in particular. He felt strangely naked just then, as though she had peered inside him and knew exactly what had happened in this room. Would she voice her suspicions to Crystal? Maybe. But if she did and Crystal confronted him, he would deny it. Deny, deny. Politicians made an art form out of denial and it worked every time. No reason it shouldn't work for him, too. It was what dictators did best.

"I'll meet you two out in the utility room."

He fled up the hallway, thinking, *I am water, I am water . . .* and knew it was a lie. If he were truly water right now, he would flow around these events and not be touched by them. He wouldn't be so spooked about what Mira had said to him. Did the incident qualify as a sign? *But of what?*

And then it hit him. Mira wasn't a psychic; she was water in its purest form, able to fill the vessel of whomever she touched so completely that she absorbed that person's memories, emotions, thoughts. It explained why she'd known about Crystal's experience with the nuns, why she'd known about what his mother had done to him.

She was the very essence of water, his counterpart in every way.

An almost religious fervor seized him. He ducked into the utility room, welcoming the embrace of its darkness.

18

"Take in all the official information, then make your own decisions."

Tia Lopez

As soon as the cellar door slammed shut, Sheppard's claustrophobia seized him. His chest tightened, his head spun, his stomach lurched. He barely made it to the bottom of the stairs before his knees gave out and he sank to the floor, legs tucked under him, forehead against the floor, hands clutched to his head. Objects crashed against the trapdoor—banging, clattering, clanging, everything echoing hideously, as though he were inside a metal box.

Will it hold? Will the door hold?

The possibility of the door collapsing and the debris of the garage caving in and burying him alive overrode his claustrophobia. He scrambled forward on his hands and knees, away from the stairs, the noise, and crawled onto his sleeping bag like some little kid who was afraid of the dark. He wrapped his arms around his head and lay there, breathing in the moldy stink of the sleeping bag, of his own sweat and fear.

Goot touched his back. "You okay?" he asked, voice too quiet for Dillard to hear.

"Gimme a minute." Sheppard groped blindly for his pack and dug around inside until he found a roll of mints. He stuck three in his mouth and started sucking.

Goot understood what was happening to him. Even though he hadn't gone through the black water, he'd been there during those events and had been the first to comment on the change in Sheppard eight or nine months ago. They'd been working a missing person case in Orlando and had followed someone onto a ride that whisked them through a dark, wet tunnel and Sheppard just about lost it. He had emerged from that tunnel so violently ill that he had bowed out of the investigation for the day and had gone back to the motel. Over the ensuing months, the symptoms had gotten worse and fit the mold for claustrophobia so closely that he finally had sought professional help.

"What's wrong with *him?*" Dillard asked Goot.

"Exhaustion," Goot replied. "The big question here, Leo, is what the hell's wrong with *you?*"

"Nothing's wrong with me," Dillard snapped.

Yeah, nothing that a lobotomy wouldn't fix, Sheppard thought, and realized that he *had* to function, that Dillard would use this against him if he got the chance. He threw off the sleeping bag and rocked back onto his heels, the last of the mints dissolving on his tongue, the taste working its magic. The room didn't spin, his stomach didn't turn inside out. He actually could focus his eyes—and his attention—on the situation.

"What's wrong, Leo, is that we're now buried under a collapsed garage, thanks to you."

"To *me?*" His thick fingers poked at his own chest. "*Me?*" He burst out laughing. "Yeah, right, Shep. I'm to blame for the garage collapsing. Uh-huh." He paced back and forth through the cellar, wiping his face with a damp towel. "Right.

Yeah, you got that right. Me. I'm the big bad wolf and blew the sucker down."

Sheppard ignored Dillard. It was the only way he could function. He noticed drops of blood on his arms where dirt had bit into his skin, but his physical injuries were minimal. He crawled over next to Goot, crouched at the side of Emison's sleeping bag. *Not good,* Goot mouthed.

"Did you get through to nine-one-one?" Sheppard asked.

"No. The cell cut out."

Sheppard pressed his hand to Emison's forehead. Shit, shit, he was hot, burning up again. If he gave Emison an Advil or a Tylenol, would he bleed to death? If he didn't give him something, would his fever spike, hurling him into convulsions?

He had no idea.

Go with your gut, Mira usually advised him.

Yeah, well, right now his gut was shrieking, but Sheppard couldn't decipher its language.

"I don't know what to do," he confessed to Goot.

"My *abuelita* always said that if you're on fire, the fire has to be tamed before you can tackle the real problem."

"Your grandmother is a santera, not a doc."

"In her world, she's as good as a doc, amigo. I say we give him a full dose."

"Of . . . ? Advil or Augmentin?"

"Advil. Get the fever down. Toss sand on the fire."

Right. Sand. Hell, he would toss sand and then spray down the sucker with water. Sheppard shook two Advils and another dose of Augmentin into his palm. Goot lifted Emison's head. "Doug," Sheppard said. "C'mon, open your eyes. Hey, Doug . . ."

Emison's eyes opened, but they were glazed with pain, fever, confusion. Emison said something, but Sheppard didn't understand him. His words slurred, everything ran together.

"Doug, you need to swallow this." Sheppard pressed the

Advil tablets against Emison's lips. "*Safeopemoneythere,*" he murmured, words running together like warm butter.

"What're you saying, Doug?" Sheppard leaned closer to him. "Speak more clearly."

For a brief moment, Emison seemed to join the real world. He sucked the tablets between his lips, sipped from the water bottle that Goot held to his mouth, swallowed. Goot lowered his head back onto the sleeping bag. "Jesus, what's happening to me?"

"You're in good hands, Doug. Just go to sleep," Sheppard said.

His eyes fluttered shut. Forty feet above them, all sorts of shit continued to thud and ping and clatter against the cellar door. "We need to secure that door," Goot murmured, and got up, knees creaking, to see what he could do.

Sheppard started to rise as well, but Emison grabbed his hand and tried to speak again. "Listen t'me," he hissed. "Money. Safe deposit. Tango Federal. If something happens to me, make sure the wife and kids get it. Promise me."

What the hell?

"You got my word, Doug." *But what money? From where? What's the safe deposit code? How much money?* Before he could ask these questions, Emison shut his eyes and went away again.

On the other side of the cellar, Dillard stared at Sheppard, then at Emison. "Hey, Leo," Goot said from the stairs. "Since you haven't helped with anything, we're appointing you the cook. Why don't you rustle up something to eat?"

"Why don't you take a fucking hike?" Dillard snapped back.

"Then you fix the door and *I'll* cook," Goot said.

But Dillard was already going through the provisions, getting out bread, tuna, mayo from the little fridge, cans of soup. "I'm on it, Gutierrez. Just secure that door."

On it only because *he* was hungry, Sheppard thought, and

pressed his palms to his thighs and stood. He went over to the boxes he'd brought down from Franklin's van and began rifling through them, looking for cell phone accessories. At this point, he would be grateful for anything—a new battery, a charger, it didn't matter.

"Leo, how well do you know Doug?" Sheppard asked.

"Probably about as well as you do." He slapped mayo on pieces of bread. "Why?"

"Did Doug come into some money recently or something?"

"Money?" Dillard's small, dark eyes darted toward Sheppard, as quick and hungry as mosquitoes. "What're you talking about?"

It seemed to Sheppard that Dillard looked apprehensive, edgier than he had moments ago. Then again, they were all edgier and more apprehensive now. "Just something he muttered. It's probably nothing."

"What'd he say?"

"That if anything happens to him, I should make sure his wife and kids get the money."

It seemed that relief flowed back into Dillard's eyes. He turned his attention to the dinner preparations once again. "He's probably talking about insurance money."

"Yeah, probably," Sheppard replied, but didn't believe it for a moment. "Did you know that Emison picked up Crystal when she was moved to the Tango jail?"

Dillard glanced at him quickly, sharply, almost furtively. "How the fuck would I know who Emison picks up and when? What's your point, anyway?"

"My point is that something stinks about DeVries's transfer to the Tango jail. Maybe Emison was paid off and—"

"Paid off by whom?" Dillard's eyes narrowed, a frown turned his forehead into a chaos of folds and wrinkles. "You're beginning to sound like one of those conspiracy theory nutcases."

"How did Franklin know where she was? As far as I know, there's no public information site on the Internet or anywhere else that reveals where inmates are. That means Franklin had inside information."

"From whom? Emison? Is that what you're saying, Shep?"

Maybe. He sensed he was onto something, but wasn't quite clear yet on the specifics. "He'd be the logical choice."

"Hey, Shep," Goot called. "Come take a look at this."

Sheppard left Dillard to his food tinkering and went over to the foot of the stairs, where Goot stood, his flashlight aimed at the trapdoor. He had fitted a broomstick through the handle.

"It's the best I can do with what we've got." He glanced back at Dillard, whose back was to them, and leaned toward Sheppard and whispered, "I figured out a way to power up the phone. A typical cell draws less than half an amp at five volts—less than three watts. That's not much. I think I can power it up enough for a couple of calls."

Sheppard slipped the cell out of his pocket and handed it to Goot. He popped off the back of the phone and examined it, nodding. "I need two flashlight batteries and some wire. Insulated wire if we have any, otherwise some paper clips, a ballpoint spring, a garbage bag twist tie, aluminum foil, whatever we've got around here. I'll need a rubber band and some tape, too."

"I'll see what I can find."

Thanks to Franklin's supplies, it didn't take Sheppard long to find what Goot asked for. What bothered him, though, was that Franklin seemed to have thought of everything *except* a way to charge a cell phone, which was unlikely. Sheppard figured the charger might be in the van's supplies, in the house, or even in Franklin's pocket, none of which was useful to him.

He set everything on the kitchen table, where Goot now

sat, the back of the cell phone removed, its innards exposed. "Now what?" Sheppard asked.

"We make magic."

Goot worked with the precision of a clockmaker, his fingers quick, yet certain. Within a few minutes, he had the wires connected to the flashlight batteries and to the cell phone's battery, juice running into it. "The current's weaker than what I want, but I'm afraid of blowing out the cell battery."

"How long will it take to charge up?" Sheppard asked.

"Beats me. I've never tried this with a cell before."

Dillard nodded his approval. "Innovative, John. Very innovative. So when it's powered up, we're going to be fighting over who uses it first." He glanced up as if challenging one or both of them to dispute what he'd said. Neither Sheppard nor Goot said anything. "So I'm proposing that our first call should be to nine-one-one so we can get Doug treated."

"That's fine with me," Sheppard said. "Too bad you didn't think of that earlier, Leo."

"That was then," he replied. "This is now."

Whatever *that* meant. Sheppard went back to the supplies, wondering what was really behind Dillard's concern about Emison's welfare. *His own ass:* that was what it always amounted to with Dillard.

In the fourth carton, Sheppard found batteries for the ham radio. He inserted them, then moved the radio against the wall, hoping it would work. He turned the knob, seeking a voice, static, anything at all. Dillard hovered behind him, his breath warm against the back of Sheppard's neck. It made him uneasy to have Dillard behind him, so he moved slightly to the right, allowing him to see Dillard in his peripheral vision.

A burst of static, then: ". . . Ralph . . . broadcasting for residents of the Lower Keys . . . bringing updates on Danielle as we hear them from other ham radio operators. Portions of the highway out of Key West have been washed away . . . everything on Sugarloaf Key east of the bridge on Sugarloaf Boulevard is underwater. The new high school on Sugarloaf—one of the shelters—has lost its roof in what's believed to be a tornado . . . a number of fatalities . . .

". . . a ham radio operator in downtown Tango reports that he's on the fourth floor of a building and the water is already washing through the second story . . . Danielle is pushing a twenty-foot storm surge and the downtown area of Tango already is flooding . . ."

"Christ," Sheppard said hoarsely.

". . . the Tango hospital, another shelter, has sustained massive damage on its eastern side and people are being evacuated to another wing in the hospital . . .

". . . the last we heard from the National Hurricane Center is that Danielle stalled offshore and that winds up to 145 have been reported in the outer bands. The center suddenly went off the air a while ago and we think it's a repeat of what happened during Andrew, when their instruments were knocked out . . ." Ralph went on to ask any ham radio operators in the Lower Keys to contact him on a certain frequency, then began his broadcast again.

The generator sputtered like a heart skipping a beat and the lights flickered, as if to remind them just how vulnerable they were even forty feet down. Sheppard quickly tuned to the frequency Ralph had given.

"Mayday, Mayday. Is anyone there? Over."

More static, then: "This is Ralph, I'm reading you, my friend. What's the nature of your emergency?"

Sheppard identified himself. "We're in the cellar of a cabin in the wilderness preserve on Tango Key. We're several miles in on Papaya Road and have a critically injured man, Sheriff Emison, chief of police on Tango, who needs medical attention. Can you get a message to the Tango PD or to the Tango hospital or EMT services? Over."

"I'll do what I can, Agent Sheppard. I'm on Sugarloaf, holed up in a house that's about ten feet above the water level. Winds are gusting to 140 or so here. I can't venture a guess at what the winds have done to the woods. It could be difficult for anyone outside the preserve to get in. From the reports I'm getting, nine-one-one has been inundated with calls and the conditions are so bad outside that they aren't promising anything. But stay tuned to this frequency and I'll get back to you as soon as I hear something. Over."

"The two cons who broke out of jail on Tango are holed up in a house on the island." He spat out his and Mira's address. "They're armed and extremely dangerous. If it's possible, can you get that information to the Tango PD? Over."

"What?" Dillard exclaimed. "How do you know that?"

"I spoke to Mira's daughter."

Ralph said, "I'll be back in touch shortly, Agent Sheppard. Over and out."

Sheppard sat back. No one said a word, not even Dillard.

19

In a twenty-four-hour period, Hurricane Gilbert's central pressure dropped from 960 to 888 millibars, a drop of three millibars per hour.

The relentless pounding of the rain, the shriek of the wind, the banging of *things* against the shutters: Tia just wanted to crawl into some dark, safe place and huddle until the storm was over. But that wasn't in the cards right now.

"You think she's really psychic?" Crystal asked as they carried Mira into the bedroom.

Tia rolled her eyes. Spare her the dopes and stupids of the world. Spare her the idiotic questions. "Yeah, girl, I think she's the real thing."

"Then why didn't she know about us before we broke in?"

"She's not God."

The strain of carrying Mira caused the pain in her shoulder to flare up again and by the time they set her on the king-size bed, Tia was breathing through clenched teeth and covered in sweat. She sank to the foot of the bed, brought her knees up to her chest, and pressed her forehead against them.

"You okay, Tia?"

Crystal squatted down in front of her and for moments here in the dim light of a bedside lamp, the white girl looked like some throwback to simpler times, a woman who lived in a hut, washed her clothes in a river, and gave birth in this same squatting position.

"Tia?" she repeated.

"Damn shoulder," she murmured. "Emison's baton did a number."

"I'll make you a sling."

"Look, I just need to sit here a few minutes. When you go digging around in the pantry, see if there's anything stronger than Tylenol, will you?"

"Yeah. Sure. I'll come back and check on you in a while. And I'm bringing a sling with me."

Tia nodded and dropped her head to her knees again.

"Listen, I'm sorry Billy's such an asshole sometimes," Crystal said quietly, in a cell mate tone of voice that invited exchanged confidences in the dead of night.

Not half as sorry as I am.

"I don't know why he had to make such a big deal out there in the family room."

"Because he's a guy with a gun. Why're you still with him?"

Crystal, still in the same squatting position, clamped her hands to her kneecaps and moved them slowly, as if massaging them. "I've known him a long time, he put his ass on the line at the jail . . ."

"Aw, c'mon, girl. We've talked about this plenty. He ditched you at the bank, let you take the fall. What's the real reason?"

And when she raised her eyes, all that blue had gone rock hard, resolute. "Half that five mil is mine. Except he says he spent about two million just getting me out. So that leaves a million and a half. I earned it. I want it. I aim to get it."

Well, well, Tia thought. The stupid white girl wasn't all

that stupid. Tia started to confide her suspicion about what had happened between Franklin and Mira in the bedroom, but thought better of it. If Crystal blew up—which she probably would—she would confront Franklin and he would deny it. It would become his word against Tia's suspicions. Crystal would side with him. She had to, if she ever wanted to see her share of the cash.

Tia understood that. She would remember it, too. "Could you get me a cold washcloth before you leave?"

"Sure. Be right back."

A few minutes later, Crystal left and Tia remained seated at the foot of the bed, the cold, damp cloth against her swollen shoulder. She wasn't sure when she first realized that Mira was conscious and that she probably had been conscious all along. Tia waited for her to speak first, but when she didn't, Tia said, "I know you're hearing me. I figure you heard most of what Crystal and me said."

Silence.

"You don't have nothing to say?"

Silence.

Tia dropped the wet cloth and moved to the side of the bed, where Mira lay still, eyes shut.

"Okay, you don't have to say anything. But I can't just leave you here wrapped up like a mummy because I know he's going to come back in to finish what he started. Dipshits like him always do. If my shoulder wasn't such a mess, I'd take him myself. But I can't even go into the Red with my shoulder like this. I've been waiting for that taste of hot peppers in my mouth, but it just hasn't come. I can't risk getting shot."

As she peeled the layers of tape off Mira's wrists, she talked the whole time. She told Mira about having seen Sheppard on CNN last Christmas, when Mira had been snatched, about how he and his copper buddies were in the preserve, probably holed up in the cabin's cellar now, and about herself, why she'd gone to jail and why she wouldn't go back. Ever.

"I know I'm intruding on you right now, while I'm getting this tape off. Like when you touched Crystal. I'm sorry for that. But I don't have scissors or anything to cut the tape."

And as she spoke, a strange sensation came over her. It was as if hands patted the inside of her skull, cupped her heart, slipped and slid around inside her. It felt eerie yet oddly pleasant, and although it disturbed her, it didn't frighten her. For the first time in she didn't know how many years, Tia felt connected to something larger than herself.

Is this God? Is this what God feels like? Is God talking to me?

Memories suddenly lit up the inside of her head and flashed across the inner screen of her eyes in psychedelic colors. Andrew, her dog, her baby, the human ruin, the horror, all of it ugly and immediate, as though it had happened yesterday. And behind these memories rushed more of her life, choppy images from her abusive marriage, of how she smothered her husband, of the support groups. All of it seemed to rush out of Tia and—where? *Where the fuck's it going?*

Into Mira.

Tia jerked her hands away from Mira's body, where the duct tape at her hands and ankle now hung in ribbons. "What the hell *are* you, spooky lady?" she whispered.

Her shoulder throbbed and sang with such pain she didn't know if she could stand, walk, function. She heard noise in the hallway and knew one of them was headed this way. "Shit," she murmured. "It's her. Or him. I gotta touch you again." Tia quickly rearranged Mira's hands and feet so they looked as if they were still bound, flipped the pieces of tape loosely back in place, but did it without any of the side effects this time, then resumed her position at the foot of the bed. "Stay still and we'll both get out of here alive."

Crystal hurried into the room. "I found some extra-strength Advil, Tia." She thrust a bottle of water at her, dropped a couple of tablets into her hand. "And I've got a sling fixed up. Billy wants everyone at the front of the house. He's real agitated, okay? I don't want to piss him off more."

"We can't move her," Tia said. "I think she's in a coma or something. What the hell did he do to her, anyway?"

"He said she hit her head."

"Then she could have a concussion. Or a fractured skull. Leave her be. She's no threat to us." As Tia rocked onto her knees and stood, agony tore through her shoulder again. "Help me up, Crystal."

Once she was on her feet, she imagined giving Crystal one hard shove into the wall and grabbing her weapon. But the pain in her shoulder was so bad it took everything she had just to remain conscious, alert, mobile.

As she and Crystal left the room, the strangeness washed over Tia once more, the sensation that the spooky lady had slid inside her again and was poking around in her memories, her secrets. Tia felt heat just under her breastbone, as if someone were holding a flame to the skin, and an image burst into her head—of Mira's eyes snapping open. Tia *saw* it, saw it in the sanctity of her own mind, and knew the spooky woman had heard every word she'd said.

Even before they left the bedroom, Mira watched them through the slits of her eyes, her body tense, ready to spring off the bed. She could still feel Franklin's hands and tongue on her, could still hear his insidious whispers—*"You like this, I know you do"*—and knew that he would have raped her if she had not tuned in on him. She also knew he would be back, alone.

Tia and Crystal vanished through the doorway. Mira counted to fifty in her head, then bolted forward, tore the loose tape away from her hands and feet. Shock and awe, like some military strategy, but that was what she felt just then. Shock, awe, and most of all, gratitude that Tia had helped her and that she'd been so easy to read. Her entire life had been there at the surface of her consciousness, floating like cream on milk, and if Mira had wanted to, she could have skimmed it away with ease. But she had seen enough of Tia's life to know she didn't want to see more. She couldn't risk opening any more doors between herself and them.

Mira leaped off the bed and scurried into the closet like some terrified insect escaping the crushing, final blow of a human shoe. She pressed her face into a mound of old sweatshirts and sweaters that muffled her explosive sobs. She felt sullied, violated by Franklin's touches, licks, pinches, whispers. A profound hunger for revenge seized her.

This feeling disgusted her more than anything he had done to her. Revenge wouldn't change what had happened and might tie her to him in karmic ways. One thing was sure: she never would read another crime scene. Not for Sheppard, Dillard, or anyone else.

Mira groped through the darkness of the closet and found her cell phone, and charger, abandoned earlier on the old dresser pushed up against the far wall. In this chapter of her life, the dresser held linens; thirty years ago, the dresser held the clothes of an adolescent. More recently, she had used the dresser as a stepladder so she could reach through the attic trapdoor to put away boxes. Unlike the attic in the garage, it didn't have a fold-out ladder, so they used it to store smaller items like Christmas and birthday gifts.

Her fingers fumbled across the cell phone keypad. No signal. *Shit.*

Could she pick up a signal in the bathroom? Maybe. But first she had to buy herself a little time. She dug into the organizer, pulled out a pair of stockings. She tied one end to the knob of the closet door, shut the bedroom door, turned the lock, and tied the other end of the stocking to the bedroom knob and pushed a chair up against the door. None of this would stop Franklin. A fingernail could turn the lock, the chair could be pushed out of the way. But even fifteen or twenty seconds might prove crucial for her.

She jerked a backpack off an upper shelf and unzipped the small, plastic cooler she'd brought in here earlier. She took two bottles of water, a bag of peanuts, another bag of baby carrots, and put them in the pack. She added a T-shirt, shorts, a pair of running shoes, a flashlight, and anything else that might come in handy.

Mira ran into the bathroom, shut and locked the door. Rain hammered against the skylight over the shower and set up a thunderous echo that pounded inside her skull. She plugged the charger into the socket, the other end into the cell phone, and turned the phone toward the window, seeking a signal. She found one, but could maintain it only if she didn't move. She quickly punched out Annie's cell number. A *No Service* message came up.

Mira pressed the two-way radio button on the phone. "Annie? You there? Over."

Her daughter's soft, frightened voice came through. "Mom? Oh, Mom. I heard gunshots. I thought you were . . . were . . ."

Dead: the word Annie couldn't bring herself to say.

"I'm okay, hon. You've done great, staying hidden all this time. Look, I'm coming to you. I'm going out the window in the bathroom. Over."

"Mom, don't risk it. It's too dangerous. Over."

"The front of the house faces away from the storm's approach. I can do this. I want you to unlock the side door of the garage so that I can get in. Make sure the shovel is next to the door. Once you've unlocked it, you and Ricki should hide behind the metal shelves near the circuit breaker."

"It's a long way from your bathroom window to the other side of the house. It'd be better if I open the garage door just enough so you can slide under. I'd do it manually. They'll never hear it inside the house."

"I think the wind is too strong. But if I change my mind once I'm out there, I'll send you a text message."

"But the cell service isn't working."

"I can do this."

"What about Nana?"

By now, Nadine would be wrapped up in duct tape and wouldn't be able to reach her cell phone even if Franklin hadn't found it. Would it vibrate on the radio function? She didn't know.

"Nadine will do what she can."

"I heard from Shep. He's in a cabin in the preserve. He gave me directions. Dillard, the sheriff, and Goot are there, too. I told him what was happening here. He's using someone else's cell phone."

Annie reeled off the cell number and Mira filed it in the back of her head. The fact that Sheppard knew where the cons were didn't comfort her at all. No one would dare a rescue now. Forget white knights in SUVs.

"Keep your cell on. I'm on my way. *Eu coosi dao, Suki.*"

"*Eu coosi dao, Mikono.*" Then, in a soft, scared voice, she added, "Bigger than Google, Mom. That's how much I love you."

Bigger than Google: Mira smiled. It used to be bigger than infinity, but now nothing was bigger than Google. "Ditto," Mira whispered.

They disconnected and Mira went to the text message box on her cell phone and composed two separate messages: *open garage* and *almost there.* She saved these in her draft folder. She sent a text message to Sheppard, at the cell phone number Annie had given her, but got another *No Service* message. She would keep pressing the *Send* button every few minutes, she thought, and slipped her phone and the charger inside a zippered compartment in her pack.

Mira turned the locks on the top edge of the window, raised it. Many of the bathrooms in the newer Florida homes either had no windows or just had panes of frosted glass. The rationale was privacy because the trend in most planned communities was to build on zero lot lines, where three to five feet separated your home from your neighbor's. Developers made more money that way. But her house sat on plenty of land and was private, so the bathroom window was large, reaching from two feet above the ground to several feet below the roofline. It obviously wasn't the original window and the man who had custom-made the shutters had commented on the unusual dimensions of the window. Quarter inches instead of whole inches, that sort of thing. No wonder the shutters for the house had cost eight grand. And they weren't even electrical.

How many people throughout the Keys couldn't afford plywood for their windows, much less shutters? What were they using? Masking tape? The kitchen table wisdom used to be that if you put huge crosses of masking tape across each of your windows, the glass wouldn't shatter. That wisdom was along the same lines as Homeland Security's initial call for Americans to buy sheets of plastic and duct tape to protect themselves against a biological attack. But the big sticky X of tape provided hope for people who couldn't afford anything more.

Just then, something nibbled at the edge of her awareness, an impression about the new school on Sugarloaf. Something bad.

Roof flying off . . .

Mira instantly threw up a wall to block the impression. Even so, bits and pieces of the image bled through—tiles lifting into the dark wind, people screaming, water pouring into the school . . .

No more.

The images faded.

Why could she pick up so easily on a school thirty miles from here and not pick up anything at all on her own predicament?

With the window open, Mira ran her fingers along the inside of the hurricane shutter, looking for the latches that would allow her to slide it open from inside the house. The latches clicked, she pulled the shutters open about a foot, and rain and wind howled through the opening, stinging her face and eyes, a raging tempest that shook the windowpane, rattled the door, and whipped the bushes in front of the window back and forth. Mira suddenly saw herself outside, sprawled on the ground, motionless . . .

She jerked her hands away from the shutters, shocked that she had picked up psychic information about herself. Had she been hurt or dead? She didn't know, couldn't tell. Either way, she couldn't ignore the warning, couldn't risk going out the window. She stood there a moment longer, rain blowing through the narrow opening in the shutters, water pooling on the floor, then quickly closed them and shut the window.

The attic, up through the door in the closet.

She wasn't even sure if she would fit through that door. She never had gone up into the attic through the closet.

You'll make yourself fit. Hurry.

20

Dr. Robert Sheets, former director of the National Hurricane Center, characterized the damage in the path of Andrew's eye wall in southern Florida as that of a twenty-mile-wide tornado.

Maybe fatigue was playing with his perceptions, Sheppard thought, but it seemed that the winds had picked up, that rain whipped the metal trapdoor, that everything inside the cellar echoed, sang, trembled.

Ignore it. Eat.

He looked down at the food in front of him. Okay, so Dillard wasn't a culinary wizard. The soup was barely lukewarm, the sandwich was just plain tuna—no celery, radishes, pepper, cucumbers, just a bit of mayo. But to Sheppard, it tasted like a feast. He hadn't eaten anything since—when? Breakfast before dawn? He couldn't remember.

The radio continued to sputter with static, voices, unofficial reports on Danielle. Now and then it went silent, the signal lost. Sheppard moved the radio to the stairs, closer to the hatch. Nothing more came from Ralph. Emison moaned and the lights flickered, reminding Sheppard that the generator wouldn't last indefinitely. And when it went, he thought, the air would heat up quickly and a few flashlights weren't going to ease his foreboding that the cellar could become their tomb.

Sheppard finally pushed away from the table, poured the remainder of the soup into a cup, stuck a straw into it, and went over to Emison. Goot got up to help but Dillard, naturally, stayed on his skinny ass, stuffing his face.

"Doug, wake up," Sheppard said. "I've got some soup." Sheppard touched his cheek. Not as hot now. "Can you open your eyes?"

Tiny slits appeared in his cheeks, a grotesque parody of consciousness. Goot slid his hand under Emison's head, lifting it, and Sheppard coaxed the straw between his lips. "Suck on it, Doug."

But Emison suddenly struggled up on his elbows and puked on himself. "My God," Dillard muttered, hurrying over with a wet towel that he tossed at Sheppard. "He's getting worse."

"Keep him upright, Goot." Sheppard wiped the vomit off of Emison's face and shirt. Some of it got onto his hands and he envisioned bacteria crawling along his skin, seeking tiny cuts and pores into which they would dig, infecting him with whatever ailed Emison.

Granted, the slice in his leg was bad and infection had set in, but Emison seemed to be suffering from something else as well. Was the Augmentin outdated? Was Emison allergic to it? But if that were true, wouldn't he have reacted sooner?

"Lower his head, Goot. I'm going to roll him onto his side. Leo, can you grab a clean sheet out of the supplies? And roll it up so we can elevate Doug's head a little more."

Dillard tossed a rolled-up sheet their way and Goot slid it under Emison's head. Sheppard turned him onto his side and realized that Emison's bedding and clothes were wet, that he'd soiled himself again. A putrid stink emanated from him also. Goot smelled it and made a face.

"What is that?" Goot whispered.

Dismay washed through Sheppard. He knew exactly what it was. Once you'd smelled this odor, he thought, you never forgot it. Years ago in college, he'd owned a cat whose fur had smelled like this after the animal had gone into renal failure.

"His kidneys are going."

"Why?"

Sheppard shrugged. "I don't know."

He got up, went over to the sink to wash his hands, and put on the last pair of latex gloves. Even forty feet down, with the cellar door buried by debris, he heard the intensity of the storm and knew he wasn't imagining it. As if to underscore the tightening in his chest, the lights winked off—then on again.

"We're running low on gas in that generator," Dillard said.

"Then you better make sure we have fresh batteries in all the lanterns and flashlights."

"Yeah, good idea."

To Sheppard's surprise, Dillard proceeded to do exactly what he'd suggested. Then again, batteries didn't moan, piss, bleed, or puke. Compared to dealing with Emison, batteries and flashlights were clean.

Sheppard stripped off Emison's soiled clothes, spread several dry towels under him, covered him with a fresh sheet. He stuck the soiled sheets, clothing, and gloves into a pillowcase and tossed it under the stairs with another pillowcase filled with soiled linens and clothing. Goot hurried over to him, his swollen eye now almost black. It seemed to Sheppard that Goot looked worse than he had earlier.

"We've got enough juice in the cell phone for one call, Shep."

"Who're we going to call?" What organization would brave category four or five winds to come out here? "There's a Red Cross chapter on Tango, but will they risk coming out here?"

"I don't know. Let's start with nine-one-one." Goot disconnected the cell phone from his homemade battery and went halfway up the stairs. He moved the cell phone in one direction and then another, seeking a signal. "Shep, look at this."

Sheppard, washing his hands at the sink, turned and Goot held the cell phone up so he could see the window. A text message: *situation critical am going to annie luv me.*

The screen went black before Sheppard could respond. Fighting despair, terror, and frustration, he stifled the urge to snatch the cell from Goot and hurl it across the cellar. "Can you get us more power?"

"I'll try. How the hell is Mira going to Annie?"

Sheppard shook his head. "I don't know."

The radio crackled and the voice of Ham Radio Ralph came through. "Hello, this is Ralph. Anyone there? You copy?"

Sheppard shot toward the stairs before Dillard could grab the mike. "This is Shep, Ralph. What've you got? Over."

"I passed on your message about the escaped cons to the Tango PD, but I don't know what kind of response there'll be. They've been flooded with calls and the winds are holding steady at a high four, or at least that's the estimate. I doubt if anyone is venturing anywhere. How're you holding up there?"

"The garage collapsed and there's debris over the cellar door now. The sheriff has taken a turn for the worst. Is there any—"

Dillard snatched the mike out of Sheppard's hand and shoved him roughly to the side. "This is Leo Dillard, assistant director of the Southeast division of the FBI, and you'd better listen very closely, Ralph. It's essential that the escaped cons now at Doubloon Drive be brought in as soon as—"

Sheppard grabbed the back of Dillard's shirt and pushed

him away. Dillard tumbled into a stack of boxes at the foot of the stairs. Then Goot was on him, straddling him like a cowboy on a bucking bronco, and Sheppard scooped up the fallen mike. "Forgive my colleague's bullshit, Ralph. We're having a few problems here. Over."

"I hear you, Shep. Stay tuned to this frequency. Over and out."

Sheppard dug rope and electrical tape out of one of the boxes and within minutes, Dillard was bound up, flat on his stomach, hands secured to his taped feet. When he thrashed, he resembled a human cradle.

"You're fired, both of you are fired, and I'm filing assault charges as soon as we're outta here," he shouted. Veins stood out at his temples, throbbing hard and fast.

"Yada yada," Goot murmured.

"Relax, Leo. You look like you're about to have a stroke and if that happens, there's no one here to help. In fact, I think you're better off not talking at all."

"My thoughts exactly." Goot snapped up a dish towel and gagged Dillard.

He shrieked into the gag, writhed on the floor, and his face got redder and redder. They decided to move him into the corner and as they hoisted him, the gag slipped out of his mouth. He hollered obscenities and threats like some schoolyard bully who'd realized that the jig was up.

They set him down on a sleeping bag several feet from Emison. When Sheppard attempted to wedge the gag back into Dillard's mouth, he snapped at him with all the ferocity of a rabid dog and bit down so hard on Sheppard's hand that he drew blood. Sheppard grabbed him around the neck, forced his head back, and squeezed at his cheeks until he was forced to open his mouth. Goot jammed the dish towel into his mouth, then wrapped electrical tape all the way around to the back of his head.

"You'd better wash that off," Goot said, looking at

Sheppard's hand. "No telling what sort of shit is swimming in Leo's mouth. Rabies. Ebola. AIDS."

As Sheppard stood at the sink, rinsing and scrubbing the bite with soap, the radio sputtered and crackled again and a new voice came through. "Shep, hello, you there? Shep? Over."

"I know that voice," Goot exclaimed.

Sheppard realized he knew that voice, too, and strode quickly up the stairs and to the radio. "Ace? Hey, man, is that you? Over."

"Shep, yeah, Ace and Luke here. In the hills. We've been monitoring you. Had some trouble with the radio so we couldn't send until now. We may be able to get to you when the eye moves onshore. Don't know when. Last we heard, the storm had stalled offshore. Over."

"It's more important that someone gets to Mira's. The cons are there. Over."

"I've been calling her place, but no one answers. Her cell isn't responding. You okay?"

"We're maintaining," Sheppard replied, glancing at Dillard.

"How's the sheriff doing?"

"Not good. Is your place holding up?"

"We've lost trees, our storage unit collapsed, we've had some flooding, but basically we're safe. National Hurricane isn't transmitting. We aren't sure what that means. Or we're not receiving if they are. We're going to try to get our own readings. Be back in touch shortly."

"How far are they from Mira's?" Goot asked.

"I don't know. I'm not sure where they live. But if it's possible for them to get out, they'll do it."

The generator coughed, wheezed, and the lights went off again, on again. Was air piped into the cellar by the generator? He didn't know. But when it cut out, how long would they have before the air ran out? An hour? Two hours? Thirty minutes? Most Florida homes were far more porous than

T. J. MacGregor

their northern counterparts, but he didn't know if that applied to cellars.

In all of Sheppard's years here, he'd seen exactly three cellars—one at a horse ranch outside of hilly Ocala and two here on hilly Tango. The Ocala cellar originally had been built as an underground bomb shelter shortly before the Cuban missile crisis. The other on Tango was a wine cellar. Neither compared to *this* cellar.

According to the real estate records that Dillard had shown Sheppard, Jerome Carver—aka Billy Joe Franklin— had owned the cabin for about six months. Unlikely that he'd built the cellar. It didn't look as if it had been built recently and besides, construction of this magnitude would require contractors, tractors, engineers, activity that would draw attention, the last thing Franklin would have wanted. Sheppard guessed the cellar might be as old as the cabin.

The original cabin had gone up just prior to the Civil War, when the property had included fifteen acres tilled for cotton. It even had included slaves' quarters. In 1890, the cabin and five acres was deeded to a liberated slave and his family and his descendants had owned the property until Franklin had bought it. For some reason, this information seemed important to Sheppard. He tried to reason through it, but fatigue had turned his brain to slush.

"Shep, you hear that?" Goot asked.

"You mean the silence from Dillard?"

Goot snickered and scooped a sliced hard-boiled egg onto a piece of bread. "No, something else."

Sheppard listened. He heard it also, something that struck him as grossly out of place, like hearing a scream on a hot, still night. Even though this wasn't as obvious as a scream, it nagged at him. It didn't *fit.*

He wrapped a towel around his hand and hurried over to the stairs. The stairwell magnified the noise of the storm. The metal door trembled and clattered, but the broomstick that Goot had shoved through the handle held fast. So whatever they heard wasn't the wind, trying to get in. He doubted if the wind could even get through the pile of debris that covered the hatch.

But water could get through.

He climbed to the top of the steps and the tight space immediately triggered his body's usual responses—something clutching at the inside of his chest, his heartbeat accelerating, a knot in the pit of his stomach. He ran his fingers around the edges of the door, but didn't feel any moisture.

"We got a leak?" Goot called.

"Not here."

Sheppard hastened down the steps—and realized where the noise was coming from. He took his flashlight out of his back pocket and ducked under the stairs, into a space thick with shadows. His bare feet met water.

He tipped the flashlight down. The beam struck a drain in the floor where water bubbled up and spilled over. Not a lot of water, not a river, not even a stream. But the water itself triggered so many internal alarms for Sheppard that he just stood there staring at it, as if the act of staring could make it reverse directions and vanish down the drain.

The drain puzzled him. Why was it here in the first place? In South America, drains were fairly common in the kitchens, courtyards, and bathrooms of older homes, where hoses—not brooms—were taken to the floors at the end of the day to wash away crumbs, dust, whatever. Maybe it originally was intended as a place to piss.

He finally dropped into a crouch and leaned forward, sniffing at the water. It didn't smell like sewage. It smelled like earth, redolent with greenery—weeds, grass, flowers, the stuff that came uprooted and washed away in deluges. He ran his fingers through it. Gritty. It looked discolored.

How many pipes lay under this cellar? Or close to it? Were they backed up or busted? As he squatted there thinking the unthinkable, the grate over the drain suddenly flew loose and water erupted from it, a miniature geyser. The metal grate skittered this way and through the water; then chunks of mud and weeds spewed up and squeezed through the opening like pus from a boil.

Sheppard slapped his hands over the open drain. Water squished up between his fingers, ran over the backs of his hands. His horror lent itself to instantaneous worst case scenarios, of water rising steadily, rapidly, and turning the cellar into a death trap. Death by drowning.

His thoughts flew into hyperdrive, scrambling for solutions that would buy them time. But the bottom line was simple. They were trapped in a cellar forty feet underground, their only exit blocked with debris, had a dead cell phone, a ham radio that provided voice contact and information but little else. The hurricane was stalled offshore, their power source was running dry, Emison desperately needed medical attention, and Dillard had turned into the maniac who had lurked for years beneath his coiffed veneer. Could it get any worse?

It might take hours for the water to build up enough to become life-threatening, but it could take days for anyone to dig them out of here.

In short, they were fucked.

21

"... you never forget something like Andrew. We're all different because of it."

Sun-Sentinel.com

With the utility room door shut, the terrible howls of the storm seemed muted and distant, Franklin thought, almost like manufactured sounds in a movie. They had cleared space for themselves on the floor by moving boxes of books into the living room. They had brought in the cooler, quilts, pillows, a first-aid kit. They had replenished the water in the utility room. They were ready.

"We need a toilet," the Amazon said.

"We just use the bathroom," Crystal said.

"The idea of a safe room, babe, is that you don't go into it until you absolutely have to and that once you go in, you don't come out." To the Amazon, he said: "A garbage can and some garbage bags would do it."

"I'll see what I can fix up." She weaved out of the room. Even though her arm was now in a sling that Crystal had made for her, she kept it pressed tightly to her side, immobilized. He could tell she was still in pain.

"Billy, there isn't enough room in here for Nadine and

Mira. There's hardly enough room in here for the three of us. Let's just keep them where they are."

"They're our tickets off the island. Go get the old lady. I'll get Mira."

"We're all going to crowd in there now?"

"Uh, *yeah*, that's the idea." What the hell was wrong with her, anyway? "*Go,* Crystal."

She frowned, the crease jutting down between her eyes, and regarded him as though she were seeing something that deeply disturbed her. He had the distinct impression that she suspected his true motive for sending her off to get the old woman while he fetched Mira. But then she rocked forward, gave him a quick kiss, and hurried out.

Franklin rubbed his hand across his mouth, wiping away the taste of the kiss. It repulsed him. Now that he'd encountered the purest essence of water, it was obvious to him that Crystal was no longer water. Jail had turned her into something else, into air, yes, that was it. She was air, infinitely changeable, as mutable as a chameleon. One instant she agreed with whatever he said, the next instant she agreed with whatever the Amazon said. He couldn't love air.

Franklin fled down the hall, through the chaotic hammering of rain against the skylight in the living room. His eagerness to see Mira, touch her, talk to her about his revelation nearly overwhelmed him. It now seemed so apparent that a series of signs had led him here, to her, and that both Crystal and the Amazon were just catalysts in that journey. He would convince Mira of the rightness of their union and she, the paragon of water, would flow into him and understand his sincerity. They would merge. Creeks flowed into streams and streams flowed into rivers and rivers ran onward toward seas, oceans, each merging more powerful, more perfect, until water covered most of the earth's surface. That was how it would be with them. Together, they would be stronger than they could ever be separately. She would see it as clearly as he did.

He reached the bedroom—and the door was locked. The lock must have engaged when Crystal shut the door, he thought. The knob had a flimsy grooved button in it; he turned it with his fingernails, pushed it open. The door snapped back and nearly struck him in the face.

What's going on?

Franklin pushed the door open more slowly, ducked under the stocking tied to this knob and the one on the closet door, and hit the wall switch. He immediately saw that the bed was empty, the bathroom door was shut, and knew she was hiding inside. *Hiding from me.* Well, who could blame her? He hadn't exactly won her trust yet. She didn't realize how entwined their destinies were. But she would. In time, he would make her understand.

Franklin unlocked this door, pushed it opened with his foot. The bathroom was empty.

Impossible.

Franklin jerked open the linen door, the shower stall door, the cabinet doors. Water glistened on the floor in front of the window. Frowning, he crouched in front of it, raised the window, and felt along the inside of the shutters for a release button. He found it. "Crazy bitch." She had escaped into the storm to . . .

What? Run away? Get help? Retrieve a weapon or a cell phone? Maybe she intended to break into the house the same way he, Crystal, and the Amazon had, through one of the windows on the other side of the house. But in winds like this, that would be insanity.

Franklin ran out of the room and up the hall, his fury and sense of betrayal propelling him.

Crystal, pushing the old woman's wheelchair into the kitchen, saw him. "Billy, what's wrong? What happened?"

"Mira escaped."

"Escaped? But she . . . she was unconscious. Out of it."

"Take her back into the family room," he snapped, pointing at Nadine. "Tell Lopez to cover the porch doors."

He stepped into the utility room, pressed his ear to the door that opened into the garage, but didn't hear anything except the storm. He plucked a headlamp off a shelf in the utility room, fitted it around his skull, and clutching his shotgun, opened the door and stepped down into the garage. He flicked the wall switch, but the light didn't come on.

Okay, no lights. Mira had done something to the lights. He pressed the switch on the head lantern and the bright beam burned through the garage, exposing the delivery van directly in front of him, the Jetta crammed in beside it. To his right lay a workbench piled high with more boxes of books and the side door to the yard. To his left were shelves that held windsurfing gear and more boxes. Directly above him dangled a rope attached to the attic door.

I'm Mira, scared shitless, in search of a weapon, a phone, something to give me an edge, and I need a place to hide.

Not the attic, he thought. Like the van, it was too obvious. Just the same, he tugged on the rope and the hinged ladder unfolded with maddening slowness. As its feet touched the garage floor, he pushed on it, making sure it was secure, then climbed it. His head popped through the opening, into the roaring chorus of the hurricane. *I'm terrified and I won't hide up here because the storm sounds too close, too horrifying . . .*

Down the ladder, nudge it back into the ceiling. He turned slowly, then made his way to the side door. Unlocked. *I am water and I'm being poured into a vessel called garage. Where are you, Mira?*

Somewhere close. He could almost smell her. He turned the dead bolt. Now she wouldn't be able to escape quickly.

Franklin crouched, checking under the vehicle. No shad-

ows. No feet. She, too, had become water. He turned off the
lamp and stood for a few moments in the darkness, absorbing it, tasting it, listening to it. Then he flowed into it, filling
this wondrous vessel called *darkness,* and was swept over to
the van and up the ramp into the back of it. He waited in the
van's darkness, in its heat, listening. Then he turned on the
headlamp, confirming what his senses had told him: except
for boxes stacked at the far end, it was empty.

Just to be sure, though, he moved quickly to the front of
the van, checking behind the boxes, in the front seat. No
Mira.

Headlamp off. *Think, think. You're water. You can figure
this out.*

She hadn't made it to the garage yet.

She was already across the street, banging on some
neighbor's door or inside that neighbor's house, on the phone
with 911.

She had broken into the house and now held Crystal and
the Amazon hostage.

Franklin pressed the heels of his hands against his eyes. *I
am Mira, desperate, terrified . . . and . . .*

Ha-ha. Tricked you. I'm in the house . . .

Franklin whirled around and hastened back through the
van. As he ran down the ramp, something slammed against
his shins, an explosion of pain burst through his lower legs,
and he threw his arms out in front of him to break his fall.
The shotgun clattered away from him and he struck the floor
of the garage, his right side taking the brunt of the fall. He
rolled, but wasn't fast enough. Something whacked his thighs
and he grabbed for whatever it was, his fingers clamped over
it—*wooden, not too thick, a broomstick? Mop? Stick?*—and
he jerked it toward him. A person fell against him, grunting,
breathing hard, kicking—a woman, but not Mira. This person was too small to be Mira.

Annie's your kid?

I sent her to Miami with friends when the warning went up.

He'd fallen for it, fallen for her lies. The kid was here, not in Miami, and Mira had gone to her and here she was.

And Christ, she was a fighter. She bit and clawed, kicked and shrieked, and they rolled across the garage floor, locked together. Now other noises pierced his awareness—howls, snarls, fierce barks, and they were close, uncomfortably close.

Where's the dog?

Those are cat bowls, the old lady had replied.

Another lie. So many lies. *How could water lie like this to him? How?*

Franklin flipped the girl over, straddled her as if she were a horse, and pinned her down. The door to the house suddenly flew open and Crystal ran out, her flashlight darting about in the darkness like a drunken firefly. The dog went ballistic and the kid kept kicking, writhing, trying to throw him off. Franklin clamped his hand over her mouth and she bit him.

He pinched her nostrils closed with one hand and held her mouth shut with the other. She struggled for a few moments and finally lost consciousness. By then, Crystal was dancing around in front of him with a roll of electrical tape from which she had torn long strips. He slapped them over the kid's mouth and around her hands and feet, incapacitating her completely.

He rocked back onto his heels and stared at the dog, tied up in a corner of the garage, snarling and leaping to break free of the leash tethered to a pipe that jutted out from the hot water heater. *Goddamn stupid dog,* he thought, and scrambled up, looking around for his rifle.

"Jesus, Billy, what—"

"Get the kid in the house and check her and the old lady for cell phones."

"But—"

"Now!" he shouted.

"Where the fuck did *she* come from?" Crystal shouted back, her face bright pink.

"Just get her outta here." He turned on the headlamp.

"What about the dog?"

"It's not going anywhere. Go on, get the kid. Get outta here."

She scooped up the girl and carried her inside the house. The dog had gone rabid, its feral sounds pounding in his skull. He found his shotgun near the van's front tire, swept it up, and as he turned, swung the gun up to shoot the dog. But Lopez stood between him and the dog.

"Get out of my way," he demanded.

"I'll deal with the dog. We need the dog. They sense things in storms."

"You won't even be able to get close to the dog, Lopez. Now get the fuck out of my way."

Just then, the door to the garage opened again and Crystal hollered, "Billy, I found their cell phones."

The Amazon smirked, her eyes locked on Franklin's. "Don't."

He held the shotgun and she was giving him orders. He almost laughed, almost pumped the weapon to blow her and the dog away. But something poured into the Amazon's face, something so fierce, so primal, that he hesitated. Then Crystal marched over to him and grabbed his arm. "C'mon. Let Tia deal with the dog. I need you inside."

The Amazon held his eyes a moment longer, then turned toward the dog. Infuriated, he wrenched his arm free of Crystal's grasp. "You've got five minutes to shut up the mutt."

The Amazon already had turned away from him and moved slowly toward the dog.

Franklin followed Crystal into the house, wondering what the hell had just happened.

Tia's throat closed up as soon as she saw the dog, a golden retriever just like the one that had saved her life during Andrew. Her beautiful Mandela, named after the man she admired most in the world, had fur just like this dog, thick and golden, highlighted with red. This pretty thing was beginning to gray around the muzzle; Tia guessed she was at least five, maybe older.

"It's okay." She spoke quietly and squatted in front of the animal at a respectful distance. Her swollen shoulder throbbed and ached, but she struggled to ignore the pain and focus on the dog.

Tied to a pipe in a recessed area of the garage, where the hot water heater and master circuit box were, the retriever growled and bared her teeth, something Tia never had seen a retriever do. Generally, they were peace-loving animals, eager to please. "I'm betting you've seen your share of heartache and it probably wasn't from these folks."

Tia moved slowly toward a metal shelf close to the retriever, where three sweating bottles of water stood. She picked up one, twisted the top, and sat down about a foot from the dog. "You're thirsty. I can tell." She poured water into her hand and extended her arm slowly.

The dog barked fiercely and snapped at the air.

"Listen, I know how you feel," she went on in the same quiet voice. "My Mandela was a rescue dog. I got her when she was two, a year before Hurricane Andrew." She kept her hand extended, water spilling over the sides of it. "When I was lying in the rubble, she rarely left my side. And when she did, she always brought back food that she shared with me. One time, I remember, she brought me a can of beans, just came trotting toward me with that unopened can in her mouth, her tail wagging. I broke open the top with a rock and we shared that can of beans. Another time, she'd found this freezer half-buried in the rubble. We raided it together, both of us licking moisture off the ice that remained." She felt tears coursing down her cheeks now and the dog, panting hard, cocked her head and sat back as if she understood every word that Tia was saying. "Please drink. Please trust me. I need to make it up to Mandela for helping me by helping you. Sh . . . she . . . died . . . in that horrid place. I can't let you die."

She inched a little closer and poured water onto the floor in front of the retriever. The dog eyed the water with obvious thirst, looked at Tia, then lowered her head and lapped it up, her tail wagging slowly. Tia moved closer still and poured the water into her hand again. The dog sniffed at her fingertips, her tail wagging a bit more quickly, and finally lapped it out of Tia's palm and kept licking even after the water was gone. Just the feel of it, the soft warmth sliding over her skin, reminded her of Mandela and she moved even closer and ran her fingers through the dog's fur. She looked at the tag on her collar. *My name is Ricki.*

"Ricki," Tia repeated.

The dog wagged her tail furiously now and licked the tears off Tia's cheeks. She wrapped her arms around Ricki's neck and buried her face in all that luscious, sweet-smelling fur and wept for Mandela.

Suddenly, Ricki began to whine, to tremble, and a breath later, something slammed into the garage door. A falling tree? Flying debris? Airborne chairs? No telling. The door clattered, then shook, and the wind howled along the outside edges. Tia tightened her arms around the dog's neck, her body braced for disaster, her mind frozen twelve years in the past. When the clattering diminished, she shot to her feet, untied the leash from the pipe, ran into the house with the dog.

As soon as Ricki saw Franklin, she went nuts, snarling and

barking and jerking on the leash to get to him. Annie, sitting up, the tape off her mouth now, shouted, *"No, Ricki, no!"*

Franklin spun around, pumped the shotgun, and fired.

Shrieking and sobbing, Annie leaped to her feet and hurled herself at the man who had shot her dog. But because her ankles and wrists were still taped, she lost her balance and fell to the floor and lay there, sobbing, her heart broken into a million pieces.

He grabbed her by the back of the shirt, hauled her up as if she weighed no more than a rag doll, and shoved her roughly onto the couch. "Your dog's a coward. It's hiding under the kitchen table. See that? Lopez caught its leash. But if you don't tell me what I want to know, I'll shoot again and I won't miss. We clear?"

Annie's senses filled with so many odors, all of them foul, that she barely could catch her breath. She looked away from his despicable face and saw Ricki cowering under the table, and a hole in the pantry door. "Just . . . don't hurt her. Let her come over here with me."

"Nope. Can't risk that. Lopez, put the mutt in the room with the cats."

The tall black woman didn't move. She glared at Franklin, her eyes small, dark, homicidal. Her face had frozen in an expression that terrified Annie, but she didn't know if it was rage, grief, or some wretched internal struggle. When she finally spoke, her voice was sharp, low, cold. "Never shoot at this dog again, Dipshit, or it will be the last shot you fire."

Franklin laughed. "Chill, Lopez. Just get the mutt outta my sight."

"Help us!" Annie screamed at the black woman. *"Please help us, don't let him hurt my dog, please."*

"Hey, yeah, good idea," Franklin said. "Help her, Lopez. Help the kid and her dog."

The bimbo leaped into it, waving her arms like a referee calling time out. "Back off, Billy. Let her get the dog outta here."

Lopez turned away, coaxing Ricki to follow her. She looked back once at Annie and for just an instant, her eyes and the black woman's connected. Annie felt Lopez was trying to communicate something to her, but she couldn't decipher it. They disappeared into Sheppard's office.

"You're a prick bastard and Shep knows you're here and he's going to beat your ass!"

Franklin grinned, the shotgun cradled in his arm.

"Hey," the blond bimbo burst out. "No kid talks like that to Billy."

"Shut up, you fat bimbo."

"You little shit," she breathed, and lifted her hand to hit the kid, but Franklin stopped her.

"We need information from her, babe." Then, to Annie: "I suppose you communicated with Shep the same way you communicated with your mom, right?" He scooped the cell phone off the table that the bimbo had dug out of her pocket. "And how was your mother supposed to get to you, Annie?"

"I'm not telling you shit."

"Suit yourself. I'll have Lopez bring the dog back in."

Annie blurted, "Through the garage's side door. She was going to climb out the bathroom window."

"Uh-huh. What's her number?"

Annie spat out the number and prayed he wouldn't be able to pick up a cell signal here in the family room. Whether he did or not, his words terrified her: "Hello, Mee-rra. This is Billy Joe. I now have your daughter and grandmother here in the family room. You have twenty minutes to get your ass in here. Otherwise I shoot one of them. Call to tell me you're on your way. Or you can just come in through the porch door. Now I'll put Annie on the phone."

He held the phone up to her ear. "Mom, it's me. I'm okay.

He . . . he nearly shot Ricki." Her voice broke and she started to cry and he brought the phone to his own ear again.

"See you in twenty, Mee-rra."

22

Nearly a million and a half people were left without power in the wake of Hurricane Andrew. Some of them were without power for up to six months.

Mira scrambled across the attic floor on her hands and knees, sweat pouring off her, the roaring of the storm so raw that she felt as though it were inside the attic with her. Something struck the roof. She curled up in a fetal position on the floor, arms covering her head.

Like that would make a difference if the roof tore away.

The blow to the roof echoed throughout the attic and was particularly loud where she was, curled up under an area sloped down so steeply she couldn't sit up. How long had it been since Franklin had left that insidious message on her cell phone? Ten minutes? Twenty? Thirty? She didn't know. Her cell didn't record the time he'd made his call. Her cell didn't work at all now.

Hello, Mee-ra. This is Billy Joe. I now have your daughter and grandmother in the family room. . . .

She choked back a sob.

When the powerful reverberations faded away, she moved forward again, inching along on her stomach like a centipede. Her flashlight barely dented the utter blackness of the attic. Here and there, the light struck massive cobwebs with spiders in them that were at least half the size of her hand. She knew these spiders had a name, but she couldn't remember it. Were they poisonous? She couldn't remember that, either.

Her only memory of these creatures came from when she was six or seven years old. She and her mother had been visiting Nadine and her second husband here on Tango and had been running down to the beach one moonlit night, through sea grape trees, and Mira had plowed right into one of these massive webs that connected the trees. The spider had moved quickly toward her and she'd shrieked. Her mother had run back to her, clawed at the web with her hands, and freed Mira. Then she'd scolded her for not watching where she was going, as though it were her fault the web was there.

Why should she remember that right now?

Because Franklin is that spider. He'd spun his web and Annie and Nadine had gotten trapped in it and she had to free them. The pattern would repeat itself until she learned the lesson—no more crime scenes. Reading a crime scene was like running through the dark and plowing into the web.

It's not that simple and you know it. Think, c'mon. It's right there in front of you.

And she got it. Franklin couldn't possibly know she was in the attic, that she'd gone through the door in the closet ceiling. She'd left a trail of water by the bathroom window, had locked that door, made it appear that she'd gone out into the storm. For all he knew, she was dead and the phone call had been to intimidate Annie and Nadine and exhibit his prowess as the guy in charge.

But could she stake their lives on that assumption?

She crawled faster and then the floor suddenly ended. She shone her flashlight around and realized this part of the attic floor consisted of pieces of plywood laid down here and there against the horizontal beams of the house. In between lay the drywall that probably wouldn't sustain her weight if she slipped off the beam. The nearest piece of plywood was four feet away. Two giant steps would do it, she thought, but one of those giant steps could be onto the drywall.

Mira flattened out and pushed herself to the very edge of the floor and pressed her palms down against the drywall, testing it. Spongy. *Too risky. Stay on the beam.* She rolled onto her back and aimed the flashlight upward, wincing as the rage of the storm echoed throughout the attic.

Just beyond where she lay, the roof rose and there was enough space for her to stand nearly upright. The horizontal roof beams might help her cross the sections that lacked plywood. But they were much too high for her to reach.

Move, decide, do something.

Perhaps if she crossed the drywall on her stomach, so her weight was more evenly distributed, it would support her. She rolled onto her stomach again, stuck the end of the flashlight in her mouth, and began to crawl slowly and carefully onto the drywall. Forearms, torso. Then her thighs slid over the edge of the plywood beam. She couldn't hear anything but the ravages of the storm, but imagined that the drywall creaked. It seemed to sag a bit, like a water bed or a sponge pillow, and she went still, sweat oozing into her eyes, fearful that if she brought any more weight onto the drywall, the entire piece would crack or collapse completely.

Mira took the flashlight out of her mouth, aimed it at the sheet of drywall below her. No cracks had opened up. She stuck the flashlight back into her mouth, brought her knees down, flattened out on her stomach, and inched forward, a centipede again, her body partly on the beam, partly on the drywall. Something else hit the roof and whatever it was struck more forcefully than the object that had hit minutes ago. It filled her with such a profound dread that she scrambled across the dry board on her hands and knees. She hauled herself onto the next piece of plywood and then lay there, her heart hammering, the humidity and heat clinging to her. She felt as if she'd been inside a sweat lodge for hours.

Up, move.

She rocked back onto her heels, moved the flashlight around again. In front of her lay stacks of cardboard boxes that held *stuff*—hers, Annie's, Nadine's, Shep's, even some things that had belonged to Tom which she couldn't bear to part with. Every box was filled with someone's memories. But the boxes meant she was much closer than she'd thought to the attic door in the garage.

She stood on legs that felt as if they'd been hollowed out and filled with feathers and tried to wedge her way between the stacks of boxes. But they were jammed so tightly together she was forced to climb on top of them. As she crawled across them, she began picking up stray bits of information about Sheppard, Nadine, Annie, even herself, pieces of their emotional lives stuffed away in boxes. Distractions. But she couldn't shut off the impressions, couldn't disentangle herself, perhaps because these details were intrinsic to who she was.

There, her mother, tall and thin, a workaholic who had become an attorney because it had seemed to be the profession farthest removed from Nadine's world. She had become left brain to Nadine's right. Here, her father, a biologist who had left science to become a science fiction writer.

She uncovered a memory of one Christmas when she and her father had decorated the tree with hundreds of tiny, multi-colored lights. Before turning them on, he had switched off all the lights in the house, told her to stand back, as though the tree might burst into flames, and turned on all the Christmas tree lights simultaneously, an explosion of light so magical that it had stolen her breath away. That sort of magic was absent in her father's books and, for the most part, had been absent in her childhood with her parents. Nadine had been her source of magic as a kid.

She supposed that was why she rarely saw her parents. It wasn't that they were terrible people. They were simply clueless about being parents, both of them caught up in their careers, with Mira as a postscript to their lives and their relationship. Because of it, she had grown up closer to Nadine than to either of her parents. Even though she understood the roots of this situation lay in other lives—that they had owed her a birth and no guarantees beyond that—despair suddenly filled her. A tsunami of emotion swelled inside her and threatened to explode.

Mira pulled her hands away from the box she was touching, clenched them against her thighs. She couldn't go there now.

She wiped the back of her arm across her forehead, brushed cobwebs off her arms, and tried to close herself off to the distracting bits of psychic information about the past. The past couldn't help her.

Her hair, sopping wet from the heat, hugged her skull. Beads of sweat rolled down the sides of her face. The noise of the storm, the dropping pressure, pushed down hard against her spine. *And what's the central pressure now? Below Camille's 909 millibars? Below Gilbert's 888?*

Mira slid off a stack of cartons to a bare spot on the sheet of plywood, dropped to her knees, pressed her palms to the wood. *Give me something useful.*

Nothing came. She pressed harder, as though the pressure would force information to flow into her, and then she begged and begged and the choked emotions that she'd managed to hold back until now erupted all at once. She started sobbing, rocking back and forth, her arms clutched against her. This made her even angrier and she got up and scrambled across the next stack of boxes, then the next. When this sheet of flooring ended, she didn't even bother estimating the distance to the next plywood island. She didn't inch across it, either. She leaped, landed hard on the sheet of plywood, grabbed on to a box to keep from falling back.

Steadying herself, she shoved boxes to the side, frantic now to reach the door. Instead, she reached the end of this piece of flooring. Mira shone the light back behind her, puzzled by where she was in relation to the house, and realized that she somehow had become disoriented and strayed too far to the back of the house. But where at the back of the house? Nadine's bedroom? The living room? Kitchen? Family room? Where were the skylights?

Again, she shone the flashlight around. No skylights, of course not. The attic bypassed the skylights. She recalled Sheppard telling her that. He was the only one of them who had explored the attic at any length, and a month ago had told her that the attic floor over his office wasn't straight. It had been too hot in May, like now, to crawl around in the attic, but come late fall, Sheppard had said, he intended to come back up here and find out why that particular piece of flooring wasn't straight. At the time, she'd written it off as a typical Sheppard thing: *give me a riddle and I'll try like hell to solve it.*

Maybe she was imagining it, but it sure seemed that the floor where she was crouched wasn't straight. She set the flashlight on the plywood; the beam slanted down. *Yeah, so?* She crept forward to peer over the edge of the plywood and her foot hit the flashlight and it rolled, picking up speed. Mira grabbed for it, but she wasn't fast enough.

The flashlight rolled over the edge, went out, and darkness closed in on her. The roaring rage of the storm now sounded worse than moments ago when the flashlight had been on. She thought of those huge spiders, sitting motionlessly in their giant webs, alerted to the fact that she had no light. She imagined them advancing on her as though she were some huge and exotic bug on which they could feast for the rest of their lives—and she panicked.

Mira threw herself forward, in the same direction where the flashlight had rolled, and didn't just fall off the edge of the plywood. She plummeted.

Tia Lopez thought she heard something behind her, but when she glanced around, saw only the cats, huddled together in the office closet. She turned back to the dog, talking to Ricki, calming her. Tia was no doggie shrink, but she knew a lot about trauma and figured that animals felt it just like people did. And this dog was traumatized by gunfire, no doubt about it. She guessed Ricki had had some horrible experience with guns in the past and might be reliving it now, a sort of canine version of post-traumatic stress syndrome.

She petted Ricki with one hand and massaged her swollen shoulder with the other and talked quietly to the dog, getting her settled on the floor. The three cats now ventured out and came over to the dog. They sniffed her, rubbed up against her, licked her snout, and loved on her until she raised her head and nuzzled each one. Maybe it was this unconditional display of love that got to Tia or that she was sick to death of bully Dipshit. Or maybe it was just that she had lived most of her adult life struggling against the bully/victim syndrome and despite the fact that Franklin was inadvertently responsible for her freedom, that freedom came with a mighty steep price this time.

Too steep.

The taste of hot peppers surged first in the back of her throat, rose quickly to her tongue, then flooded the inside of her mouth. She knew what it meant. She knew.

And suddenly she was moving through the office, door, slamming it shut, the taste of the peppers so strong that she was breathing it. And there was Dipshit, screaming at the kid, waving the shotgun around, and the girl was sobbing—a girl only a few years older than her own daughter would be now.

Crystal saw her first. "Hey, did you get the dog—"

"No more, Dipshit."

He glanced around, his face livid, limned with everything she'd seen in the face of other abusers, other men who took such perverse delight in wielding their physical strength, power, and whatever else they believed they possessed, against women. "Get lost, Lopez. And do it fast."

Her muscles tightened, her pain vanished. The hot pepper taste burned the inside of her cheeks, coated her tongue and the backs of her teeth, and reached way down deep into her throat. Then the odor permeated her brain, catapulting her into the Red, and suddenly she was airborne.

Tia's feet struck him in the chest, knocking him back. She heard air whooshing from his lungs, a noise not unlike the sounds of choppers as they swept in low over a target. The shotgun fell away from him and he crashed into Nadine's wheelchair. Crystal was screaming, the storm was screaming, her heart was screaming.

Tia whirled and her right leg kicked out and hit Crystal in the stomach. She doubled over, gasping, stumbling back like a drunk. Dipshit shot to his feet, his face vampire white. He pulled something from his pocket and aimed it at her—*not a gun, what is it?*—and she danced to the right, a move that he anticipated. The object struck her in the thigh and she suddenly knew what it was, what it did, and thought, *I'm fucked.*

He had shot her with a taser, a favorite weapon of riot police. Upon firing, compressed nitrogen projected two air taser probes. The instant these probes made contact with clothing or skin, an electrical signal scrambled the person's neuromuscular control, stealing his or her ability to coordinate movements. The pulsating electrical current, she knew, was pretimed and covered about thirty seconds, ensuring that the person—*me, I'm that person*—wouldn't recover instantly and pull the probes out. It could be lethal. It knocked her legs out from under her and sent her body into violent convulsions as her muscles contracted. She jerked like a splayed frog until her body finally curled in on itself, into a fetal position.

Her bladder let loose, Tia felt it, the warmth streaming out of her just as it had done when her water had broken and she had gone into premature labor during Andrew. And then she was gone, her mind stuck in the terror twelve years in the past.

PART THREE

LANDFALL

"In the twentieth century, U.S. hurricanes destroyed $73 billion in property. During the 70-year period from 1925 through 1995, the toll was $61 billion. During these 70 years, 244 landfalls occurred. The average landfall would have resulted in $1.5 billion in damage with today's prices and coastal development."

www.firstscience.com

23

"The strongest winds in a hurricane are found on its right side. But the right side is determined with respect to the storm's motion. If the hurricane is moving to the west, the right side would be to the north of the storm."

www.aoml.noaa.gov

The generator shuddered, let out a terrible gasp, and died, plunging the cellar into blackness and cutting off the fans, the fridge.

With the generator silenced, the full orchestra of the storm's violence echoed around Sheppard. Fiddles shrieked notes two octaves too high, horns and trumpets blared, cellos and harps and violins were played by novices, cymbals banged discordantly. And behind all this, the noise of water coming up from the drain created a strange auditory backdrop, that of a gurgling brook or a slow-moving stream. Under other conditions, that particular sound might be relaxing. But now it only increased Sheppard's general anxiety about their ultimate fate.

Sheppard turned on his flashlight and moved quickly around the cellar, switching on the battery-operated lanterns they had removed from the boxes of supplies. He placed them in strategic spots around the cellar, which allowed the light to spill even into the darkest corners. The illumination forced his darker thoughts about dying in the cellar back into the abyss from which they had sprung, but also woke Dillard.

He went through all the expected antics like a hungry dog performing its usual tricks. He rolled around on his sleeping bag, screamed into his gag, jerked on the ropes that held his arms and legs together.

"You'll have to wait your turn, Leo," Sheppard told him, and crouched next to Emison to check his vitals.

He felt Emison's head: the fever seemed to be down. But his breathing was quick and shallow and his heartbeat much too rapid for a man who had been flat on his back for hours. Since Sheppard had gone through Franklin's limited supply of latex gloves, he was extremely careful not to get his hands soiled as he checked the sheet under Emison to make sure it was dry. It was. He didn't know if that was good or bad. When your kidneys failed, could you still take a piss?

Sheppard folded back the lower part of the sheet to take a look at Emison's leg. The wound didn't appear to be seeping blood now. That was positive. He unwrapped the bandage. The stitches had stemmed the flow of blood, but Sheppard didn't like the rest of what he saw. The skin around the stitches looked puffy, pus seeped out. Streaks of red shot out from the center of the stitches, like roads on a map. Infection. Did it mean Augmentin wasn't the right drug? That the stuff hadn't kicked in yet? That he hadn't given Emison enough to fight the infection?

Sheppard squirted Betadine on the wound, let it dry, then used a Q-tip to spread antibiotic salve over the stitches. As he wrapped a fresh bandage over the wound, Goot woke up. "What's going on?" He lifted his head from his sleeping bag.

"The generator died."

"Is water still coming up out of the drain?"

"Yeah. I made a barricade of boxes, towels, and linens to keep our area here dry, but water's starting to seep through." Sheppard turned his flashlight on the wall he'd created with cardboard boxes. The beam exposed the dark marking at the bottom of the boxes where the water had penetrated.

"We're going to have to shuffle everything around," Goot said.

Dillard made more noises, animals sounds, and started wiggling around again, too, as if he were telling them he had to take a piss or stretch or had a cramp or some other damn thing.

"Here's the deal, Leo," said Goot. "I'll take the tape off your mouth but only if you promise not to annoy us with your bullshit."

Dillard nodded his fat head.

"Fine. You can wait until I've used the can." Goot disappeared behind the bamboo screen.

Sheppard turned his attention back to Emison and saw that he'd opened his eyes. They looked rheumy, glazed, and Sheppard didn't think he actually saw anything. He lifted Emison's head and reached for the bottle of Gatorade on the floor next to him.

"Doug, it's Shep. Sip from the straw. The stuff has electrolytes your body needs."

Emison groaned, blinked, and his mouth closed around the end of the straw with all the greediness of a suckling infant. Then he let the straw drop away and the hoarse whisper that issued from his dry lips wrapped around Sheppard's senses as intimately and urgently as Emison's fingers tightened around his wrist. "She . . . t'th . . ."

"You want more to drink?" Sheppard held up the bottle of Gatorade.

Emison shook his head and touched his chest. "Ta . . . ih . . ."

Sheppard didn't have any idea what Emison was trying to

say. It was like trying to converse with a young toddler whose grasp of English consisted mostly of sounds. "I don't understand what you're saying, Doug."

With excruciatingly slow motions, the sheriff reached inside his shirt and pulled out a cloth cord with the memory stick on it that Sheppard had noticed hours ago in Emison's office.

"Take. Keep."

"All right. I'll keep it safe for you." Sheppard removed the cord from Emison's neck, put it around his own, and tucked it inside his shirt. "I'll hold on to it."

"All you need," Emison murmured, taking great care to enunciate his words.

All I need for what? Was his laptop still powered up? Would it have enough juice in it to transfer the files?

"Doug, what's on this thing?"

Emison murmured incoherently—and lapsed back into a profound silence, his eyes fluttering shut, his mouth slightly open, his breathing ragged. Sheppard covered him with the sheet and got up.

To reach the sink, he had to climb over the wall of boxes he'd built and came down in about three inches of water. The water from the drain was pooling on his side of the barricade, the towels and sheets he'd pressed up against the boxes were now soggy with water, and the stuff pushing up from the drain wasn't slowing down at all. It scared him. On the positive side, the water *accumulated* slowly and maybe they wouldn't drown. Maybe they would be long gone by the time the cellar flooded completely.

Goot came out from behind the bamboo screen and removed the tape from Dillard's mouth. "Could you please cut me loose, guys? My legs are cramped, I need to piss."

It was the most contrite tone of voice Sheppard had heard yet from ole Dillard. "Cut him loose, Goot."

"Totally loose?" Goot looked troubled by the mere suggestion.

"I think he's gotten the message."

But Goot pulled out his kitchen knife and held it up to Dillard's cheek. "I could shave you with this sucker, Leo. And personally, I'd just as soon slit your throat. But Sheppard's sticking to the Geneva conventions, so I'll play along unless you fuck up. We clear on that?"

"Sure. Of course."

Goot sliced through the rope that connected Dillard's hands and feet and his legs dropped to the floor. An expression of utter relief swept over his face, he briefly shut his eyes. Sheppard almost felt sorry for him.

But only *almost*. The bottom line was that Dillard was the sort of man whose insight into himself was limited; he just wasn't the introspective type. He lived in a black-and-white world, where things were one way or another, with a clear boundary drawn between the two. No gray areas, nothing in between. Sheppard knew that he and Goot always had existed in the bad-guy zone in Dillard's world and nothing that had occurred here had changed his opinion in that regard. But he would do whatever he needed to do to get along until he was in a position of power again, even if that meant agreeing to whatever Goot said.

Goot untied the rope around Dillard's feet and hands and he rolled onto his back, massaged his hands, then sat up and massaged his ankles. He grunted, groaned, and finally stood and went into the bathroom. Sheppard mouthed, *Don't trust him,* and Goot grinned and took up guard duty next to the screen that shielded the bathroom from the rest of the cellar.

Sheppard removed his laptop from his pack and went over to the stairs. He climbed to the fifth step, well above the water, and sat down, the computer balanced on his thighs.

The battery usually lasted about three hours. But he'd been running it off and on all day and suspected it was low.

He connected Emison's thumb flash to the USB port and a single folder appeared entitled *Insurance.* He copied it onto his hard drive documents and clicked the folder. Two more folders appeared: *specifics* and *category 5.*

He clicked *specifics* and a message appeared on the screen:

> *To access this file, you must answer the following questions:*
> •*When did Doug Emison begin at the Tango PD?*
> •*When was Emison elected sheriff of Tango County? (month/year)*
> •*What is Emison's current monthly take-home pay?*
> •*Who is Emison's boss?*
> •*What was the true nature of the black water mass?*
> *Once you have answered these questions correctly, the file will open automatically.*

What Sheppard found so intriguing about these questions was that anyone willing to do the research could answer the first four. But only a handful of people knew the exact nature of the black water mass, and Emison, despite whatever suspicions he had, wasn't one of them.

A light came on indicating that the battery was low. "C'mon," he murmured. "Give me just a few more minutes."

He took a stab at the first, second, and fourth questions, based on his knowledge of island politics. For the last question, he typed: *The black water mass is nature's wormhole, a time tunnel.*

The computer made a whirring sound, as if it struggled with the encryption on the file, then a window popped up: *Access denied. All questions must be answered.*

"Okay, okay," Sheppard muttered irritably, and thought about the third question, Emison's take-home pay.

The Tango Police Department fell under the jurisdiction of the county, which had a hierarchy of grade levels similar to that used by the federal government. He knew that entry-level positions for cops began at grade five but didn't have any idea what that grade level paid. The elected officials, like the sheriff and the mayor, began at level sixteen, but again, Sheppard didn't know what that grade level paid. Even though Emison hadn't been elected, and was called Sheriff, he technically was the Chief of Police, an appointed position. Unless he had a bottom line, he couldn't estimate what Emison made, much less what he took home every month.

"Hey, Goot. What do you think Emison takes home every month?" Sheppard asked.

"I don't know about take-home, but I know he's at grade level nineteen with the county and that they pull in around sixty-five grand a year."

"That much?"

"Tango County ranks way up there for property taxes and taxes pay the county wages."

Sheppard did some quick math in his head, deducted taxes, an approximate figure for what Emison paid to the county for health insurance, divided by twelve, and entered that figure. He hoped the encryption program only looked for certain key words or figures rather than exact answers. But that would mean that Emison couldn't encrypt for the last question unless he had theorized the black water mass was related to time or to time travel or some other word that meant the same thing.

Access denied.

Dismayed, Sheppard prayed the battery would hold out a little longer.

Third question again. *What is Emison's current monthly take-home pay?*

Sheppard typed: *Not enough.*

Then the file opened to a Word document and Sheppard

laughed out loud. Two Word documents came up—*dates &
figures* and *details*. Sheppard clicked on the first document.

> *What I've written here is true to the very last word.
> On November 12, 2003, Leo Dillard and I culminated
> a deal that had been in the works for months. My part
> is simple: I arrange the transfer of a con from the
> Dade jail to the Tango jail. For this, I have been paid
> $150K, with another $150K to be paid when the trans-
> fer is completed. Please click the next folder.*

Sheppard's blood boiled. How much had Dillard made?
Five hundred grand? A million? From the moment Emison
had called Sheppard before sunrise this morning, Dillard's
only goal had been to hunt down Franklin—and silence him.
Not only would he win accolades from his superior, but the
man who had made the payoff would be dead. Dillard figured that Emison wouldn't be a problem; he was as guilty as
Dillard and had benefited, too. But Dillard probably hadn't
counted on Emison having insurance in the event that
Dillard tried to double-cross him.

His computer made odd sounds, as if a rat had gotten into
his hard drive and was busily gnawing away at the data. The
battery light now flashed, and a window popped up: *Battery
is low.*

Rather than waste whatever time remained on the battery
by clicking on the next file in this folder, he exited and
clicked on *category 5*. Since he already had broken Emison's
code to get into the primary folder, there were no riddles to
solve this time, no twenty questions. The document appeared and Sheppard scanned it quickly.

But every glaring and horrifying detail leaped out at him,
one travesty after another. He sat there scrolling through the
pages, the photographs, the damning evidence. Once the
media got a hold of this, Dillard not only would be finished

with the bureau, but would be known as the perpetrator of a cover-up.

Low battery! Computer will shut down in 15 seconds! Save all work!

"Shit, no, don't do this." He quickly exited the file, clicked the icon at the bottom of the screen to safely remove hardware, and the computer shut down.

Sheppard stared at the black screen, his mind screaming. His hand trembled as he slipped the memory stick from the USB port. He flipped the cloth cord over his head again, tucked the memory stick inside his shirt. He saw red when he raised his head and realized Dillard stood there with a little smirk on his face worthy of most politicians.

"That's Doug's thumb flash, isn't it?"

Sheppard could barely speak around the surging swell of his mounting rage. "He asked me to keep it for him."

"Doug slept with the damn thing. He wouldn't ever entrust it to anyone else. Guess we'll be adding theft to your list of transgressions, Sheppard."

Sheppard set the laptop on the step, pressed his fists to this thighs, and stood. When he spoke, his voice was sharp, brittle, but very quiet. "If I were you, Leo, I'd be less worried about my supposed transgressions than I would be about the deal you and Emison culminated on November twelfth of last year." *And let's go farther back, Leo, ole buddy, ole friend. Let's go back twelve years, back to . . .*

Emison looked as if he'd swallowed a brick and it had blocked his windpipe. "What the hell're you talking about, Shep?"

"Emison and Dillard making deals?" Goot said. "Do tell. What sort of deals?"

Blood rushed into Dillard's face and he waved his container of juice around. "I caught him stealing Emison's thumb flash and he tries to turn it around with some bullshit story."

"Three hundred grand hardly qualifies as bullshit, Leo.

And all Doug had to do was arrange for an inmate transfer from Dade's jail to Tango's. So let's connect the dots and figure out who that con was. It's twenty questions time."

"Ding-dong," Goot said in a singsong voice. "I've got the answer."

"You're on, Goot."

"Crystal DeVries."

"And *you,* my friend," Sheppard shouted, pointing at Goot, "win the million-dollar prize! Because here's how I figure it, Leo. Someone pays you a shit load of money to get Devries transferred to the Tango jail, and since you don't have all the right connections, you bring Emison in on the deal. You pay him three hundred grand to do it. He not only arranges the transfer, but he drives to Dade to get her himself—and conveniently loses or misplaces the transfer papers."

"You're a fucking nutcase, Sheppard." His voice sounded as if rubber bands were tightening around his vocal cords.

"It gets even better. The Tango jail's more lax than Dade. It's easier to spring a con. Franklin knew that. And Franklin had five million from his bank heist to play with. How much did he pay you, Leo? A million? Two? It's all right here." He held up the thumb flash. "That's why Doug slept with this thing. It was his insurance." *And he could blackmail you in more ways than one. Let's talk about that category-five folder, Leo. Oh yeah, let's, you son of a bitch.* "And now it's on my laptop. The big question, Leo, is how far back does it go? If memory serves me, you were overseeing banking investigations for the Southeast bureau at one time. I don't think it's a stretch to speculate that you helped Franklin arrange that heist."

"You're really out to lunch, Sheppard."

"We'll see. At the very least, Doug's got enough evidence on here to charge you with bribery."

Throughout this little exchange, Dillard had moved away from the sink and kept stepping back slowly and carefully through the water. Now he was up against a stack of boxes and had nowhere to go. Sheppard and Goot approached him slowly, as though he were a ferocious beast that might strike out at them any second now. But he didn't have a weapon, he was outnumbered, what harm could he possibly do?

Quite a bit, as it turned out. Dillard lowered his head and charged Sheppard like an enraged bull. And Sheppard, his reflexes already slowed with fatigue and anxiety, didn't move quickly enough. Dillard slammed into him, his ribs shrieked, and Sheppard fell back over a low ridge of boxes. They crashed into the water that continued to spew from the drain and rolled through it.

Dillard fought with the fierce tenacity of a scrappy street kid and although Sheppard was taller and also outweighed him, his ribs were screaming and he couldn't get the fucker off him. But he got an arm loose and grabbed Dillard's perfect hair and jerked his head back, back. The skin on his skull and across his forehead tightened and pulled at his eyelids until they had narrowed to slits. The tendons stood out in his neck. He gasped and snorted and Sheppard snapped his head forward and slammed it into Dillard's nose, nearly knocking himself into next week.

Sheppard rolled away, his ears ringing, stars bursting inside his eyes. The thumb flash was so wet it clung to Sheppard's chest like a soggy leaf. *Destroy the evidence:* that had been Dillard's intent. Sheppard shook himself, came up slowly on his knees, and through the haze of his vision, in the spill of light from the lantern, saw Goot holding the kitchen knife to Dillard's neck, blood streaming from Dillard's nose, and his laptop facedown in the water.

"Hey, amigo, you all right?"

Sheppard swept the laptop out of the water and carried it over to the kitchen table. "Slice the bastard's throat."

"That's *murder,*" Dillard squeaked, barely breathing, his eyes wide, startled, terrified.

Sheppard grabbed the few paper towels that remained on the roll and wiped off the thumb flash and then went to work on the laptop. Water streamed from the spaces between the keys, beaded on the screen, dripped from the ports.

"Good try, Leo, but one way or another, I'll extract the evidence."

"There's nothing to extract. You're living in a pipe dream, Sheppard."

"No one gave you permission to speak," Goot snarled, tightening his arm around Dillard's neck and pressing the tip of the knife harder against his neck. Beads of blood appeared.

"Jesus, you're cutting me," Dillard breathed.

"That's the idea, *pendejo.* The big question is how you and Franklin connected."

"It's all in Emison's files." Sheppard actually wasn't sure of that at all. Knowing Emison, the promise of three hundred grand had been enough to quell whatever misgivings or questions he might have had. "And in the event it isn't, then there's always Emison himself. I'm sure he'd be delighted to turn state's evidence to keep himself out of prison."

Dillard smirked. "I hate to tell you this but Doug doesn't look like he's going to be here for breakfast."

Goot pressed the tip of the blade more deeply into Dillard's neck. "Neither will you, asshole. But death's too easy for you. I think I'll just slice out your tongue so I don't have to listen to your horseshit."

"You . . . you talk like a thug, Gutierrez. But you're no killer."

Goot grinned. "Jesus, Leo, you are tempting me so bad, I just can't tell you."

While Sheppard had taken great pleasure in seeing Leo Dillard squirm and pretend that he wasn't scared shitless, the water had been rising steadily. Sheppard grabbed the roll of electrical tape from the table, tore off a long strip, and splashed through the water to Goot and Dillard. He slapped the tape across Dillard's mouth, then jerked his arms behind him and wrapped the tape around his wrists. "I'd love to do your feet, too, Leo, and let you lie in the water as it rises. But I'm more interested in seeing you go to trial."

And more interested, he thought, in the story that he would release to the media about the other file on Emison's memory stick. He pressed his hands down hard against Dillard's shoulders, forcing him to sit on a box. "You move, and I press your face into the water."

He and Goot went over to the kitchen table. While Sheppard put his laptop into his pack, Goot whispered, "We should move to the higher boxes. The water's breaching the barricade pretty fast."

Sheppard nodded and pulled the wet T-shirt off over his head, his ribs complaining. He thought he heard something, a small, odd noise that didn't belong in here. "You hear that?"

"What?"

"I don't know. Probably nothing."

He unwound the wet Ace bandage, dropped it on the floor, wiped his skin dry with a dry black T-shirt that belonged to Franklin. Then he asked Goot to wrap the electrical tape tightly around his ribs. As he did so, Goot said, "Is there enough on that memory stick to indict him?"

"Yes. And then some."

"Such as?"

"Later," Sheppard whispered, eyeing the rising water. "We should move the supplies, too."

"We can move Doug onto the kitchen table and push the table over the barricade and flush with the other wall," Goot suggested. "Then we can put the supplies on top of the boxes stacked around the table."

"Let's do it."

As soon as Goot finished wrapping Sheppard's ribs, he pulled on Franklin's T-shirt and he and Goot went to work. Dillard didn't move. Blood continued to seep from his nose.

He watched them the way a cornered mouse watches a cat, his eyes darting here, there, seeking an exit.

They moved everything up and back away from the barricade of boxes and, gradually, Sheppard realized that a foul odor had crept into his awareness. He thought the toilet had overflowed or backed up and then realized the obvious: it was the water. Sheppard hurried over to the drain, the water now well above his ankles, and shone his flashlight on it. In addition to clumps of mud and grass, he saw bits of shit.

Somewhere up the line, sewage pipes had burst or, more likely, a septic tank had sprung leaks and he, in his bare feet, was standing in it. His mind immediately threw up all the dire possibilities: typhoid, cholera, e-coli, hepatitis. That was just for starters.

"Jesus, what's that stink?" Goot asked.

"A septic ta . . ." Water exploded upward from the drain, a volcanic powerhouse that eclipsed the rest of Sheppard's sentence. It splashed into his face and he stumbled back, frantically wiping the backs of his hands across his eyes, spitting until he had no spit left in his mouth.

As Sheppard spun around to flee for the higher boxes, Dillard shot to his feet and scaled the boxes like a terrified mountain goat. Then the three of them stood on the boxes, paralyzed with horror as raw sewage continued to shoot upward, spraying shit and piss on everything within a five-foot circumference. The geyser gradually shrank to a bubbling shit hole, but by then the cellar floor was covered with half a foot of discolored water with turds bobbing in it like pieces of cork.

Sheppard no longer heard the storm—no wind, no rain, just the rushing tidal wave of his own mortality. And then he didn't even hear that. He seemed to pass into a place of utter and complete silence. For the briefest moment, he wondered if he had died and simply didn't know it yet.

He heard the noise again, a soft, plaintive sound that might break his heart if he followed it. But because it was so out of place, so glaringly odd, he turned his head, listening, trying to determine its source. He crawled across the top of several stacks of cartons, vaguely aware of Dillard's grunts. The noise stopped—and so did Sheppard, head cocked as he listened, as a part of him pleaded with the noise to return.

And it did, just ahead of him and to the left, coming from the wall. His flashlight died, he set it aside to fill with fresh batteries later, and pulled a headlamp out of a zippered pocket in his pack. He wondered where it had come from— Franklin's supplies or his own. He seemed to be losing sight of details like this.

Once he put it on, it freed his hands. He moved another box and exposed a metal grate in the wall. Behind it, a cat meowed and rubbed up against the grate, begging to be freed. It was a soft, buttery yellow mixed with white.

"I'll have you out of there in a second," Sheppard said, and the cat rubbed up against his fingers as he stuck them in the grate.

He pulled at the grate, his mind racing. The cabin had been built during the Civil War, had been given to a freeman and his family after the war, and Tango Key had been strategic in moving slaves off Tango to the mainland. Whatever lay behind the grate, he thought, might very well lead them to freedom.

"Hey, Goot, it's a cat," Sheppard said.

Goot climbed over to Sheppard, but Dillard, uncertain of his status in this sequence of events, hung back, grunting, making faces, trying to make himself understood. Sheppard and Goot ignored him.

The grate was rusty and old and popped off easily. Sheppard set it aside and picked up the cat, a skinny little female with soiled fur and a pink nose smeared with dirt. He set her down on the carton where he sat and Goot dug a can of tuna out of their supplies, popped it open, and set it in front of her. She went after it as if she hadn't eaten for days.

"So can we get through that opening?" Goot asked.

Sheppard turned and shone the headlamp into the hole, the mouth of a concrete pipe. It looked to be about four feet in circumference, large enough for a grown man to crawl through, but questionable, he thought, for a man who was claustrophobic. It seemed to angle uphill and the inside walls were rough and dry to the touch. A memory broke loose and bobbed to the surface of Sheppard's mind. "This leads to that concrete storage unit at the back of the property. We saw it when we came in here."

"That's close," Goot exclaimed with unmistakable hope in his voice. Then he tilted his head toward Dillard. "What about him? He can't crawl with his hands taped behind him. So we either free him or leave him."

"We give him a choice. He can stay or he can leave with us and pull Emison. He'll be between you and me, Goot."

Goot nodded, thinking about it. He and Sheppard both glanced back at Dillard, who waited, watching them, no longer grunting. He knew they were deciding his fate for the next few hours. "What about Emison? We'll have to drag him in the sleeping bag."

"We can't leave him," Sheppard said.

"I know, I know. But the sleeping bag will catch on the floor of the pipe. We need to rig something."

"We'll cut up one of the boxes, tape it to the bottom of the sleeping bag, and make a cardboard sled."

"Good. Yeah, that's good, Shep."

With Dillard's fate still undecided, they prepared Emison and his sleeping bag.

Dillard didn't make a sound, didn't make any sudden moves. He was now on his best behavior.

When they were finished, the cardboard clung like a second skin to the bottom and sides of the sleeping bag and Emison was wrapped up inside it. It wasn't the greatest sled in the world, but it might hold long enough for them to get Emison through the pipe.

"Okay, what about Leo?" Sheppard whispered.

"Shit, man, truthfully? I'd rather leave him."

"Me too." Leave him, yes, until he thought about that *category 5* file. "Leaving him is too easy. The files on that memory stick . . ." Surging anger snagged the rest of his sentence and he just shook his head. "Let's give him the choices."

Goot pulled his kitchen knife from his belt.

They climbed over the boxes to where Dillard sat, staring at the rising water. His eyes moved quickly to Goot and Sheppard. His face shone with sweat. "Here's how it goes down, Leo," Sheppard said. "You can stay here or you can leave with us. If you go through the pipe, you'll be between Goot and me and pulling Emison. Make your choice." Sheppard peeled the tape off Dillard's mouth.

"I want to get out."

"The person behind you," Goot said, "will be carrying the knife. If you fuck up in there, if you do anything, you're a dead man. We clear?"

"You got it. Clear. Definitely."

Nature was a power greater than man, greater than God, Sheppard thought, and Dillard understood that. He would agree to anything to escape the cellar.

Goot held the knife to Dillard's throat as Sheppard freed his hands from the tape. "You don't need the fucking knife, Gutierrez," Dillard said. "I want to get out of here as badly as you two do."

"Oh, so I should trust you?"

Dillard looked contrite. "I won't cause trouble."

Goot let Dillard sit up and Sheppard pulled a rope through

loops on the sleeping bag. Once they got Emison into the pipe, the other end of the rope would be tied around Dillard's waist. They gathered up the cat and their packs.

"Can you do the pipe, amigo?" Goot whispered.

Sheppard glanced out at the putrid water rising on the other side of their barricade and seeping through it to their side. "I don't have a choice."

"I'll lead."

Smart, Sheppard thought. That way, if he froze up in there, he wouldn't block Goot and the others from getting out.

"That means you get the knife." Goot passed it to him, handle first.

The knife didn't have a sheath, nothing that convenient. Sheppard clutched it. "And you get the headlamp."

Goot removed it from Sheppard's head and fitted it onto his own. The light was bright, the batteries strong.

"Let's get moving," Sheppard said.

The cat went in first, eager and quick. Then Goot climbed inside and turned, helping Dillard lift the front of Emison's cardboard sled, while Sheppard picked up the back. The sheriff groaned softly, just once, and lapsed back into silence. Sheppard slipped the last of the mints into his mouth, conjured mental images of vast blue skies and gorgeous, deserted beaches, and repeated his mantra: *I am safe, I am safe.*

But as soon as he was inside the pipe, with the grate snapped back into place, he didn't feel safe. He faced the narrow confines of this new world and realized the pipe wasn't wide enough for him to extend his arms to either side, and that he couldn't sit up without hitting his head. Tons of wet earth pressed down against this pipe. *Against me.* His chest seized up, tightening like an elastic band. Mints, mental images, and mantras weren't going to cut it, he thought, and began to crawl, fighting back one crippling wave of claustrophobia after another.

24

"The government never told the full story about Andrew. Twenty-one communities disappeared that night. Hundreds of people died. The confiscated bodies were hauled out on Burger King trucks."

K.T. Frankovich
Hurricane Andrew survivor

Crystal screamed, the girl shouted and sobbed, the dog howled, the Amazon had fallen and now twitched gracelessly on the floor. Then, as Franklin hauled himself upward, he heard pounding.

The storm? Something against the roof? The shutters?

Pounding at the front door.

Sweet Christ.

He grabbed Crystal by the shoulders and shook her, hissing, "Shut up, shut up. Someone's at the door."

"Wh . . . what?" Crystal stammered.

Pounding again. Harder and louder this time.

The kid suddenly shrieked, *"In here, help, please, in here!"*

Franklin lurched toward her and clamped his hand over her mouth, snapped at Crystal to bring him some electrical tape. Moments later, he slapped a strip over the girl's mouth.

"They'll go away, Billy," Crystal whispered. "If we just stay here, they'll go away."

"We don't know that. Stay here. Secure Lopez."

He scooped up the shotgun and ran into the kitchen, the living room. He couldn't peer out the windows because the shutters covered them. Answer the door and blow whoever it was the fuck away? Christ, Christ, what the hell was he supposed to do?

More pounding. "Help, we need help out here!" a man shouted.

Help? Yeah, right.

Franklin raced into the master bedroom, the bathroom, and skidded to a stop on his knees, in front of the window where Mira had escaped. He raised the window and ran his fingers along the inside edge of the shutters, seeking the button that would enable him to slide them open.

As he pulled the shutters apart just enough to see out, the howl of the storm swallowed the sound they made. The wind sucked away his breath, a succubus that intended to devour his soul as well, and hurled rain into his face. It shrieked through the opening, blew the bathroom door shut, whistled along the edges of the shutters, and tore at the hedges just in front of him. Squinting, Franklin stuck his head through the opening and parted the bushes with his hands.

Bright, powerful lights sliced through the coruscating sheets of horizontal rain, revealing trees that shook with paroxysms of fury, palm fronds flying like dark angels through the wet air, rivers sluicing over the sidewalk and rushing into lakes that now stood in the front yard. It took Franklin a few moments to recognize the lights for what they were, the headlights of a Hummer that had been driven over the lawn and onto the sidewalk, stopping just short of the screened porch. The lights exposed a person in a yellow raincoat who stood just inside the porch, the screen flapping around him.

A cop. He could *smell* it.

Mira had escaped to some other house and called the cops.

Shoot him.

But did he have a buddy still inside the Hummer who would call in reinforcements? Would there be reinforcements during a hurricane? The winds, he guessed, were well into category four and only a warrior cop with visions of heroism would be stupid enough to come outside in this tempest.

I am water, I am water, I am . . . a warrior cop in a raincoat, in the middle of a hurricane, banging on the door of a home where the escaped cons might be. I'm shouting for help so they won't think I'm a cop. . . .

Franklin couldn't tell if there was anyone else in the Hummer. It could be that the cop at the door had left the engine running, the lights on, so that he could see or that he'd just left the headlights on with the engine off. Even more to the point, it was possible his partner was circling to the rear of the house, preparing to break in through one of the shuttered windows.

Either way, the Hummer could provide him and Crystal with a way out of here when the storm had passed. It was a more formidable vehicle than the cars in the garage, capable of traversing any kind of terrain, even debris and ruin. It could get them back to the cabin so he could pick up his money, and although it couldn't cross water, it certainly could make it onto a ferry and get them to the mainland.

Choices, choices.

I am water and . . .

. . . a good Samaritan cop. Doing my civic duty. Tonight I have rescued old ladies, wet cats, stranded children, and dogs. I have escorted ambulances, emergency vehicles, and personnel. I am a hero, I am . . .

. . . here.

Franklin brought the shotgun up, poked it through the moving bushes, aimed, and squeezed the trigger. The clamor of the storm swallowed the explosion—and the cop toppled forward like a tree.

If he had a partner who was in the Hummer, then the partner would see the cop fall and would check it out. Franklin quickly closed the window, the shutters, and raced out of the bathroom. The lights in the hallway blinked off and on several times, then the power died completely. The violent chorus of the storm sounded closer now. Rain battered the skylight in the living room, wind shook the shutters, the house itself seemed to shudder. Franklin groped blindly for the wall to orient himself, pulled out his flashlight, turned it on. The bright beam of Crystal's flashlight appeared at the other end of the hall, bouncing up and down as she loped out of the kitchen.

"What happened?" Breathless. "Who was it?"

"A cop. I shot him." He peered through the door's peephole; no partner raced toward the house. The cop he'd shot was still on the floor of the porch. Good, that was good. "He's on the porch. There's a Hummer in the yard."

"Is there . . . another cop?"

"Not in the Hummer."

"He's somewhere else?"

"Maybe."

"How're we going to find out? Suppose he tries to break in here?"

"Calm down. We're in good shape." He sounded so convincing he almost believed his own lie. "Look, I'm going to pull the guy into the house and we'll have to do it so a minimum of wind gets in here. The porch is set back. That'll help."

"Open the *door?* Are you nuts, Billy? And I don't want a dead person in here." The glow of the flashlight made her features look unbalanced, disproportionate, grotesque. "It's bad luck to bring a dead person into a house. We've had enough bad luck."

"It'll be worse for us if the battery on that Hummer dies. It's our way off the island. If the keys are in his pocket, I might be able to turn off the headlights with the remote." If the Hummer had that option.

"And suppose the keys are in the Hummer?"

"Then I'll get them out of the ignition. I might even pull the Hummer closer to the house."

"After we find out if there's another cop."

"Right."

Hand on her hip: she looked like a skinny little teapot that might tip to the side at any second. "And how're we going to find that out exactly?"

"I don't know yet. First we pull the dead guy in the house. I'm going out there to get him. When I pound on the door, open it just enough so I can pull him in. Don't let the wind jerk the door out of your hands."

"Okay, okay, just go. Hurry."

He turned off his flashlight, tucked it into his back pocket again, and he and Crystal traded weapons. He flicked the dead bolt to the left, disengaging it. Even as the door cracked open a couple of inches, he felt the inexorable power of the wind, a hungry monster eager to get into the house and consume everything.

He slipped out, Crystal yanked the door shut, and Franklin suddenly felt as though he were on one of those spinning carnival rides where the force of gravity plasters you to the walls of the ride and pulls your face and mouth into weird contortions. The wind sang across the metal porch door and whipped the screens so they twanged like an out-of-tune guitar. Even as he stood there with his back pressed up against the wall, a section of screen was torn away and lifted off into the wet light like some exotic bird.

He dropped to his knees, crawled over to the fallen cop. Wind lashed across his spine, rain stung his cheeks. In the illumination of the Hummer's headlights, Franklin could see that the cop's blood ran pink through the water streaming across the porch floor. He saw where the slug had penetrated the back of his raincoat. He turned the guy over, his hood slipped off. Definitely dead. Young, too, maybe thirty. He wore a Tango PD badge.

Franklin grabbed him by the forearms, pulled him over to the door, and kicked it, signaling Crystal to let him in. As she opened the door, the wind tore it out of her hands and she stumbled forward, chasing it, tripped over the body, and fell into the porch door. Franklin shouted at her to get up, fast, and kept pulling the body into the house.

Once he crossed the threshold, he dropped the cop's arms and lurched back onto the porch. Door, Crystal, door, Crystal. *I am water, I am water . . .*

Crystal was on her feet, but barely. Franklin grabbed hold of her arm, shoved her through the doorway, struggled with the door, and somehow got it shut. He turned the dead bolt and sank against the wood, breathing hard, his heart hammering furiously. Crystal was on all fours, shaking her head, sobbing, water streaming off her, but still gripped her flashlight, the beam shooting off across the hallway floor.

The dead man lay between them.

"You . . . you . . ." She rocked back onto her heels, glared at him, looked down at the dead cop, and scrambled to her feet. "Get him outta here!" she shrieked, backing away from the cop.

Franklin didn't have the energy for this. For her. He blocked her out. He became water and flowed across the floor toward the cop. He went through the cop's raincoat pockets and pulled out a handheld radio. It was on, filled with static. He set it aside, unzipped the raincoat, reached inside.

He took the cop's gun, removed his badge, wallet, a set of keys. Hummer keys. One look told Franklin that the remote clicker didn't have the headlight option. That meant this turkey had left them on and that he would have to venture out into the yard, where he wouldn't have even the moderate bit of protection from the porch, to turn them off. He went through the wallet, looked at the cop's badge. Corporal Jim Kilner. When the time came, Franklin would become Corporal Jim Kilner.

He tucked the weapon in the waistband of his jeans. "Would you help me move him into the back bedroom?" Franklin finally looked up at Crystal, who stood about four feet from the cop's body, fist at her mouth, hair plastered against her skull, eyes wide, shocked. She wasn't sobbing now. Wasn't making any sound at all. "Hello? Crystal?"

Blink, blink. Her eyes slipped so slowly toward him it was like watching the movement of molasses. "What?"

"Could you help me pull his body into the back bedroom?"

Blink. "Shit. Yeah. Okay."

Just then, the radio crackled. "Jimbo, Miller here . . ." The transmission broke up with what sounded like wind roaring through a tunnel. ". . . copy?"

Franklin and Crystal looked at each other. *Answer it,* she mouthed.

He scratched his nails across the surface of the radio, mimicking static, and muttered, ". . . copy . . . your position?"

". . . side of the house . . . door?"

"No one home. Let's split. You copy?"

"Copy . . . okay? Your . . . sounds different."

Your voice sounds different: Franklin felt certain that was what Miller had said.

"He knows," Crystal whispered.

Franklin shook his head. "He suspects."

"Jimbo?"

"Meet you at the car." He turned the radio off, removed the dead cop's raincoat, put it on.

"Great idea, Billy. I'll cover you."

"From the bathroom window." He explained how to open

the shutters, what sort of view she would have, where he would be. She threw her arms around his neck, hugging him so tightly that he thought she might squeeze the air from his lungs. Her wet body clung to his—and she kissed him passionately.

"Be careful," she whispered.

Now that he had fallen in and out of love with Mira and had seen her for what she really was—a duplicitous bitch who lied to him, lied repeatedly—he discovered that he was attracted to Crystal again. He kissed her back and slipped out the door in the dead cop's raincoat.

A seamless darkness. Mira's mind instantly slammed into left-brain mode and raced through a physical inventory. Did she ache? Was she bleeding? Was anything sprained or broken?

She seemed to be relatively intact and realized she was sprawled on top of her pack, which apparently had broken her fall. She brought her palms to the surface on which she lay and immediately knew it was concrete, not plywood. A floor, not the attic. Mira pressed back against her feet—it felt solid. She raised her arms above her head, testing the height of wherever she was. Her fingers brushed air. She rocked back onto her heels and patted her pack, fingers fumbling for the zipper. She found it, unzipped a compartment, dug around inside. Matches.

She struck one. Nothing happened. It occurred to her that she might have fallen into some other space and time, just as she had a year ago when she'd pursued the madman who had snatched Annie and taken her through the black water mass and into 1968. No telling where she was now—another dimension, where the usual laws of physics broke down; a nuthouse in the nineteenth century; a flatland of two dimensions.

Mira struck another match. It flared and barely dented the darkness. But it illuminated enough of the area for her to see that she was in the strange little room behind Sheppard's office closet, the place she and Annie had explored in that moment lifetimes ago before Franklin and his entourage had broken into her home. Their *safe* room.

It held a cooler, a couple of blankets and pillows, and whatever else they had stored in here. Mira could hear the wind and rain, but the sounds seemed distant, remote, like background noise in a nightmare. The match burned her fingers, she blew it out, lit two more. She held the matches up above her head, dispersing the glow of the exiguous flames, and glanced around for her flashlight. She found it in a corner of the room, but it no longer worked.

She peered upward. No hole in the ceiling, just the weird half staircase that ended almost where the ceiling began. Was there a door at the top of it that she couldn't see?

She would figure it out later, she thought, and made her way over to the cooler. It was a fraction of the size of the cooler in the kitchen, one of those portable things that Sheppard took with him when he windsurfed. And like the smaller cooler she'd left in her bedroom closet, it didn't hold much.

She blew out this match, lit two more, then unzipped the cooler and reached inside. Even though she wasn't hungry or particularly thirsty, the cooler represented what was familiar, known, something that had existed before the intruders had arrived. It calmed her. She scooped out a handful of ice and ran it over her forehead, eyelids, her cheeks. It cooled her down. She sucked from a container of juice, lit another match, and wondered about how she had come to place a cooler in each of the rooms where she had ended up.

Because you're living in a deeper layer of existence.

Right. Yeah. Uh-huh. She was living in such deep layers now that she didn't know if she would ever dig her way out.

A maniac had her daughter, murderers were loose in her house, Shep was in a cabin in the preserve somewhere, Danielle gripped Tango Key by the balls, and she couldn't pick up squat about anything. If and when she ever got out of here, she needed to go away some place by herself and puzzle through what now seemed to be a central question in her life: why her ability didn't work for her and the people she loved with the same predictability that it worked for everyone else.

She had peered into the darkest corners of Franklin's life, Crystal's life, and had connected at a strange and disturbing level with Tia Lopez. But she couldn't seem to find Shep or Annie or Nadine in any of it. She couldn't catch even the barest glimpse of their futures. It was as if she were trapped in that cellar room six months ago, prisoner of a wacko hellbent on revenge against Sheppard, her abilities lost to her. She felt like half a person, stripped to the bone.

Mira went over to the shelf where she and Annie had stashed some supplies. They weren't in any order, at least no order that Sheppard would approve of, and she rifled through them, hoping to find a flashlight. Or a candle. Or some other remnant of an earlier civilization that would provide light—sticks that she might rub together, flint, anything. Her need for light struck her as primal, as basic to her continued existence as water.

Much to her surprise and delight, she uncovered a package of aromatherapy candles in a variety of colors. She'd bought them when she'd been into feng shui during a brief period of madness and chaos following her experiences with Wacko six months ago. She'd hoped to bolster the health, prosperity, and relationship sectors of her home and business. But even with a compass in hand, she'd gotten the directions wrong and had placed the wrong colors in the area of her home and her bookstore that represented what she hoped to achieve. So much for her short foray into feng shui.

Mira tore open the box and lit a red candle, set it on the floor, then lit blue, green, and yellow candles. With enough light, finally, to see what the hell she was doing, she pawed through the rest of the supplies. Plastic utensils, paper cups and plates, garbage bags, a jar of instant iced tea: all of it was useless. Mira moved rolls of toilet paper, packets of paper napkins, boxes of Kleenex, and there, under several rolls of paper towels, she found Annie's Swiss Army knife. Sheppard had given it to her several months ago, for a Girl Scout trip.

Mira gripped it in her right hand, moved to the door. Ear to the wood, she listened, straining to hear anything that would tell her where Franklin was. All she heard were the cats, meowing, and Ricki, whimpering, all of them close to or inside the closet. Was that a good sign? Or did it mean the intruders were in the office and had closed the animals up inside the closet?

Wouldn't Ricki be barking outrageously if they were in the office?

Maybe not after being shot at.

She listened harder, trying to block out the animal sounds. She heard the relentless fury of the storm and felt as if she were trapped inside a huge conch shell that held the echo of breaking tidal waves and the violent shifting of the ocean's tectonic plates.

Mira brought her open palms to the door and silently begged for information, input, something, anything, anything at all. She felt a violent tug at the back of her neck, as if invisible hands had grabbed the sides of her head and jerked it backward, and she abruptly went elsewhere.

. . . goddamnbastardsshotme . . . twitchinghurtingcan't-controlmusclesbladderoh, Christ, Christ . . . where's my baby . . . oh, Christ, Christ . . . pain . . .

Mira threw herself to the floor and rolled, struggling to shake off the intensity of Tia Lopez's emotions. She felt as if she were suffocating or drowning or being buried under a ton of hot sand. She slammed into the wall, raised herself up on her knees, her hands, and sucked air through clenched teeth.

Then she dived, her mind screaming, into Tia Lopez again.

Tia, snap out of it, stop, you're not alone.

Stupid white girl went and—

It's Mira, calm down, you're okay, let me help. Let's help each other.

Huh? Wha . . . get outta my head, you psycho freak.

Help me. C'mon, we did this before, you and me. Open your eyes. Let me see Annie and Nadine. Hey, you with me? You here? Hello?

Mira heard breathing that was not her own, a hammering heartbeat that didn't belong to her. The taste of jalapeno peppers flooded her mouth so completely that the fumes stung her sinuses and her eyes started watering.

You're in my head, really in there this time . . .

Let me use your eyes, your ears, please . . . Where is he? Where's Franklin?

You can see what I see?

If you let me. Where's Franklin?

Not in here. The doorbell rang. Stupid white girl's around, has a gun. That's all I know.

My daughter, let me see Annie . . .

Darkness. Silence. Mira never would be completely certain whether the conversation, as she had heard it, was what actually took place. Or if any mind-meld had occurred at all. It was entirely possible she'd watched too many episodes of *Star Trek*, too many science fiction movies, and had imagined the whole thing, that she was, at this very second, locked in a delirium triggered by panic and desperation. Possible, but she didn't really believe any of that.

Other sensations and images rushed into her, emotions and experiences from Tia's life, similar to what she had experienced earlier in the bedroom, but now it came to her in greater detail and depth. Mira fought to keep from drowning in Tia's energy. She didn't want to sympathize; she just wanted information on her daughter and Nadine.

She opened herself completely and the images came at her fast, furiously, in no particular order or time sequence, without pause to process what she was taking in.

And when the images dried up to a trickle, Mira's fingers turned in on themselves like claws, her leg muscles tightened and contracted, her eyeballs felt huge, hot, desert dry, and she was suddenly so thirsty it was as if she hadn't had anything to drink in hours. Her bladder filled to aching, her toes cramped, and her shoulder throbbed with acute and terrible pain. Mira suddenly understood that the physical sensations belonged to Tia, that she was so fully immersed in the woman that she felt what Tia felt, and now she saw what Tia saw.

Annie and Nadine. Bound, mouths taped. Annie is on the couch in the family room, Nadine in her wheelchair—and Crystal paces back and forth in front of the French doors, the glow of her flashlight darting about like a firefly in the darkness.

Mira's shock shattered her psychic connection with Tia, returned her own body to her, but also rendered her blind to the other room. She scrambled toward the closet door, the candle in one hand, the Swiss Army knife in the other, and pressed her ear to the wood again.

All she heard was the muted noise of the storm.

She wiped her sweaty hands on her shorts, set the candle on the floor, and opened each blade in the knife, looking for the one that was the longest, sharpest, most deadly. A knife wouldn't do much against a gun, but it was better than nothing.

Mira blew out all the candles except one, turned the knob. The door creaked as it inched open, her knees popped when she slipped into the closet. The cats greeted her with soft purrs, rubbing up against her and begging her for attention and comfort. Ricki whined and licked at her, wagging tail whipping against Mira's arms.

Whispering: "Okay, guys, okay. Everyone needs to go in here now." Mira pushed open the door to the safe room and Ricki led the way inside, with the cats scurrying in behind her.

Mira shut the door and, heart thudding like an old, tired engine in her chest, blew out the candle. She pinched the wick with damp fingers, slipped it into her pocket, and crawled toward the door, through a blackness like coal.

25

"The nine-year period from 1995 to 2003 produced a record 122 named storms, 69 hurricanes, and a near-record 32 major hurricanes."

Palm Beach Post

Annie ground her bound hands together, struggling to loosen the duct tape. The darkness worked to her advantage because the bimbo couldn't see her unless she aimed her flashlight directly at the couch. And so far, she hadn't done that.

In fact, since the doorbell had rung, the bimbo was hyped, edgy. She paced relentlessly, the shotgun cradled in the crook of her arm, the glow of her flashlight bobbing up and down in the darkness like a luminous cork in black waters. Now she paused to press her face to the glass in the porch door and tried to see outside. Annie felt sure the shutters were open slightly to give her a limited view of the porch and its outside door.

Several times, the bimbo Crystal had hurried past Tia Lopez, slumped against the door frame, and into the kitchen and down the hall, out of sight, and Annie wished she would do it now. All she needed was a few more focused minutes to get her hands loose.

Suddenly, the bimbo whipped around and turned the flashlight on Annie, who went completely still. She hurried over and leaned in so close to Annie that she could see the sheen of sweat on the bimbo's face. She smelled sour, scared, but these odors didn't lead Annie into any images. "Here's the deal, kid. Two cops arrived. One of them is dead and the other one is still out there. I ran into the bathroom and opened the window, okay? Billy's in the Hummer, waiting for the cop. But I figure the cop knows we're in here, that he didn't fall for Billy's voice on the radio. Just a few seconds ago, I saw a light outside, off the back porch. I'm sure of it. The shutters are open just a crack and I swear I saw light. So you're going out onto that porch and you're going to shout for help, you're going to . . ."

Blood roared through Annie's skull, drowning out the rest of what the bimbo said. Crystal tore the tape off Annie's mouth and Annie gasped and pulled air into her lungs.

"You got the rules, kid?"

Annie's head moved up, down. The inside of her mouth was so dry she couldn't form words.

"Say something, for Christ's sake."

"Yes." She whispered it. *Let me loose, Bimbo, so I can kick you in the jaw.* "I get it."

"And I assume you understand I'll shoot the old lady if you fuck with me."

"Yes."

"You're going to tell the cop that someone inside the house is injured and you're going to bring him in here. Through the door." She gestured at the French door.

"Okay."

The bimbo tore off the tape at Annie's ankles. "Lean forward so I can get your hands."

"I . . . I could blow . . . away out there," Annie stammered. "The storm is worse at the back of the house, where—"

Nadine shouted into the electrical tape that covered her mouth, banged her cast against the footrest of her wheelchair, shook her head wildly.

"Yeah, yeah," Bimbo said. "I hear ya, ole lady. Tell her to shut the fuck up."

"Nana. It's okay, I'll be okay." But Nadine's eyes, as shiny as wet paint, signaled alarm, a warning, something other than the obvious. Annie didn't know what it meant, what Nadine was trying to communicate.

"Move forward so I can get your hands. C'mon, fast."

Annie scooted toward the edge of the cushion, leaned forward. As the bimbo stooped over to remove the tape from Annie's wrists, Annie snapped upward. The top of her skull slammed into the bimbo's esophagus, and she stumbled backward, gasping for air, and tripped over the coffee table behind her.

The coffee table rolled and slammed into one of the porch doors with the bimbo half on it, her feet grappling for purchase. The shotgun went off and pieces of the plywood that covered the skylight broke apart and rained down. Annie leaped up and grabbed the end table lamp, tearing it from the wall socket. She hurled it. Even though the bimbo's flashlight was now on the floor, there was enough light to see and she rolled right, off the table and onto the floor. The bimbo snapped the weapon upward and fired at the lamp.

The shade tore apart, the bulb shattered—and the slug kept right on going, through the opening in the plywood, and the skylight exploded.

Rain poured through the breach and the wind howled into the family room, a vortex of energy so furious and powerful that it toppled the floor lamp, tore books off shelves, cracked the TV screen, shattered the panes of glass in the porch doors, and shook the hurricane shutters from the inside out.

And suddenly her mother was *here*, in the room, shrieking like some madwoman who had risen from the depths of hell. She grabbed Annie's arm, jerked her down to the floor, and shouted at her to get Nadine and hide in Sheppard's office.

Annie crawled as fast as she could behind the couch. She came up behind Nadine's wheelchair, grabbed on to the handles, pulled back, and gave her a hard shove toward the open office doorway. The last thing she saw was her mother, Warrior Queen, hurling a knife at the bimbo.

The knife sank into the front of Crystal's shoulder and she fell back, shrieking like a terrified baby, and struck the far wall. Before she could rise, before she could recover, Mira dived behind the coffee table and shoved it through the water, against the swirling wind, and it slammed into Crystal as she struggled to stand and knocked her sideways. The shotgun hit the floor and spun through the water.

As Mira shot to her feet to get it, Crystal shoved the coffee table back at her. She leaped out of the way only to trip over something behind her. And suddenly Crystal was on top of her, fighting like some feral alley cat, biting and clawing, scratching, kicking, punching. The prolonged and violent physical contact blew open all of Mira's psychic circuits. Images from Crystal's life poured into her—past, present, future, possible futures, probabilities, all of it coalescing in a single, throbbing instant in which Mira saw Crystal blowing her away.

Everything inside her shut down, as if a divine hand had thrown her master psychic switch, and she kicked and punched and bit. They rolled through the water, closer to the weapon . . .

*   *   *

Alarms shrilled in Tia's head, all of them screaming, *breach, breach*. Wind and rain swept through the room, a swirling tempest that shook windows, banged doors open and shut, hurled books around, toppled boxes and figurines, and ripped pictures off the walls. Water poured across the floor.

Tia ground her wrists, but the tape, wrapped to her elbows, held. She struggled to jerk her legs free, rubbed her face against her shoulder to roll back the tape that covered her mouth, strained the muscles in her legs again. Her feet abruptly snapped loose and she propelled herself across the wet floor on her stomach like some huge, grotesque worm.

The shutters that covered the porch door suddenly flew apart, the door banged open, and a man in a yellow raincoat blew inside—a cop, he was a cop—his hood gone, his shoes gone, his gun drawn. The stupid white girl saw him, reached the shotgun, and fired once, twice, and the cop catapulted backward, crashed into the door, and didn't move. Tia shouted at Mira to run, then leaped at Crystal. Time slowed, sound vanished. In a moment of terrible clarity, a moment that seemed to stretch through eternity, Tia saw Crystal squeeze the shotgun's trigger, and knew that she wouldn't be able to move fast enough to get out of the way.

But nothing happened.

The weapon was empty.

Her bare feet struck Crystal in the chest, knocking her back. As she fell, Tia couldn't maintain her balance, not with her arms still taped up behind her. Crystal slammed into the couch, the impact sent the couch sliding toward the wall, and Tia crashed to the floor, her hip and injured shoulder absorbing the impact. She must have passed out briefly, because she came to with Crystal standing over her, shrieking and hitting her with the shotgun—across the thighs, the legs, the arms.

She rolled, the gun hit the wet floor, and then it was gone and Crystal sprawled facedown. Mira helped Tia up, up. Her head swam, her body was on fire, the wind lashed her. The next thing she knew, she lay flat against a cool, wet floor, her hands and legs completely free of tape. Although she still heard the wind, it wasn't Andrew, it wasn't God. She raised her head and saw Mira and her kid pushing a desk in front of the door. She nearly laughed at that, a desk as a barricade against the end of the world.

Tia blinked again and now the old lady was crawling into the closet. Another blink and she was inside some other place, a small, tight room where the air reeked of human horror, that peculiar and ineffable horror that surfaced when you knew you had only minutes left on the planet.

A shudder went through the room, the walls seemed to shake. The dog howled, the kid sobbed, the cats cowered. The candles someone had lit flickered and danced, threatening to go out. A body, hunched in front of the door, shoved towels and sheets up against the crack, a flimsy barricade against water.

Tia crawled over to the figure—to Mira, it was Mira—and for a moment or two, they just looked at each other, the unspeakable passing between them. The flickering light from the candles played over the surface of Mira's face and her eyes whispered, *You're no longer the enemy, you can stay.*

Tia grabbed quilts and more towels, twirled them into tight rolls, pressed them up against the crack in the door. Her entire body hurt in so many different places that her shoulder no longer held center stage in the pain department. She couldn't feel it at all. It seemed to be dead to her.

When she finally sat back on her heels, so did Mira. When she pressed her hands to her thighs, so did Mira. They were still connected, she thought, and dimly wondered how such a thing could be possible. They pushed back simultaneously from the door, back into the deepest part of the room, the candles flickering, dancing, the heat like some terrible curse. And they huddled there as the stupid white girl banged and kicked at the office door and Danielle roared ashore.

The Hummer shuddered and shook, rain hammered the roof and the doors and pummeled the windshield. Franklin huddled low in the seat, the Sig clutched in his right hand, and waited for the cop. But the minutes ticked by—*how many minutes? How long have I been out here?*—and the cop didn't show. He realized he'd made a very bad choice. One more bad choice in a day of bad choices.

He bolted upright in the driver's seat, rubbed frantically at the fogged glass, but couldn't see a damn thing. The headlights had gone out automatically some time ago and nowhere was there a source of external light. He felt like Jonah trapped in the belly of the whale.

Stuff slammed against the roof and hood of the car. Franklin instinctively jerked his head in toward his body. *Branches? Power lines? What the fuck was that? Get out and run for the house.* But the wind was so much more powerful now that it would fling open the door and seize him by the scruff of the neck as if he were some mongrel dog—or it would exert an inexorable pressure against the door and prevent him from opening it. Wind was air. He didn't know how to become air. *I am water and I . . .*

". . . am in deep shit."

He slammed his fist against the steering wheel, knocked his forehead against it, squeezed his eyes shut. He tried to become water, tried to put himself in that frame of mind, pretended that he was a kid again and that his old man was shouting and his mother was shouting and everyone was shouting, but none of it touched him because he was water.

But he couldn't become water. *Drive closer to the house, pull up parallel to the porch.*

His head snapped upright. Of course. The house would provide some shelter from the wind and he would be able to get out and into the house, into the safe room. Better that room than the car. Never stay in a car during a hurricane: primary rule of the National Hurricane Center. But a Hummer was no ordinary car. It weighed . . .

"Who gives a flying shit how much it weighs?" He turned the key, flicked on the headlights—and saw that a tree had fallen across the sidewalk and branches and leaves covered the hood. Dozens of dark shapes moved across the windshield. Frowning, Franklin leaned forward and brought his fingers to the glass—and abruptly wrenched back, horrified.

Snakes. Jesus God, snakes writhed and slithered across the windshield, some of them trying to burrow behind the windshield wipers and into narrow crevices in the hood. He hit the lever for the wipers and as they whipped back and forth across the glass, some of the snakes were knocked off to either side of the window, others tumbled down onto the hood. Then he started the engine and threw the Hummer into reverse and weaved back down the sidewalk and into the yard.

When he was far enough back, he gunned the accelerator and the Hummer shot forward, aimed at the top of the fallen tree, where the branches were thinner. Seconds later, the tires slammed into it, bounced up over it, slammed down again, and Franklin turned sharply to the right to bring the Hummer parallel to the porch. But he miscalculated his turn and the rear end clipped the metal porch frame. Already weakened by the battering of the wind, the frame collapsed, leaving only the porch roof, jutting out like a misshapen tongue.

And then the roof collapsed, blocking the front door.

Sheets of screen slapped the side windows of the Hummer, whipped away into the darkness, blew up against the walls of the house. Franklin killed the headlights, grabbed his gun, and threw open the door. The wind hurled rain into his face and tore at his hair, his raincoat, his clothes, his skin. He couldn't breathe. He crawled over the pile of debris and somehow made it to the front door. But it wouldn't open, debris blocked it. He scrambled across it, cutting his hands and knees, the wind tearing at him, the rain so harsh that it felt like acid against his cheeks, his eyes. He got the shutters open, raised the window, and crawled into the house. He slammed the window shut and collapsed against the floor.

Franklin lay there, gasping, his heart thudding, his fingers moving impotently against the cold, hard floor. Then he rolled onto his back, his side, and followed the beam of his flashlight up the hall. Where the light ended, he saw Crystal, sitting against the wall, arms covering her head, knees drawn to her chest. He knew he heard sounds that he should not have heard inside the house, but he couldn't make sense of them. The entire spectrum of his perceptions had shrunk to nothing more than a visual: Crystal huddled against the hallway wall.

Why the hell was she against the wall?

He heaved himself up, crawled over to the flashlight, got shakily to his feet, and moved swiftly up the hallway. Sound returned to him, as though someone had turned up the volume on a TV, and suddenly everything fell into place. The sounds he heard were wind and rain, right here inside the house with him, an auditory vortex of violence. He moved through water that ran freely across the floor, a swollen river filled with dirt and leaves and bits of wood.

Breach, there's a breach, my hostages, where the fuck are they? I am water, water, I am . . .

Crystal.

He slid to his knees in front of her—and saw a knife sticking out of her shoulder. Swiss Army knife. The entire blade embedded. Blood had turned her wet T-shirt a pale pink. The shotgun lay on the floor beside her.

"Jesus." He tucked the weapon under his arm, scooped her up into his arms, and hurried toward the utility room.

The doors to the family room banged open and shut repeatedly, water streamed out of it, into the kitchen. Wind whipped through the kitchen, water ran everywhere. He knew what had happened. He knew. No Lopez, no kid, no old lady. The skylight, gone.

He set Crystal on one of the quilts in the utility room, slammed the door, locked it, and shoved another quilt up against the crack beneath the door. Then he turned his flashlight on the knife.

Had it hit an artery? Would she bleed to death if he pulled it out?

He didn't know. He pawed through the stack of towels on the dryer, folded a hand towel in two, set it on the floor beside him. "Babe, can you hear me? Hey, Crystal, you with me or not?"

"With," she murmured, her eyes fluttering open.

"Good," he said, and slid out the knife.

She screamed and snapped upward, her eyes wild, and he pushed her back against the quilts and pressed the towel over the wound. "Keep pressure on it. I—"

A shrieking banshee eclipsed the rest of his sentence. The utility room door shuddered, the walls shook, the entire house seemed to be on the verge of collapse. And then a sound he would never forget filled the room, the house, the world, a thousand freight trains applying their brakes at the same instant, a screech of metal against metal.

He grabbed one of the other quilts, threw himself to the floor, jerked the quilt up over them, and flung his arms across Crystal's body, holding her tightly against him. He wasn't sure whether he was providing protection or seeking it. A moment later, such distinctions ceased to matter. The wind ripped away the roof as though it were no more substantial than the tin lid of a tuna fish can.

26

"Do not venture out after the hurricane has passed. There will be debris, flooding, fallen power lines, and possibly live wires that can electrify entire areas."

Tango Key Gazette

Extreme heat, low ceiling, darkness, echoes: all of it exacerbated Sheppard's certainty that he was being buried alive.

As he crawled along behind Dillard at the end of the line, it took all his resources just to move and to keep his claustrophobia sealed up in a metal container in his head. His mints were gone and the images he conjured of vast blue skies and oceans didn't do much. He kept repeating his mantra, *I am safe,* but he didn't feel safe. It helped, though, that the sound of Emison's cardboard sled scraping across the floor of the pipe remained soft, rhythmic, a focal point for his concentration.

"Got to stop," Dillard announced, breathing heavily.

"If we keep stopping, we're never going to get there," Goot griped.

"It's your turn to pull the sled, Gutierrez," Dillard barked.

Sheppard whacked the flat edge side of the knife across the sole of Dillard's foot. "That hurt," Dillard bellowed.

"That's the idea. The deal was that you pull the sled. Keep moving."

"Just let me catch my breath."

Can't stand it in here much longer, gonna lose it, gonna freak . . . Sheppard slipped back, arms stretched out in front of him, nose touching the cool concrete, his butt resting against his heels. He brought his arms back alongside his body, like folded wings. The child's pose, a yoga position Mira had suggested, sometimes mitigated an attack, a fact as mysterious as the effects of the mints on his claustrophobia.

Sheppard forced himself to breathe, to visualize those fields and beaches and vast, open skies. Despite his best efforts, he began to feel the weight of the wet earth pressing against the pipe, embracing it, squeezing it. His breath balled in his chest, his fingers now gripped his thighs, sweat seeped from his pores. He squeezed his eyes shut to close off any visionary input that would exacerbate his nausea and the attack. The only alternative to this, he reminded himself, was to turn around and head back to the cellar, where he surely would drown in sewage. That realization helped calm him.

When they began moving again, the cat—now named Liberty—trotted back through the pipe and meowed at Sheppard, as if urging him to hurry up. "Just lead the way, girl." He stroked her briefly, then she scampered away from him, pulling out ahead of Goot and Dillard.

Sheppard concentrated on his movements—left hand, right knee; right hand, left knee; repeat—and fell into the rhythm of it. After a while, the rhythm mesmerized him. He had become a pack animal no different than a burro, an elephant, a llama, a horse, following the rest of the herd to wherever they were going. He realized the pipe seemed to be slanting upward, that his pack now scraped the roof, that the walls were closing in on him. He immediately dropped into a child's pose again, groped frantically for another mint, but remembered he had finished the last one. He brought up his stock images. Nothing worked. His mouth flashed dry, sweat streamed from his pores, his head spun. He was seconds away from a full-blown attack of claustrophobia.

"The pipe's climbing and narrowing," Goot reported. "And it smells damp up here."

Sheppard resisted the urge to tear off his pack and either hurl himself upward or scramble back toward the cellar. If he hurled upward, he would knock himself out. And he couldn't go back. But the bottom line was that anything remotely resembling panic would feed into the claustrophobia. So he forced himself to stretch out on his side, to remove his pack slowly, to reach inside. *Get bottled water. Roll across face, back of neck. Okay, better now, keep eyes shut. Find a wide, open space in your head.*

"Shep? Are you okay?" Goot called.

"Just getting water from my pack." No problem. None at all.

But Goot knew him nearly as well as Sheppard knew himself and also knew that he had to be tactful or his claustrophobia would become one more weapon in Dillard's arsenal. "Leo and I are going to keep moving ahead, amigo. Just take your time."

"What's wrong with him?" Dillard asked.

"He's got fractured ribs."

Sheppard sat up as much as he could without hitting his head on the pipe's ceiling, tilted the bottle to his mouth, drank. He slipped the bottle back inside his pack, set it on the floor of the pipe, then rolled onto his hands and knees again. He crept forward, pushing his pack along in front of him. The flashlight provided just enough light so that he could see a foot or so in front of him, but not so much light that he would be able to see just how confining the pipe actually was.

"Shep?" Goot called.

"Yeah, I'm behind you."

"The pipe curves, climbs, and narrows a lot of up here." Goot's voice echoed eerily. "You'll have to, uh, move through on your stomach."

Curves. Climbs. Narrows. The verbs nearly collapsed the walls Sheppard had built around himself. He crawled faster, faster. And then the line came to an abrupt halt and Sheppard raised his head—only to wish that he hadn't. The combined beams of their flashlights reflected off the curved walls of the pipe and reached out far enough ahead of them to reveal a pipe so narrow it amounted to little more than a crevice through which they would have to slither. *For how far? For how long? Suppose the flashlights die?* Sheppard's breath hitched in his chest, blackness swam in his peripheral vision.

Can't do it. Gotta turn back.

A bright light struck Sheppard in the face and he squinted against it. "Shep, you're looking green, like a kid who just got off a carnival ride." Dillard laughed. "I don't recall ever seeing any mention of claustrophobia in your psyche records."

Just the idea of Dillard reading his psyche evaluations was such an affront to Sheppard that he blurted, "You'd better be more worried about your Andrew cover-up, Leo, about the Burger King trucks that you ordered into the containment area to haul out the dead bodies, about the mass graves for the migrant workers and the radiation leaks from the Turkey Point nuclear plant. You'd better be very worried about all that, Leo, because when I get finished with you, you won't have a job left, much less a fucking career."

Dillard moved with the speed of a professional assassin—divesting himself of the sleeping bag rope, spinning around on his stomach, scrambling over Emison—and lunged at Sheppard. It happened so fast that Sheppard reacted instinctively. He pushed back and jabbed out with the knife.

Dillard bellowed, *"My hand, you cut my fucking hand!"* He propelled himself toward Sheppard again.

Enraged, Sheppard turned with more dexterity than he thought possible in such a confined space, snapped his legs up close to his chest—and kicked. His bare feet struck Dillard in the head and he collapsed against the floor of the pipe. For moments, Sheppard lay there on his back, his ears ringing, heart hammering, sweat pouring off him. He stared at the ceiling of the pipe. Too close to his face. Tons of earth on top of it. Tomb, tomb . . . Sheppard rolled onto his side, lifted himself up onto his hands and knees, and shook his head like a dog with ear mites.

Gradually, Goot's voice pierced his awareness. "Shep, Leo's out cold. Let's leave him a flashlight and get Emison outta here. Can you get past him?"

Sheppard turned again, more slowly and with far less dexterity this time. Dillard was sprawled directly in front of him. "I think so." Sheppard found his pack, shrugged it on, and moved up against the side of the pipe. He crawled slowly past Dillard, careful not to touch him for fear it would rouse him. He paused at the foot of Emison's sleeping bag and Goot passed him a flashlight to leave next to Dillard. Sheppard turned it on and set it next to Dillard's hand.

"I'll pull," Goot said. "But we'll get outta here faster if you can push, amigo."

Push. Sure. He could push. He took off his pack and set it on the sleeping bag, and as Goot pulled, he pushed. It gave him something to concentrate on. As long as he kept his eyes on the pack, he could ignore the proximity of the pipe's walls in his peripheral vision.

"Is all that shit true?" Goot asked. "About Andrew?"

"It's on this memory stick Doug gave me."

"But is it true? I never heard anything about Burger King trucks and—"

"I saw the Burger King trucks, Goot. I spent five days in that wasteland and when I resigned, I turned in a letter detailing what I saw. And Dillard showed up at my place with some DOD guys and told me I was suffering from post-traumatic stress and could be treated at the government's expense."

"In other words, shut up about this or we'll make sure you end up in a padded room."

"So I left the country."

"Then we're going to do whatever it takes to bring the fucker down."

Amen to that, Sheppard thought.

"We've known each other—what? Five years? How come you never mentioned anything about this?"

"Because every day I do my best to forget it happened. Until now, I never had any proof that Dillard was involved."

"Where'd Emison's information come from?"

"I'm not sure. My computer died before I got through the whole document. But I think he got the information as insurance, just in case Dillard tried to double-cross him."

"Shit, man. This is huge. But I doubt if Dillard was making decisions in a vacuum. FEMA had to be involved, too."

"FEMA was in charge and Dillard was their bureau liaison."

Sheppard realized that Goot intentionally kept the conversation going to distract him. It seemed to work, too, until the pipe shrank in size with shocking quickness, the walls compressing, pulling in, the roof sloping downward so steeply that he was forced to flatten out on his stomach. The mantra didn't work. His visualizations didn't work. And now Goot was silent, conserving his energy for the uphill struggle. For long, terrible moments, the only noises were the rhythmic scraping of the cardboard sled and the heaving of their collective breaths.

Then, behind him, Sheppard heard Dillard, grunting and

groaning. He glanced back and saw Dillard's flashlight bouncing erratically in the dark. The only thing worse than Dillard
in his face was Dillard at his back. *Move, move.*

Suddenly, Emison began thrashing about and shouting,
"No! No! Don't let them, no!"

Sheppard realized that Emison was trying to escape the
sleeping bag and it placed a tremendous strain on Goot, who
still struggled to pull him uphill. "Goot, hold on. Let me get
him quiet."

Goot's headlight, Dillard's bouncing flashlight, even the
beam of Sheppard's flashlight, exposed the interior of the
pipe in such excruciating detail that Sheppard saw more than
he needed to—that the roof of the pipe was barely six inches
above his head, the pipe was no more than two and a half feet
wide. He couldn't extend his arms in either direction, couldn't
sit up, couldn't do anything except struggle against the urge
to rear up and claw at the roof of the pipe like some caged
and crazy beast.

He squeezed his eyes shut, forced himself to breathe
more deeply. *You will do this.* He opened his eyes and inched
forward, across the bottom of the sleeping bag, over his own
pack, and stretched out alongside Emison. "Doug, it's Shep.
You need to calm down, man. We're nearly out of here.
Don't struggle."

Emison turned his head and his eyes opened wide, eyes
filled with shock, pain, terror—and recognition. "Flash," he
murmured.

"Got it right here around my neck." He held up the memory stick so Emison could see it.

"Good," he rasped.

"Doug." Whispering now. "Where'd you get the information on Dillard and Hurricane Andrew?"

Emison's mouth seemed to twitch into a small, sly smile.
"Buddy . . . at FEMA. All there. Names, dates, you'll see."
He shut his eyes and slipped away again.

"Touching," Dillard muttered from behind him.

Sheppard turned his head and shone his flashlight down the pipe. Dillard was maybe five feet behind him. He froze when the beam of the flashlight hit him in the face, and in those moments, Sheppard saw malignancy in Dillard's sweaty face, his cunning eyes. But in the same moment, he realized that Dillard's corruption was the human face of American imperialism. He'd been cut from the same cloth as the people who had invaded a sovereign country for greed and profit, who claimed to know nothing of torture in Iraqi prisons, who waged a religious war against Muslim countries that might last as long as the Crusades, and who had plunged the country into a debt so massive that Annie's grandchildren would still be paying it off. Dillard, a lifer bureaucrat, symbolized the greedy, beating heart of darkness that had infected the country since the theft of the 2000 election.

In the end, Sheppard thought, when charges and counter charges were brought, when an internal investigation was launched into the Franklin fiasco, Dillard might very well come out with a promotion while he and Goot would be fired. If you didn't toe the line, you got kicked out of the line.

But one way or another, Sheppard would make him pay for all of this, from Andrew to Franklin.

"Let's move, Goot. He's quiet now. Get in front of me, Leo." Sheppard waved the kitchen knife and moved to the side of the pipe.

Dillard squeezed past him without saying another word.

They inched forward. Every few moments, Goot announced what was coming up—a curve, dampness, he could see the cat, they were close to the end. Sheppard suspected he did it for his benefit, to reassure him they were making progress. But as his usual bag of tricks failed him, Sheppard felt the tightness in his chest now expanding and spreading throughout his entire body. He suddenly couldn't move at all. Fear paralyzed him.

Sweet Christ, move . . .

Can't, his mind screamed.

"Goot, hey, Sheppard's locked up. He's frozen. He's not moving."

"Leave him alone," Goot called back. "Let's get Emison out first."

Can't move, can't go another inch.

The paralysis ratcheted the level of his panic, his paralysis, and increased his difficulty in breathing. His heart roared like a jackhammer.

"I can see the end, Shep," Goot hollered. "I can see it, fifty feet in front of me."

Right now, fifty feet might as well be fifty miles.

"He's still not moving," Dillard repeated.

Sheppard heard every word they said, but it was as if he were a bystander, an outsider, eavesdropping on strangers.

"Leo, I'm going to pull Doug on through and then come back in and get Shep out."

No, don't leave me the fuck here. Sheppard screamed at his muscles to twitch, at his body to move. But sweat poured off him, his brain screamed for air, space, light.

Fields, beaches, skies, please . . .

Then he smelled smoke. He didn't know where it was coming from, but he could see it in his head, balls of fire tumbling through the pipe and burning him alive. Air exploded from his mouth, his feet flew upward, struck the roof of the pipe, and his arms jerked into action. He clawed at the floor of the pipe, fingertips now on fire, raw and bleeding as he pulled and pushed his way forward. His body writhed, his primal brain screamed, blood roared in his skull.

"Not much farther, Shep," yelled Goot. "I've got my flashlight shining on you. See it? Can you see it? Say something, Shep."

His mouth fell open, but nothing came out except the anguished sound of his breathing.

"I'll grab your arms," Goot shouted.

And suddenly Goot was right in front of Sheppard, angled down into the pipe like a diver from a high board, and he grasped Sheppard's forearms and pulled. Sheppard pressed the balls of his feet against the pipe, pushing himself forward faster, faster, toward the promise of fresh air, space, light. And when he finally popped free, he sprawled on a cool, concrete floor, his chest heaving, his fingertips and toes bleeding, and was unable to move another inch.

His stomach heaved and he pushed up fast on his hands, rocked back onto his heels, and puked.

27

"Hurricane Andrew was the most expensive natural disaster in U.S. history, It caused more than $26.5 billion in damage, left 250,000 people homeless, and more than 700,000 insurance claims were filed."

from cnn.com

Since emerging from the pipe, Sheppard no longer felt as fragile as newly blown glass. Sound had returned to his world—howling wind and rain lashing the building with a kind of malevolent glee—and he could breathe normally again. Stand upright. Stretch out his arms. Dillard was no longer at his back. Even though the storage unit wasn't much larger than the cellar, it seemed larger because there weren't any nooks, crannies, stairs, or shadowed places. The ceiling was higher.

The building was windowless, concrete block, with a cement floor. No water seepage. The front door was heavy-duty metal. There was a cat door at the bottom of it, but it was latched. A Harley and a boat stood on the opposite side of the room. To his right lay a workbench, a full-size fridge, a utility sink. The fridge was running off a large propane tank, which led Sheppard to believe the building didn't have electricity. Too bad. He would love to boot up his computer and read Emison's files in their entirety.

He unzipped his pack, handed Goot the ham radio, and removed the first-aid kit and a large electric lantern. Goot, kneeling next to Sheppard, nodded his head toward Dillard. "What do you want to do about him?"

Dillard now stood at the utility sink, running water over his cut hand. "Nothing for now. He's not going anywhere. Let's keep our distance. He knows the score. Besides, I lost the kitchen knife in the pipe."

"We don't need a weapon to take him. There're two of us. If he gives us trouble, we just tape him up again." He tapped the ham radio and set it down. "Right now, we need news on this storm. And maybe I can get a cell signal here. If there's enough power in the phone."

Sheppard picked up the lantern, the first-aid kit, and stood. Was he imagining it or did the wind and rain seem less vicious now?

"You need help with Doug?" Goot asked, already fiddling with the radio.

"Nope. By the way, thanks."

"For?"

"Getting me out of the pipe."

Liberty trotted over to Sheppard and rubbed up against his leg. Goot aimed his index finger at her. "Thank *her* for getting us out of that death trap. In fact . . ." He dug into his pack, pulled out a can of tuna, popped it open, and set it on the floor. Liberty went after it, but she had company—a larger cat that looked exactly like her, except that her nipples sagged, heavy with milk. The mom.

"Looks like you and Mira now have two more cats."

Great. And they could open their own animal shelter.

Sheppard went over to Emison. He appeared to be sleeping, but his breathing sounded ragged. His skin was cool and clammy, not warm and dry. Changes, but what did they mean? Sheppard ripped the tape off the sides of the sleeping bag, unzipped it, folded it back from Emison's body. His T-shirt was sopping wet, the bandage around his wound had soaked through with blood, and fresh blood seeped from the edges of it.

Shit, shit. He didn't have any fresh bandages, latex gloves, or fresh clothing or linen. If he unwrapped the wound to squirt Betadine over the stitches, he would have to wrap it up in the bloody bandages again. Was it time to give him more Augmentin? Water, he thought. Maybe Emison just needed something to drink.

Then Emison gasped, struggled upward on his elbows, his hands, his eyes as dark as walnuts and as wide as dinner plates. "Dad," he whispered, and fell back against the sleeping bag. His body twitched, went still.

Alarmed, Sheppard scooted up to the other end of the sleeping bag and shone his flashlight into Emison's face. His eyes stared vacantly at the ceiling. He touched his fingers to Emison's neck, seeking a pulse.

Nada. Nothing. Zip. Gone.

"You're not doing this, Doug," he muttered, and quickly slipped his hand under Emison's head and lifted it upward, so it was slightly tilted. He placed the heel of his other hand on Emison's forehead and pressed downward, elevating his chin. With the hand that was on Emison's forehead, Sheppard pinched his nostrils shut, took a deep breath, and brought his mouth tightly over Emison's. He breathed in, counting in his head, one breath every five seconds, for a total of twelve breaths per minute.

CPR. How easily it came back to him when he needed it.

But would it hot-wire Emison's heart, his lungs?

Emison's chest expanded, but when Sheppard paused and brought his ear close to the sheriff's mouth, he didn't hear any air escaping. Christ. Nothing. He pressed his mouth to Emison's again, kept breathing, twelve breaths a minute, over and over again. And then he slammed his fist against Emison's chest, shouting, *"Breathe, you bastard. Breathe."*

He felt a hand on his shoulder. Goot's hand.

"Shep, he's dead. You can't do anything else."

Sheppard tried for another two minutes, but air never whispered from Emison's mouth.

He finally rocked back onto his heels, feeling as if he'd been sucked dry. Emotions, all of them negative, scrambled around inside him like prisoners seeking their position in the higher scheme of things.

It didn't matter that he and Emison hadn't agreed on everything, that they hadn't been close. The point was that throughout this ordeal, Sheppard had become Emison's guardian, his nurse. Emison, in turn, had entrusted Sheppard with something that illuminated events that had led not only to this moment, but to experiences Sheppard had had twelve years ago, in one of the defining periods of his life.

Now he was dead. Sheppard had failed him. Maybe if he hadn't frozen up in the pipe, if he'd gotten out faster, if he had made different choices . . . If, if, if.

"Christ," he whispered.

Already, Emison's lips were turning vaguely blue. Goot closed Emison's eyes, folded the top of the sleeping bag over his face, and zipped it shut. Sheppard finally raised his head and there stood Dillard, staring at the sleeping bag. His eyes met Sheppard's and, for the briefest moment, his mouth shifted into a mocking smirk. *Ha, ha, Sheppard. Guess he won't be testifying against anyone.*

Rage propelled him to his feet, arm swinging. His fist connected with Dillard's chin, and he staggered to the right, but didn't fall. He lunged for Sheppard, bellowing and snorting like an enraged and injured bull, and punched Sheppard in the side. His ribs lit up with pain, air rushed from his lungs, and then adrenaline flooded through him. He blocked Dillard's next blow with his forearm and kicked him in the balls. Dillard doubled over, gasping. Sheppard grabbed the back of his shirt, threw him to the floor, and straddled him, the weight of his own body holding Dillard down. He sank his fingers into Dillard's usually perfect hair and slammed his head against the floor. No telling how far he might have gone if Goot hadn't pulled him off.

"What the hell're you doing, man? You want him to stand trial, remember?"

Sheppard slid off Dillard's back and rolled onto the floor, appalled that he had lost control in such a violent way. Maybe everything Nadine believed about him was true. He rubbed his hands over his face, the fury bleeding away from him now. "The bastard was smirking about Doug's death."

Goot tore off strips of duct tape. "So let him smirk with his mouth taped. With his entire body taped. And he's going to stay like that until we get him into a jail cell."

Sheppard sat up, nodding, struggling to shake the deepening malaise that he felt. He got shakily to his feet and weaved across the room, eager to put as much distance as quickly as possible between himself and Dillard. He finally stopped at the Harley.

He walked around it, a black monster of a bike, all spiffed up and polished, with room in the back for a second person and bags hanging on either side for supplies. The key was in the ignition. Sheppard turned it, checking the gas tank. It was full. To Sheppard, the Harley symbolized the depth of Franklin's hubris, his escape in the event that all else failed, the vehicle that would whisk him and his *chiquita* off into the sunset.

Sheppard straddled it, placed his hands on the handlebars, allowed his body to remember what it was like to ride one of these. Had the eye come ashore yet? Was the storm still stalled or on its way out? Would it be possible for him and Goot to escape the preserve on a Harley and make it to Mira's?

It would mean leaving Dillard here, with Emison's body, but without a vehicle, Dillard couldn't escape. Even if he managed to free himself from the tape and walk out of the preserve, he couldn't leave the island any more than the cons could. In a best-case scenario—minimal damage to the island—the ferries wouldn't start running for a day or two and traffic wouldn't be allowed across the bridge until it was deemed to be safe. And that was only if the Tango bridge hadn't collapsed. Short of swimming to the mainland, Dillard would be stranded here like everyone else.

Sheppard took inventory of the contents of his pack and removed everything that was nonessential. That left him with his laptop, an extra flashlight and batteries, a change of clothes, and a raincoat, and with room to spare for water and food.

"Hello, Ralph, Ace, Luke. This is John Gutierrez and Wayne Sheppard. Anyone copy? Over." Crouched at the radio now, Goot continued to attempt making contact with someone—and only got static.

Sheppard opened the refrigerator. His flashlight revealed plenty of cold water, juices, Gatorade, several bags of dried fruit and trail mix. He took a bag of dried fruit, several bottles of water and Gatorade, and opened the side door to the freezer. It was jammed with stuff—frozen pizzas, frozen burgers, vegetables, muffins, breads, everything pushed back deeply on each of the four shelves. From the looks of it, Franklin had been planning on lying low here at the cabin for a prolonged time. Even so, there was enough food in here to feed Tango Key's entire population for a week.

Puzzled, Sheppard moved stuff around, then took out some of the items so he could see better. Pressed up against the back of the lowest two shelves were four brown paper bags, like the lunches Mira prepared for Annie during the school year, except the bags were much larger.

He removed one of them, opened it—and turned, his back to Dillard just in case he had come to. He didn't want Dillard to see what he was doing. What he held. What he'd found. Each paper bag contained twelve to fifteen freezer-size Baggies stuffed with hundred-dollar bills. He couldn't tell how many bills because the Baggies and the bills were rolled up like sausages and had frozen. But even if each Baggie held, say, a hundred hundreds, that would mean ten grand per Baggie. If each Baggie held two hundred hundreds, it was twenty grand.

Sheppard did the math quickly in his head and nearly choked on his tongue. It was possible that these four paper bags held as much as a million bucks. It was a small percentage of Franklin's total bank take, but it was more money than Sheppard had ever seen in his life. And it would be of enormous interest to Dillard, he knew. In fact, it probably would be of such great interest to Dillard that the cash could disappear into a Dillard black hole.

He unzipped his pack, fitted his extra shirt around his laptop, and stuffed the bags of money inside. It wouldn't take long for them to thaw in this heat and he didn't want the water to seep into his laptop. Thanks to Dillard, it already had suffered water damage.

The radio continued to spew static. Goot finally came over. "What'd you find?"

Sheppard showed him. Goot's eyes widened, he murmured in Spanish, removed a Baggie filled with the frozen bills, and held it up to his flashlight. "Holy Christ. Franklin's bank take?"

"At least part of it."

The radio crackled. "Shep, Goot, it's Ace. You there? Over."

They both hurried over to the radio. "Shep here, Ace. We had to evacuate the cellar. We're in a concrete storage unit behind the house, close to the woods. Over."

"We don't have any official readouts on the storm, guys. We lost touch with most of our operators like Ralph and our regular radio just picks up static. But we think the winds are falling off. We don't know if it's because the eye is making landfall or if the storm is passing. Either way, if it keeps falling like this, we can get out. I need specific directions to where you are. Over."

Sheppard gave Ace directions from Old Post Road. "How far are you and Luke from us?"

"Distance isn't the problem. It depends on the damage in the preserve. We've got the refrigerated truck we use for street performances."

Plenty big for what Sheppard had in mind. "If you can get us out to the road, we can get to Mira's from there."

"Yeah? On what?" Ace asked.

"A Harley."

"Risky, Shep. There's going to be a lot of debris and live wires lying around. If the storm actually is moving on, the winds are still going to be strong enough to knock you off that bike. Even if this is the eye that's making landfall, we have no way of telling how fast the storm is moving, so we don't know how long the window of opportunity will last."

"The eye's fifty miles wide, right?" Sheppard asked.

"The last I heard, it had shrunk to about thirty miles," Ace replied. "Even so, that's big enough to cover the entire island. In theory, there won't be much if any rain, the winds should be relatively calm, it may even be possible to see some stars. But as the eye moves on, the higher winds will start up again with a vengeance, in the opposite direction."

"Just get here," Sheppard said.

Goot asked, "What damage reports have you heard?"

"News has been spotty. Hours ago, we heard that the Tango pier vanished in the storm surge, the downtown is flooded, the jail and the library are gone, and so is part of the hospital. We had an operator up in Pirate's Cove who was giving us periodic reports. He was taking in neighbors whose homes were damaged. Our last report from him came in some time back. He said a freight train was on its way through his place— then the transmission went dead."

Sheppard's heart flopped around in his chest like a dying fish. Pirate's Cove was just up the road from his and Mira's place. "Ace, do you have any weapons?"

"Three semiautomatic Glocks."

A regular arsenal. "Bring them."

"You got it. We'll call you as we're leaving, so keep the radio tuned to this frequency. Over and out."

Rain continued to batter the building, but now Sheppard definitely heard a difference in the storm's fierceness. Dillard had come to and rolled onto his side so he could watch them. "How fast did Andrew's eye move over Miami?" Goot asked.

"I don't know. I slept through most of that storm. But Andrew's eye was only twenty miles wide. Blink and it's gone."

"How the hell are we going to know if it's the eye or if the storm is moving on?"

"Beats me. C'mon, let's move everything closer to the door."

They spent the next thirty or forty minutes moving their belongings, Emison's body, and the Harley up close to the door. Sheppard found a cat carrier on the storage shelves above the workbench, small but large enough to accommodate both cats during the move onto the truck.

Dillard occasionally grunted and shouted and rolled across the floor, a regular mummy man. But when his antics refused to elicit any response in either Sheppard or Goot, he fell strangely silent, eyes widening and filling with abject terror. Sheppard figured he thought they were going to leave him here in the building, wrapped up as tightly as meat in a sausage, defenseless against the hurricane.

The radio came alive again. "Shep, Goot. It's Ace. We're shoving outta here in a few minutes. Be ready."

"Done," Sheppard replied. "Over and out." He picked up the radio and set it on top of his pack, then he and Goot went over to Dillard and crouched on either side of him.

"How's it going, Leo?" Goot asked.

Grunts, muffled shouts.

"I think he may have a few words to say, Goot." Sheppard peeled the tape off Dillard's mouth.

Dillard stammered, "You . . . you can't leave me like this. I'll . . ."

"We might be open to negotiation," Sheppard said.

His eyes turned as flat and secretive as the dark side of the moon. "How much?"

Sheppard and Goot regarded each other as though they were seriously considering it. "Naw," Sheppard said, shaking his head. "I'd rather see you rot in prison."

"You fucking moronic asshole, you—"

Goot pressed the tape back over Dillard's mouth. "Get his feet, Shep."

They carried him over to the door and set him beside the sleeping bag that held Emison. Sheppard cracked open the door and shone his flashlight into the darkness. Rain whipped through the beam of the flashlight and although the wind blew furiously, it was nothing like before, when the garage had collapsed.

He stepped out the door, then shut it and held it closed with his body. Rain stung his face and the wind howled around him, shaking the darkness as though it were some huge tambourine. But he reveled in the sense of space, the blessed space denied him in the cellar and later, in the pipe.

He inhaled the cloying wet scent of the earth, greenery, and felt strength and hope flowing into him.

Goot banged on the door and Sheppard moved away from it so he could come out. He held an electric lantern high above his head and stood there next to Sheppard, a Diogenes lighting the way to their rescue and redemption.

28

On September 8, 1900, the Galveston Hurricane slammed ashore in Galveston, Texas, and killed six thousand people, making it the deadliest natural disaster in the U.S.

Groans, whimpers, labored breathing: the noises are so close to Mira they nearly touch her. Somewhere beyond herself, she hears hums and hissing, shrieks and howls, animal sounds. Her eyes are open, but just barely, and all she sees is blackness. Her eyelids feel as if they are weighted down with chunks of lead the size of her hands. She smells blood and jalapeno peppers. Her throat, the surface of her tongue, even the backs of her teeth are bone dry, coated with grit, sand, gravel. When she breathes, she inhales dust.

She desperately wants to sit up, to move, but realizes something is on top of her. Rubble? Debris? Rocks? Jesus God, what's happened here?

Mira commands the fingers of her right hand to move, but the most they can muster is a pathetic wiggle. She commands her toes to move, her legs, her arms. Nothing happens. And the pain, the excruciating pain in her belly, sweeps over her again, and she screams. Her baby is coming, her daughter is pushing her way out four months early, and she screams again and the darkness claims her.

When she comes to again, the dog is licking her face, her arms, her fingers. The dog whimpers, barks, howls, and then licks and licks and begins to dig. The dog struggles to dig her out of wherever she is buried. Eventually, she feels wind and wetness on her face and she sucks at the air, sucks it deeply into her lungs, and starts coughing. The coughing brings on the waves of intense pain and then a rush of warmth between her thighs and she cries out—for help, salvation, redemption.

No one comes.

There is only the dog, licking her face, struggling to comfort her, to free her.

Now she stumbles through the debris, her baby cradled in the crook of her arm, her soft, beautiful body covered by a dirty towel that she found in the ruin. Her thirst pushes her forward. The dog, just ahead of her, barks, signaling that he has found something. Mira sees his wagging tail, his snout buried deeply behind rocks, chunks of cement. When she reaches him, she drops to her knees and she and the dog lick frantically at the melting ice inside a freezer half-buried in the rubble. It soothes the desert in her mouth, but moments later her stomach cramps painfully and she gags and throws up.

Now it is night. She doesn't understand how time flows in this place—darkness, light, darkness, light, everything quick and erratic, here one moment, gone the next. The monkeys sneak in as soon as it's dark, eager to steal the food she and the dog have gathered—bits of garbage, rotting fruit and vegetables, containers of thawing Stouffers frozen dinners, pasta as hard as rock. And one night, the panthers come and she and the dog and her baby hide inside the freezer where they once feasted on putrid water.

It seems that the panthers eat her daughter, but this memory may be false, a product of hunger and terror, she isn't sure. She can't be sure of anything now. It's possible that her daughter dies of hunger and thirst because she refuses to suckle. It's also possible that her daughter was born dead.

Her hair starts falling out in clumps. Her dog is so thin his ribs show. She aches all over, she wants to cry, but only anger and rage pour from her.

She and the dog find a place to hide at night, safe from the monkeys, the panthers, the starving skeletons that rattle across the ruins in search of food. It's like a cave, this place, tucked up under collapsed concrete and trees. She doesn't know how long they spend in this place, breaking open cans of food with rocks. But one day, the trucks find them. Soldiers in bulky suits leap off the trucks and demand to know who she is, how long she has been here, and she laughs and laughs and then collapses, sobbing, begging them to help her, to take her out of this place. The dog leaps at them, snarling, his teeth bared, and they ask no more questions. They open fire.

She buries him next to where she buries her daughter, among the rocks, in the blistering white sun, in an unmarked grave. And then she goes away.

When the trucks roar in again, she returns to herself, hopeful that they are bringing food, water, medical supplies. They are Burger King trucks and carry soldiers who collect the bodies. She hides in the rubble, digs herself a hole in the rocks, and fits her body down deep inside a crevice and doesn't move for hours.

She drifts away, into a dreamless sleep, and when she crawls out, it is dark again, but no quieter. Ghosts now roam the ruins. She sees them, transparent, aimless, confused, the dead floating like low-lying clouds across the ruins.

Mira clawed her way to the surface of wherever she was and realized she was sprawled on her back in water, that something heavy lay against her legs, trapping her so that she couldn't turn in either direction and couldn't get up. It was completely dark. She heard the soft patter of rain, a gentle, almost friendly sound, and beyond it, a steady wind. But not a hurricane's wind. Nearby, she thought she heard someone splashing through water.

Her shoulder throbbed and felt swollen, misshapen, and she suddenly understood that she was still connected to Tia and had taken on her injury in the safe room. Beyond that, she remembered nothing, didn't have any idea how she had come to be where she was right now. Even as she puzzled over all this, the throbbing began to ebb. Her body absorbed the injury, transmuted it, released it, something that had happened to her since she had first taken on the injuries of a frog years ago. With the pain bleeding away from her, she shouted for Annie, Nadine, Shep, Ricki, the cats, someone, anyone, but never heard a sound. It seemed that she couldn't form words. The most she could muster was an animal sound, part groan, part plea.

A light burned into her eyes, a man's voice said, "She's alive."

Shep? Is that Shep? Why's he aiming the flashlight into my eyes?

"Grab her legs, babe, pull her out."

Babe. Sheppard never called her that.

"She stabbed me. I'm not pulling her out. You do it."

"For Christ's sake. We need her to get off the island."

"We need to find the others," Crystal said crossly. "Especially Tia. She turned on us."

"Forget them. They're buried under the rest of that wall. Grab her arms, I'll get her legs. We'll carry her out to the Hummer. Hurry up, c'mon."

"But we aren't sure if this is the eye of the storm or if the worst is over. And those chairs fell on her, Billy. Her legs might be broken. We can't take her if her legs are broken. Just leave her."

"Nothing's broken. She's just banged up. Look, I'm checking, okay?"

He ran his fingers over Mira's right leg, supposedly looking for broken bones. But Mira, remembering what had happened hours ago in the bedroom, knew that he took enormous pleasure in touching her like this in front of Crystal, under the pretense that he was doing it just to placate her.

Waves of revulsion crashed over Mira, sourness filled the back of her throat. When he bent her legs to show Crystal that nothing was broken, Mira allowed her eyes to open to narrow slits and suddenly jerked her legs upward. Her bare feet smashed into Franklin's face, he fell back, Mira rolled to the left, away from him, and scrambled to her feet before he'd even gotten up.

And then she raced down the hall, splashing through water, her heart clanking, blood roaring in her ears. She stumbled over something in the hallway and even though she couldn't see it, she sensed it was the corpse of whoever had rung the doorbell. She fumbled with the dead bolt, pushed, but it refused to open all the way.

Shouting behind her, Crystal, then Franklin, then both of them. Mira threw her body against the door and it gave just enough to enable her to squeeze through. She stumbled through the debris that blocked the door—*from my porch, it collapsed*—and lost her balance. As she lurched forward, her arms flew out to break her fall and she crashed into something as huge as a whale. Only then did she realize it was a Hummer, the car the man on the floor had been driving.

Mira slammed down onto her knees, air exploded from her lungs. *Get up, get up, lead him away from the house, away from Annie, Nadine. Fast.* She knew she had bought some time because he wouldn't be able to squeeze through the opening in the door as she had. But how much time? *Enough, keep moving.*

She made it to her feet and tore around the back of the Hummer, scrambled over a fallen tree, and dashed into the yard. A wall of wind and rain struck her and her feet sank into the lake the yard had become. Water rose to her knees, mud squished through her bare toes, something stung the soft, tender flesh there. Ants? Scorpions? *Oh God, God . . .*

She cut toward the road, struggling against rain and wind that slammed into her out of the east.

The mud sucked at her feet, trying to hold her in place, but her terror was stronger. She reached the street, splashed into the water, her thoughts frantic, wild. She had no plan other than to lead Franklin away from the house, away from Annie and Nadine. Mira glanced back—and saw Franklin's dark silhouette race out of the garage. She fought against the weight of the rushing water, moving as quickly as she could across the road, her plan born of desperation. She would run north and plunge into the trees that grew on the side of the hill.

Annie, huddled in the back of the safe room, where she had come to after the freight trains had roared through the house, heard it all. And she didn't move, barely breathed, until the blond bimbo shouted, "Hey, you can't leave me in here, Billy!"

"Get our stuff and follow me in the Hummer," he shouted back.

Feet slapping the wet floors. Crystal swearing. Beside Annie, Ricki growled, but Annie touched her snout and the dog fell quiet. Then she sensed that Crystal had left the house or gone into another part of the house, so she crawled forward, whispering Nadine's name, praying she wasn't hurt or dead.

"Nana?"

"Right here, *mi amor.* Are you okay?"

"Yes. You?"

"Wet, with ringing ears, but okay. Do you have matches? A flashlight?"

"I do." That came from Tia, who lit a match and held it up. "There's a big hole in the wall."

"And rain, soft summer rain," Annie breathed. "Is it the eye? Or is the storm leaving?"

"Don't know," Tia whispered back.

Annie moved over next to Tia, peered out the hole in the wall. It was too dark to see anything, but she didn't have to see to know how much water had accumulated in the kitchen; it reached to her forearms. "The skylight in the family room is gone," Annie whispered. "And so is part of the roof."

"I think the roof was breached in the utility room, too, or maybe over the dining room. Look, I'm going after Dipshit and your mother. Can you and Nadine get into the back of the house on your own? It'll be safer."

"We'll manage," Nadine told her. "Just get going."

Tia blew out the match and handed the pack to Annie. "The back bathroom or your mother's closet should be safe. Make sure you have plenty of towels and stuff to soak up water."

"I know what to do."

Tia reached for Annie's hand, squeezed it. "He won't get your mom. I promise you that."

"Wait."

"What?"

"Why're you doing this?"

"I wish I could give you the bullshit answer, that my soul got redeemed or I found God or I'm rehabilitated or something. But the truth is that when you suddenly hear someone speaking to you in your head, when that kind of impossible thing happens, it's not so easy to just say, Well, fuck you, I'm outta here. It changes things, to know that the impossible isn't impossible at all."

With that, she crawled on out of the hole.

Tia's first stop was the pantry, where she retrieved a flashlight she'd seen here hours ago. Then she moved swiftly through the ruined utility room, where most of the roof was gone, rain pouring through it, and out into the garage. The door was open. Tia shone her flashlight around, swept a hammer off the workbench. She heard the roar of an engine at the front of the house.

She ducked back into the garage and seconds later, a Hummer weaved down the sidewalk, its blunted nose aimed at the street. In the dim light of the stars it looked like some sort of hulking, awkward, and amphibious creature out of a Jules Verne story.

It had to be Crystal driving.

Tia fitted the hammer lengthwise between her teeth and ran after the Hummer, her body hunkered over so that Crystal wouldn't see her. The rain stung her eyes, the wind threatened to flatten her, but she was fast, determined, relentless. Also, her shoulder no longer ached, it wasn't swollen. She was bruised, battered, scraped, but no longer in pain.

Why not?

Tia reached the Hummer seconds before it shot free of the driveway, grabbed on to the ladder that climbed the back of it, and hauled herself upward, onto the roof. She nearly fell off when the Hummer made a sharp right turn. She hooked her feet over the top rung of the ladder and groped blindly for something to grip to either side of her. The vehicle banged into a hole, jarring her. Then she raised her head, following the beams of the headlights. Eight or ten yards in front of the car, she spotted Dipshit, racing through the rain like a madman so that he could reach Mira before she plunged into the trees.

His stupid white girl laid heavily on the horn, warning him that she was coming up behind him. Like he wouldn't know it even though the headlights impaled him. Franklin, supreme dipshit of the universe, dove for Mira, tackling her as though he were a football player trying to save a touchdown.

Crystal slammed on the brakes and the abruptness hurled Tia to the side, her legs whipping left, her torso whipping right. She held on, but just barely. Crystal threw open the back door and, seconds later, no more than that, Dipshit ran toward the Hummer with Mira draped over his shoulder as though she were a Neanderthal female he had caught and would take home to his cave for dessert.

Tia flattened her body against the roof, cheek squashed down against the cool metal, the hammer still tight in her hand. *Not yet,* she thought. *Not yet.* The Hummer already was on the move again, racing downhill and weaving from one side of the road to the other.

And suddenly, the inside of Tia's head lit up like high noon in a southwestern desert and she saw what Mira saw, Crystal driving like a drunk, Franklin tying Mira up in the back seat, and both of them shouting. Then she heard Mira's voice just as she had when *she* had been tied up in the house: *Help me, Tia.*

The refrigerated truck slammed through the preserve, dodging fallen trees with massive trunks hunched up against the ground like huge alien creatures. The truck bounced in and out of lakes of standing water. The truck shuddered and shook in the wind.

"What do you want us to do with Dillard, Shep?" Ace asked. "The jail's gone. But I think the Tango PD set up an emergency center in the hospital."

"Take him and Goot there." Sheppard was loading two of the three semi-automatic Glocks that Ace had brought. Goot had the other one. "If Old Post is impassable, the bypass road might be a good place to let me off."

The bypass cut across the island from east to west and was lined by monster trees, some of them at least a century old, that had deeper root systems than the trees that lined Old Post Road. His hope was the trees would shield him from the worst of the wind.

"Yeah, the bypass should be safer," Ace agreed. "But I still think you should let me take you to the house, Shep. Even if the wind starts up before we get there, the truck's a safer bet than the Harley. This baby weighs more than a Hummer."

"Let's see what the situation is like when we get out—"

The truck slammed into a hole, eclipsing the rest of Sheppard's sentence. The tires spun. "Shit," Ace muttered, and threw the rig into reverse, forward, reverse again. The engine whined, then the rig shot out of the hole and barreled through the dripping branches and out onto the Old Post, rear end fishtailing. Ace tapped the brakes, bringing it to a gradual stop.

Ace and Sheppard threw their doors open at the same time and climbed out. They gazed across ruin and devastation so vast and horrifying that Sheppard couldn't wrap his mind around it. Fallen trees blocked the road, piles of debris created miniature dams, cars were overturned, colossal pieces of concrete lay everywhere. It looked like the aftermath of Andrew.

Rain and wind gusted across the road, as if to emphasize the need for action. "The bypass is a quarter mile south," Ace shouted over the din of the engine.

They swung back into the truck and Ace turned the rig south. He drove slowly, dodging obstacles, water splashing up against the sides of the truck. Now Sheppard was deeply worried that he might not be able to get to the other side of the island. If the bypass was blocked or if the western section of Old Post was as bad as the eastern side, then the only other route would be a two-lane road that cut directly north to Pirate's Cove. From there, he would have to jog west, along a dirt road that was probably underwater. The idea that he would get to the house on the Harley now struck him as impossible.

Ace turned onto the bypass. Here and there, trees had been uprooted, but for the most part the bypass looked to be in better shape than Old Post. Decades of wind had sculpted the trees to bend in the same direction that wind usually blew and they formed a tunnel of dripping green through which they drove. The road climbed steadily upward, through a rushing river of water.

"Uh, Shep, I think you'd better forget the Harley. The water will be up to the handlebars."

"Then either Goot or I should drive and you and Luke should stay in the back with Dillard. I don't want anyone getting hurt."

"You ever driven one of these rigs?"

"No, but Goot has."

Ace slowed, pulled on the emergency brake, and banged on the door to the back compartment. It swung open and Goot stuck his head inside. "We're there?"

"Change in plans," Sheppard said. "You're driving." He handed Ace the other Glock. "Stay inside until we bang on the door."

"Right."

Moments later, Sheppard and Goot were in the cab and Goot put the vehicle into gear, glanced at Sheppard, and said, "Let's roll."

It didn't take them long to climb the hill. But as soon as they turned right onto Old Post, the wind and rain struck them head-on, fierce and relentless.

29

"You survive something like Andrew and forever more, your life is divided into Before and After."

Tia Lopez

Mira was conscious, alert, but taped up just as Nadine and Annie had been in the family room. She had fallen to her side during Crystal's maniacal driving and couldn't push herself into a sitting position. If she could sit up, she might be able to maneuver her bound feet so she could slam them into the back of her head or Franklin's.

She dropped her legs to the floor of the Hummer and, using her feet as leverage, pushed up on her elbow, struggling to a seated position. But she realized the distance between the back seat and the front seat was too great. Her legs wouldn't reach.

Now and then, some stray bit of information about the men who had been inside this car earlier slipped into her awareness, circling her like rogue planets in her personal solar system. She didn't want to know anything about them—like that they were both young men, with families, and were now dead, part of the mounting body count that could have been avoided if she had refused to read that site for Dillard.

She kept wiggling her hands, struggling to free them from the tape. But Franklin had incapacitated her as quickly and efficiently as a cowboy bringing down a steer for branding. *Tia*, she called in her head. *Did I imagine it or are you nearby?*

Silence.

Crystal and Franklin were arguing again, shouting at each other, and the Hummer veered right, left, right, again through the driving rain and wind, its path forming an S across the road. Mira shut her eyes, desperately seeking psychic information that, even now, was denied her. She could pick up bits and pieces about the dead men who had driven the Hummer, but her abilities failed her when it came to what she should do.

She scooted her hips to the edge of the seat and knew that if she thrust her legs away from her body, she might be able to reach the front seat. But if she struck Crystal in the back of the skull, she might drive the Hummer into a tree or down over one of the ravines. If she hit Franklin and didn't knock him out, he might shoot her.

As soon as she considered this possibility, she knew that he wouldn't kill her because he seemed to think he needed her to get him off the island. Instead, he would do things to her that would make her wish she were dead.

Then she heard Tia calling to her in a voice both sonorous and eerie, a ghost voice that was barely a whispery noise in her head. Mira focused on it, concentrated on clearing the static from what she heard, on bringing greater clarity to it.

Hey, psychic lady, you there? You with me?

With you. Where are you?

It wasn't as if she heard Tia's voice with the certainty of a voice on the radio or on TV or in person. At best, this was an approximation, the way her brain translated the experience. And yet, when she asked for Tia's location, an image took shape in her mind: a body plastered to the roof of the Hummer,

splayed out like some ritualistic arrangement for human sacrifice.

Do something. Do it fast.

Let me see and hear what's going on.

Mira adjusted her senses for receptivity and felt it the instant that Tia's awareness slipped into her own, the energy
fitting perfectly and comfortably, like Cinderella's shoe. But
this time there wasn't any transfer of emotions or memories,
only a download of information as Tia used Mira's eyes and
ears.

Lie low, Tia told her.

And Mira rolled off the seat and onto the floor. . . .

Franklin rolled his lower lip between his teeth and sat forward at the edge of his seat, moving his hand frantically
across the glass to clear it. Rain drummed against the windshield, the wind rubbed it around like spit, and the wipers
couldn't move fast enough to clear it. With each gust of
wind, the Hummer shuddered, skidded, fishtailed. His head
ached, his body ached, his bones ached.

"Control the car, for Chrissakes," Franklin shouted.

"Stop yelling at me," she yelled. "This was *your* idea. We
should've stayed in the house. You're the weatherman and
you can't even tell if this is the eye or the last of the hurricane. How could you not know that? And if this is the back-
side of the storm and we're in the open . . . Jesus, I never
shoulda listened to you. And where the fuck are we going?
There's no way we can get off the island. We—"

"Shut up, just shut up and stop the goddamn car. I'm
going to drive."

"Everything you've done since breaking me out has been
one big fuckup. I'm not dying out here because of choices
you make." She turned abruptly in the middle of the road,
floored the accelerator, and the Hummer shot forward.

Franklin grabbed the steering wheel and they wrestled for control of the car, Crystal grunting and screaming, clawing at his arms and face, a wild, rabid woman who had never been water. Never. He seized her by the hair with his left hand and shoved her head against the window once, twice, and then again and again until she slumped against the door.

Unfortunately, her foot was still pressed against the gas pedal. He tried to push her body closer to the door so he could move into the driver's seat and get her foot off the pedal. But her butt was fixed fast to the seat. He finally got his left foot hooked up under her right leg and kicked it away from the accelerator.

The Hummer instantly lost speed. Franklin gripped the steering wheel in both hands and shifted his body around so that he sat partially in the driver's seat. Just when he thought he had things under control again, an explosion blew out the Hummer's back right-side window, and the hungry, rushing wind hurled glass everywhere. Certain he'd been shot at, he swung to the far side of the road, the tires bounced down onto the shoulders. He quickly checked the right-side mirror, expecting to see a car coming alongside him.

But there wasn't a single vehicle.

Now the back left-side windows exploded and pieces of glass struck him in the sides of his face, piercing his cheeks, the back of his neck, into his skull. No cars on this side, just wet trees whipping in the wind. Whoever had done this was on the roof, he thought, and slammed on the brakes, hoping the abrupt stop would hurl the person off.

But no one tumbled off.

It had to be the Amazon up there—who else could it be? She probably expected him to scramble through the driver's door. Instead, he threw the Hummer into reverse, careened back up the shoulder of the road, pushed his door open, and rolled Crystal out. She tumbled into the road like a bag of dirt. He felt a pang of regret, but it was brief. She wasn't water and he couldn't love her unless she was.

Now he jammed the Hummer into drive and tore into a sharp turn in the middle of the road. As he came out of it, he stuck his arm out the window and fired wildly across the roof, certain that at least one shot would hit the Amazon.

Something rolled onto the windshield, blocking his vision. It was her, the Amazon, her head and torso pressed against the glass, the rest of her dangling over the short hood. He hit the switch that turned on the four swamp lights lined up on the roof, just above the windshield, and thought: *I am water and she is dead.* He grinned and burst out laughing and tapped the brake, slowing down.

"Hey, Mee-ra," he called. "It's just you and me now and once this hurricane heads out into the Gulf, you're going to get us off the island. But first, we get the Amazon off the windshield."

He laughed again, inordinately pleased with himself, and the Hummer rolled to a stop. He turned off the engine, pocketed the keys, kept the headlights and swamp lights on, and leaped out of the car. He sank into a rushing torrent that lapped at his calves. Rain snapped at his face, the wind nearly bowled him over.

Franklin grabbed the Amazon by the feet, pulling her off the hood, her cheek scraping against the windshield—and suddenly she reared up. For just a moment, in the backwash of the headlights, she looked like some mythical creature that had risen from the blackest depths of the sea, her face vivid and bright with insights or wisdom or some other goddamn thing that he knew he never would understand.

"Fuck off, Dipshit."

Even as she uttered the words, her arm flew up and slammed down, sinking the prongs of a hammer into the back of his hand, impaling it in the crack where the hood fit.

Bones snapped, tendons were severed, he felt it, felt all of it, and lost his grip on his gun. She tore the hammer upward, a pain so excruciating that the world listed to the right, then left, and he knew he was seconds from passing out.

He stumbled back, clutching his hand, sucking air in through his clenched teeth, and she spun toward him and kicked out, her concrete foot crashing into his stomach, his jaw. His head snapped back, he tripped over his own feet, and crashed to the ground. Even before he hit, the Amazon was on the move, swinging her hammer as though it were six feet long. She smashed the headlights, the swamp lights, ushering in darkness once again. But it didn't matter. He was a creature of the darkness. He didn't have to see to know her intentions. She was about to free Mira.

I am water and I can burst free of this vessel . . .

Goot drove like the Latino he was, carelessly and fast. The truck careened from one side to the other, and pressed onward, against the assault of wind and rain. As it came out of a turn, the headlights on high beams, Sheppard saw something off to the side of the road, something moving, raising up, something human that rain and wind played with like a cat with a mouse.

The person tottered and weaved into the road and fell down again. Goot murmured something and shifted gears, slowing down. Before he had stopped completely, Sheppard jumped out and ran over to the shape in the middle of the road.

It was Crystal DeVries, who looked as sorry as an abused dog, a gash in the side of her head leaking blood that the rain washed away nearly as fast as it appeared. As Sheppard helped her up, the truck stopped and Goot ran over to help. He took her other arm and together, they got her into the back of the truck, where she slipped to her knees, shaking her head repeatedly and rubbing her palms hard and fast against her thighs.

"Fucker, fucker, fucker," she murmured. Then, looking up at Sheppard, Goot, Ace, and Luke and Sheppard again, she said: "Where am I?"

"At the end of the line."

Which was pretty much where he was, too. "Where's Billy Joe?"

"With Mira. He thinks I don't know what happened in the bedroom. He thinks I'm stupid. He thinks I don't have a clue. But I know. He believes she's water."

Sheppard and Goot exchanged a glance, a gust of wind shuddered across the side of the truck, and they quickly slammed the rear doors and got back into the cab, leaving Crystal with Ace, Luke, and Dillard. Neither Sheppard nor Goot spoke. The vehicle clung to the road with the tenacity of a spider to its web.

. . . what happened in the bedroom. . . . . His hands balled into fists against his thighs and he sat at the edge of the seat, peering through the half-moon that the wipers cleared against the glass.

As they came out of a turn three hundred yards later, the headlights struck a Hummer, parked at an angle in the middle of the road. No headlights. No doors standing open. Every instinct Sheppard had told him the Hummer was empty, but just the same, he and Goot approached it warily on foot, weapons drawn, following the twin beams of the truck's headlights.

The back of his neck tightened, prickled.

. . . what happened in the bedroom. . . .

He refused to go there. Not now.

The Hummer was empty, the windows blown out, glass everywhere.

Sheppard wasn't sure what tipped him off, but he suddenly whipped around and saw Franklin dashing out of the trees to his left. "FBI!" Sheppard shouted. "Stop now!"

He kept on running and Sheppard and Goot fired simultaneously.

Franklin fell back and collapsed against the pavement.

They ran over to him. He was still alive and blustering that his knee was gone, that his shoulder burned, that they were lousy sons of bitches who were going to lose their jobs when Dillard got wind of this.

Dillard.

They carried him over to the refrigerated truck, got him into the back. "Where's Mira?" Sheppard demanded.

Franklin moaned and lifted his head and then he saw Dillard. *"You fucking prick, this wasn't part of our deal, this . . ."*

If a facial expression could convict a man, Sheppard thought, Dillard would be lynched. Dillard turned his head away from Franklin.

"I'll tell them everything," Franklin went on, shouting now. "Everything. How we met, how you helped us pull off that heist, all of it."

Dillard began to squirm and writhe. Ace stuck out his long leg, pressed his huge foot against Dillard's stomach, tore the tape off his mouth. "Start talking, asshole."

Dillard glared at Franklin. "I don't know him. He's nuts."

"Two million," Crystal suddenly burst out, glaring at Franklin. "That's where the two million went. To *him.*" She stabbed a finger at Dillard.

Sheppard grabbed Franklin by the front of his wet and filthy shirt. "Where's Mira? Which direction did Lopez take her?"

"The trees closest to the Hummer, that's all I saw. I swear."

Sheppard slammed the doors and took off toward the trees.

*   *   *

They crashed through the trees, but Mira wasn't sure whether they were fleeing Franklin, the storm, or something else altogether. She tried to see it, but couldn't. Even though she and Tia were still connected, like Siamese twins connected at the brains, she couldn't see what she needed to see.

Tia, where're we going?

Keep moving.

But where?

Away.

From what?

Dipshit.

Mira stopped. "No," she said aloud. "He's not chasing us now."

Tia stopped, head cocked, listening. In the glow of her flashlight, she looked like the fugitive she was, desperate, her face glistening with sweat, rain. "We don't know for sure."

"I know for sure. I can't feel him back there."

"Then what *do* you feel?"

"That we need to go back."

"Back to what? What the fuck is *back* there for me?"

"I don't know."

"How the fuck can you not know? You're the one who sees things. You're the one who . . . who . . ."

And she grabbed Mira's arm and the trees, the storm, the darkness, all of it abruptly vanished. . . .

She is living somewhere in the Northwest, in Seattle or Sacramento, in a place that begins with an S, and she is a wife, the mother of two children, a boy and a girl, and she counsels abused women. She is Tia but not Tia, a woman who has claimed the fork in the road, who has found the road that, in another version of her story, she might not have taken . . .

But unless she had a chance to claim that path, she would end up on death row. "Run, Tia. You have to run. You have to keep running until you get off the island."

"And just how the hell am I supposed to do that?"

They stood in the trees, these two women, one black, one white, their lives and souls merged in ways neither of them fully understood. Mira removed the malachite necklace that Nadine had given her and pressed it into Tia's hand. "Hide in the woods until dawn. Then go to the marina at the southwest side of the island. A tall black guy named Ace will meet you there. He'll get you off the island and—"

"Stay right where you are, Lopez," Sheppard shouted.

Mira whipped around, hands flying upward as though they were shields. "Back off, Shep," she called. "I'm okay."

He didn't lower his gun, but he didn't shoot, either. He came toward them slowly, warily, the gun in one hand, his flashlight in the other, and pieces of Mira's life slammed together like bumper cars at a carnival, except these bumper cars formed a picture. And she didn't like what she saw, what she felt. A line had been drawn with Sheppard, symbolic of authority, on one side, and Tia—renegade, murderess—on the other. And she was in the middle.

"She saved my life," Mira said. "You're going to let her go."

"She's awaiting trial for the murders of four men, Mira. She broke out of jail, cops died, I can't let her go."

"Knock it off. You're not Elliot Ness. Never have been, never will be." Mira kept her hands up in front of her, patting the wet, terrible air, and moved toward Sheppard. She touched his gun, pushing it down. "She saved Annie's life. She saved my life, Nadine's. If you take her in, Shep, then you take me, too."

His flashlight was still aimed at her—not into her eyes, but at her chest—and in its glow she saw the expression on his face. He regarded her as though she had lost her mind. "You're asking me to do something I can't do."

"I'm asking you to do what's *right.*" Mira fully understood what she was demanding. But she also knew she was right and that Sheppard, when it came to Tia Lopez, was wrong. "A door blew open when I read that site for you and Dillard. That won't ever happen again. That's my choice. What's yours?"

He didn't say anything.

"Well?" she asked.

"Why?" he whispered.

And right then, his eyes were filled with such pain that she couldn't help herself. She put her arms around him and pressed her head against his huge and wonderful chest. After a moment or two, his hands came up over her back and he held her tightly, his body wet, shaking.

"Because she deserves a chance." *Because I saw what's possible. Because I know I'm right. Because she saved my fucking life.* "Because this is where her life forks."

"This is where everyone's life forks, Mira . . ."

She didn't hear the rest of what Sheppard said because right then, she knew he wouldn't let Tia run. So she screamed, "*Run, Tia!*"

But Tia Lopez was already gone.

"What the hell have you done?" Sheppard demanded, and started after Tia.

Mira threw herself at him, the gun exploded, and they both went down, rolling through the wet leaves, across fallen branches, their bodies entangled. She caught fragments of what Sheppard had been through, but these images were interspersed with what Tia was seeing, hearing, feeling. Then the connections between her and Tia snapped and she was alone within herself.

Sheppard clambered to his feet and Mira raised herself

up, shocked that he still stood there, staring down at her. His face looked ravaged. Neither of them moved or spoke.

She finally broke the silence. "Shep . . ."

He just shook his head and walked quickly away from her, back through the trees, into the rain and wind. Mira sat there for a few moments, wind whipping through the trees, shaking loose branches and leaves. She struggled to make sense of what had happened, what it meant.

But she knew what it meant. Soon the sun would rise, Danielle would move on out into the Gulf, and people would start picking up the pieces. But none of it would happen soon enough for her and Sheppard to salvage what they had lost.

30

"How often does anyone get a second chance?"

Tia Lopez

July 2

Mira finished pushing a mound of dirt and refuse out the front door of the bookstore, then stepped outside to turn on the hose. The sky, a deep July blue, held a few clouds shaped like animals—there, an elephant, here a stretching cat. Even though it was only midmorning, the sun burned white and hot, without a breath of air to relieve the relentless heat.

She turned on the hose and washed the dirt down the sidewalk and out into the street. The water that poured out of the hose came from the reservoir that supplied drinking water to the island. It was filthy, just one of the many reasons that health officials had told residents to boil water before they drank it. At home, they were using the propane grill to boil water and cook. But that would last only as long as the propane did.

She looked down the street, as she had countless times in the last ten days, and still felt a terrible void. Four out of five businesses on this road had been destroyed—not just damaged, but flattened, gone. Her store and Mango Mama's were the only survivors at this end of the block.

At least 50 percent of the store's stock was damaged, 60 percent of the roof was gone, and she and Annie were still sweeping out the half foot of mud that had covered the floor. The waterline on the walls reached to three feet, four inches. She and Annie had measured it. Only her office and the yoga room had emerged relatively unscathed from the storm. In the larger scheme of things, Mira considered herself fortunate. Overall, 90 percent of the homes and businesses in the town of Tango had been damaged or destroyed. Pirate's Cove, to the north, had fared marginally better, with just about 50 percent of the homes and businesses damaged.

Countless hundreds were homeless and housed in a few paltry shelters that FEMA had set up. FEMA also had set up staging areas around the island for food and supplies, but these were a joke. Since they were keeping the media away from the areas where most of the worst damage was, you couldn't get into the staging areas unless you were searched first for cell phones, cameras, recording equipment, or anything else that might allow you to get the truth out to the rest of the world. After all, the governor wanted to present the best possible picture to the media, that he and his cronies had responded quickly to the crisis and that aid was pouring in.

The governor, in fact, had sent ancient equipment to Tango—all of the modern stuff was in Mideast. The equipment had broken down on I-75 and the untrained personnel who were driving didn't have any idea what to do. Forget water purification trucks. All they got were old water tankers and old communications and storage trailers. Suddenly, there were two versions of reality, she thought, the one the media told and the one she was living.

The professional thieves were out in droves. Electronic thieves intercepted phone calls to the insurance claim lines and demanded credit card numbers for up-front payments of five hundred dollars to have claims processed in twenty-four hours. Recycling companies were stealing aluminum siding from destroyed mobile homes. Roving gangs were stealing personal possessions from damaged homes and businesses that weren't guarded. The National Guard was supposed to be patrolling the streets to prevent looting, but they were a travesty—untrained and unequipped. Gougers were selling bags of ice for ten bucks, charging thousands to cut up and remove trees from homes, and demanding money up front to file fake insurance claims.

In her neighborhood—and in countless others around the island—people had banded together for protection twenty-four-seven. Signs had been posted making it clear to gangs and other trespassers that neighborhoods were protected by Smith & Wesson. All together, her group of thirty-two people had two rifles and eight handguns.

The official number of dead was supposedly fifteen; that was what the media reported. But Mira and her neighbors and other similar groups around the island had conducted their own count—over four hundred dead. In short, the aftermath of Danielle wasn't so different from what she had seen through Tia of the aftermath of Andrew. Cover up and lie.

Power hadn't been restored yet and although she had gotten a generator from one of the FEMA staging areas, she ran it only when necessary. There wasn't any gas on the island. The ATMs still didn't work, the banks were closed, and although the Publix had reopened for a few hours a day, they sold on a cash basis only and her cash was running low. Two nights ago, she, Ace, Luke, and the rest of her band had pooled their meager resources so they now ate communally.

So much for life in paradise.

As she was about to turn to go back inside, a bicycle sped up the sidewalk, Ace pedaling fast and wearing his usual headphones. He stopped at where the gate had once stood, hopped off, wiped his T-shirt across his sweaty face, and pushed the headphones off his head so they hung around his neck.

Every day, he showed up at about the same time to bring her news—who was in the hospital, where the best deals could be found on food and other supplies, the latest body counts, who had fresh ammo for the security patrol, and whatever other news might prove useful. It was a far cry from normal life, but because normalcy was what they all craved, these new rituals and habits provided the appearance of normalcy. And Ace's ritual had begun the day after he and Luke arranged to have Tia Lopez smuggled off the island on a friend's fishing boat.

Today, he unzipped his pack and brought out a small package and a packet of mail. "The ferry brought mail and parcels today. Can you believe it?"

"All that's for me?"

"Every last piece. I'm now working part-time as a messenger for the post office, so, honey, things are looking up." He snapped his fingers and did a little jig right there on the sidewalk. "And did you hear? The mayor got the street performers together last night and asked us to put on a show in the park for the Fourth of July. He thinks everyone needs a boost in spirits."

"That's great, Ace. It's work." She noticed the box didn't have a return address. Frowning, she tore off the wrapping. "It's a start."

"Yeah, it's work, but I don't know how much we'll make since everyone's short on cash, but what the hell, right? The post office is paying cash. And tomorrow, some contractors and builders are arriving from Miami to donate their time in rebuilding homes."

Now that was the best news she'd heard yet. Only half of her house was livable—the back half—and even it didn't have running water or plumbing. "Fantastic. By the way, if you need batteries, I came across a box filled with undamaged ones, all sizes. C'mon inside and take a look."

"I'll—"

The arrival of a car interrupted them. Cop cars were the only cars on the streets these days. As Sheppard got out, Ace stammered, "I'll, uh, go inside and look at those batteries."

He hurried off before Mira could object. Ace believed that he was on Sheppard's shit list because he and Luke had gotten Tia off the island, but she knew otherwise. There was only one person on Sheppard's shit list: her. For the last week, he had been living at Goot's place.

"Morning," Sheppard said.

Very formal and businesslike. "Hi, Shep. What's going on?"

"I just wanted to let you know that Dillard is going to be arraigned in federal court in Miami tomorrow."

"Congratulations."

"Franklin was eager to talk and the state attorney's office may cut him some slack because of it."

"How much slack?"

"He'll still do time, Mira. He's got a slew of charges against him, including the assault against you, kidnapping, murder." He gestured toward the store. "How's the cleanup going?" he asked.

She shrugged. "It's going."

In the hot, bright light, Sheppard fidgeted and squirmed, as though his shirt were too small for him. She sensed he had more to say and just wished he would get to the point. She didn't want to prolong the conversation. It was too stiff, unnatural.

"I'm, uh, going to move the rest of my stuff into Goot's today."

Her heart seized up, she felt tears stinging the backs of her eyes, and quickly looked down at the ground. What had she expected, anyway? That the rift torn open between them would heal itself magically, that it had all been just another bump in the road?

"Oh." She kicked at a pebble on the sidewalk.

"Would it be okay if I go inside and see Annie?"

So you can break her heart? Mira raised her eyes. "I'll tell her what's going on, Shep."

Now he looked stricken and when he spoke, his voice sounded choked. "That's unfair, Mira."

"*Unfair?* To whom? Her? Or to you?"

"Look, what you did concerning Lopez was wrong. You interfered in a federal case, you allowed a fugitive to go free, and you really compromised me with the bureau."

"Since when have you followed all the rules? She saved our lives."

"She killed at least four men."

"Knock it off, will you? Get out on the island and tell your federal cronies to do something useful. We've had to organize our own security group because you people aren't doing your jobs. We've banded together for meals, supplies, and that's just for starters."

"There's only so much we can do, Mira. FEMA is in charge."

"Yeah, yeah, whatever. I've heard it all before, Shep. Your litany doesn't change."

"And neither do we."

With that, he turned and walked back to the cruiser. It enraged and saddened her that he walked away now just as he had done that night in the woods. She stood on the sidewalk, watching him, pieces of her heart sliding away from her and running after him, shouting, *No, don't go, please, I love you, don't do this, let's talk . . .*

But her feet never budged and Sheppard never looked back. Within thirty seconds, the car had turned the corner and disappeared from sight.

Blinking back tears again, Mira looked down at the unopened box and tore it open. Inside, nestled in a soft bed of colorful tissue paper, was her malachite necklace and a thick wad of hundred-dollar bills. Under the tissue paper was a note:

> *Spooky lady, the least I can do is contribute to the reconstruction of your life so you don't have to wait around for the insurance guys.*
> *You are forever in my thoughts.*
>
> > *Tia Lopez*